HOW TO KILL A STREET RAT

JENNIFER M. EATON

How the Kill a Street Rat © 2019 Jennifer M. Eaton

Published by Galactic Razor
Cover by Christian Bentulan
Interior Artwork by Nicole Conway

DEDICATION

*For anyone carrying around the burden of past mistakes.
If an evil sorcerer can find redemption, so can you.*

1

Soon, the golden city of Bisnagar would bow to the whims of a sorcerer. Its people just didn't know it, yet.

Amir's horse's hooves crunched in the desert sand as the massive dome towers of the palace rose in the distance, glinting in the sun.

"Look Xerxes!" Amir leaned forward to pat the horse's shoulder. "We've made it. We will be there before sundown."

Amir wiped the sweat from his brow. The first time he'd heard stories of the palace plated in gold had been around a campfire. Henry Smith, his father's trusted friend, had strode around the glowing embers, spouting tales of huge domes visible from a great distance, and streets paved in gold. Amir had listened, wide eyed, salivating for more. He'd vowed to see the golden city for himself one day, and now it lay before him: the ultimate prize, ripe and ready to be conquered.

Amir's fingers dug into the reins. Henry Smith had taken everything away from Amir only a month after that fated night. Now that tiny boy he'd left to die in the ocean with the rest of his family would rule the city Smith had adored. A fitting revenge, since ale and debauchery had beaten Amir to the pleasure of killing him.

Dismounting, Amir gave his stallion half the remaining water. Xerxes was built for speed in short bursts, not long, strenuous journeys through a parched wasteland. But the animal had served him well, as always.

Amir's fingers slid over one of the creature's raised scars, now hidden beneath Xerxes's healthy black coat. He grimaced, remembering the open, bloodied wounds riddling the beast's hide when he'd first found him.

The horse shivered.

"Fear not, my friend. Your former owner will never torture another helpless animal again." Amir had been merciful, though. The man was still alive. It was more than he deserved.

"Come. Our kingdom awaits our arrival." He tilted the waterskin, giving the stallion another drink, and took only a few drops for himself. If he passed out, Xerxes could carry him to the city. It was more important that the horse stay fit. Of course, he very much preferred the idea of entering his new home conscious, if at all possible.

As Amir approached the slick white stone walls surrounding the city, a group of men lit torches on either side of a gate that seemed primed to thwart an attack by elephants.

Amir took a swig of the water, dismounted, and gave the last of the waterskin to Xerxes. "I'll get you more as soon as we're inside."

A large man, bare-chested and wearing a black turban and sash about his waist, approached Amir. He scowled, eyeing the horse. "Where are you traveling from?"

Amir took a deep breath, readying his planned response. "I am a student, traveling from Bagdad to attend your university."

The guard nodded. "Well, you're lucky to have made it here before sundown. You'd better find yourself lodging before your horse drops dead."

Amir wiped the froth from Xerxes's mouth. "That is advice I would be all too glad to heed, sir. Where is the nearest *khan*?"

"Straight on toward the palace domes. There are plenty places willing to board both you and your horse."

"I thank you." Amir bowed his head and coaxed his horse forward.

He maneuvered Xerxes past the carts, peddlers, and people walking about. The streets were not lined in gold, but dirt like any other. Perhaps the outskirts had expanded beyond the central city's original opulence.

"Some coin, sir?" A man in rags held out his hand.

A large guard wearing a red and yellow sash wrapped around his waist—the sultan's colors—pushed the beggar aside. "Back off, street rat. Let the man walk."

"It's no problem, I assure you," Amir said, but the sentry had already passed, a huge curved scimitar blade hanging unsheathed at his hip.

Amir frowned at the weapon as the crowds parted, making way for the large man. Such a display should be unnecessary in the most wealthy kingdom in the world.

A street peddler walked toward him, pushing a cart of fruits and whistling a tune as he called out his wares.

"You there!" Amir held up a hand. "I'll take a half satchel."

The merchant smiled as they exchanged a stack of coins for a bag of apples.

Amir held one up to Xerxes. "Here you go. This is well-deserved, my friend."

The beggar stood back, lips parted as he watched the horse eat. Amir handed the man two fruits. "Here, sir. Enjoy a good meal."

The man stared at the produce, agape, before he snatched the apples from Amir's hands and ran, disappearing into the throng.

"You are welcome," Amir whispered.

What kind of place is this where a man would be afraid to

accept a simple kindness? He scratched the back of his neck. None of Henry Smith's stories chronicled such poverty or the need for armed guards. He considered the golden domes of the palace, still more than a *parasang* away. The site was irrefutable. This was the gilded city he'd been plotting to subdue.

Apparently the current sultan was not taking good care of Amir's future kingdom. Dealing with the poor may be one of his first challenges, once he took the crown away from the doddering old fool.

The last of the pink sky winked out behind the palace domes as they pressed farther into the city. Lines of torches flared to life one at a time as the lamp-lighters cast the city in a soft glow.

The darkening sky didn't seem to discourage people from taking to the streets, though. Amir had to slow as the multitudes pressed in around them. Luckily, the stream of humanity flowed deeper into the city, toward the palace, taking Xerxes and Amir along with them.

A child in a soiled white long-shirt scuffed up the dry ground with his sandals as he grabbed Xerxes's muzzle. "Look at this horse! This is a beautiful horse!"

"Why, thank you, young man," Amir said.

A group of three men reading from a handheld parchment bumped into them. Many of those about them appeared equally distracted.

"Can you tell me what's going on?"

The boy's eyes narrowed. "That accent...you are not from here."

"No, I'm not."

The boy pointed down the street. "The day after the full moon, riders compete against each other for coin. The people make bets and watch the sport."

Lovely. Hopefully, that would not mean the *khans* were full.

Xerxes coughed, spraying froth on the ground. Amir wiped his mouth again. "Sorry, my friend." And to the boy, he said, "Could you direct me to a place to water my horse?"

"Yes, there are stables and a well near the entrance to the competition. You may as well place a bet while your horse drinks." An impish dimple gave away a hidden smile as the boy studied the coin purse hanging from Amir's belt. "You can even pay me to draw water and brush your horse while you watch the riders compete."

Amir considered the boy's sunken cheeks and gaunt limbs. It had probably been ages since the child had eaten a decent meal. Amir's stomach twitched, the memory of hunger and fear of being alone still gnawing from within, but that had been many moons ago. Amir had vowed to never go hungry again, and that meant no one else should, either. This was one of the many things he would fix, once Bisnagar was his.

"That sounds most agreeable." Amir reached into his purse and dropped three coins into the boy's open hands.

The boy's eyes widened as he examined each copper. He nodded and took Xerxes's lead, pushing through the crowd.

On the street corner, a teenaged boy held open his vest, showing the frayed violet lining to the crowd. "Now, see me make a stone emerge from the air." The boy flicked his wrist, and a rock appeared in his hand. The crowd about him cheered, throwing coins into an unfurled sack.

Amir smiled as the boy made the rock disappear as well. Impressive, but this was street magic at best. Trickery and sleight of hand. This land probably had never seen what a real sorcerer could do. Still, Amir appreciated a lad working hard for his coin. He threw a silver in the sack.

The teenager bowed. "Thank you, sir."

A tiny girl ran up to him. "The guards!"

The boy straightened, grabbing his sack of coins. "Time to go!" He grabbed the girl's hand and vanished into the masses. Two guards wearing sashes of the sultan's colors gave chase. Apparently, performing on the streets was frowned upon just as much as requesting alms.

Amir continued to follow the younger boy leading Xerxes through the crowd, squeezing between men and women in embroidered, colorful frocks, while others were in tattered rags. The people smiled and laughed, rich and poor alike.

"They look like they are having fun," Amir said.

The boy smiled. "Of course. It *is* a festival!"

A rotund woman on the street corner screeched out a song at the top of her lungs. Many passersby held their hands over their ears.

A man standing on a wooden crate shouted an old Arabic poem up to an open window. An attractive girl perched on the sill above, surrounded by a gaggle of her friends, who snickered and whispered to one another, probably mocking the poor fool.

Amir shook his head, turning his attention once again to the small boy leading his horse. Although Amir had been born wealthy, his father had come from the most humble of beginnings, not unlike this young man. Every year his father had told the tale of the day he'd been seeking work in the marketplace when he'd come face to face with the most beautiful girl he had ever seen. When he'd tried to speak to her, she wouldn't give him so much as her name. Amir smiled, wondering if that market where his parents had first met had looked much like this.

Xerxes's ears twitched as the sound of drums echoed through the city. Amir put a soothing hand on the horse's neck. "Easy, friend."

The revelers divided as nine veiled women burst into the

street, dancing with lit torches. Amir's cheeks warmed, taking in their exposed mid-sections as their supple curves undulated in perfect time with the rhythm of the drum. Now this, Mr. Smith had chronicled well in his stories. As a child, though, Amir hadn't understood the man's emphasis on women exposing so much skin.

He gulped as their torches painted glowing streaks through the dark. One of the women made eye contact with him, swaying and moving her arms and body as if she were a silk curtain flowing in a breeze. Amir turned away, unnerved by the intimacy of her gaze. Bisnagar certainly wasn't home, nor like any other city he'd visited.

Beyond the square, a young man dressed in a hooded brown leather riding outfit made his way toward a muscular black stallion pawing the ground. Judging by his stature, Amir judged that he couldn't have been more than thirteen or fourteen. The lower half of his face was covered and he appeared to be communicating with hand signals to the man tending his horse. It was a strange thing to behold, but between the young man's hand signals and the expressiveness of his fierce green eyes, no one seemed to have any trouble interpreting what he wanted to say.

The boy nodded and mounted his horse as the other man handed him a bow and quiver filled with arrows. Just beyond them, several men swept back debris from a series of alleyways while others hung various targets from clotheslines strung between the windows and along the sides of the buildings.

An audience gathered on every rooftop along the route shouted down at the four riders readying themselves at the starting line. A smile burst across Amir's face as he moved closer. His skin tingled as the crowd began to chant someone's name. Maybe this event would be interesting after all.

"You go," his young helper said. "I will take good care of our friend." He patted Xerxes's side.

Amir glanced at the staff sticking up out of the travel bag tied to the back of Xerxes's saddle. Everything he owned was in that simple sack, the contents worthless to most. But his most valuable possession displayed itself in plain sight, presenting itself as no more dangerous than a worn, wooden walking stick.

The child touched the bag. "I watch your baggage, too. No worries. We are friends!"

Maybe not quite friends, but Amir had to trust the boy's entrepreneurial heart. "See that you do, and the coin will keep coming."

He threw him a silver piece. The boy grabbed the coin from the air like the greatest of prizes.

The child's eyes turned to saucers before a smile burst across his face. "I will! I will!" he shouted, pulling Xerxes toward the well.

Amir smiled. The boy probably had never seen a silver in his life. He reminded him of himself at that age, full of hope and promise. Still, it didn't hurt to be cautious.

Staring at the staff, Amir held up two fingers and whispered, "*Exortus lunae quartae metuentibus.*" A simple spell, but a potent one. He trusted the boy, but anyone else who might accidentally find the staff in their possession would be in for a disagreeable surprise once the moon rose high.

The music stopped and a hush fell over the people. The wide-eyed anticipation in the throng left Amir salivating, excited for the start.

It had been ages since he'd attended a sporting event. The air about him tingled with anticipation, and his heart pulsed in time to the chanting voices.

A loud whistle sounded and the four riders bolted from their starting positions. The gatherers cheered, and Amir climbed a nearby ladder so he could see the riders on their horses racing down the alleyway.

They fired arrows at their targets as they hurtled through the narrow passage. The hooded rider hit four bullseyes in a row while his competitors barely hit the edges of each target. One of the riders, a large man with flowing, gray hair, threw his elbow, knocking the boy from his horse.

The onlookers shouted, booed, and cursed in disapproval. The hooded rider, barely fazed, sprang to his feet, leapt to a windowsill, and pulled himself up amidst applause from the people overhead.

Someone knows how to please an audience. Either that, or he needed the winner's coin as much as the child tending Amir's horse needed a good meal.

"You can do it, boy..." Amir whispered beneath the ruckus as the boy climbed up the side of the building like a spider. He ran and jumped from one rooftop to another, firing arrows and hitting targets as he went.

The observers whooped as he changed directions. The racers rounded the center marker of the track and began coming back toward the stables. Not wanting to miss the end of the race, Amir climbed the rest of the way up and pushed around the other spectators just in time to see the hooded boy cut across the rooftop through a group of women before flipping backward off the edge of the building.

Landing square in his horse's saddle, the hooded rider ripped the quiver of arrows off his back and flipped around to face the man who had elbowed him off his horse earlier. The boy swung the quiver like a mallet and the man's head whipped back. His bulky form teetered before he tumbled backward off his horse and hit the ground in a cloud of dust.

Amir threw his fist in the air with a *whoop* that was echoed throughout the masses.

Turning himself back around, the boy shot the last two targets and crossed the finish line in second place.

Hooking his elbow on the edge of the ladder, Amir clapped his hands in appreciation. Now this was the type of entertainment he could get used to.

After receiving a small sack of coins for his prize, the hooded rider slunk off the stage and headed away from the ceremony as everyone's attention drew to the winner. Amir made his way back down the ladder. As the boy passed, Amir caught a sweet floral scent. The boy must have lived somewhere near jasmine flowers.

"You there!" Amir held up a hand, but the rider only wove more quickly through the people, barely stopping as many congratulated him.

Interesting, that he would compete, but not be interested in the accolades. He'd out-ridden riders with twice his size and years of practice, yet he hadn't stayed to be recognized past getting his purse, despite being an obvious favorite. A conundrum, indeed.

Amir stepped quietly, keeping his distance as the boy made his way into a narrow unlit alley where several children waited. He bent down and handed over the sack of coins before darting off into the shadows.

Amir straightened. *Interesting...* All that trouble, just to forfeit his prize in secret. Bisnagar, it seemed, was full of surprises.

Amir made his way back to the well. "Thank you for taking care of Xerxes." He handed his helper two more coppers. "Where shall I find you, should I require your services again?"

The boy stared at the coins before clutching them to his chest. His lower lip trembled, before he corrected his posture.

"My name is Iman. I always seek work around the marketplace. Please, come find me. I will look for you."

"I shall seek you out should I need assistance."

"I'm at your service." Iman gave a courteous bow before running off to the street vendors, making his way straight for a cart filled with fruit.

Good boy. I hope you eat well tonight.

The crowds eventually died down and Amir was finally able to find a room at a *khan* that could provide lodging for both himself and Xerxes. Closing the door to his room behind him, he dropped his staff and travel bag on the pitted floor and stumbled, grabbing the wall.

He licked his dry, cracked lips. Perhaps in tending to Xerxes, he'd been too lax on his own body's needs. This was not the night to be sick. Too much depended on his success. He needed to be clear. Focused. After tonight, he'd be the master of the cursed temple of dark knowledge, and once the spells of the ages were his, the palace and the throne would follow.

A pitcher of water waited at his bedside, and he drank half straight from the container before he collapsed on the hard lumpy linens and straw laid out on the floor. The room spun around him while his ears buzzed. Maybe if he closed his eyes for just a moment...

Amir's staff hummed, drawing him from a deep sleep. He blinked twice in the blackness before sitting straight up in his bed. "Is it time?" He ran to the window and checked the placement of the moon.

Sands! He'd nearly missed it! He needed to be more careful.

He made his way back down to the stables, retrieved Xerxes, and headed out to the main gates.

A guard approached, his face red with torchlight. "It's dangerous outside the ramparts at night." He glanced at the staff lying across Amir's lap. "And that isn't much of a weapon."

Amir tapped the staff like an old friend. "Oh, I assure you, I'll be just fine."

The guard pursed his lips. "I'll send someone to look for your horse in the morning, but we'll leave your body to the dogs."

Amir lowered his head and tried not to laugh. By morning, he'd be one step closer to owning this land and everyone in it.

Xerxes shot into the desert, confident in his swift strides, as they'd practiced driving through the dark sands countless times in preparation for this night. For the first time in a century, if Amir's calculations of the star patterns were correct, the dark oasis would appear a half a *parasang* east of Bisnagar. Certainly this was a sign that the timing was right, and a new day would soon dawn for the golden city—the dawn of the sorcerer.

Amir tightened his grip on Xerxes's reins and pulled back, slowing the horse's gait as he calculated the moon's trek across the sky. Only a few more moments. He checked the constellations and backed Xerxes up a few spans. Too close meant death. Too far, and they'd miss it. There was no room for error.

Xerxes tapped his hooves, skipping to the side and leaving indentations in the sand.

"Easy, boy." Amir stroked the stallion's neck. "It'll be soon now."

He gulped, afraid to blink. If he missed it, he'd have to wait another year to get his chance, and the next prophesied location was half-way around the world. He straightened in the saddle. There would be no waiting. Tonight, he'd secure his future.

His heart rattled as the moon crept to its peak. He grabbed his friend's mane. "This is it."

The sand beneath them trembled and a creaking sound echoed across the dunes. A hundred paces ahead, directly under the North Bastion Star, a massive black obelisk shot out of the desert, growing and widening until it loomed above, a black horror glinting in the moonlight.

Amir gaped as greenery sprouted from the sand. Rolling vines wrapped around the base of the monolith and spread out across the ground as leaves and flowers unfurled. The desert settled as the moon cast an iridescent glow over an oasis that didn't exist in the world of man.

Xerxes snorted and backed away. Amir patted the stallion's rump and slid from the saddle. "It's okay. Stay here."

Removing his black cloak, Amir draped the thick cloth over his horse's body to make him less noticeable under the brightness of the moon.

Xerxes whinnied.

Amir petted his neck. "I'm trusting you not to abandon me." Because it would be most upsetting to have come this far, only to die in the desert without a horse.

He eased toward the leaves, searching within the verge for any movement. He took in a deep breath, steeling himself. He couldn't waver, or he'd run out of time. The cursed oasis only appeared to the world of man for thirty clicks at a turn. When that time expired, he needed to be back out in the desert with Xerxes and on his way to destiny.

He breached the verge and the grass shifted, just as real grass would. A smile burst across his lips. He was actually here. He'd found it!

Still, he needed to work quickly to find what he was seeking. Everything depended on it.

His hands only trembled slightly as hundreds of tiny multi-colored diamonds winked in the moonlight, clinging to thick, black leaves. An interesting trick: keep the wayward traveler out here, collecting trinkets, while the real prize lay inside. Dozens of his readings chronicled those who'd filled their pockets and lost track of time, only to find the obelisk disappearing before they could reach the door. Amir would not be so unfortunate.

He treaded onward until the entrance at the base of the tower beckoned him into the dark. The pull of a millennia or more of dark magic pulsed, prodding him from all sides. Better men had fallen to this malevolence. Amir focused, centering his thoughts.

He'd get through this. He would not fail like so many others before him.

Amir's foot slipped on a step. In the darkness, he could only hope that the slick surface was covered in algae and not some something unthinkable. He steadied himself by placing his hand on the damp wall. The stench of death churned around him. Another ruse, he hoped. He took shallow breaths. Once he was through, the wonders inside would make any toils worthwhile.

He whispered an incantation and the jagged raw crystal embedded in the top of his twisted driftwood staff pulsed to life. A myriad of roaches hissed and retreated back beyond the reach of the light. Good riddance. Nasty creatures.

Finally, he reached the last step, turned toward a large room, and gasped. Shelves of scrolls lined the walls and reached far beyond the range of his light. At the center sat an alchemist's table covered with various bottles and scraps of paper with scribbled notes on them. Amir held his staff higher, trying to determine the height of the room, but the shelves seemed to go on forever.

His fingers twitched. He was more than ready to pull out the scrolls and learn the knowledge of the ancients, but for this night, only a single scroll mattered. Commanding his staff to stand on its own, keeping the room illuminated, he selected a scroll and unrolled the yellowed parchment only enough to read the title.

Will of the Dead: Raise an army from the grave.

THAT CERTAINLY COULD BE USEFUL, BUT NOT RIGHT NOW. Putting it back, he repeated the process with a scroll held closed by a red ribbon.

Breath of Demons: Exhale with intention and summon flames to scorch your enemies.

ALSO INTRIGUING, BUT NOT THE ONE HE WAS SEARCHING for.

Again and again, he peeked at the first few lines of each scroll, hoping that somehow he would get lucky and find the spell he needed. His chest tightened and he forced a deep anxious breath. He needed to lean on logic rather than fate, for every second was too precious to gamble. Once the stars faded, the oasis would move again, leaving him alone in the desert, no closer to his goal than he had been this morning.

No. He'd spent too much time preparing. All his research told him the Sumerian text should have been right here. It would have been the last enchantment used by the unholy cleric who had created this place. Amir examined the alchemist's table, reviewing the lists of components for potions unrelated to the magic governing the oasis. Sands! He was running out of time!

With a roar, he flung his staff across the room and sank to his knees.

He closed his eyes, trying not to count the passing minutes, imagining himself as the fated keeper of the scrolls, practicing dark magic in secret. According to the ancient texts, the cleric had been discovered, persecuted, and sentenced to death. However, he'd escaped, returning to his temple, where he'd amassed all the world's mystical knowledge. He'd sat in the dark, waiting for the murderous throng to surge down the stairway.

Amir imagined the man's last moments on Earth. The keeper's time was running out. He needed to summon a dark spell to spirit himself away.

Saving himself would mean nothing if he lost his temple, though. He had spent centuries gathering all the knowledge cataloged within these walls. So he took his knowledge with him.

The keeper had created the most powerful binding spell of all time—a curse on this place, and a curse on himself. It spirited the entire building away from harm, jumping from place to place, keeping the keeper, and his knowledge, safe.

Until now. Somewhere in this room was the spell he'd used. Amir just needed to find it.

The floor trembled slightly, as if a horse had run past. That was not a horse, though. It was the temple preparing to wink out of existence again.

Amir took in the smothering darkness that loomed overhead. If the cleric had a spell to see in the dark, maybe he'd hidden the text up there?

Jumping to his feet, he retrieved his staff and started inspecting the walls. Yes! Just as he had hoped, a jagged metal vein ran from the floor, up and out of view. Touching his staff to the vein, he spoke the same incantation that had illuminated his staff. If his research proved true, the metal vein was infused with copper, thus capable of conducting magic.

A faint hum droned above as a soft light appeared high overhead, then intensified until it spread. Soon dozens of glowing crystal spheres replaced the entire ceiling, as if the night sky had come alive for his pleasure.

"Allah," he whispered.

Amir hadn't felt wonderment like this since he'd been a boy, taking in the sight of the Great Sphinx for the first time. He shook the astonishment away. He could gape later. The spell he sought was not there. He would not admit defeat, though. He'd come too far.

He took in the architecture's perfect symmetry, the high shelves of scrolls, the tiled floor beneath his feet, and...

There, above the entrance, were ancient Sumerian characters expertly etched into the archway.

"Clever demon," Amir whispered.

Taking a piece of chalk from the pocket of his robe, Amir faced the doorway and began drawing symbols on the floor, mirroring the arch in perfect reverse.

The ground trembled once more, stronger this time. Sweat broke out on his brow and he narrowed his eyes. Each letter needed to be perfect, not only the spelling, but the placement, the thickness of the line. He took a deep breath, checked his work, and then spoke the words aloud.

The drip in the far reaches of the chamber heightened. Darkness continued to loom around him.

The floor trembled with enough force to make him stumble, and then it stopped.

Blast it! The sands of time still ran, counting down to his defeat. His Sumerian was perfect; he'd been practicing for years!

He checked the lines on the floor, panting—each breath harder to draw in than the last. Could he have pressed too hard on the chalk? Made the lines too thin? He took a step back. Did he have time to write the words again?

No. His teachers had spoken of intent. He needed to speak the words and press their meaning through his mind. This was not a lecture, but sorcery. He held out his hands, gripping his staff, and called the words out to the temple walls. He would be the master of this place. He would control all. He was not a child to be tossed aside, but a warrior, a sorcerer. No. He was *the sorcerer* heralded in ancient texts. He was *the next*. He was *The One!*

The tile beneath him hummed, then shook. Several squares dislodged and popped from the floor.

No! It was too early. The obelisk could not be moving again!

A deep, guttural growl echoed through the dusty library. Amir held out his staff before him like a weapon as the air about him fogged and coalesced into an ancient, decaying face with an unshapen beard.

"You can't get rid of me so easy, boy!" The apparition hissed through teeth filed into needle points.

Amir concentrated on not stepping back. He'd imagined the caretaker old, but the demonic features were unexpected. Showing fear, though, would be his downfall. He was in charge of the situation, and he needed to stay that way.

"I don't intend to get rid of you." Amir waved his staff across the room. "I am taking your oasis as my own personal study and you along with it."

A gust of cold sulfurous wind whipped though the chamber.

"I am no slave, you fool. I will be your undoing."

"We shall see." Amir grinned, raising his hands and tilting his head back, channeling the last of his power into the binding.

He spoke the enchantment, holding firm as the unnatural wind whipped around him. Amir stumbled, fighting against the torrent of a thousand storms. He toppled forward, trying not to step on or smudge the carefully placed letters. He refused to be thwarted when he was so close.

"By the sun, the moon, and the very sands that surround you, I hereby bind you, Iago, demon cleric of Eleses!"

The creature's bloodshot eyes grew wide as the lights overhead brightened like the sun.

Magic flowed through Amir's body like a river through an open floodgate. Every nerve in his body sparked and crackled with vicious heat. Amir called on everything he had been, everything he was, and everything he would be. His mind opened like a flower and reached out to grasp the infinite universe. A chaotic symphony of stars, planets, and swirling colorful dust...the fabric of space, time, and the essence of all living things obeyed his call.

The heat swelled, overwhelming his mortal body. Amir screamed, falling to his knees. Moisture rushed back into the room, filling his lungs. He grabbed his chest, gasping for air. His hands slapped against the tiles, smearing his perfect Sumerian.

The ruined chalk-work mocked him in the unearthly silence. The ground beneath him rumbled. Sand poured into the room.

No! He clawed at the roiling sand, struggling to keep his head above the tumult. He'd done everything right. It should have worked. He'd invested so much time...

The sand piled in around him, filling every crevice. The lights above winked out, leaving him in darkness. He clawed his way to the top and struggled for a last breath before the sand covered his face.

3

Amir's temples throbbed as sunlight raked across his eyelids. He tried to roll over, but his muscles screamed in protest. He drew his hand across the fabric below him to find coarse linen and a hard surface beneath.

He sat straight up, breathing heavily, blinking as the walls of his room at the *khan* came into focus. Harsh light streamed through the window, dust dancing within the sunbeams. Across the room, his staff lay on the ground beside the door, exactly where he'd dropped it.

Sands! Had it all been a dream?

He bolted from the room, down the stairs, and through the dirt street to the adjoining stable.

"Xerxes!" he shouted, pushing through his stall.

The horse raised his head, whinnied, and stuck his nose out for a pat.

"Ho, there." A man in thick, brown britches scratched his shirtless chest as he approached. "Is everything all right?"

Amir turned to him. "Who brought my horse back?"

The man cocked his head. "That horse has been here all night."

Sweat dampened Amir's brow. "Are you sure?"

The man nodded. "I locked him in myself."

Amir stumbled back and grabbed the pillar in the center of the barn. Had it all been a dream? It couldn't be!

Then again, the idea that a single man could walk down the ancient steps and take control of the most powerful magical place in the world seemed unthinkable. Yet the fear in the demon's eyes had been palpable. The great Iago knew he'd been outmatched.

Of course, even if it hadn't been a dream, there was still a chance that Iago had fended him off, and the magic temple had spewed him out like garbage. Why, then, would he wake in his bed, and not in the middle of the desert?

He gritted his teeth and straightened, storming out of the barn. The power that had coursed through his veins last night, the fury of the temple as the ancient priest had tried to fend him off...that could not have been a dream.

He marched to his room and locked himself inside. Last night was not a dream, and he could prove it.

He grabbed an apple from the bag of fruit he'd purchased the night before, took a bite, and settled on the ground. Pulling his saddle bag closer, he unbuckled the leather cords and carefully unwrapped a bundle of cloth to retrieve his ceremonial incense burner. After lighting a small pile of slow-burning powder in the delicate vessel, he pulled a scroll from his satchel and unfurled the yellowed parchment.

He rolled the words around on his tongue, practicing his annunciation before setting his staff across his lap. This was it. The truth would soon be known.

Taking a deep breath, he shaped the streams of fragrant smoke, moving his fingers in the patterns of the constellations as the scroll instructed. Inhaling the tangy, sweet mystical vapors, he recited the spell.

The room seemed to stretch, and his body with it. Something sparkled within his stomach before the room around him faded to black and then exploded in yellow light. The smoke shrank into a puffy billow, then thickened, blocking out the light and pulling him into a murky haze. The fizzle in his stomach became a jitter, then a pinch. He kept repeating the incantation into the spiraling smoke, tracing the figures in the air before him until he found himself once again in darkness—the absence of everything, even sound. His pulse pounded in his ears. There was simply...nothing.

A bright light flashed. "You!" The demon caretaker of the scrolls materialized, his pasty naked body glowing in the dark. "I had hoped the buzzards would be dining on you by now. Instead, I get the pleasure of smelling more of your human stink."

Amir pressed his lips together to hold back a celebratory yelp as the radiance of the demon illuminated the scrolls lining the walls. He'd done it! He was back in the temple!

"Get used to it. You'll be smelling a lot more of me over the next few centuries." He stood, grabbing his staff.

"Time is nothing to me. Your human body will rot to dust before one century has passed, and I will still be here."

"I guess we will have to wait and see." Amir found the copper vein and illuminated the room with a touch of his staff.

Amir returned to the wall and began searching through the scrolls, trying to find some kind of order. "If I can find a spell for immortality, we might get to spend a lot more time together."

"No one can cheat death. I tried."

"That is a challenge for another day."

Snickering, the demon's shimmering form shrank into the body of a pale, shriveled, naked man.

Amir averted his eyes. "Clothing, please."

Iago scoffed, but a dull, gray frock materialized over his head and dropped onto his shoulders.

Good, at least the ancient keeper would listen to him. That would make things much easier.

He returned his attention to the scrolls. "The first thing on my agenda is taking the kingdom of Bisnagar as my own."

"Bisnagar? Why?"

"Why do you care?"

"I don't. But if you're going to be digging through my library, I'd like to know why."

"Revenge."

The demon cocked a brow. "You want to take revenge out on a city?"

No, he wanted to control the one thing in the world that Henry Smith seemed to love. Amir would not cast Bisnagar into the sea, as Smith had done to his family, though. Amir would make the golden city his own, mold it into an image of perfection with the knowledge in this room.

First, though, he needed to sit on the throne. "How would you go about taking control of the grandest city in the known world?"

"I'd start there." Iago pointed a bony finger. "The best way is usually the simplest."

A tattered scroll floated from a shelf toward Iago's open hand. Handing it to Amir, he flashed a smile of blackened, sharp, pitted teeth.

Amir carefully unrolled the brittle scroll, squinting to make out the faded characters. The words referred to a magic lamp that contained a powerful, malevolent spirit—one that was forever doomed to grant the wishes of whomever possessed it. Below the text was a drawing of a simple ancient lamp.

"This doesn't interest me." He hastily rolled the scroll back up and placed it on the shelf. "Even if the jinn still existed, which they don't, they were known for being tricksters. Only a fool would tamper with something whose only desire is for you to wish your own life into ruin." Amir turned and glared at

Iago. "Although I suppose that would have been a clever way to rid yourself of me."

Iago shrugged, his countenance as innocent as the child who'd tended Amir's horse. "It would have been convenient."

Amir picked up another scroll and started reading. "This is a list of ancient law surrounding the royal family. I'm going to start here. In the meantime, I'd like you to clean the temple up." He drew a line in the dust on the apothecary table. "I refuse to live in such filth."

Iago's eyes bulged. "You dare to presume to command me?"

"That, or I can bring someone else in here to mop and straighten. I do so love to give back to the community by giving work to the less fortunate."

The demon grew larger, its nostrils flaring. "You wouldn't dare! It would expose you."

"I could erase their memories afterward. It would be simple." He tapped his lips with his fingers. "I wonder if I can find that old woman who likes to sing. She can't hit a single note, poor dear. But oh, does she try her hardest."

"Fine!" The demon shrank to his regular size. "I will comply, but if you ever bring another mortal in here, I swear on all my demon gods..."

"You'll what? Curse me? Try it and I'll banish you to wander the desert for all eternity. You can either help me, or by the dark gods, I will find a worse fate for you than even you could imagine."

Iago's eyes transformed into red glowing orbs before returning to their hollow black. "Yes, *Master*," Iago hissed through clenched teeth as he picked up a flask from the floor.

Amir concentrated on the scroll as Iago made repairs and blew away the dust. In time, the ruined temple began to shine with its original evil brilliance. The words of the scrolls began to blur together, but Amir forced himself to concentrate...

History of the families...the original sultan who'd formed the small village that had grown to what Bisnagar was today...his sons...his son's sons. He read for hours before finally finding something that made him back up and reread.

"A few hundred years ago, there was a princess who refused to marry." He leaned back in his chair and rubbed his chin. "So her father, the sultan, wrote into law that if she didn't choose a suitor by her eighteenth birthday, she would have to marry the Grand Vizier." He unrolled the scroll across the alchemy table. "The vizier was ninety-seven years old." He smiled. "The ploy worked and she chose a suitor that spring."

Iago scrubbed a coppery-colored stain from the floor. "What does this have to do with you?"

"Rumor has it that the current princess of Bisnagar is also a bit of a shrew. All I would have to do is place myself into the role of Grand Vizier and remind the sultan of this law."

"Stupid boy. How are you going to become vizier at your age?"

Amir leaned back and stared at the twinkling lights in the ceiling. "I have my ways."

Iago grimaced. "With any luck, your idiotic scheme will get your head properly separated from your shoulders and I will regain some peace and quiet."

"You'll see." Amir picked up his staff and gazed into the raw crystal. "All I need is to place myself inside the palace."

4

Amir paced the now-clean floor of his haven temple. The first thing he needed was the ability to heavily influence the mind of a human being. Searching the scrolls, he found a spell that would imbue an object with powerful hypnotic energy. The focusing agent for the spell was gemstone, and the augmenter was gold in its purest form. He had two rubies in his coin purse that would do for the gemstones.

"Gold in its purest form," he whispered to himself.

Iago leaned against a row of shelves, pushing a box on the lower shelf back with his heel.

Amir stood. "What are you doing?"

The demon folded his arms and looked away.

The damn fool had been away from humans for far too long if he thought feigning innocence would work. "Get out of the way." Amir knelt and pulled the box out and opened the lid. Within a partially desiccated cloth wrap lay a golden idol of an Egyptian snake deity. "Gold in its purest form," Amir whispered, holding the idol up to the light.

Iago hissed. "I've had that for a thousand years."

"Such a beautiful treasure is meant to be seen, not hidden away in a box."

Calling up a fire spell, Amir melted the bottom of the deity.

Iago gasped. "What are you doing?"

"Fear not. I'm only damaging the base." When the gold began to drip, Amir whispered another incantation and set the snake head atop his staff, right over the raw crystal. The liquefied metal spread and covered the wood until the two objects became one. The gold solidified as the spell ran its course, but not until he eased the rubies into the eye sockets of the snake.

Smiling, he pointed the serpent at Iago. The demon winced, turning away. "I take it this is enough to invoke the spell."

The demon priest scowled. "That, and then some. You are dabbling in power you cannot understand."

Maybe, but Iago knew nothing about Amir, his struggles, or the years of practice to bring himself to this level. All he needed now was the invitation into the palace.

Over the course of several weeks, he spent time amongst the people of Bisnagar, learning all he could about their society and those in power.

After hiring the boy who'd helped him water Xerxes when they'd first arrived, Iman told him that the Grand Vizier, Jai'far Hazim, spent a great deal of time lecturing at the university, and also that the man payed far below standard wages for a day's hard work.

"Unlike you, sir. You are a great and generous master." Iman's grin was enough to light a dark room.

Amir patted him on the back. "I simply appreciate a day of good, hard work and believe one should be compensated accordingly."

Amir smiled. The wealthy considered the poor with the same regard as furniture. They were invisible and overlooked. That resulted in the peasants and servants being a wealth of wonderful information.

Iman had just relayed that the vizier was overly frugal with his wealth, which would make him the easiest of targets.

Amir entered the university, posing as a student to sit in and listen to the old man speak in circles for hours on end, day after day. Most of the audience seemed to doze off. Apparently, the only person who was enthralled with the sound of the vizier's voice was the vizier himself. Normally, this would be an annoying quality, but this suited Amir just fine.

He stroked the lush beard he had been growing since he had arrived in Bisnagar, hoping to hide his youth. Too bad the man didn't use his extensive knowledge to better the state of the kingdom's foreign relations, or Bisnagar would be an even grander city than it already was.

Amir approached the old man after a class. "Vizier Hazim, I very much enjoyed your lecture," he began. "The part about the various trade routes really opened my eyes to the scale of the global economy."

The man shifted his oddly-high black turban. Creases formed around his eyes as he smiled. "Really? That's delightful, my dear boy. I don't believe I have seen you at my lectures before."

"I tend to stay in the back. It's easier to take notes."

"Is that so?" The old man squinted. "And what did you say your name was?"

"I am..." Amir didn't want to put his true identity on the table should someone try investigating his past. It made him too vulnerable and the last thing he needed was for some weakness from his past to be exploited. However, it might be worse if they researched a house name that did not exist. Anyone searching his real name would come up with a wealthy house. What happened to that house, he'd done his best to keep hidden. So in this case, he decided, truth might be his best disguise. "Amir of the house Haddad." He bowed. "I would be so honored, sir, if you would allow me to buy you food and drink in exchange for an encore of your research into the history of our great kingdom."

"Well..." The elderly man shifted his weight, and tugged his long, white beard. "I am rather thirsty and I try my best to share as much knowledge with you young people as I can."

Amir sensed a 'but' and readied his staff in case the old man tried to excuse himself.

Instead, the old man nodded. "Yes, I will join you for dinner and tell you everything I know."

Amir led the old man to a local establishment known for serving strong spirits. As the meal came, and the drinks continued to pour, Amir asked question after question, lowering the defenses of the self-absorbed man. Soon the two were laughing at stories about Hazim's childhood.

As the vizier sipped his third cup of wine, Amir lifted his staff, as if he were examining it. This drew Hazim's attention to the dark red stones. Amir extended his mind into the ethereal plane, connecting with his higher self, causing the snake's eyes to give off the faintest glow.

The vizier blinked, leaning closer. "Is that pure gold?"

"The purest."

Hazim lifted his cup and sipped away once more. "I've been going on and on about myself. Please tell me about you, dear boy."

Amir considered making something up, but his family deserved better. They'd been wiped out...erased from existence. They deserved to be remembered.

"My father was a poor man, who was in love with a slave girl. She belonged to a wealthy sheik who refused to set her free." Amir closed his eyes, picturing his father as a young man. "After seeing how persistent my father was, the sheik demanded one hundred times what he had paid for the girl. This would have been an impossible feat for a man of my father's means, except my father made freeing her his life's work."

Amir sat up slightly taller at the mention of his father's tenacity. He hoped, wherever his father was, that he looked down on his last remaining son with approval.

"He took every job he could, working night and day, saving every penny. But my father wanted more than to simply rescue the girl from the sheik. He was a man with vision. He wanted to give her a life beyond anything she had ever dreamed."

Laughter erupted at a table across the room, and the vizier gazed disappointedly into his empty cup. Amir called for the cup to be filled, and Hazim's eyes drew back to the scepter.

"My father kept saving until he was able to buy the materials he needed to build a ship. He hired a few hard-working, trustworthy men, and soon they were trading spices, cloth, and other goods to every country across the sea." Someone dropped a glass, and a server ran to pick up the pieces.

"Please, continue," Hazim said.

Amir leaned back. There was so much to tell, so many adventures, but the most important of all, was the final result. "It took years, but after his third voyage, he came to the sheik offering not only the required gold, but also gifts of wine and precious jewels. At last, the sheik allowed my mother to leave with him, and my father was able to have the one thing he wanted: a family."

Amir's eyes drew to his ring, a family crest of sorts. His father had one fashioned for himself, and each of his children— a perfectly cut sapphire representing the sea, and five ships sailing on forever. His father was a dreamer, whose life had been cut short long before his time.

The vizier continued to stare into the jeweled eyes of the scepter. Amir only hoped that it was the spell and not the priceless beauty that had enthralled him.

"I am also a man of vision," Amir said. "That is why you will take me on as your apprentice."

"Is that so?" Hazim chuckled. "The foreign son of a merchant trader and a slave girl advising the sultan." He broke down in a fit of drunken laughter, spilling his wine and pounding his fat fist on the table. "Even if I weren't completely appalled by the concept, there is no way convention would ever allow it."

Amir's cheeks burned and he clenched his teeth. *This pompous fool thinks that merely being born of noble blood entitles him to besmirch those who actually manage to claw their way up from the muck.*

He took a deep, determined breath and buried the rage beneath his stone-hard will. "All the same." The eyes of his staff began to gently pulsate, matching the heartbeat of the Grand Vizier. "You are going to forget everything I just told you about my past." Hazim leaned away, his brow drawn together, but his face slowly relaxed into a visage of contented bewilderment.

"What was it that you told me?" The old man's eyes grew wide as he gaped at the subtle glow of the red jewels.

"You know me well," Amir spoke intently.

"Yes, I've known you for years." Hazim nodded with a trusting smile.

"I come from a noble and well-educated family from Bagdad."

"Your father and I are good friends." He blinked slowly.

"I have been your apprentice for the last three years."

"I have taught you well, my boy. I'm so proud of you."

"You are feeling ill as of late."

The vizier tugged at the collar of his shirt, sweat beading up on his forehead. "My declining health has slowed me down a bit."

"You fear your mind is not as sharp as it used to be."

Hazim took a handkerchief from his robe pocket and dabbed his furrowed brow. "Oh my word! It's a good thing I took you on when I did. The kingdom would be in terrible trouble if I were to step down without someone qualified to take over my position."

"I'm so pleased to hear you say that, old friend."

Amir grinned and leaned back, leisurely letting the satisfaction of a spell well-cast wash over him. It was like soaking in a lovely hot bath of smugness.

He folded his hands across his chest. "Tomorrow after you've had time to rest, you are going to introduce me to the sultan and tell him what must be done."

"Yes, it's time, my dear boy. You're ready…I have every confidence in you."

"I'm flattered by your confidence, Hazim. Now go home and sleep until morning. Then come to the university entrance to find me."

The vizier stood and left the room, rubbing his head.

Amir's skin tingled. *All too easy.* He placed a few gold coins on the table and pushed through the door. He needed to keep his wits about him, though. Just because the vizier was so easily manipulated didn't mean the sultan would be. He needed to remain focused. Now was not the time to be overly confident.

Making his way back to the *khan,* Amir stopped at the stables. Xerxes whinnied when he entered, and Amir scratched between the horse's nostrils. "His coat is looking healthy. That oil seems to be working."

"I told you." Iman finished brushing out the long, flowing tail. "If you put good things into an animal, they give good things back to you. You should have seen my father's milking goats when…" His elated expression faded as his shoulders sank. "Never mind."

"Finish your story, boy."

"My father's goats produced a lot of milk, even the small ones. He fed them well, sang to them, made them happy." He brushed through the tail again. "They gave us more milk than we could ever drink. We used to sell it in the marketplace."

"Your father has passed?"

Iman nodded. "Plague."

Amir cringed. "I see. I lost my family too." Losing a father hurt, no matter your age.

"I still have my mother and sisters. When they are old enough, they will marry and be taken care of. Until then, it's up to me to make sure everyone is fed."

"And you do a good job." Amir held out the boy's wages. "Does your mother work?"

"She got sick when my father got sick. She lived through the fevers, but she hasn't been the same since. She sleeps a lot. Doesn't eat much, which is good since work is hard for me to come by. My sisters take care of her while I'm gone. They are still small, though. They can't do much."

Amir shook his head. This was so much responsibility for one so young. "It was a blessing for me to have been left on my own. I had no one to worry about except myself."

Iman frowned. "I am grateful that I have them. No one wants to be alone."

Amir's chest clenched. His mother's smile, his father's wit, his brothers' teasing...so many things lost, pushed aside and forgotten in the name of vengeance. He wondered what it would feel like to be needed by someone who cared about you. He shook the thought away. He'd been fine without a family. No use dredging up old ghosts now. He patted the boy on the shoulder and excused himself, heading up to his room.

The lumps in his mattress reminded him of the time his brother Omar had hidden Milef's shoes under Amir's futon. The two of them had always been pranking each other. His mother used to stamp her foot at them, all the while fighting back a smile. Father would pretend not to notice. Amir had tried his best not to get caught in the middle.

He rolled over, facing the wall. Telling his father's story, and hearing the plight of young Iman had reopened an old wound, one that Amir had convinced himself was no longer something that had power over him. But as soon as he drifted off to sleep, he was drawn into memories of a great storm on an angry sea—waves crashing over the wooden deck of a ship, his father shouting orders that were lost in the howling wind and cracks of thunder.

Omar had thrown a rope about Amir's waist. "Hold on, Amir. You'll be okay." He'd smiled rustling Amir's already soaked hair. That was the last time Amir ever saw him.

Amir opened his eyes and sat straight up, clutching his chest as his heart pounded so hard, he thought it might burst. The sound of the storm still filled his ears even as he covered them, clenching his eyes shut. He'd spent too many years and too many spells shutting those nightmares out. He refused to let them back in again.

He breathed deeply, steadying his trembling hands. The screams of his father and brothers gradually morphed into the normal sounds of the bustling marketplace outside. Daylight was good. Nightmares didn't come during the day. Tonight, he'd be sure to ward himself against dreams again. He did not have time for childish night terrors, not when he was so close to finally avenging their deaths.

Pushing himself from the bed, he washed, combed his beard, and put on his best robes. He smiled at himself in the warped mirror. The frightened child who nearly died in that storm was gone. Forgotten. The man left behind was about to meet his future father-in-law.

5

Hazim stood on the steps in front of the university entrance with his arms out to his sides. "Are you ready? This is a big day, my boy."

Amir bowed. "I am, Master."

"Very well. Come along!"

They made their way toward the palace. Amir took note of the changing scenery as they grew closer to their destination. The architecture became more ornate, the people walking in the streets wore finer, more brightly colored clothes, and the streets themselves were clean and devoid of beggars. It was as if the poverty he had seen only a stone's throw away didn't even exist.

This was the golden city that Amir had originally expected when he had arrived at the gates. He wondered if the artists who'd painted the palace had lodged in the part of the city where he had been staying. He wondered why no one ever painted the blind cripples with their hands outstretched for coins, or the passersby spitting in those open hands.

Several spans from the palace, the dirt-covered road turned to clay, and then the clay turned to glistening gold. Amir gasped. Such opulence seemed out of place when the poor lived within walking distance.

"Come, boy," Hazim said. "Don't dawdle."

At the entrance to the palace, two large guards in brown

britches and yellow and red vests blocked their path. They both wore crisp beige turbans and each sported thick, well-groomed beards. Amir was unsure if the resemblance was due to blood relation or if they'd simply trimmed their beards side by side in the mirror together in the morning.

"Who's this?" The larger of the two gestured to Amir, who was still smiling at the image of their morning routine.

"Someone who will shortly be above your station, Nadir, you great fool!" Hazim snapped.

"I'm sorry, Lord Jai'far." Nadir bowed. "You know it's my responsibility to ask."

The guards both stepped aside. Amir nodded to them cordially. The guards bowed out of respect, though the larger one—Nadir—looked up, his gaze sweeping over Amir.

Amir smiled and passed him with his head held high. *That one will most likely be a problem, but no matter.* Once Amir was sultan, he could choose his own guard.

As he passed through the gates, a giddy rush of energy tickled up from his core. He had just done what no other invader in the world would have dared. He'd walked in through the front door in the open with a weapon in hand. His staff tingled in his grasp as his excitement flowed into the golden serpent with the ruby eyes. Little did they know what chaos they'd just committed themselves to.

The colossal marble pillars and archways towered overhead like polished mountains. The entrance of the throne room could not have prepared Amir for the scope of the immense dome-shaped chamber that glistened with golden brilliance from floor to the center of the dome, where an ornate candelabra hung suspended holding dozens of round oil lamps.

An unimposing older man with a plump kind face sat motionless on the brilliant throne as if he were a statue.

Another man stood before a large canvas, painting a stunning likeness of the sultan.

The vizier folded his arms, staring at the artist. Judging from the man's clothing, light skin, and the painting style, he was from Florence or studied under someone from the same region.

Hazim lifted his chin. "Your Majesty, our own country is known to have birthed the greatest artists who have ever lived. Why lease this rabble?"

Amir rolled his eyes. The painter was more than likely traveling to avoid the dangerous political tensions brewing in Europe. It was obvious the man was highly skilled, though, and Hazim only made himself look like a fool in mocking him.

The sultan turned toward them. "Our kingdom will one day be ruled by a prince from another land, Jai'far. You would do well to learn respect for our foreign neighbors."

"Royal blood transcends geography." Hazim moved closer and bowed. "Sire, I have an urgent matter that I must discuss with you."

"Very well." With a wave of his hand, the sultan shooed away the artist. The guards excused themselves behind him. "I assume whatever you wish to discuss is not something you wish to keep from your guest."

"Naturally, sire. This has to do with him as well." He pulled Amir forward. "This is Amir. He has been my loyal apprentice for the last three years and I have known him and his family for much, much longer than that. He comes from the noble house of Haddad and has a rich education pertaining to political and economic matters."

The sultan's brow wrinkled with concern. "I had no idea that you've had an apprentice. How is it that I'm only hearing of this now?"

Amir felt his heart skip a beat. Would this highborn little man actually question the reality presented to him?

"Forgive me, Y-Your Majesty." Hazim gulped. "I planned to tell you only when I was sure that Amir was ready. Today, the time has come for you to meet him."

What Amir needed now was to earn trust. He could not let his ego ruin all that he'd worked for. He took a knee and bowed deeply. "I'm humbled to be in your presence, sire." He gritted his teeth. *Today I kneel before him so that tomorrow he will kneel before me.*

The sultan's eyes narrowed, his gaze resting on both of them.

Hazim continued his explanation. "My health has begun to fail me. I fear my days advising the throne must come to an end." Hazim put his hand over his heart. "As my last act as Grand Vizier, I strongly advise that Your Majesty accept Amir as my replacement. I will be available to offer him guidance for the rest of my life, of course. However, I feel most confident that he will take hold of the challenge most competently."

The sultan's jaw dropped. "Jai'far, this is most irregular. How is it that you've never brought this man to meet me before today?" His voice grew louder as his distress trickled in.

"If I may address His Majesty?" Amir lowered his eyes, showing the deference he would one day demand of his own people.

The sultan took a long pause, as if to decide whether or not to entertain the idea. "Very well."

Amir raised his eyes. "Bisnagar has made many enemies, men who would wish to plunge the kingdom into chaos. I am a mere apprentice, unworthy of living within the palace walls; for this reason, Hazim feared for my safety and we conducted our studies in secret."

The sultan's eyes narrowed on Hazim, before returning his attention to the stranger.

Amir continued. "Over the last year, I have discovered that there are spies operating here within the city. In his wisdom, my master ordered me to gather as much information as I could without the traitors learning of my identity."

The sultan straightened. "Spies! In my kingdom?"

Good. He had the man's attention. "Now that Hazim no longer feels capable of fulfilling his duties, I am uniquely qualified to serve in his stead. I assure you, I only want what's best for Bisnagar and its people."

The sultan looked down his nose at Amir. This man was used to unflinching loyalty. If he sensed anything but abject devotion from Amir, his quest would be over in a snap of this man's fingers. Amir needed to prove, without any chance of doubt, that his trustworthiness was unwavering.

He closed his eyes, swallowed the bile pooling in his throat, and bowed lower. "If Your Majesty feels unsure of my abilities or faithfulness, he should take my head now. For a life not spent serving my sultan would be no life at all."

The sultan harrumphed. "You speak of taking heads as if it is a light matter. That is not the sort of sultan I am."

"No sire, nor would I want you to be. That is why I must serve you. My entire life has been in preparation for this moment, and nothing short of death could separate me from my duty."

The sultan glared at him. "I do admire your determination. Tell me your name again."

"Amir Haddad, sire."

The sultan shook his head. "That won't do at all. You will be called Jai'far, like my family's viziers before you."

Amir pressed his lips together. Had he actually convinced this fool to allow him into his house?

The sultan continued. "I will allow you to advise me for the next forty days, at which point I will decide if you belong in my service."

"His Majesty is most wise." Amir bowed once more. He might not have been given the job outright. However, if the sultan was as easy to hypnotize as Vizier Hazim had been, the kingdom would be his before the sun set forty nights from now.

Hazim bowed. "I will show him to my old chambers. I have men already moving my things to my family home outside the palace."

The sultan cast formality aside and put a kind hand on the old man's shoulder. "My physicians and servants are at your disposal. I thank you for your years of loyal service to my kingdom and to my family."

"Your thanks humble me, sire. I thank you for all you have done for me as well."

Hazim and Amir bowed and exited to the great hall.

"Don't be upset by being renamed," Hazim said. "My name isn't really Jai'far, either."

Amir smiled. That little tidbit had escaped his research.

"Allow me to show you around so you don't get lost. Navigating the palace can be confusing at times."

Gold inlayed walls, grand columns, and statues from around the world—the palace certainly did not disappoint. Amir's days of begging for food and striving to better himself were over. From now on, the world would do his bidding. And Henry Smith would look up from his fiery toils in Jahannam to see that the boy who survived the wretch's attempt to wipe out the Haddad family now owned a grand portion of the world's wealth. His family would finally be avenged.

The Grand Vizier's chamber opened up to a massive balcony that faced a courtyard at the center of the palace. Across from his balcony, stood another identical to his;

together, they overlooked a lavish garden that was inhabited by an array of exotic creatures. This was a pleasant surprise, like having an oasis of his own to gaze upon every morning.

Amir inhaled, taking in a familiar sweet, floral scent. "Jasmine flowers."

Hazim smiled. "Yes, I will miss that." He reached over the edge of the balcony and plucked a white blossom. "They're everywhere."

He pointed across the courtyard, where the vines grew up the other balcony as well. In this setting, they probably never stopped blooming. The sultan, at least, had good taste.

A fountain in the center of the garden cast water straight into the air that fell to the circular pool below in a bowl pattern that mirrored the trees around the base. A woman with long, billowing black curls sat alongside the outer edge, trailing her fingers in the water. Judging from her magnificently embroidered *lehenga,* this could only be the Princess Badroulbadour.

For some reason, he had expected her to be rather unattractive. While rumors of her beauty ran rampant throughout the kingdom, such things were often exaggerated if not fabricated entirely, and Amir had assumed the issue of her refusal to marry had been due to a lack of effort on the part of her suitors. Thankfully for him, this was not the case.

Amir straightened his robes and ran his fingers through his hair. With her station, and the pompous nature of most princes, she'd probably never met a man with the skills required to woo a woman properly. He needed to make the best first impression possible. He puffed out his chest and stood tall.

"I suppose you want to meet the princess. If I'm being honest, she's rather unpleasant company but for her pretty face and what-have-you."

Amir continued to stare. Her hair caught the light and her

skin glowed. He'd been prepared for the worst. This was maybe the best surprise of all. "I'm sure we'll get along quite well."

"Bless you for your optimism, dear boy."

Hazim led the way down the stairs to the lower floor and out into the garden. She stood as they approached. Her exposed midriff would have shocked him before seeing the fire-dancers in the square that first night. While it took some getting used to, he was finding that he appreciated the customs of his soon-to-be kingdom.

"Your Highness, may I present the new vizier, Jai'far Haddad," Hazim said. "He will be taking over my position, as I have decided to retire."

Her eyes were the most brilliant shade of green that Amir had ever seen. He stopped walking and nearly stumbled as that gaze alighted on him. "Pleased to meet you," she said. "How is it that this is the first time we've met?"

"Oh child." Hazim laughed condescendingly. "These are matters of state. Nothing for a woman to concern herself with."

Her plump, red lips thinned. "I can't help but be concerned if I'm about to share my home with a complete stranger. Is Father aware of this?"

Amir held up a hand. "Forgive me, Princess. I would be happy to explain everything to your complete satisfaction if you would grant me the pleasure of a walk in the garden."

Something in her eyes became predatory, like a tiger in a cage, more than ready to rip the throat out of its handler. "Very well. I would like to hear your explanation." She glared back at Hazim. "In spite of the fact that a mere woman has no right to know what's going on within the walls of her own home."

Hazim forced an insincere smile and blinked, deliberately ignoring her. "With that, I think I'll take my leave. I need to rest my old bones." The old man wasted no time making his exit, leaving the two alone.

Perfect. Now Amir had no one to watch directly over him, and time to engage in more important matters.

He held out his arm for the princess, but she simply walked past him. She held her head high, not unlike a man. "I'm sure you'd like to see the various flowers and trees that adorn our grounds. Come with me and tell me who you are and how you came to be our new vizier."

As Amir walked alongside her, he retold the lie that he had committed to when he'd hypnotized Hazim. She listened quietly, shaking her head.

"I can't believe he's kept a secret apprentice for all these years." She turned to Amir. "I am usually adept at rooting out deception."

With those piercing eyes, he wasn't surprised. "I only wish to serve your family and your kingdom." He gave a slight bow, his hand on his chest. He would win this woman's trust, and then her heart.

"That's a somewhat soulless introduction of yourself. Surely, you're not merely defined by your position—or rather, a position you *aspire to*." She waved a finger. "Let's not forget that your being here is tentative until my father says otherwise."

Ah, so now her reputation comes into focus. No wonder men were intimidated by her. She said exactly what she thought without tiptoeing around his ego. Amir smiled. Things were getting more interesting by the moment.

"Of course, Your Highness. However, this position is more than a social grace for me."

They stopped in front of a cage of large white birds. Cockatoos, or was it cockatiels? Birds were not his forte. He ran his fingers over the bars until one of the blasted creatures snapped at him.

He backed away. "My aspirations define me because I

believe I have a destiny to fulfill. Surely, that does not make me soulless."

"What of your father and mother? You said that your family was noble, but you mentioned nothing else about them."

"I, uh—" A cold chill spread over him as he recalled the screams of his father and brothers. He blinked the nightmare away. He'd lain that horror to rest fifteen years ago. "My mother was actually a subdued woman, not confident like you are. But she was kind and I would even say strong in her own way."

A red and blue parrot squawked as they passed. The princess took a fruit out of a box and handed it to him, scratching the back of its neck.

She began walking again. "And your father?"

"My father was...relentless. He never felt entitled to anything he didn't earn. His soul was the most noble part of him. It was something I always felt inspired to try to live up to."

She frowned. "You speak of them in the past tense. What happened?"

His pulse quickened. Screams. Shouting. Waves crashing over the deck. "It was partly nature." He reached out and touched the petals of an orange lily. "Partly human nature." He needed to stop. This was too close to the truth, and if his true past was discovered, he'd lose this chance at the throne. He should try to talk about it more, though. Revisiting the events might tame the demons haunting him at night. Still, it would be all the better if she had no memory of this conversation, only a charming stroll with a tall, handsome stranger.

He lifted his staff and she gazed curiously into the eyes of the Egyptian snake. "I'll thank you to forget this conversation and never bring up my family again."

"Excuse me?" She stepped back, shoving his staff away. "Get that ugly thing out of my face. If you didn't want to talk about it, you could have just said so." She turned and stormed from the garden with the thickened gait of a soldier marching into battle.

Amir spun the snake scepter and stared into the idol's eyes. Had it not worked, or had it not worked *on her*?

He trembled, staring at the doorway she'd disappeared into. Wooing her might prove more of a challenge than he'd expected.

6

Princess Badroulbadour pushed through the garden gates and stomped down the hall. "Imbecile!" Three servants pressed themselves against the wall as she passed, but they had to know they were not the cause of her wrath.

Before this pompous new vizier had waved the ridiculous snake cane in her face, she had decided she almost liked this Jai'far more than the original. It wasn't just because of the dark, wavy hair and those light brown eyes with amber shards that caught the light of the afternoon sun.

She shivered like she had a chill. No. It had nothing to do with his looks. He'd put her at ease in a way the old Jai'far never could. However, something about him did set off a kind of warning alarm in the back of her mind, which could have had everything to do with the tall, dark, and handsome problem.

She turned a corner, heading for the throne room. She needed to make sure that this new vizier hadn't been trained to manipulate her father into making poor decisions that would benefit the former vizier's wealthy friends.

She winced. Vizier Jai'far Hazim didn't care if half the country was starving while the other half lived in the lap of luxury, never doing an honest day's work as long as they lived. If she never saw the old man's smug face again, it would be too soon. However, she would not let this tall, dark stranger simply walk into the palace without finding out exactly who he was.

If he were lying, she'd most likely be able to sense it, just like the imprudent suitors who lined up to meet her, spouting words of love and devotion after only a few moments. Their words were always lovely, and their intentions were sickeningly clear. Money and power, nothing less.

She'd shrouded her prodding questions to the new vizier as cordial small talk, and his responses about his family seemed genuine enough. The sorrow on his face made her feel a twinge in her heart for his loss. He'd made a terrible mistake, however, ordering her to never bring it up again, as if he were the sultan and she a mere servant.

"Gah!" She threw her arms in the air.

He had forgotten his place and the royal in her wanted him to pay for his insolence. She didn't want to play the role of spoiled princess, though, but if he didn't want to open up to her on his own, he could have just said so. She would have to find alternative ways to ferret out his past.

A young servant girl ran by, one of the children tasked with polishing the bases of the golden columns. The children of Bisnagar saw and heard many things and always managed to go unnoticed. Outside the palace, their hungry outstretched fingers and cries for help were merely background noise to most of the people walking by and having dealings in dark allies. If anyone would know about this man, it would be them.

First, though, she needed to understand what had gotten into her father's head, allowing this.

Standing outside the throne room, she took a deep breath before pushing through the doors. "Father?"

The painter was focused on the portrait he had been working on for days. He'd been standing in that same spot for so long, it was almost as if he were part of the scenery.

"Who is that man now taking up residence in the Grand Vizier's room?"

He sighed. "Darling, it's so heartwarming to see you fussing over our old Jai'far's retirement. I know that you have not always—"

"I don't care about anyone retiring. I care that you let a stranger into our home."

"Jai'far Hazim has vouched for the boy, Badroulbadour, and that's good enough for me."

"Even if you believe that he is trustworthy, he's not much older than I am! How much experience could he possibly have? What are his qualifications?"

"According to our Jai'far, the boy has been groomed for this his entire life. He has shadowed our vizier on every decision made over the last three years. I owe it to Jai'far to give his protégé a chance to prove himself."

"But Father," she pleaded.

"Babedra."

Badra tensed. Her mother used to call her that. The warmth the pet name normally provided failed to fill her, though, when her father used the designation in an argument.

"You will stop worrying over things that should not concern you, my dear." He put up his hand and made it clear he was no longer listening. "You must learn to trust and submit to those who have stronger logic than you."

She cringed. *Submit? Stronger logic?* Men were the only people on this planet who had no idea that they could be imbeciles at times. She ground her teeth to keep from screaming.

"Your feelings cloud your judgement," her father continued. "Your mind shouldn't be forced to bear the weight of these matters, and I will hear no more of this nonsense. Besides..." He pointed to a servant who held a bound tome open to him like an inert bookstand. "Yes, yes, it says here that we have a new suitor set to arrive at any minute. You must be on your best behavior. Please *try* to act like a *proper* woman this time."

Proper woman? Biting her lip, she turned and marched back to her room with clenched fists. Why couldn't she have been born a boy? It would have made everything so much easier.

7

THE COUNTLESS LIGHTS ABOVE SPARKLED AS AMIR TAPPED his fingers on the edge of the alchemy table in the cursed temple. "She's not a shrew at all. It's obvious that she is sensible...dare I say, intelligent."

Iago nodded, paging through an ancient text.

"She's very strong and sure of herself. I honestly find that she's a breath of fresh air. Women in general would be more pleasant company if they nurtured these qualities."

Iago held up a finger to request a pause. "So, just to be clear, you want a woman who acts more like a man."

"No, she's nothing like a man. The qualities I described are not specifically male qualities." Amir stood. "She's a human being with a personality. She has a grasp on who she wants to be." He scratched his beard. "Honestly, she seemed receptive to my charms until I tried to hypnotize her."

"Tried? What do you mean, you *tried?*"

"I conjured the power from within, the same as I had done when I hypnotized the vizier, only she wasn't affected by it at all. She even looked straight into the eyes of the serpent and it was as if I had no power over her whatsoever."

"That's troubling."

Amir spun toward Iago. "Why? What do you mean?"

"Involuntary hypnosis only works on people of average or less intelligence. Strong wills have been known to be a problem.

The only way you can get her under your power is if she *wants* to be."

Amir shook his head. "That will never happen. I can tell you right now—she won't allow herself to be treated like an object."

"Then as soon as you are crowned sultan, you'll have to kill her. We can work out the annoying detail of the heir easily enough."

Amir grimaced at the sour taste in his mouth. Taking such a jewel from the world would be unfortunate, but..."If that is what must be done, then that is what I will do." His stomach clenched as a deep dread swept over him. He shook it away. "That is a task for another day. For now, my greatest worry is the suitor who has come to woo her."

"Competition, how grand!" Iago clapped his hands. "There are thousands of ways to murder a person chronicled in these scrolls." He pointed to the shelves, licking his lips. His eyes whirled with a red glow. "And where does this walking corpse hail from?"

"I can't just start killing everyone who gets in my way."

"Why not?" The demon's brow furrowed. "Oh, you have a conscience all of a sudden?"

"Of course not, you fool. If dead bodies start piling up in my wake, I'll be discovered." He picked up a flask from the table and considered the purple liquid inside. "The sultan and Badroulbadour must both be dealt with once I am on the throne. Until then, I need to draw as little attention to myself as possible." He started pacing again. "This prince from Reahah Krihh shouldn't be too difficult to manage. I can use my staff to hypnotize him. Or I can make a potion to banish him."

"Poison is easier."

"Again, I do not want to draw suspicion, but thank you."

"I still prefer killing. It's much more fun to watch the life drain from their eyes." He rubbed his palms together, grinning.

Amir folded his arms. "What you are saying is that you'd prefer I got caught so you can sit here in the dark for another thousand years."

"That's not entirely accurate." Iago looked down, his long teeth still protruding from his closed mouth. "It did get rather dull after a few hundred years. I used to enjoy leaving the temple and watching the birds fly through the clouds when I was bored." He shrugged. "Since that is no longer an option, you are all I have."

Amir smiled.

"I'm not saying that I like you!" The demon put his hands up. "I just find you somewhat amusing. I'd like you to succeed in your quest seeing as I've become invested in seeing how this drama plays out." He closed his book. "The longer you live, the more entertainment I get out of you."

"I'm glad I could amuse you, but I need to get back. The second born son of the fifth kingdom of Reahah Krihh will be in the garden with my future wife as we speak. I have work to do."

"If the shrew hasn't already killed him for you!" Iago cackled.

"She's not a shrew," Amir insisted as he faded back into his room at the palace.

He made his way down the stairs and out toward the garden. Hearing an unfamiliar male voice, he halted and hid behind a pillar.

A tall, gangly man, probably ten years Amir's senior, had one foot on the edge of the fountain. "You are like a delicate flower. I would be honored to have you decorate my arm," the prince cooed.

"I'm sure you would." The princess leaned away as a peacock feather stuffed in the prince's turban fell forward.

Amir found himself smiling. She didn't bother trying to sound impressed at his feeble attempt to win her affections.

She stood, suddenly. "You need a fragrant flower to hide the stench of your ignorance and utter uselessness."

"Excuse me?" the prince retorted.

"Over the last several hours, you have told me all about yourself, and yet you seem to know nothing of your country or your own people, let alone mine. You have never fought a single battle in spite of the fact that your father has continuously waged war against neighboring kingdoms. Your territories are constantly on the brink of civil war due to political unrest. Your brothers all will most likely start trying to have one another assassinated to take control of one or all of the outlying regions. I have no idea why you think I would want to be in the middle of that mess. I certainly wouldn't ever offer up my kingdom's treasury to fund your father's warmongering. Not to mention, your breath is the foulest thing I have ever encountered in my entire life."

Amir's eyes widened. *Bravo! And she didn't even take a breath!*

"How dare you speak to me in such a fashion! I could have you beaten, princess or not!"

*Oh, he did not...*Amir chanced a peek around the column. This was something he refused to miss.

Badroulbadour's expression of benign irritation faded and she became something so much worse. She walked aggressively to her suitor with all the confidence of a queen. "You come as a guest into my home to take advantage of my father's hospitality. I spurn your pathetic advances and confront you with a harsh truth, and your first response is to threaten me like one of your slaves?" She jabbed his chest with her pointer finger. "I suggest you gather your possessions and remove yourself from my kingdom while you still have all of your manly appendages intact."

The prince gaped at her. "Are you mad?" He pulled down the edge of his shirt, sticking out his chin. "My father will be marching his five armies to your gates within a month's time."

"Please..." The princess held up an arm and turned from him. "Unless you have another rich princess lined up to meet every one of your brothers, there is no way your father could afford to sustain an army large enough to mount an attack on my kingdom. Half of your men would die on the journey here and the other half would arrive too weak to fight. If you know what's good for you, you'll simply say that you tried and failed, just like all the other men who have come before you. There is less shame in that." She folded her arms. "Rest assured, if you ever threaten me again, you may not live to regret it."

The prince glared at her and spat on the ground before storming out like an angry toddler.

Badroulbadour turned to see Amir casually leaning against the pillar with a satisfied smirk. "Are you spying on me?" Her eyebrows came together and her cheeks flushed as she stalked up and shoved Amir off his perch. "How dare you slink around in the shadows?"

Amir couldn't help but laugh, even with her tiny hands swatting at him.

"My apologies, Princess." Amir put his palms up in surrender, still laughing. "At first I thought you might need someone to step in and remove that pompous prat. But it became very apparent that you were perfectly capable of handling the situation on your own."

She stepped back, her eyes softening. "You're not going to scold me for my poor diplomacy?"

"That illiterate swine got exactly what he deserved." Amir

laughed again, shaking his head. "I thought it gracious of you to let him leave without a good beating."

Her brows rose and her stance loosened. Could it be no one had ever congratulated her on this wonderful strong spirit of hers? People in this kingdom needed to rethink their priorities.

The princess finally freed a frustrated laugh. "I wish they would just stop coming. Being forced to choose one of these morons as a husband makes me wish I had never been born." She sighed. "I hate that the most I can offer this world is to be a wife to an imbecile and have his children."

"You don't really think that will be your fate, do you?"

She held up her hands. "What choice do I have? I am covered head to toe in jewels and satin, but they're merely lavish chains to represent my enslavement. I'm expected to live and die within these walls, and I don't see any way out of it."

"I suppose I know how you feel to some extent."

"How do you figure? It was your choice to come here."

Maybe, but it was a choice thrust upon him by another man's greed, a greed that had driven Henry Smith to murder.

Amir pursed his lips. "I made a decision long ago about who I was going to be. I spent every breath of every day working toward this monumental dream and somewhere along the way, I lost sight of why I wanted it."

Which was true. For years, the anger, frustration, and the sickening loss had enveloped him, pushing Amir to find the most adept sorcerers in the world to train him. With their combined knowledge, Amir had become a force to be reckoned with. And now he was here, on the brink of his destiny. For the first time in fifteen years, though, he questioned whether avenging his family would truly abate the ghosts that haunted his dreams.

The princess gazed into the sky. "You could always change your objective."

"I feel like it's too late. After spending two-thirds of my life studying and working toward this life I've designed for myself, what sort of man would I be if I just gave up moments before I reached my goal?"

"So you're a captive to your own ambition?" Her tone had an aftertaste of sarcasm.

"I know it sounds foolish, but my sense of duty is stronger than my desire to be free of it."

"I do know how that feels."

"Badroulbadour..."

"Please." She held up her palm. "I loathe the sound of my name. If we are to be trapped here for the rest of our lives, you should call me 'Badra.'"

"Badra." Amir smiled as he spoke. "It does roll off the tongue a bit easier than Ba..."

"Don't say it!" She covered his mouth with her fingertip.

"It means 'full moon of full moons,' doesn't it?"

Badra rolled her eyes. "Thanks for reminding me. You're one of about five people who actually know that."

"Your secret is safe with me." Amir bowed.

"I have more than one. I have a feeling the same can be said of you." Her eyes smiled despite the bite in her words.

He smiled back. "One can never tell."

She walked around the fountain, running her fingers along the edge of the water. "If you studied with our former vizier, you must be a scholar."

Amir nodded. "It is one of my true loves."

She turned to him. "In all your studies, have you ever read anything that could assist me with my suitor dilemma?"

His cheeks heated. He pushed aside whatever tainted emotion pressed him. He'd been waiting for exactly this opportunity to offer himself as a solution. He should speak, tell her about the scrolls...yet, he found himself considering his own reflection in the water. His beard had thickened. He ran his fingers through the course hair. The vision was him, yet at the same time, it wasn't.

He turned to her. "I can consult some ancient texts in my personal library. If there is a way around your marrying an imbecile, I will make it my mission to find it."

The sound of an explosion echoed in the distance, causing them both to look toward the eastern desert. A starburst shot up and a white line of smoke appeared, starting behind the wall and drawing a white line across the sky. Magic, Amir was sure of it.

"That's strange." Badra squinted into the distance. "I don't believe there are any pyrotechnics scheduled."

Of course she would think it a celebration. Only a sorcerer would notice the subtle difference.

Amir found himself feeling an unexpected desire to protect her, even though *he* was the thing she needed protection from the most.

"We should go inside." Amir placed his hand on the small of her back to coax her along. Her eyes darted to his, as if to assess his intentions. Seemingly satisfied that her safety was his main motivation for touching her, she relaxed and walked with him. A subtle smile may even have crossed her lips.

Looking back, he saw a shape flying through the sparks that glistened in the distance. He whispered a spell to sharpen his vision. It almost looked like a person riding on a magic carpet.

A cold sweat beaded up on his forehead. The magic resonance in the ethereal plane quaked, and he swallowed down the nausea left in its wake.

Something was on its way to Bisnagar and the shift on the wind told him it was even more dangerous than he was.

8

THE FOLLOWING EVENING, AFTER SHE'D TAKEN HER MEAL, Badra strolled toward the gardens. Once again, at dinner, her father spoke of new princes for her to meet. Unfortunately for her, it seemed there was an unending supply of pompous buffoons to parade in front of her like peacocks.

If their new Jai'far could actually find a way for Badra to avoid having to wed one of these ridiculous suitors, she'd be first in line to convince her father to keep him as the new Grand Vizier.

Oh, to be done with sitting and listening to idiotic princes talk about themselves for hours! She didn't think she could sit through another droning attempt to win her affections.

Just outside the throne room, she caught her reflection in a mirror. A deep purple bruise shone on her cheek. She hoped no one had noticed. Covering her face, she bolted to her room and excused the servants who were turning down her bedding and replacing the flowers. They all bowed and exited.

Once alone, she opened a drawer and placed a smooth layer of makeup over her cheek.

When Alagan had pushed her off her horse during the race, she hadn't realized she'd been injured until the thrill of the competition was over, and the excitement waned from her veins. She rolled her shoulder, testing the ache. The injury was worth it, though. With the purse she'd won, three deprived children would eat for more than a week.

However, she needed to be more careful. She'd been fortunate no one had noticed her injuries thus far. The bruises that had covered the left side of her face were almost completely gone now, but even the slightest mar on her complexion would lead to questions.

Bruises covered, she smiled into the mirror, recalling a conversation she'd overheard between the old Grand Vizier and her father the week before.

"Makeup is clear evidence that women excel at deception," the vizier had said. Little did he know how right he was, at least this time.

Her father, on the other hand, believed that women were two-dimensional: innocent, pure, delicate creatures, whose only job should be to bear and raise children.

"There is a reason Allah only allows women to carry children," her father had countered. "Their minds cannot even comprehend things like hatred, war, or treachery. They are the closest thing to divine beings that dwell here on Earth."

Jai'far Hazim had shaken his head. "Sire, I had three older sisters. Hatred, war, and treachery were daily visitors at my home, and that was just before breakfast."

Badra had loved to eavesdrop as the two men debated. It was obvious that neither of them knew much about women, and while he often frustrated her to no end, she loved her father. He looked for the best in everyone, and that made him an easy target for those who would take advantage of his kindness.

Her monthly excursions to the races had taught her a great deal about the world beyond the walls of her golden cage. Her father would have her believe that starvation was a problem that didn't exist within the borders of their kingdom. It wasn't until she'd seen children begging in the street that it had become part of her reality. While she'd refused to steal from her father, she resolved to find a way to make a difference, and winning the race purse was a means for her to make that difference. Even if she could save one life, hers would mean something. She would be a worthwhile person. Not just an empty womb waiting for a future prince or princess to take up residence.

When she'd learned of the races, she could think of nothing else. The time had come and she'd watched in wonder as men on horseback competed against one another. From then on, she'd devoted all of her free time to riding lessons, and the dance lessons her father had insisted upon had proven helpful as well. She'd focused every day on strengthening her body as well as her mind.

Stretching her shoulders, she winced. Another day or two of healing and she might be ready to restart her training.

In the meantime, she had servants fetch volumes of scrolls from the university in secret. While her father's idea of an education revolved around learning manners and etiquette of various cultures around the world, she wanted to learn about the world itself.

The world... She shook her head. The world had requirements for a woman of her breeding.

She walked to her balcony and took in the sounds of the

fountain and the songs of the caged birds that had been brought out to enjoy the fresh air. She sympathized with them. Of course they had everything their little hearts could desire, except the choice to fly away.

With the sun going down on this, the night of the full moon, Badra yearned for her brown hooded riding outfit. She had loved it so much when she'd first stitched it together. Now, the thought of hiding her femininity felt shameful. She was proud of who she was. Women could be strong, powerful, and just as good at riding as any man. She wished she could show the audience, especially the young girls lining the streets, who the hooded rider really was.

The only time she ever felt free was when she raced. She told herself that it was because she wanted to help the children. But somewhere deep down, she couldn't help but wonder if her motivations were truly so charitable. Some part of her did it because she wanted...no, *needed*...to feel like she was more than the mindless doll everyone thought she was. The day would come where she would be trapped in the role of princess forever.

The moonlight caught a shadow moving through the garden. Jai'far—the *new* Jai'far—stole through the bushes. What would their new vizier be doing out after dark? This was too intriguing to pass up, so she climbed over the edge and down the trellis, following quietly behind him.

The gardener's entrance at the rear of the orchard was always locked, but Jai'far mumbled something to himself as he pushed against the door and the latch popped. He hesitated, scanning the verge concealing the princess. Ducking behind a tree, she held her breath, standing perfectly still.

Hearing nothing, she peeked out from behind the tree to see that Jai'far had disappeared, leaving the garden door slightly open. She crept up and peered out, gasping as two strong hands grabbed her from behind, spinning her around and shoving her against the wall.

"Now look who's spying on whom." Jai'far growled.

She straightened her *lehenga*. "Well, where are you sneaking off to at this hour?"

He released her, taking a step back. "In the shabby district, the people hold horse races. I'm going to watch them."

Really? This new vizier grew more interesting by the moment. "Observing social gatherings for your research?"

"No, I just like watching a bunch of barbarians on horse-back bludgeon each other in competition." He laughed. "I'd tell you there was a more profound reason, but it would be a lie."

"It sounds fascinating." Badra donned a mischievous smirk.

"I assure you it's nothing that would ever interest a princess."

"You'd be surprised." As would anyone. Her father had done a good job of hiding her womanly inadequacies.

"Would you like to come with me?" Jai'far took off his black cloak and slipped the thick fabric over her shoulders. "I would escort you and it would be our secret."

Was he serious? Leave the palace, just like that, with her father's advisor?

It was insane. Irresponsible. She barely knew this man. Then again, if he tried anything unsavory, she could easily lay him out flat on the ground before he knew who'd hit him.

Besides, she planned on going to the race herself, anyway. This was a much better option than them accidentally running into each other at the event.

A smile burst across her face. "How could I refuse?"

Badra brimmed with glee as they passed through the gates. It seemed odd, and even more nefarious to be sneaking out with someone else, rather than alone.

At the second perimeter, Jai'far whispered something to

himself, and when they reached the final gate, it lay open. Had he paid off a guard?

She looked back at the exit when she passed though. "Will it lock?"

He pushed on the door. "No worries. I would never allow the palace to be unsafe."

Which was good to know. However, every time she'd left, she'd propped the door open with a small stone. The door appeared just as locked as ever, but the mechanism couldn't engage. This time, they were actually locked out. "But how will we get back inside?"

His smile was dazzling. "Fear not, Princess. I would not have left if I didn't have plans on how to return."

She took his arm. This new vizier was interesting indeed.

The wealthier district seemed completely deserted, except for the lit windows. However, once they crossed into the shabby district, the streets came alive, bustling with the usual liveliness of the common population. Badra breathed in the scents of smoked meat, dirt, and horses. She'd heard people describe the smells of the shabby district as foul. They were anything but.

Jai'far tugged on her arm, a huge smile on his face. "Come, I want to show you—"

They walked toward an assemblage gathered around a small stand. As they approached, the group cried out, and then simultaneously droned "aww" as Badra had heard them do when their favored rider lost a race. A man stepped away, his head bowed low. A little girl pouted beside him. "Can you try again, *Baba*?"

He shook his head. "That was the last of our festival money, *hubun*."

Jai'far pulled Badra to the front. "What is our prize today,

Tiffin?" he asked the rotund, black-bearded man beside the table.

"This lovely doll." He pointed to the center of the table. "A perfect likeness of the princess."

Badra cocked a brow beneath her hood. The doll had long, straight dark hair and green button eyes, but other than the colors, it looked nothing like her.

Jai'far paid for two balls and handed them to her. "You need to bounce the balls on the cups at least once. If you knock the vase in the center of the table over, you win."

A game? How delightful! Badra bounced her first ball, but it landed inside a cup.

"Losing ball!" Tiffin called.

Badra gaped. "But the cups are all upward. It's impossible not to land in a cup."

The man bowed. "If it were not hard, it would not be a fun game."

She tried again. Her ball bounced twice before hopping off the board and rolling back toward her on the ground.

"Dead ball!" Tiffin called out again.

Stupid, idiotic...Badra snatched the ball off the ground and flung it at the stand, smashing the vase off its perch to fall onto the glasses.

The crowd laughed, but Tiffin waved his finger. "Alas, you didn't pay for that ball, and it has to bounce at least once."

"Stupid game," Badra whispered.

Snorting, Jai'far pulled her aside. "Did you really want the doll? We can try again."

His smile dazzled, abating her anger. A laugh bubbled up from her core. "No, of course not. I just—"

"Don't like to lose." He snorted again.

She folded her arms and glared at him. He just laughed harder.

He waved a finger at her. "That won't work out here, Your Highness. In the shabby district, we are all equal."

She smiled, taking his arm. That was one of the reasons she found this place so grand.

To their left, an archer shot the outer white rim of a target and won the prize of a small elephant toy.

She scanned the prizes, and her eyes widened over a larger doll, maybe two of her feet tall. This one, with vibrant green eyes and flowing curls of black hair that easily matched her own, couldn't have looked any more like her if she had sat for the artist like her father sat for his yearly portraits.

"I want to play this," she said.

Jai'far clucked the roof of his mouth. "I'm not much of an archer."

She flashed her best smile. "Come on. It's supposed to be fun, right?"

He made a show of rolling his eyes like a child but still handed money to the games keeper. The arrow fell out of his hand when he tried to cock the bow. She supposed there was no need for a scholar and advisor to study archery.

Jai'far shot the arrow, but it landed in the dirt a few feet in front of the target.

She covered her mouth so she didn't laugh.

He frowned. "Have you ever tried to pull back a bow? It's hard!"

"I'm sure it is."

The games keeper handed her a bow. "Maybe the lady would like to give it a try?"

"A woman archer?" An observer scoffed. "How ridiculous."

Half-baked fool. Badra accepted the bow. "I'd love to try."

Jai'far raised a brow as he handed the money to the games keeper. Badra cocked the arrow, being sure to fumble twice to make it appear she'd never held a bow before.

"Can I help you?" Jai'far asked.

She opened her mouth, ready to spit a retort that he'd done no better, but his eyes were so sincere. He only wanted to help, not to do it for her. She nodded, concealing her smile.

He moved behind her, pressing her back against his chest. "Now, I've heard people say that holding it steady is the hard part."

Yes, it was. That and aiming. Badra raised the bow and let him help her feel the tug of the strings. Her own bow was more lightly weighted, but if she only needed one draw, she would not tire from the tension of the strings.

"Be careful the feathers don't slice your hand."

That safety motto she'd learned months ago.

He leaned closer, his warmth overcoming her as their bodies pressed together. Such closeness was forbidden, especially with the staff. She couldn't remember ever being this close to another person. Not even the most pushy prince. She leaned back into him for a moment and could feel his smile against her cheek.

"Are you ready?" he asked.

She closed her eyes, drinking in the last seconds of his contact before nodding.

He backed away, leaving her completely off target. She smiled, knowing it was unintentional. She corrected her aim and let the arrow fly free. The arrow sank into the target with a satisfying *thunk*. It wasn't dead center, but it was pretty close.

All the women in attendance jumped up and down, screaming. A few of the younger girls cried out that they wanted to be archers, too. The men crossed their arms, shook their heads, and grumbled, "Luck."

Jai'far scooped her into his arms, swinging her around in a circle before placing her down. His smile faded for a moment as he stepped back, no doubt remembering himself.

His smile returned. "You never cease to amaze me, you know that?"

She shrugged. "I like to keep things interesting."

"What prize would you like?" the games keeper asked Jai'far.

Badra tensed at the snuff. After all, she was the one who'd hit the center of the target.

Jai'far pointed her to the prizes. "Which would you like?"

A large pillow shaped like an elephant caught her eye, but she had ulterior motives in mind. "I'd like the doll, please."

The games keeper smiled. "All ladies want to play princess, able to lie about the palace with servants attending to her every wish."

Badra bit her tongue. If they only knew how stifling that life could actually be.

The games keeper wrapped the doll in white linen and handed it to Badra. She hugged it tightly to her chest. Beautiful things normally appeared in her room, gifts from suitors or traveling dignitaries. She'd never actually chosen any of her dolls, let alone earned one herself.

Jai'far placed his palm on her back. "Come. We can still make the races."

She looked up from her doll. It had been ages since she had attended the races as an observer. Would it be as exhilarating as a spectator, now that she knew the thrill of actually competing? Excitement bubbled up from within. This was so much more fun than a bath and studying all night!

They moved with the mob, toward the main alley that made up the race path. Several paces in front of them, a man with silver highlights that glowed in the torchlight strolled toward the race. Through the people, she could just make out a little girl holding his hand.

She waved her arm. "Wait!"

"What's wrong?" Jai'far asked her.

She pointed ahead. "I need to talk to that man."

His grip on her tightened as he pulled her ahead, pushing through the crowd until Jai'far grabbed the man's shoulder. "Excuse me, sir."

The man turned, wide-eyed and holding up the hand that was not gripping the child as he stepped back. "I have no money."

Jai'far's brow furrowed. "I don't want or need your money."

Badra crouched to the child's height. "Hi there. What's your name?"

The girl put a finger in her mouth. "Jamila."

"That's a gorgeous name, Jamila." She handed her the package. "I have a present for you."

The child's eyes widened as she removed the cloth, revealing the doll. "*Baba*, look!"

The man's posture drooped. "I can't pay for that. It's not fair, teasing the child."

Badra stood, shaking her head. "It's a gift. I saw how sad she was when you didn't win earlier."

The man pursed his lips. "I can't accept."

"You can," Jai'far said, handing the man a small purse. "And take this, too. Bring your family home a nice, warm meal tonight."

His eyes widened. "Wait, you're that vizier, aren't you? The young one."

Jai'far lowered his face. "I have no idea what you're talking about."

Not taking credit for his high station? Interesting. Badra stood. The old Jai'far practically shouted his title in the streets, seeking every bit of recognition he could muster.

The man stared at Jai'far for a moment, then at Badra. His eyes widened.

Jai'far's hand touched the father's chest. "We prefer not to make a scene."

The man slipped the coins in his pocket. "You'll have none from me, sir."

Jamila held the doll up to him. "Can I keep her, *Baba?*"

The man pulled her close. "Yes, child, you can." And to Badra and Jai'far, he said, "Thank you, and please thank our most wise sultan."

Badra laughed as Jai'far pulled her back into the throng. Little did the man know the sultan had no idea they were even out here.

"That was a little closer than I would have liked," Jai'far said. "We need to be more careful."

"Nonsense," Badra said as he led her to a seat. "That was amazing. If everyone could give just a little bit of their surplus to others, the world would be a much better place."

He nodded with apparent approval. "Wise words...from a *woman.*" His emphasis on the word *woman* prickled at her spine.

She straightened, her eyes wide, until she saw his playful smile. She had to wonder, though, did he actually agree with her? Could this new vizier be her ally in trying to convince her father to change Bisnagar for the better?

A young boy of maybe ten years in a clean, fairly-new cloak —something quite uncommon in this district—approached. Jai'far waved him closer.

"Sir, I have been taking good care of Xerxes. I take him out walking every day so that he doesn't get bored." The boy beamed up at him, then smiled at Badra. "Who is this enchanting desert flower?"

Badra pressed her lips together. *How adorable.*

"Just a friend, Iman. I'd prefer not to draw attention to her, if you don't mind."

"Of course, sir."

Jai'far handed him a coin purse. "Here are your weekly wages. Now go on and get something good to eat for you and your sisters."

The boy accepted the coins and disappeared back into the masses.

Badra watched him go. "You know, if you have a horse, you can bring him into the palace stables."

Jai'far nodded. "I could, but then young Iman would be begging in the streets again. This arrangement suits us both fine."

Interesting. Most men would look forward to the amenities her father's stables had to offer, yet he chose to better the life of a commoner. This new Jai'far continued to surprise her in all the right ways.

The dancers twirled and Badra watched the display as if it were for the first time. Her protector, however, seemed more interested in her than the dancers. She tried not to blush under his stare. His interest was only in her wellbeing, of course. Sure, she had men stare at her all the time, but their expressions were blank and covetous. Jai'far appeared amused and impressed, rather than searching for a way to raise his station by taking all her dowry offered.

The race kicked off on time, and Badra winced as Alagan, the man who'd unhorsed her in her last race, came in first place. She clapped her hands with little exhilaration.

"It's a shame." Jai'far put his arm around Badra as they fought their way through the crowd. "The best rider didn't show up tonight. He would have made it a night to remember for you."

"The best rider?"

He nodded. "A young man. He was pushed from his horse

the last time I saw him, but he still came in second place. The race was very exciting."

A shiver of adrenaline wove up her spine. What would her new vizier think if he knew that rider was a woman, let alone his princess in disguise? "I'm sure he's remarkable, but I assure you, I'll never forget this night as long as I live, best rider, or not."

While she'd made her way to the races many times, she'd never dared to move out into the market before for fear of discovery. Each month she would steal out, win her purse, and give her winnings to someone in need. The games Jai'far had shown her tonight were a delightful amusement she hoped she would have a chance to visit again.

Jai'far whispered again as they neared the first gate. Unsurprisingly, it opened as they approached.

"Someday you will have to tell me how you do that," Badra said.

He held the door open for her. "A man needs to keep a few secrets to himself." The door relocked with a click once they were through. Next, they passed through the garden gate. He scanned left and right, as if looking for a guard.

"I guarantee you, they have no idea I'm gone." She slipped his cloak off and handed it back to him. "They never check on me after I've retired for the evening." Which had made it oh-so-easy to sneak out.

He nodded. "Then I suppose I should see you back to your room so you can get a good night's rest."

"I could never sleep after all that!" She leapt onto the edge of the fountain and twirled around the edge with her arms out.

Jai'far reached for her. "Be careful. You're going to fall in."

"I'll have you know, I'm quite agile. Not to mention, my neck is tired from having to look up at you all night." She folded her arms, looking down at him for the first time. "Why are you so tall anyway? The only people I've seen that are as tall as you come from other kingdoms...except the guard captain, I suppose. He's almost as tall as you are."

"I suppose I'm just exceptional." The new vizier grinned and stepped up on the ledge to tower over her once more.

"Is that so?" Badra pushed him and he tipped toward the pool, grabbing her as he fell. They both hit the water with a splash and emerged, gasping. "You pile of weasel dung! You'll get us both caught," she whisper-yelled.

"Oh, really?" Jai'far splashed her face.

She gasped, wide-eyed, ready to spew a heinous rant of epic proportions while calling for the guards. But then the moonlight caught that confounded smile of his.

He didn't care that she was a princess. He treated her like anyone else. When was the last time she hadn't been put on a pedestal?

Probably never. This man had given her the night of her dreams, shown her what it was like to be like everyone else, and she'd never had so much fun.

She wiped the water from her eyes. He would soon find out she was not the delicate desert bloom his servant boy thought she was, though. She tackled the vizier and pushed him under the water before standing up and running away. He gave chase and the two laughed, running circles around the garden until Badra let him catch her. She allowed herself to linger in his arms for a moment. He was warm, fun, and everything those pompous princes weren't.

He was also forbidden.

She couldn't force herself to pull away, though. Instead, she moved closer, drinking in his warmth.

He held her for a few moments before tapping her back and stepping away.

"We have to dry off and get to bed." He wiped a wet strand of hair from her face.

Any other man would have taken full advantage, but this former apprentice to an old man she abhorred thought only of her wellbeing. Maybe what she wanted could not be found in the royal courts. Maybe she needed to look elsewhere.

"Have you found anything in your research about what I asked you before; something to stop the suitors from coming for me?"

He visibly gulped, staring at her as if memorizing the lines of her face. "In a way, I have." He rubbed the back of his neck. "But it's not ideal. I'll keep looking." He backed away, walking toward the fountain.

She scrambled to walk beside him. "Well, at least tell me what you *did* find."

He tried to shake the water from his clothes. "No, it's ridiculous."

She grabbed his arm, stopping him from walking. "Regardless, if it would keep me out of a marriage to someone I hate, I'd like to hear it."

He started to speak, then stopped. "Just let me do some more research. I'll give you a list of options after I find every possible answer."

She shoved him back. "I want an answer now."

His lips thinned. He straightened, somehow becoming even taller. "I am not ready to give you one."

Her hands clenched into fists. "Are you refusing to answer me?"

The vizier stared into her eyes. Red stained his cheeks before he turned away.

Heat flooded her face. "Fine!"

She threw up her arms and bounded away, grabbing on to her trellis and scampering up the side. He'd found a solution but dared to *decide for her* as to whether or not it was 'ideal.' The nerve! He had no business holding something back that could help her.

She'd thought he was different, but maybe he was no better than any other man who wanted to keep her caged up in this blasted palace.

9

Amir paced the length of the floor in the cursed temple. "She was so incredibly angry with me. I wasn't sure what to do."

Iago cackled through his pointed teeth. "The solution is simple. Give the girl her answer, and you become sultan, you fool! You should have taken that opportunity. It might not come again."

True, the opportunity may never return. In one swift, poorly conceived decision, he may have ruined an entire life's worth of planning. And for some odd reason, he didn't care.

"I couldn't." He dragged his fingers through his hair.

"What do you mean, you couldn't?" Iago's shape wavered, becoming denser, before returning to his natural, partially transparent self. "What about all that nonsense about your destiny to rule Bisnagar?"

Amir spun, pointing at him. "I will rule Bisnagar...in time." He began pacing again. "I will let the sultan live a long and natural life while I pursue my secondary goal of immortality. Badra will rule at my side and I—"

"Stop right there!" Iago stood. "You're going to let her live as well?"

"Yes, you dimwit, I just said—"

"That she will *rule at your side.*"

"That is correct. Perhaps, up to this point I haven't been

worthy of someone like her, but I will be." He picked up a halved rock from the shelf and stared at the glinting white gemstones inside. "I will give her everything she could ever dream of."

"Do my ears deceive me or are you questioning your adequacy?"

"I am one of the most adept sorcerers who ever lived. There is nothing in the perceivable universe beyond my potential." He placed the rock down. "Except her. She is the most beautiful creature I have ever seen." He began his pacing anew. "More than that, she has a brilliant mind. She's courageous in the face of her fears. Her will is unbreakable. Every other person in the world pales in comparison."

"If I didn't know better, I'd say the evil, all-powerful sorcerer has a weakness." Iago chuckled. "Could it be love?" He put his hands out, and a rainbow shot from his fingertips, arched over them, and disappeared into the tiled floor.

"Don't be foolish. I will rule Bisnagar and my son will be the greatest sultan in the history of my kingdom."

"*If* she'll have you."

"What do you mean?"

"She might decide to choose whichever prince she can dominate the easiest. There is also the possibility she might run away as soon as her father passes. That would leave you Sultan Apparent, but not sultan. You would be challenged by anyone and everyone who felt they had a right to that throne."

The rainbow winked out. Amir's stomach sank.

"For all your power, there is no magic in the world that can make someone love you." Iago lifted his chin. "We could possibly make her believe that she loves you for short periods of time, but if her will is truly as strong as you say, that might even be difficult." He smiled, showing his grimy teeth. "There is always lust—much better than love in my experience."

Amir closed his eyes as the well in his gut deepened. A month ago, he would have taken either of these possibilities. But now?

He shuddered. Spells were easy. Bending people to his will was just a matter of finding the right words and channeling his intent to the correct radiance. Fifteen years of training had made him a weapon of epic proportion. Yet he would lay it all at her feet if she asked him to.

He turned to the demon. "What if I don't need any of that? What if she actually did love me?"

Iago stared at him blankly for a several seconds before he burst into laughter. Tears poured from the demon's bloodshot eyes. "Yes, boy," Iago shrieked, trying to catch his breath. "That *would* be something."

Indignant, callous fool!

Amir snatched the scroll from the table and cast the spell to return to his chamber. Taking one last look at the words that would give him everything he wanted, he grimaced.

Iago was wrong. Not all things needed magic, or a cold heart. Bisnagar was his destiny, but he refused to bathe his fortune in blood.

He glanced at the words again. This scroll was his easiest path forward, and he needed to use these ancient words to his advantage, no matter what his heart told him.

Nadir, the burly guard captain, appeared in Amir's doorway. "The sultan demands your presence."

"Of course." Amir rolled up the scroll, tucked the parchment under his arm, and began his trek to the throne room.

The large guard followed closely behind. Badra was right; this was the only man he could remember whose height nearly matched his own, but the guard probably weighed forty pounds more than Amir. The man's size pressed him forward.

He quickened his pace. "Thank you for the escort. I feel so much safer with you hovering like that."

"I have a feeling, *sir*," Nadir stated with feigned respect, "that you have lost favor with the royal family."

Amir flinched. "Why would you say that?"

Nadir pointed toward the throne room, where Badra stood beside her father, eyes ablaze and arms folded in defiance.

Amir took a moment to appreciate how stunning she was, especially when she was on the verge of violence. Then he realized that violence might be aimed at him.

No matter. He could right his wrongs.

He glanced at the parchment, then back to Badra. A soothing warmth swept through him, and his shoulders relaxed. Why did he even need to be sultan? What point did it serve? His entire life had been pointed at this moment, and now that he stood here, he realized that the one thing that truly mattered was not what he wanted, but the happiness of the woman who stood next to the throne, throwing daggers from her eyes. He smiled at her, but she flared her nose in return. His smile only widened.

"Jai'far, thank you for coming," the sultan said. "My daughter is under the impression that you have found a way around the law that she must marry a prince. I hope, for your sake, that you didn't tell her a lie in hopes to buy yourself time to find said solution."

Ah, so that was what this was about. He supposed he should not have expected less from her.

Amir bowed. "Lying to the princess is the last thing I would ever do." Amir's words burned like acid as they passed his lips, partly because it was a lie in and of itself, but more so because as time passed, the more it felt true. He didn't want to lie to her anymore. Even the thought made his stomach turn. Yet here he was, facing the sultan, forced to tell a truth he no longer wanted to utter.

The scroll's weight hung beneath his arm. What foolery was it that made him want to win her heart, when the solution presented itself in the written word, ready for all eyes to see?

Still, he wanted real affection. *Her* affection. Without magic. Was that so wrong?

"I did find something, Your Majesty, but as I told Her Highness..." He bowed to her. "It is not ideal, and I wanted to look further."

The sultan pulled his shoulders back. "I will decide what is, and is not good for my daughter. Tell me what you found."

This was it. The point of no turning back. His stomach roiled.

This was what he'd come for, though. He should be jumping at this chance. Yet everything told him that this wasn't the way. Which was ridiculous. This scroll guaranteed his success, and he needed to take advantage, no matter what his ridiculous heart told him.

He steeled himself, and turned back to the sultan. "There was a previous sultan who had a similar dilemma to Your Majesty. His daughter refused to choose a suitor, so he wrote something into law to bend her to his will."

Badra shifted her weight. Her brow furrowed.

"And?" the sultan urged.

Everything he'd learned told him the sultan had a deep reverence for the traditions of his ancestors, believing that they had some sort of superior wisdom simply because they had lived so long before. Once Amir told him the law, there'd be no stopping this. He'd declare the law still valid, and Badra would be bound, as she so deeply wanted *not* to be.

"Jai'far?"

Amir opened his mouth, but his tongue dried. "I found...I-I found..."

The sultan stomped his foot. "I have told you that I don't take heads without good reason but you are trying my patience, sir."

Amir nodded, though his stomach tightened. Badra kneaded her fingers.

The sultan's eyes narrowed.

Enough stalling. This was what he'd come for. He shouldn't doubt himself when he was so close to his goal. Lifting his chin, he unrolled the scroll and read, "If a suitor isn't chosen by the princess's eighteenth birthday, then she is to marry..." He glanced at Badra. "The Grand Vizier."

The princess gasped.

"What? How can it be that I've never heard of this clause?" The sultan reached out his hand. Amir handed him the scroll. The sultan examined the sacred symbol stamped at the top of the document before finding where Amir had left off. "He's right. '...She is to marry the Grand Vizier, who will rule as Sultan Apparent until she gives the kingdom a true heir.'"

Badra put a hand to her forehead. Tears welled in her eyes, and she ran from the throne room.

A deep pang riddled Amir's heart. He took a step toward her, then remembered himself. She was a princess, and he was nothing. At least not yet. Everything was going according to plan, but suddenly, the thought of Badra marrying him because she had no choice made him feel more of a snake than the idol on his scepter.

"Thank you for your diligence, Jai'far. You may go." The sultan continued to peruse the scroll, enthralled by every detail. "Nadir, please fetch my historian, this needs to be properly cataloged and its texts copied for further examination."

"Yes, sire." The large guard bowed, his eyes lancing Amir.

No matter. He didn't need the guard's approval, only that of the sultan. Amir backed from the room in a bow and tried to appear casual as he walked as fast as he could to the only place Badra might have run to.

With every step, he tried to imagine what he was going to say to her. What could he say that wouldn't make her feel like a prisoner in a gilded cage?

He stopped just outside the garden. The time for thinking was over. There she sat, exactly as he imagined, tears dripping from her eyes as she stared into the water of the great fountain.

10

Badra slapped the water with her palm. She'd never be anything except a vessel to breed more royalty. More slaves to the crown.

As the water stilled, Jai'far's dark shadow fell over her. "I do *not* want to talk to you."

"I don't blame you." He kept his distance, fidgeting with his snake staff. "Now you know why I was trying to find another way. I understand if you don't want to marry an old fool like me."

"Ha!" She stiffened, realizing she'd reacted without listening to what he'd said.

Did he actually care what she thought? He could have told her about the ancient law last night, yet he hadn't. He'd hesitated, just like today, until her father had demanded the information. "How old *are* you, anyway?"

"I've seen twenty-five summers pass."

"That doesn't seem too old."

"Too old for someone like you. You're vibrant and full of life. I spend most of my time with my head bent over a table reading old scrolls and tomes."

She smiled, turning toward him but keeping her eyes on the grass. "I don't think *vibrant* is a word that most men would use to describe me."

"Those men are dullards." He knelt down on one knee close at her side. She met his gaze. "Promise me one thing, Badra—that you will never change. Not ever, for any man. The world will try to tell you that your fire is too bright. But don't you listen! You...are perfect."

Perfect?

She gaped. She was far from perfect. She was the opposite of everything she was supposed to be. She was strong willed and belligerent. She stood up for herself. But would she change any of that? Could she?

She closed her eyes. In a world that couldn't, or *refused to,* understand her, this one man defied culture and custom and chose to be her friend, boundaries be damned. He accepted her for who she was...not only accepted, but embraced her short-comings. For all that was good in the world, why couldn't he wear a crown?

But then again, he didn't want a crown, or he'd have jumped at this chance. Instead, he'd sought another solution. Her pride and her anger had backed them both into a corner neither of them wanted to be in.

"I'm sorry," she whispered.

He sat beside her. "I'm sorry, too."

She swallowed down the ball building in her throat. The only time anyone said they were sorry to her, were those backing away, hoping to avoid her wrath. She choked out a sob, leaning on his shoulder. None of this was fair. She was too young to be forced to marry, despite that stupid law. Why did she have to marry anyone by a certain age? It made no sense.

Once she let go, he wiped her tears and sat next to her on the edge of the fountain, staring at the red parrot perched in the shade, preening his feathers.

She took in the vizier's golden skin and carefully shaped

beard, his finely angled nose. He certainly was more handsome than any of the princes who had come for her. If she were forced to marry, maybe—

"I promise I'll keep looking." He turned toward her. "I won't rest until I find a way for you to be free."

Her chest clenched. Once again, he denied the power that was about to be all but thrust upon him. This man was like no other she'd met.

Reaching for his hand, she interlaced her fingers with his. "If there is no other way, would you consider marrying me?"

Jai'far's eyes suddenly glistened with the threat of tears. He closed his eyes and covered his face with his hands. Then with a deep breath, he looked back at her. "Would you actually consider me a worthy suitor?"

His amber-brown eyes searched hers as she tried to find the right words to answer. Finding none, she leaned in, bringing her lips toward his. He placed his fingertips on the soft curve of her cheek. His touch was warm, inviting, and so incredibly right. After so many years of tortuous meetings, was it possible to find the perfect man in a noble, rather than a royal house?

She trembled as his breath skated across her lips, then relaxed as all the world suddenly became right.

He closed the distance, his lips covering hers—not dominating and insistent, like some of the boorish princes who had tried to force themselves on her, but soft, unsure, and so incredibly perfect.

Maybe Hazim's illness had been fate. Maybe this was the match she'd always been destined to have.

A thunderous trumpet sounded from the great hall. They both jumped, releasing the kiss.

More instruments joined, sounding like an entire orchestra had entered the great hall.

"What on Earth?" Badra stood up and gasped as minstrels, dancers, and a massive, painted elephant marched into the garden.

92

11

Amir stood beside Badra, holding her arm as the dancers circled past them and out the rear entrance. His eyes widened as the elephant, covered in white powder and colorful paints, raised his trunk into the air and trumpeted.

Badra walked toward the massive beast. She'd probably never seen a creature so large. The goliath stared at her, its eyes oddly knowing. It seemed to smile at her as she touched his warm, painted hide. The creature shook its ears, tinkling the bells woven around his tusks with white flower vines.

Badra reached out cautiously and touched its trunk.

"Be careful," Amir said.

Badra shook her head, probably unable to comprehend how anything so grand could be dangerous.

Her father stepped into the gardens, accompanied by a young man who appeared to be in his late teen years or early twenties. Rich robes draped from the boy's shoulders as he straightened an oversized white turban on his head.

The sultan pointed to Badra, and the boy nodded—undoubtedly another suitor here to beg and plead for her affections. He was soon to find out that Bisnagar's princess was not a prize to be granted to the highest bidder, or to the fool with the flashiest ensemble.

Amir scowled as Badra laughed, petting the elephant's

trunk. They needed to be done with this boy just as quickly as the last one.

Amir stormed toward Badra's father, barely remembering to bow.

The sultan held out his hand toward the prince. "Jai'far, this young man is Prince Aladdin from the kingdom of Noblis."

Amir straightened, forcing the prince to look up at him. The boy's features were well cut, drawing attention to his clean shaven face. Or maybe he was not unshaven, but too young to grow a full man's beard.

Aladdin smiled, placing his hand over his heart. "Always a pleasure to meet a land's vizier. I'm honored."

Amir was sure he wasn't. The boy's voice seemed *off*, as if he worked to make his tone deeper. A prince unsure of himself would certainly be sent running by Amir's bold, forthright princess. Amir held back a smile, looking forward to his lovely desert bloom knocking this charlatan down off his pompous elephant-toting rear end.

"Oh!" Badra called out as a small animal leapt from the elephant's back, scurried across the grass, and jumped onto Aladdin's shoulder. A slight yellow hue surrounded the monkey, as if sunlight bathed the animal from behind, which, of course, it didn't. Amir tightened his grip on his staff, ready to throttle the beast, if needed, as a hint of magic far darker than his own wove through the air. What sort of creature was this?

Keeping wary of the cursed animal, Amir kept his eyes on the prince. "Where exactly is Noblis? I can't recall the name."

Aladdin smiled. Nice lines, pretty teeth. Yes, this one certainly needed to go. "I won't expect that you've heard of it. We are mostly self-sufficient, so we rarely trade with outside sources. We haven't been involved in a political conflict with any neighboring kingdoms in well over a century. Our kingdom is far smaller than Bisnagar, but prosperous."

"All facts of which you should be most proud, Your Highness. Where would Noblis be located on a map?" Amir persisted.

"Far to the south...er." Aladdin blinked. "East...the southeast."

"Interesting." Amir's eyes narrowed.

The sultan pulled the prince's shirt, nearly dragging him toward the elephant. "This is the Princess Badroulbadour."

Amir cringed as Aladdin's mouth fell open at the sight of Badra. She glanced at him, then continued her petting of the elephant.

"Forgive me." Aladdin placed his hand on his heart. "The rumors of your beauty don't do you justice, Princess." He gestured to the elephant that was now following Badra like a lost puppy. "I see you have met Keeko."

"Yes, he's amazing." A smile lit up Badra's face as a curious elephant trunk brushed her shoulder.

Aladdin leaned closer and mock-whispered, "I think he likes you."

A swirling ball of heat erupted in Amir's soul, shot down his arm, and stopped just under the skin of his fingertips. He gritted his teeth. The last thing he needed to do was lose his temper over this ridiculous fool.

He needed to retire and leave Badra to dispatch this one as well as she'd dismissed the last. "Excuse me, Your Majesty, Your Highnesses; I think something might not be agreeing with me." He bowed.

"Take care of your health above all things." Aladdin held up a finger.

Amir fought the desire to bite the digit off and spit it at him.

If there were a place called Noblis, Amir would have come across it in his research. He would find out who this boy was and expose him before this blasted elephant trampled the flower beds.

12

THE ELEPHANT WAS A NICE TOUCH, BADRA HAD TO ADMIT. It didn't change the fact that this Aladdin was one more grandiose royal who was walking in, hoping to own her like a piece of furniture along with the palace and the kingdom that came with her hand.

None of it mattered, though. It was only a matter of time before this fool was gone like the rest of them, and her new Jai'far would keep searching for a solution to her problem. She touched her fingers to her lips. Her skin had hummed when their lips had met. It was like touching sunshine, or a bubbling spark of joy. His deep amber-brown eyes had lacked the air of judgement most men had when she spoke. He not only listened to her, but encouraged her to speak her mind. He celebrated who she was and she knew she would never have to change for him to accept her.

How wonderful it would be to be with someone because she wanted to, rather than having a suitor thrust upon her.

"Come, Highness." Her servant, the girl who the sultan had named Red, startled her from the moment's warmth. "The prince has brought gifts for you."

Badra balked, finding several dresses draped over her bed and chair. Apparently, Red had been busy while she'd been daydreaming.

"These dresses came all the way from Noblis." Red held up

one of the garments and spun around the room. "I've never felt cloth like this in my life!"

Badra reached out and took the dress. The material glided through her fingertips, both soft and sleek. She touched the fabric to her cheek. "Why do you sound so impressed? I've never even heard of Noblis."

Red beamed. "It must be a special place to make such fine dresses, Highness." The girl picked up another dress. "And he has lots of animals."

"Most royalty owns a variety of animals."

"Yes, but he loves his."

"What makes you say that?"

"They look happy and healthy," she pointed out. "And they are not covered in scars from being beaten into submission."

"The elephant was covered in paint or something," Badra said. "If it was scarred, you wouldn't even notice."

"I just think there's something about him that's different, Highness. You must wear one of these dresses to the meal he is having prepared for you."

"He's having dinner prepared for me? How do we even know the food is safe?" Badra threw the dress down.

"Our chefs are following recipes brought by his chefs. Your father's tasters have already tested the spices he brought. Your father would never allow you to be put in danger."

Badra folded her arms. "My father trusts too much before he knows people."

"His Majesty has a kind heart." The girl bowed. "Which dress would you like, Highness?"

"I will wear my own clothes, thank you."

Badra walked to the edge of her balcony and gazed toward Jai'far's room. He'd left in such a hurry, maybe striving right now for a way to save her from another set of tremulous days until she could rid herself of this new suitor. Until he did find a way, though, she'd have to play the part her father asked.

She wouldn't make it easy on this new prince, though. "I'll not have him thinking he owns me because I dress to please him."

Red held up a thick golden collar necklace, so thin it almost seemed sheer. The metal caught the light, making it sparkle with an unearthly sheen. "At least wear this. That may be considered a compromise, rather than shirking all of his gifts. Bisnagar certainly would not want to be seen as unwelcoming."

Of course, she was right. Red's willingness to speak her mind was one of the many things that Badra loved about her.

"Very well." Badra sat and lifted her hair as Red placed the collar around her neck. When the clasp clicked, a stinging zap shot through Badra's body, as if she'd rubbed her feet on the carpet and touched the wall. The tingle dissipated and a sense of warmth came over her. The craftsmanship certainly was exquisite. Maybe she should at least give this prince a chance.

Red smiled at Badra's reflection as the girl put the finishing touches in her hair: tiny flowers that peeked out from between her voluminous locks that she'd twisted up in elaborate curls. There was something about flowers that made Badra feel beautiful—powerful in her own right, in a world where she was left powerless at every turn. She certainly didn't want to attract this new prince, but...

She scanned the balcony, and the top of the vizier's window. If a few flowers drew Jai'far's eye, maybe he'd offer her a smile, some sort of consolation that he wouldn't give up.

"We must leave, Highness." Red held up a hand and Badra followed.

She held her head high and strode from the room.

Badra was the Princess of Bisnagar. She had no one to impress. This boy with the fancy pets needed to impress *her*, and he was about to find out that her favor was far from easy to win. The necklace tingled against her skin. She reached up and touched the cool gold.

The gifts were nice, though. She should at least go to him with an open mind.

She stopped short and shook her head. What was she thinking? She couldn't be bought, not with expensive gifts, and not with exotic pets. Her chest warmed, though, remembering the prince's dazzling smile.

No. That wasn't enough. She wouldn't be tricked like a silly child. Meeting all these suitors was starting to get to her. The closer she got to the dining room, however, the more her steps slowed. She wrapped her arms around herself. Jai'far was her only hope of a real life. He *wouldn't* give up. Of all the men she'd ever met, she found she trusted him the most.

They entered the grand dining room and Badra stopped short. Red stumbled into her and apologized, but the servant's voice was in the background.

At the head of the table, in the place reserved for the sultan, sat the Prince of Noblis. Her father had taken a seat farther down the table beside Jai'far.

The vizier's gaze met hers. His lips thinned as his eyes pointed to the prince. She nodded her solidarity. This was insolence at its worst. Why had her father even allowed a stranger to take the place of honor?

The prince stood up and held out his arm, motioning for her take the seat at his right hand. She glared at him.

Her father stood. "Come, dear, take a seat next to Prince Aladdin and get to know him over this most excellent meal."

In front of so many dignitaries, she had no choice. Either she complied, or she made her father look like a sultan who could not control his own daughter. This, she would not do to him.

Easing down beside the prince, her eyes widened over the table overflowing with fresh fruits and vegetables and plates of spiced meats. Fish with long, spikey tails were arranged on circular plates with colorful garnishes. A medley of spices filled the air. She hadn't seen this extravagant a meal since they'd welcomed the King and Queen of Iscandia.

She glanced at Jai'far again. He shrugged, and then her father tugged on his tunic to engage him in conversation. This may have been the oddest meal she'd ever attended.

Aladdin turned to her. "You seem troubled, Princess."

"A prince who is perceptive of a woman's mood is a rare thing indeed." She fumbled with her napkin before shoving it onto her lap in a ball.

"Please, I would like to know what plagues you."

She held up a hand. "Nothing out of the usual. Power-hungry suitors who pour into our gates by the dozen to ask that I submit to them, surrendering my home, my freedom, and my body to appease their appetites and ambitions."

The boy's eyes widened and he gawked at her before bursting into irreverent laughter. Badra stood from her seat with clenched fists and burning cheeks. This one was no different than the others!

Aladdin put a hand on his chest and held up the other. "Forgive me. I meant no offense. It's just that I understand how you feel more than you know." He motioned for her to sit back down. "Please, allow me to explain myself."

She sat but continued to glower at him. How dare he laugh at her, and in front of all these people?

"I am my father's youngest son, a trophy prince, if you will." He touched his chest, and she nodded in understanding. "I will never be the Sultan of Noblis, nor would I wish to be. Honestly, I wouldn't wish such a position on my worst enemy. There is so much responsibility involved, so many people depending on a sultan." He fingered his goblet. "Nonetheless, my father believes if I am to be worth anything, I must secure a crown through marriage."

Badra furrowed her brow. "You don't want to be sultan?"

He leaned back and played with his goblet. "Don't get me wrong. The palace, the servants, the food, these are all things anyone would want, but I understand there is more to ruling than all that."

She leaned back. "Then why are you here?"

"Ever since I came of age, my father has pressured me to accept an arranged marriage. I am here at my father's bidding." He took a drink of his wine before setting the goblet down and meeting her gaze. "But then I saw you."

Clenching her teeth, she folded her arms. If she had a ruby for every pompous ass who had said that to her over the last year, she would drown in them.

He laughed again. "I understand your frustration. You are intoxicating, and you have the biggest dowry within four hundred *parasangs*. I'm sure you've seen your share of liars and cheats trying to squirm their way into your heart."

"I have." She prepared for him to tell her that he was different, that she was the moon and stars and he can't live another day without her.

He nodded. "I understand. I don't want to marry anyone I don't love, either. Especially if it means I'll have to be sultan."

She gaped at him.

"It isn't my wish to impose on you. I will only stay for as long as my father has commanded, then I will bid my farewell to your splendid kingdom, and you will never have to see me again. What do you say?" He held out his hand to her, like European men did when they were bartering a deal.

Could it be true, could this boy be in the same horrible situation, born royal, and being forced into an unwanted union?

He leaned closer. "If you will allow me to stay seven days, my father will be leaving for Emirates. He will be negotiating trade agreements for at least a year. That would give me three hundred and sixty-five more days of freedom. That's all I ask of you: a gift of time, from one condemned to another."

Badra's heart warmed. This boy was far from what she'd expected. How could she say *no* to such a heartfelt request?

His eyes were wide and hopeful. Surely, she couldn't throw him out and doom him to the very fate she was trying with all her wit to sidestep herself.

"You are welcome to stay for seven days. But make no mistake; I am not prey waiting to be overtaken by some hunter."

"I am no hunter, my lady. A creature like you should live free and wild."

She pursed her lips. "Like your elephant, or the monkey?"

"They are as free as they have ever been. They made this journey with me because they wanted to."

"Is that so?"

He leaned his elbow on the table and smiled. His gaze lowered to the necklace he'd given her before returning to her eyes. "I am rather good company, don't you think?"

She laughed. "I've had worse."

13

Amir stomped through the garden. The thought of Badra being forced to spend an entire dinner beside another pompous, arrogant, self-ambitious imp made his skin crawl and his magic tingle on the edge of release.

By now she must be spitting thorns, ready to kill someone.

He smiled. Oh, how he would love to see her take this new prince down to his true size—and she would, in time. Tonight, she played the part, most likely to keep from embarrassing her father. Once the dignitaries left, though, Aladdin would feel the bite of her lovely tongue, and Amir fizzled with glee, ready to watch her in action again.

Tonight, though, she must be raving in anger. She'd had no warning about Noblis's arrival. She needed to know that Amir was still here for her, that he was still someone she could count on. He checked over both shoulders. As usual, the guards were on the outer boundaries. Here, there were no eyes to thwart him. Pushing his fingers through the jasmine vines, he grabbed on to the trellis below Badra's balcony, and climbed.

The sweet smell of the flowers overwhelmed, just like that first night in the city.

"Badra," he whispered as loudly as he dared. "Princess!"

"Jai'far?" She came to the edge and peeked over the railing. Her grin rivaled the setting sun. "What are you doing? Have you lost your mind?"

"Not my mind." He smiled up at her. "I am still looking for a loophole to save you. However, I was wondering if you would like to accompany me on another adventure. We could venture beyond the palace walls and I could show you more of the city."

Her eyes saddened. "I would love to, but I promised Aladdin that I would show him around the palace."

"I see." His chest tightened as he searched her face. "Dinner went well, I take it."

"He's not as bad as most of the others." She looked out over the gardens. "Not that I'm ready to throw myself at him, but Aladdin is my guest and I am happy to be a hospitable hostess as long as he treats me with respect."

But that would put them in close proximity to each other for far too long.

What was it about this boy that didn't make her want to draw blood? He grimaced. He needed to find out more about this strange land of Noblis and its enchanting prince.

"I'll leave you to your duty, then. Please forgive the intrusion." He took a step down the vines.

"No apology necessary, my friend." Her words cut through him like cold steel.

Friend? Was she really going to act like what had happened in the garden earlier was nothing? No. It hadn't been nothing.

He dropped down to the ground and plodded through the garden, kicking over a basin left by the horticulturists. He and Badra had shared a connection he'd never experienced with a woman, something deep and meaningful. He refused to let that drift away on the wind because a pompous prat had shown up with a decorated elephant.

Back in his room, he closed the curtains to his balcony. He would do some digging and find out exactly who this intruder was and what he was really up to. Careful not to make a mistake in his haste, he set up all of the components for the ritual and cast the spell that brought him safely to his study.

Iago reclined on an old couch off to the side, examining one of his scrolls. It seemed that since Amir had made him clean up, the demon had rediscovered his love of reading, even if he had read these volumes all at least once before he'd collected them.

The demon priest looked up from his studies. "Is everything going according to plan?"

"How do I use the temple archives to learn everything about someone who is alive in the current time?"

Iago tilted his head. "That's easy; the scroll of Kenard."

Amir's magic tingled on the edge of his fingers. "I don't have time to play games with you. What is it and where can I find it?"

"You don't have to be rude!" Iago snapped his fingers and called to the ceiling. "The scroll of Kenard!"

A rolled parchment shimmied off the top shelf and floated down into Iago's hand.

"Clever." Amir snatched the scroll and spread the parchment out on the table. His gaze drew over the pristine, unblemished paper. "Why is it blank?"

"Because you didn't state who you wanted to learn about before you opened it. You have to say the name out loud after you recite the prayer of Kenard from memory."

"What is the prayer of Kenard?"

Iago frowned. "You call yourself a sorcerer?" He taught Amir the prayer. It was relatively short. Three verses in an ancient nomadic dialect.

Amir recited the prayer perfectly, and then spoke, "Prince Aladdin of Noblis." His eyebrows drew together as he slammed his fist down on the table. "I don't have time for this, Iago!"

"What exactly is your predicament?"

"It's still blank!"

"Interesting." Iago scratched his veiny throat. "I have a thought. Try looking for him in the lineage archives in the palace."

"Why would there be a record of him in the sultan's library?"

"Don't argue with me. Just walk into the palace library with the clear intention of finding out who he is. Open up the first scroll that jumps out at you."

"If you're trying to make a fool of me, I swear..."

"I don't need to make a fool of you. You're doing a fine job of it yourself. You're panicking like a live rodent in a lit oven and you can't see the situation for what it is."

"Which is what?" Sparks danced on his fingertips. He drew the magic back in, lest he ruin a priceless scroll.

"Just do as I say, and if I'm right, we will decide how we should proceed."

Amir did as Iago said and walked into the palace library, determined to find some record of Aladdin. Just as Iago said, the first scroll that he opened had a map of their continent with a clearly marked country to the far southeast called Noblis. The next scroll had a record of Aladdin's family lineage and even a sketch of the prince looking as dashing as ever holding a small puppy.

Amir rubbed his eyes and groaned. He took the two scrolls, rolled them up, and took them back to his room and again to his study.

He spread the scroll that had Aladdin's picture out onto the table. "Iago, I have to kill this man." He gritted his teeth. "It has to look like an accident, though, preferably an embarrassing accident."

"Now we're talking." Iago's face lit up as he approached, rubbing his hands together. Lifting the parchment, he tilted his head and raised a condescending eyebrow. "King Egbert the second? I'm fairly certain he's already dead."

"What?" Amir perused the scroll. Confused, he unrolled it farther. "Not ten minutes ago, I looked at this very scroll and it had a picture of that little piece of camel dung's smug face. He was holding a puppy!" He slammed his fist on the table again.

Iago scratched his flakey head. "Then it is as I feared."

Amir threw his hands up. "I would greatly appreciate your insight as to what in the name of Allah is going on!"

"It's obvious, you simpleton!" Iago stood. "The boy is a magic user, and quite a powerful one if he can alter sacred documents that have been blessed by a royal cleric. This is something far more ancient than you've ever encountered."

"I doubt that." A chill ran up Amir's spine as he recalled the storm from his nightmares. That sorcerer had emitted true power.

"You shouldn't doubt it. With that kind of strength, he must have some sort of magical item enhancing his power." The demon pointed at the scroll. "It could be completely covering who he is. He could be older than I am, for all we know."

"So he's an imposter. He's using magic to alter sacred documents to hide his true identity. Why does the spell no longer have an effect when I bring the documents here?"

"No trickery has any power in my temple. This place and everything inside will always hold the truth."

"Interesting."

So, Aladdin's death would leave no complication of an international incident.

Amir stroked his beard. "Attempting to kill the boy outright would be far too risky without knowing the source of his power. We don't know what failsafe he might have in place." He paced the tiled floor. "There must be a way for us to use what we know to our advantage. We must learn all his weaknesses and exploit them to the full extent of our ability."

"Things just became more entertaining." Iago's fiendish grin widened as he rubbed his hands together. "I hope it gets bloody."

14

Badra strolled around the deeper section of the garden, staying out of the central area normally frequented by staff and guests. Showing Aladdin around the night before had been uneventful. The boy had hardly spoken, and had acted unimpressed with the palace, frequently remarking that he had more and bigger versions of everything back home.

He wasn't all together unpleasant, but the whole time she was catering to him, she couldn't help but wish she had been able to go with Jai'far on whatever excursion he had wanted to sweep her off to.

Taking her dinner alone in her private dining area, she thought over the night before. She'd treated Jai'far harshly, shooing him away like one of the servants. The way his lips had thinned broke her heart...today.

It was almost like she'd been oblivious to everything last night but getting back to Aladdin. Which was ridiculous. She certainly would have had a better time with Jai'far. She stood, leaving her meal half-eaten. She needed to find the vizier and apologize. At this time of the day, he was most likely discussing the day's events with her father.

Placing her napkin on the table, she walked out into the great hall toward the throne room. The large, empty space echoed as Aladdin spoke in a hushed tone. Badra stepped quietly as she made her way toward the sound of his voice.

"I can almost taste it!" he hissed.

She stepped out from behind a column. "What?"

"Princess!" Aladdin turned around.

The monkey, perched atop a golden statue of her great-grandfather, screeched.

"What can you almost taste?" she asked.

Aladdin's mouth opened and closed several times, as if having trouble deciding on the words. His gaze drew to her neck. "You're—You're not wearing the necklace I gave you. Don't you like it?"

Her eyes narrowed. "It's fine, but a bit too ostentatious for every day."

He nodded. "Something less flashy. I'll work on that."

"What?"

"Nothing."

She felt her hands clench. "What can you almost taste?" she repeated.

"Uh, tonight's dinner." Aladdin adjusted his posture. "Your chef is going to prepare your favorite tonight. I thought it only fair since last night your staff was so accommodating to my wishes."

"What is my favorite?" she asked.

"I-I don't know." Aladdin scratched his head. "I wanted it to be a surprise."

She raised her eyebrow.

"For me, I mean. I want to *be* surprised and learn your favorite food."

The monkey looked wide-eyed back and forth between the two of them.

"You know," he continued, "by trying it."

The animal's eyes trained on her. She'd never seen a monkey before yesterday, but the knowing gaze made her stomach sink.

"Were you talking to the monkey?" she asked.

"I feel silly when you say it like that, but yes." Aladdin tapped the beast's head while the monkey batted his hand away. "I get lonely in the palace at home. My brothers all have their own lives to live and sometimes it feels like Monkey is the only real friend I have."

"I suppose I understand that. When you're royalty you're put on a pedestal by everyone around you. It creates distance between you and every other person in your life. Everyone serves you, but you never really feel loved."

The memory of Amir's words washed over her.

Promise me one thing, Badra—that you will never change. Not ever, for any man. The world will try to tell you that your fire is too bright. But don't you listen! You...are perfect.

A spark ignited in her heart and warmth spread over the previously cold, bleak universe. It suddenly seemed possible that she could be loved and accepted exactly as she was. She didn't need a prince to have a fulfilling life—that was for certain.

She nodded toward Aladdin as if to say farewell and walked back to the sanctuary of her room.

After closing her door behind her, she rushed toward her balcony and threw the curtains open. Straining to stand on her tiptoes to see over the palace wall, she could only detect the faint glow reflected by the street lanterns on the night sky. She longed to look out over the city, but the wall was just a little too high.

"Are you looking for a better view?" Jai'far's voice didn't startle her. Rather, she had hoped he wouldn't be too discouraged after last night to come back.

"Not necessarily a better view, but a different one." She came to the side of her balcony that she frequently climbed down to get to the races. "I've been staring down at this delightful garden every night since I was tall enough to look over the edge." He was almost at the top of the trellis. "My home is lovely and I don't want to seem ungrateful for everything that I have." She looked toward the city, again. "There are many who will live their whole lives having never seen a view like this. I just wish I could get a little more scope of the world."

"Your wish is my command." Jai'far held his hand out. "Come with me. We may not have many more nights like this if you get swept off your feet by a handsome prince." His tone was playful, but her stomach clenched. Something about the idea of marriage—any marriage—seemed so final. But not tonight. There was nothing final about tonight.

She scanned the garden for guards before throwing her leg over the edge and climbing down with him. Navigating the vines was much harder in slippers than it was in her sturdy riding boots. They had to step carefully and Jai'far's long arms reached around her more than once. When he stepped onto the ground, he took her by the waist to help her the rest of the way. His hands were just as warm as she remembered, and she turned away in case she flushed. How could one man have such an effect on her?

They crept through the darkness, past the garden, through a series of halls until they came out near the outer fortification, beside a watchtower that was built into the palace wall.

"Nadir and Salem will be along soon," Jai'far whispered. "We will have to climb up here."

He hoisted her up and she grabbed the top window ledge, pulling herself up to the roof of the watchtower with ease. Below her, Jai'far stood agape.

"What?" she asked.

His smile caught the moonlight. "You never cease to amaze me, you know that?"

He lumbered up the stone wall and sat beside her. Voices carried on the breeze, and he held her back in the shadows.

Nadir's and Salem's silhouettes came into view.

"I'm telling you," Salem said. "The girl that sells figs in the market is the most beautiful woman in the city. I don't even like figs, and I spend half my salary just to get close to her."

Nadir laughed. "Figs stand nothing against that fire dancer. That one gets my breeches ablaze, let me tell you."

Badra blushed, hiding her face, despite the shadows.

"Is your vantage clear?" Nadir asked.

Salem leaned over the edge, practically looking straight at them. Badra did her best not to breathe. "Yes, we're clear."

"Then let's go. We're already behind schedule." The silhouettes disappeared with the sound of footsteps.

"My goodness," Badra whispered. "Thank the stars that we were not brigands trying to break into the palace."

Amir nodded. "It is possible that our guards have grown lax after so many years of peace. I will speak to the sultan about it."

Her brows rose. "How will you explain how you found out?"

His smile dazzled. "I would never lie to your father. I'd have to tell him I stole up here with a brazen young wench."

She smacked his chest. "Wench?"

He snorted, and they both broke into hushed laughter.

Amir lay down and gazed at the stars. "You are certainly more fetching than the fire dancer."

"How about the girl who sells figs?" Badra teased, wrinkling her nose.

Jai'far simply looked at her, silent and unblinking. Her cheeks heated again, and she turned away. If any other man said such things to her, she'd have pushed him away.

Her chest swelled. Everyone wanted something from her. To be here, on the wall, with someone who only wanted to enjoy her company...this was almost more than she'd ever dreamed of. Yet she knew so little about this great man. Her station called for her to be aloof, to call on him for advice and council, but she didn't care. She wanted to know more.

"What's your name?" she asked.

He touched his heart. "My sultan has deemed me 'Jai'far,' thus, I am Jai'far."

"What's your real name?" She placed her fingers over his lips before he could say 'Jai'far' again. "What is the name your mother gave you?"

He returned his attention to the stars. "Amir."

Badra nodded. "Amir. I like it. It's strong, humble."

"Apparently too humble. Your father chose to change it."

Badra laughed. "Don't take offense to that. There is a reason all the servants dress in the same color every day. That's so he can call them by the hue of their clothing. It's easier than remembering their names."

Amir sat up.

She continued. "His father's Grand Vizier's name was Jai'far, so he deemed Hazim's name be Jai'far as well."

"And now, me."

She nodded.

He laughed quietly. "I figured my name was just too common for the palace."

She reached up and touched his cheek. His rough skin and beard warmed her hand. "I think 'Amir' is a strong name. It suits you."

He cleared his throat and spun toward the torches illuminating the city. "What is Prince Aladdin like?"

She swallowed hard. She supposed she deserved that after she'd outwardly discounted what had happened between her and Amir in the garden. Part of her wanted to jump back to that day. She wished Aladdin hadn't arrived and ruined a cherished moment.

"He's not unlike the others," she answered. "He has a little more depth to him, but not much. In the end, he is out for himself."

"I suppose everyone is out for themselves, to some extent. We all try to find who has what we want and wants what we have to offer."

"I don't want anything from him." Badra gazed at the flickering lights of the city. "I just want to get through the next six days and hopefully by then, you will have found a way for me to escape this."

He straightened. "So you still want to be free to choose?"

She nodded. "Definitely." Couldn't he see it? Didn't he know that she'd made her choice?

Jai'far—no, *Amir*—took her hand in his. His grip was strong and sure. "I will find something, Badra. No law in this world is absolute."

She didn't need any absolute law to save her anymore, though. She'd reject this Aladdin, and that would leave her forced to wed the Grand Vizier. All she needed to do would be to stave off the rest of the suitors until Amir was officially raised to the title.

She placed her head on his shoulder. "I need to tell you..."

"Shh," he cooed. "There is no need. Let's just enjoy this moment."

They watched the brilliance of the sun rising over the desert sands as if they were the only two people in existence. In some part, they were. At least for now.

Amir was right. They didn't need words. All they needed was to be together.

As the sun began to peek from the horizon, casting purples

and pinks across the sky, he brushed his lips against her forehead. "I need to get you back."

She nodded. As much as she wanted to stay, if she was not there when her servants came to tend to her, the guards would be called. Being found alone with the unconfirmed vizier would not be ideal. At least not yet.

She should have been exhausted, sneaking about and avoiding the guards all night, but she wasn't. Her senses were on fire and she couldn't stop smiling as she imagined a life filled with nights like this one.

When she was with Amir, it was like she was free to drop the mask she had been wearing all her life—a mask that had grown heavy and made her resentful of all who forced it upon her. At last, she felt she could cast it off, along with all the assumptions that everyone made about her.

All this time she had been trying to prove to herself that she was worth more than people believed. But she didn't have to prove anything to Amir. He saw her as something amazing, and when he looked at her the way he did, for the briefest moment, she could see herself through his eyes. It made her feel like she was capable of anything and she never wanted that feeling to go away.

She held her chin high, feeling powerful, maybe for the first time in her life. She'd help Amir to ascend to Grand Vizier, and then all they needed to do was wait for her eighteenth birthday.

But first, she needed to get rid of Prince Aladdin.

15

Amir stood at the bottom of the trellis watching Badra climb back to the safety of her room. As the smell of the jasmine swirled around him, he watched her gracefully ascend. It was as natural to her as walking. Her movements were so like the hooded rider, how he'd jumped up and ran along the side of the building, all the while smelling like jasmine flowers.

He plucked a flower from the vine and breathed in the heady scent as she turned and looked down at him, her bright green eyes full of emerald fire as they caught the light of the rising sun.

Those eyes, the same vibrant color as the eyes of a boy who'd chosen to ride masked.

How could he have been so blind?

As if she weren't striking enough, this new realization added another dimension to this astounding woman. She had been born into privilege, wealth, and power, yet she found her fulfilment in helping her fellow man.

Badra craved danger and adventure in her life and Amir wanted so badly to be the one to give her everything her heart desired. All the power in the world wouldn't feel as sweet as that. Even if it meant he had to risk discovery, he couldn't simply seize the throne and cast her aside. He needed her in his life, and he dearly hoped she needed him in hers.

There was a more pressing and dangerous matter at hand,

though. The real obstacle to his mission was this boy and the strange power that was at his disposal. He would have to defeat Aladdin, after which he would turn his attention toward finding a way to give Badra the freedom he promised—and then pray that when she was free to choose, she'd still decide to pick him...because she *wanted* to, not because she *had* to.

He hurried back to his room and spoke the incantation, using his hands to draw the symbols of the constellations. At last, he no longer needed the incense to assist him in his journey. One day, he would be powerful enough to conjure the spell without the use of an incantation or the hand movements. The sorcerer he aspired to be would be able to cast all manner of spells with a mere intentional thought.

"Iago," Amir called out to the dark temple. He waved his hand and the lights burst to life.

"For the love of all that is unholy, what in the dark god's names is wrong with you?" Iago shielded his eyes. He lay on the old purple couch curled up with his scrawny legs against his chest.

"Are you sleeping?" Amir gaped at the slumbering demon.

"Well, I've been holding this corporeal body since you've been popping by so often; so yes, it tends to get fatigued!" Iago sat up and folded his arms, scowling at the wall.

Amir put his hands up. "I didn't mean to insult you. I just didn't know that you physically slept."

"If I'm going to be perfectly honest"—Iago stretched his boney arms—"in my spirit form, I had no need to sleep. However, I have been studying up on taking on a physical form that would be able to venture outside the temple. But I need to be in the habit of existing on the physical plane to learn to maintain the needs of a physical body." He stood, shaking out his boney arms. "I've been conjuring myself food and water and developing a sleep schedule for a few days now."

"Does that mean you miss the world out there?" Amir tilted his head.

"Not at all." Iago scoffed. "I'm merely bored."

"Well, I'd be happy to assist in any way I can."

Iago's defensive expression softened. "What are you doing in here anyway? I thought you were going to be shadowing that Aladdin boy to figure out the source of his power."

"I took Badra out to see the sunrise from the wall."

Iago furrowed his brow and leaned forward. "You really are itching to get yourself killed, aren't you?"

"I need her to trust me and hypnosis doesn't work with her. Plus, if she is to choose me—"

"You love her."

There was a surprising lack of sarcasm in Iago's voice and something in his eyes conveyed something akin to sympathy. It made Amir wonder what in Iago's past could have made him relate to what he was going through.

"Well, I can't say I'm surprised." The demon grabbed a rag and rubbed a scuff out of the table. "Every time you come here after having spent time with her, you seem different."

"How do you mean?"

"I don't know. You seem...*happy*."

Amir couldn't deny he had developed a certain fondness for the girl. The term *love* seemed like an oversimplification of his feelings. He admired her; she made him aspire to be a better man.

Iago puffed out a breath. "Regardless of where he gets his power, there are some spells you will need if you are to defend yourself when the time comes."

"And what spells are those?"

"Oh, the basics: fire-breathing, levitation, telekinesis, mind reading, shapeshifting, et cetera."

Amir's mouth fell open. "You don't really expect me to learn all that in one night, do you?"

"For the sake of your princess, you'd better learn as much as you can. My senses tell me a great storm brews in the ether and there will be no escape for anyone who is unprepared."

After hours of memorizing and practicing various spells that Iago insisted would be necessary when going up against a rival wizard, Amir returned to his room in the palace and fell into bed just as the sun was reaching its peak. He closed his eyes and breathed deeply, attempting to clear his thoughts and get a few hours rest before...

A sharp knock jarred his consciousness as his eyes snapped open.

"Vizier Jai'far." Nadir's voice boomed from the hall.

Lovely. The last time this oaf had knocked, he'd been dragged to the throne room because Badra had been angry. He opened the door.

Nadir crossed his inhumanly thick arms. "The sultan has requested that you organize a lavish ball to celebrate Bisnagar's newly found friendship with the land of Noblis."

He opened the door. "Shall it be a farewell affair?" Amir's optimistic tone wasn't lost.

"It sounded more like a warm welcome." The guard pursed his lips. At least they could agree that this new *prince* was not to be trusted.

"His Majesty wishes to welcome the prince halfway through his visit?" Amir asked.

Nadir sighed. "I relayed the message as I was ordered. If you have further questions, please address His Majesty."

"Very well." Amir rubbed his stinging eyes. "Let's give him a nice warm welcome."

Amir sent a servant to hire the fire dancers who always performed at the races as well as a few other local entertainers.

He also asked them to try to find the magician boy. He was sure the lad could use some real coin, rather than what he earned on the street. Unfortunately, he was nowhere to be found.

All the noble families were personally invited to the event and were all too happy for a chance to dine in the palace for the second time that week. It was an event to be remembered by all who attended and the guests were jubilant in their merriment as Amir sat to the right of the sultan and tried not to seem miserable. At least he and the sultan were seated in their correct places this evening.

Directly across from Amir, Aladdin smugly reveled in the attention from the noble ladies who continued to ask him questions about himself and his kingdom.

"Jai'far, my boy, you really know how to host a celebration!" The sultan patted Amir on the shoulder.

"I'm glad Your Majesty is pleased."

"I am confident that at the end of your forty days, I will be inclined to make it official. You will be a wonderful adviser."

"There would be no greater honor, Your Highness."

He was about to say more when Badra entered the room wearing a dress that was unlike anything she normally wore. The fabric was reminiscent of the ripest of Persian grapes and hugged her womanly curves in ways that shouldn't have been allowed in public. While she always exposed her midsection to some degree, this garment pushed the boundaries of what could be worn without being considered indecent even for Bisnagar. Sands, the material was so transparent, her legs were exposed right up to a panty that barely concealed her innocence!

Amir and Aladdin stood as she approached, biting her lip and forcing an insecure smile like a little girl hoping for approval.

"You look stunning, Princess," Aladdin cooed. "Like a goddess."

"You always look stunning, Highness." Amir bowed.

Aladdin beckoned for her to sit at his side.

"Thank you," Badra said.

Amir waited for her to meet his gaze.

Instead, she sat and listened attentively as Aladdin droned on about politics and how spectacular his kingdom was. Amir couldn't help but notice that nothing he actually said made much sense, but everyone around him was captivated, nonetheless. Even the princess seemed drawn in by the boy's words. Amir felt an eerie vibration dead-center in the front of his skull and suspected that there was some sort of spell at work and he was resisting it. This boy was good. Very good.

The servants brought out large trays of food and the guests all applauded at the bountiful spread before them. A roasted pig was placed on the table between Aladdin and Amir. As the servants began carving off slices for Amir and the sultan, Badra cut a serving for the prince, carefully placing a bunch of grapes and a small loaf of bread on his plate as well. She leaned over, and her womanly curves nearly fell out of that blasted tight excuse for a top.

This was too much for Amir to bear. He flicked a finger, and on the other side of the table a glass of wine tipped over and spilled onto Badra's garment.

"How clumsy of me. I must have bumped it with my elbow." She blinked rapidly as she shook the droplets of wine from her hands. "I'll go change."

After Aladdin had turned his attention to the fire dancer who was giggling and tugging on his sleeve, Amir leaned in to whisper to the sultan. "Sire, forgive me, but I must retire."

"Very well." The old man seemed barely awake himself. "I shall most likely retire soon myself."

Amir walked slowly until he reached the hall. He rushed toward Badra's room, only to intercept her on her way back wearing another outfit that was just as bizarrely designed as the first. He caught her by the wrist and pulled her behind a column.

"What are you doing?" She shoved him, but he didn't let go.

"What are *you* doing?" He pushed her back against the pillar and released her.

"I don't know what you're talking about."

"This!" Amir gestured to her breasts that were pushed together and erupting from the thin layer of fabric that held them in place. "You dress to gratify his male inclinations and serve him as if you were the common wench we joked about the other night." He pulled her close, placing the tips of his fingers on her cheek. "This is *not* who you are, Badra."

A glassy expression crossed her features, as if she were going back over the events of the night in her head. Her brow wrinkled and she shook her head slightly. "I-I don't really..." She shook her puzzlement off. "I've never let anyone push me into doing anything I don't want to and I'm not about to start now." Shoving Amir away, she stomped back toward the noise of the celebration, turning only to shout. "You need to mind your own business. If I want your advice, vizier, I'll ask for it!"

Amir's nails bit into his palms as he took a deep breath, reminding himself that whatever power was at work was stronger than anything he had seen since he'd been a child.

He walked slowly out into the garden. The stars above twinkled down on him but offered no comfort. The utter loneliness he'd felt since his family had been murdered swept over him. He'd been so close to avenging them, only to be thwarted by a mere boy.

He took a deep breath, realizing that this was beyond him. He was alone, and dearly needed an ally.

The red-breasted parrot slept on its perch under the tree.

Coaxing the bird carefully onto his arm, he willed himself back to the temple.

Iago's voice boomed. "Master, I do enjoy your exceedingly more frequent visits, but—"

"I've brought you something." Amir held up his arm and the bird squawked, raising its red and blue wings. "A parrot from the palace garden. The placard on its perch read, *crimson rosella*."

Iago gaped, frozen.

Had Amir made a mistake? "I remember you saying you used to enjoy watching the birds when you were alive."

Iago took a step back, pressing his palms to his cheeks. An almost innocent wonderment in his eyes, he stepped slowly forward and reached a long, white finger out to stroke the soft feathers on the parrot's chest. Amir urged the bird to step onto Iago's shoulder.

The demon beamed, practically dancing in place.

"I'm glad you like him." Amir slumped onto the couch.

"Something happened." Iago crouched, preening his new friend. "You're going to tell me eventually, so you may as well just speak."

"I lost her." He leaned forward, his head in his hands. "Whatever magic he's using is powerful enough to make her fall in love with him."

"No magic is capable of that."

"No? You should have seen her."

"Magic can only make people act like they are in love. Powerful enough necromancers can even make people *think* they are in love. But it's not real."

"Real or not, she's in his power now. Yet again, a dark sorcerer has taken everything from me."

"Again?"

There wasn't any reason to keep it a secret. Especially now.

"My father cut ties with a business partner after finding out he'd used our ships to transport slaves. My mother had once been a slave, so obviously he couldn't allow such a thing." He spun his family ring on his finger. The ships circled the blue stone as if they still sailed the seas.

"Obviously," Iago agreed.

"The slaver was so angry that he told my father he would hire a sorcerer to conjure up a storm the likes of which our land had never seen." Amir put his hands up to demonstrate the scale of the impending disaster.

"And did he make good on his promise?" Iago's posture perked up.

"The storm was...well, it seemed alive, like it was screaming. The ships were all tossed about like leaves for hours. After the sky cleared and we thought it was over, a massive wave as high as the palace swept over the land."

Iago's eyes narrowed. "That kind of power is out of the realm of sorcery."

Amir turned on him, his eyes ablaze. "I'm telling you what I saw. What was left of our island was a muddy mess that slowly sank into the sea." Amir's posture sank as his shoulders slumped down.

"I know the island of which you speak. Famous for its riffraff, houses of ill repute, and a safe haven for piracy."

"Not everyone who made a life there was a scoundrel. My father was a good and honest man. Not that the storm discriminated. The reputation of the island gave birth to rumors that it was the hand of some Western God whose wrath had been incurred by our wickedness." Amir shook his head. "Those of us who managed to survive were scattered to all corners of the Earth. I searched for months, but all I could find was the wreckage of my father's ships."

"And how did an orphan come to find out about Iago and his cursed oasis?"

Amir's nose flared. "I made up my mind to become a master of the dark arts." Heat flushed through him. "I wanted to become more powerful than the sorcerer who'd killed my family so I could take some sort of horrible revenge against both him and the man who'd hired him."

"And did you?" Iago licked his lips, his eyes wild. "Did you hold his beating heart in your hands and wring the life from it?"

"By the time I was formidable enough to go after them, I discovered the slaver had drunk himself to death after squandering his riches. The sorcerer was nowhere to be found."

Iago nodded. "The jinn."

"What?"

"The slaver did not use a sorcerer. He used a jinni."

"I told you—the jinn no longer exist."

"Believe what you want." Iago waved his hand. "But a storm like you described cannot be conjured by a human, no matter how powerful." He scratched the bird's neck. "So, you can't find this supposed sorcerer. How did you end up with your sights on Bisnagar?"

Amir shrugged. "At first, it was revenge. The slaver was born here. He bragged about the city extensively."

Iago nodded. "Totalitarian, fitting. I like it."

"At some point, though, I decided maybe I should use my power to rule with wisdom and fairness—to do something in my life that would make my parents proud."

"What does it matter? They're dead."

"It does matter!" Amir spun on him.

The demon's eyes widened, and Amir realized he held a flaming ball in his hand. He flicked his wrist, and cast the enchantment away.

"It matters to me," Amir said more softly. He walked

toward a wall of parchments. "It seems, though, that no matter how powerful I become, there will always be someone more powerful to come and take what is dearest to me." Amir flexed palms now scored with marks from where his fingernails had dug in.

"I take it you're not talking about Bisnagar."

"No." Amir turned to the demon again. "Not Bisnagar."

"So how do you plan to proceed, Master?"

"Like a man in love." Amir slammed his fist into his palm. "I will go to Aladdin and confront him outright. It will throw him off-balance and hopefully he will drop his defenses and reveal the source of his power. If I know what spell he's using, I can find a way to counter it."

"That is the most half-baked, ill-conceived, ludicrous idea in the history of senseless, shortsighted, moronic ideas. You haven't slept in days. You need to get some rest before you go through with something that reckless."

Amir leaned against a shelf and rubbed his temples. "Perhaps you're right. I know I'm not thinking clearly."

"No, you're not." Iago scratched the parrot's breast bone. A smile crept over his face before his gaze dropped to Amir's hand. "That ring you wear. It is a lapis lazuli, yes?"

Amir covered the stone, pulling the ring to his chest. "Yes. Why?"

"I'd like to borrow it."

"For what?"

"I won't damage it, I swear to you. I just need a lapis lazuli to channel a spell."

Amir held out his hand. He was unaware of a spell that needed this gem in particular, but Iago's knowledge still outweighed his own. "You'll give it back?"

The demon waved his hand in front of his face. "Yes, yes, I will only need it for a few hours." Iago pointed at him. "And you should take that time to rest and get your wits about you."

Lifting his chin, the demon held out a hand, waiting for the ring.

Amir fingered the ships sailing about the stone. He hadn't taken the ring off since the day his father gave it to him, wearing it first as a necklace, and then having it fitted to him once he had grown. It had been a lifeline...his only remaining connection to his past.

"I don't have all millennia," Iago said.

Taking one last look at the bright blue stone, Amir sighed and handed it over. "If you lose that..."

The demon snatched the ring. "Yes, yes—you will banish me into eternity and curse my scrawny bones into a pit of infinite despair. I know, I know."

Amir pointed at the hourglass sitting on his alchemy table and with a flick of his fingers, it levitated, turned over, and the sand began to flow down through the small waist of the device. "I'm going to rest, as you suggested. Wake me when the sand runs out." He took off his cloak and lay down on the couch, pulling his garment over his shoulders like a blanket.

Within moments, he was back on his family's boat. A wave crashed over his head. People screamed.

"*Baba!*" he cried.

His father's wide eyes turned to him. His lower lip trembled, before a bolt of lightning lit up the sky. The *boom* cracked at the same instant, and the mast crashed down onto the deck. Water started rushing across Amir's feet, and his father...was gone.

A squawk jolted him awake. "Master, the sand just ran out. Master!"

Iago's voice sounded strange. When Amir opened his eyes,

his gaze focused not on the demon, but on the red parrot peeking down at him from the back of the couch.

The bird opened its beak. "Master?" it croaked.

Amir sprang to his feet and backed away. "Iago?"

The bird held up its red and blue wings, considering each one in turn. "I thought if I inhabited this body, I could easily accompany you around the palace. Maybe I can find something useful. I've been practicing flying. It isn't as easy as it looks, but tapping into the bird's memories and instincts is helping."

"This is *so* unsettling." Amir leaned cautiously toward the bird. "Are you really in there?"

"By the dark gods, how is it you are always so shocked when you witness my power? You do realize that I'm far more adept than you are." The bird ruffled its feathers.

"I suppose, but you're out of practice and have been hiding in your temple for a millennium."

The parrot cocked its head. "Inconsequential. Are you still planning on confronting the boy?"

"Yes." Amir cracked his neck. "It's the only way I can think of to draw him out into the open."

"Off to our graves then." The parrot cawed. "I've grown bored with immortality anyway."

16

Amir closed his eyes and concentrated on bringing himself and Iago back from the temple. They appeared in the safety of Amir's palace chamber. With Iago perched confidently on his shoulder, he marched out to find his adversary.

Finding the great hall, garden, and throne room empty, Amir knocked on Badra's door but heard no movement on the other side. He gritted his teeth and walked down the hall toward the guest space assigned to Prince Aladdin. He could hear the sound of muffled conversation inside. He pressed his ear to the door.

"You would be a fine prize for any prince to fight for," Aladdin said in his exaggeratedly deep voice.

Badra responded in a smitten tone. "If I am a prize, then I would have you win."

What in all that was holy?

Amir knocked hard and whispered an incantation to unbolt the locks. "Prince Aladdin, I wish to speak with you on a matter of the utmost importance." Without waiting for an answer, Amir threw the door open.

Aladdin sat in a large cushioned chair with Badra seated on the floor at his feet wearing another of the ridiculous outfits he had brought for her. She wore a golden band around her neck and one around each wrist.

Aladdin looked at Badra and jerked his head toward the exit. She obediently got to her feet and hurried to the doorway.

Amir gently took her hand as she started to walk past him. She stopped, her expression blank. "Are golden shackles any better than cold iron, Highness?"

She jerked her hand away and continued out into the hall without responding.

"Thank you for granting me an audience on such short notice, Prince Aladdin." Amir shut and locked the door behind him.

"Of course." Aladdin sat back and smirked. "I can always make time for my future vizier."

"That is most wise. After all, even a sorcerer such as yourself could use advice from time to time." Jai'far took a few paces toward the seated prince.

"Sorcerer?" Aladdin leaned forward. "Jai'far, I'm afraid that I have no idea what you're talking about."

Amir conjured an ice-cold wind that swept into the chamber putting out every lamp and candle, leaving the room mostly dark except for the fading light of the setting sun shining through the window. In the mirror to his left, Amir's dark silhouette was accentuated by a slight glow of fury in his amber eyes.

"Magic can be a dangerous thing in the wrong hands, Your Highness." Amir calmed himself and the glow of his eyes faded back into darkness. "What's even more troubling is the thought of someone using such skills to domesticate a noble and distinguished princess. It would be a tragedy to see a woman of royal birth reduced to a docile, gilded house pet."

"A gilded house pet lives a better life than ninety-nine out of a hundred citizens of this kingdom." Aladdin stood and struck a flint, lighting the wall lamp closest to him.

The parrot dug its claws into Amir's shoulder, swiveling its head as it surveyed the room.

"More than two-thirds of this golden city is covered in filth and governed by cruel, greedy merchants who would sooner destroy their surplus and watch children starve to death than part with a single crust of bread without receiving payment for it." Aladdin put out his arms. "I'm going to change all of that."

"How?"

Aladdin lifted his chin. "I will make wealth illegal. All treasures will be spread evenly among the people."

Amir lifted a brow. "You can't be serious."

"Oh, I am. I will make everyone equal."

More like he'd make everyone dead. "If everyone is equal what would drive a man to better himself?"

Aladdin raised his palms. "The good of the people."

Yes, Amir had experienced the *good of the people* first hand as he laid in the gutter, bleeding.

There would always be those who would take advantage of the weak. It was simply human nature. The worst brigand of all, though, stood right in front of Amir, and he had somehow managed to conquer a mind that Amir's magic found impenetrable.

"What about Badra?" Amir tightened his grip on the staff.

Iago walked to his other shoulder. His head continued to flick back and forth.

"The princess is the happiest she's ever been. You need not concern yourself with her wellbeing." The prince waved his hand as if dismissing Amir's concerns.

"This spell that you have her under, it is not true love and she is not happy, not really. I know there is no kingdom of Noblis. I know you are an imposter, and regardless of your noble intentions, I will not hesitate to expose you unless..." Amir paused.

"Unless?" Aladdin held out his hand, as if inviting Amir's offer.

"Unless you release Badra from this spell and abandon your quest to take Bisnagar as your own. You could travel anywhere else in the world and find yourself a kingdom to rule."

"I see." Aladdin scratched his chin. "That is a very generous offer, except I was born here, grew up here, and until last week I practiced the art of magic on street corners for coin."

The street magician. Of course!

"Bisnagar is my home," Aladdin continued. "Besides, I've grown very fond of Princess Badroulbadour." His face tightened into a sinister grimace. "I'm not going anywhere. And now, my friend, you have made a very dangerous enemy."

The bird inched closer and started chewing on Amir's ear. He was about to shoo Iago away when he heard a whisper. "I can't believe it! Do you remember my first suggestion when you asked how I would conquer a kingdom?"

Not now, foolish demon. Amir sneered at Aladdin. "You've made a dangerous enemy as well. Everyone will know what you are."

"And what is that?" Aladdin laughed. "If you had any proof, you wouldn't have bothered threatening me."

Another almost-indiscernible whisper erupted from the parrot. "He's found one of the lost jinn. He's not a sorcerer; just a boy with an all-powerful slave."

No. It wasn't possible!

Amir kept his voice steady. "I don't make threats, Your Highness. I make observations."

His eyes fell on a dented and tarnished oil lamp placed on a pedestal at the foot of Aladdin's bed. It matched the picture in the scroll to almost perfect detail.

Of all that was great and good in the world, it was true! He trembled but held his staff steady. If this boy was in control of a jinni, they may already be lost.

Aladdin followed Amir's gaze to the lamp. His voice shook. "Get out or I'll kill you where you stand."

"Yes, Highness."

Amir bowed, but he needed to push the boy off-kilter. He needed to make this prat doubt that his jinni could conquer all. Forcing a smug smile, he turned and used his powers to throw the door open and light all the lamps in the room at once...all except the one at the foot of the bed. Fire blazed up from each, nearly hitting the ceiling, before abating to a gentle flicker.

He strode through the door, looking over his shoulder. "I'll take my leave. I would hate for you to waste one of your wishes on smiting me."

Amir smiled as he strode down the hall. While infinitely wiser and more ancient than any other being on Earth, a jinni's sole purpose was to turn a master's wishes against them, twisting words for the creature's own diabolical enjoyment. It would be the boy's downfall, eventually.

This was not the time to become overly confident, though. Aladdin must have been a crafty one indeed to have held on to a jinni this long without having wished himself into oblivion. This knowledge would give Amir a much-needed edge, but this battle for the throne of Bisnagar was only just beginning.

He looked down the hall that led to Badra's room and trembled. Something even more valuable than the kingdom was hanging in the balance. He'd made her a promise, and he'd keep it, no matter what it cost him.

17

Badra's hands shook as she sat on the edge of the fountain. She closed her eyes and let the song of the birds lull her racing heartbeat.

How dare Amir barge in on her and Aladdin? They only had a few more days left together before her prince returned to Noblis. The vizier should understand that every second was precious!

Putting a finger in between the itchy golden collar and the tender skin beneath, she looked into the dark violet sky and took a deep breath. Badra held out her hands and considered the thick gold bands around her wrists. Yes, they were larger than her normal jewelry and uncomfortable in this heat, but they were a gift, and a lovely gift at that. How could she not wear them?

She'd never met anyone like Aladdin. He didn't demand she lay at his feet, but every time he gazed at her, she couldn't help but shed every thought except that she wanted to serve him in any way he wished. She would spend the rest of her life wearing rags, eating table scraps if only to prove her love for him. Every book, poem, and sonnet she had ever read made her feel assured beyond any doubt that this had to be love.

Sweat beaded beneath her collar. She reached up and grabbed a wide leaf from a tree, and placed the greenery between her necklace and her skin. She instantly cooled.

Touching the water, she remembered the night she and Amir had gone out to the races, and how they'd both fallen into the fountain. She smiled. That was the first time in her life she could truly say she'd had fun inside the palace walls. He had a way of freeing her and allowing her to be herself, without all the expectations of what a proper princess should be.

Her fingertips drifted to her lips at the memory of their lips brushing together as they sat at the fountain. She wished Aladdin hadn't interrupted. Even if she did decide to marry the Noblis prince in the end, she wished that she could have had a few more moments to really savor that kiss.

"My love." Aladdin appeared in a white billowing frock as he made his way through the archway and out to the garden.

Badra plucked the leaf from beneath her necklace and let it drift to the ground.

He kissed her hand. "How the sight of you under this moon enchants me."

The princess blushed. Funny, how if any other prince had said that to her, she would have wanted to throw sand in his face for lying. With Aladdin, his thoughts were perfection and a show of how much he truly cared. For some reason, though, Amir seemed furious when he'd entered the room. What could possibly have been so important that he'd needed to speak to Aladdin at that very moment?

"Is everything okay?" she asked. "What did Jai'far want?"

"Actually, we need to talk about that." He took her hands in his. His lips thinned.

Her heart sank. Had she done something to displease him? Was Aladdin angry with her? "What's wrong? What did I—"

"I think Jai'far is in love with you."

Her chest thickened. "What makes you say that?" She turned away, looking back to the darkening sky.

"Princess, neither you nor I are fond of pretenses. I beg you not to abandon your honesty now." He put a hand on his chest. "I know that the two of you are good friends and I am not a jealous man by nature." He lowered his hand. "That said, if I thought his feelings for you would not impair his judgement, I would gladly overlook them and trust him as my advisor for the rest of my life." His lips twisted. "However, after the conversation I just had with him, I can't help but think he will always be looking for a way to eliminate any and all obstacles that come between him and his ultimate prize...you."

Badra's jaw fell slack. "I can't deny that Jai'far and I have become closer than what would be appropriate for a sultana and her husband's vizier. Though I would never betray your trust, I can't speak for him."

"I hate to suggest such a thing, but I can't have a vizier I cannot trust with my own wife. If your love for me is true, you must dismiss him from the palace and allow me to place someone in the position whom I have faith in."

But... But that would leave her alone again, with no one to understand her and...

Warmth tingled along her collarbone beneath her necklace.

It didn't matter. Aladdin was here for her now. "Technically, he is not actually the vizier—not yet, anyway."

His brow furrowed. "What do you mean?"

"My father's vizier took ill suddenly and produced Jai'far, whom had been his apprentice for several years. He's already gained our trust."

Aladdin stood taller. "I fear you and your father have been the victim of a terrible plot, my love. This is going to be hard to accept, but I need you to listen with your heart." Aladdin pulled her close. "I believe Jai'far is a practitioner of the dark arts. The staff he holds seems to have magical properties. I believe he might have used it to bewitch both the former vizier as well as you and your father."

Badra pushed Aladdin away. "That's ridiculous!"

"Is it, my love? Think about it." Aladdin placed his hands on her shoulders and whispered into her ear. "Set aside your feelings for him and draw your own conclusion." He swept his fingers over the edge of her collar. The gold tingled against her skin.

When she'd first met the new vizier, he'd told her the story about his parents and then had held up his staff, ordering her to forget what he had said and to never bring up his past again. The dull ache in her stomach spread. How many other times had he done that to her that she couldn't even remember?

She dropped to her knees, clutching her middle. Tears welled in her eyes. "No, it can't be."

Amir had known how badly she wanted to be free, and he'd attended the races before. He'd probably seen her there, figured her out, and used her secret against her. He'd taken her on adventures to gain her trust, playing off what he knew she wanted. All this time, her one true friend had only been a monster lurking in the shadows waiting to pounce.

"How could I have been so blind?" Tears streamed unbridled down her cheeks and her stomach twisted into knots.

"It's okay." Aladdin knelt down, putting his arms around her.

His touch eased the agony pooling inside her, pushing it away. She curled into his comfort. He was her savior, forgiving her gullibility and rescuing the kingdom from this brigand and his black magic.

Holding tightly on to Aladdin's hand, she let him walk her to the throne room. She told her father everything they'd discovered. Aladdin corroborated her suspicions by recounting Jai'far coming into his chamber and threatening him.

The sultan spun the ring Aladdin had given him on his

thumb. His face reddened with each new piece of information until he stood. "Guards!"

Nadir, Salem, and three others stood to attention.

The sultan's nose flared. "Arrest Jai'far. Separate him from his staff and bring him before me." He pointed to the floor. "Now!"

18

THE PARROT SQUAWKED, AND AMIR TURNED OVER IN HIS bed, pulling up his sheets. "Shut up, confounded bird!"

The parrot only squawked louder. Iago was enjoying playing the part of stupid bird far too much.

The hot slap of a large callused hand met Amir's cheek. His eyes bolted open. He gaped as burly figures loomed above him.

"What is the meaning of—?" Another slap splayed him back flat on the bed.

Amir whispered the words to bring him back to the temple, but someone grabbed his collar, pulled him from the bed, and punched him in the stomach. The breath shot out of him as he slumped to the floor, coughing.

Iago squawked again, flying above the heads of his attackers and clawing at their hair until one of them swatted the parrot. The bird hit the wall and slid to the floor in a lifeless pile of red and blue feathers.

Amir groaned as cold iron shackles snapped around his wrists and ankles with a sharp click. Gasping, he reached for his scepter, but one of the men grabbed the snake head, dragging his staff from the room. "What is the meaning of this?" he repeated.

"Close your mouth, traitor," Salem hissed.

Traitor?

His soul hollowed out. *Aladdin.* What a fool Amir had been, thinking the boy would panic and wait before striking!

"I've been waiting for this since this pile of camel dung got here." Nadir cracked his knuckles. "Give me a moment alone with him."

"Me, too," Salem said.

"Yes!" Another stepped forward.

Had Amir really made so many enemies in such a short time?

He called to his magic, but the pain in his stomach broke his concentration. Blast it, he was defenseless! He turned toward his balcony. "Badra!"

Nadir punched him. "The princess will not save you this time, swine."

On his hands and knees, Amir spat blood on the floor.

"Out. Everyone." Nadir sneered.

"I can at least hold him, sir," Salem said.

What had Amir done to warrant such disdain?

"He doesn't need holding." Nadir kicked Amir in the ribs.

Burning pain shot through his core. He rolled over, groaning.

"He's nothing without that snake staff." The huge guard loomed over him.

Salem grumbled something as he left. Nadir kicked the door shut behind him.

Now the real beating would begin. Amir pushed himself up. Taking a deep breath, he called again for his powers, but the stinging in his gut left no chance of concentration.

He looked up at Nadir. "You may as well take your frustration out on me now, my friend. You may never get another chance."

"Shut up, you snake." Nadir grabbed him by the collar and pulled him up. "I know you're not who you say you are. But there may be something in the palace more dangerous than you." He tossed him on the bed. "I don't trust you as far as I can throw you, but at least you haven't bewitched the princess and made her a slave."

Amir rubbed his gut. "She's definitely under his influence."

"This is more than influence!" Nadir's forehead wrinkled. "She is like a completely different person!" Specks of the man's saliva splattered Amir's face. "I've been a guard here for ten years. I have watched her grow from a child into a strong, if not somewhat hardheaded woman. I know she would never let a man control her, let alone beg for it." He paced the room, gripping the hilt of his sword. "This is sorcery beyond whatever that snake staff of yours can do." He scowled. "I've always speculated that you were a menace to the throne, but you might be the only one with the skills necessary to stop this." He knelt before the bed and grabbed the side of Amir's head with a massive hand. "I know you care for her. Tell me the truth of what sort of man you are." Nadir tightened his grip. "If you lie, I will know."

There was no use in lying at this point. This man may be the only friend he had left.

Amir nodded. "I wanted to take the throne for myself." He lowered his gaze and tried to dig deep enough to find the words to convey what he felt. "Now I feel differently. Honestly, if anyone were fit to sit on that throne, it would be her. I have always had a lust for power, but the more time I spent with Badra, the more I found that ruling my own kingdom was no longer the thing I want most."

Nadir spat on the floor. "I don't care about your bleeding heart, Jai'far. I only care about Bisnagar."

"Then take these chains off me and give me back my staff! Let me fight the boy, one sorcerer to another."

Nadir shook his head. "You know I can't do that. That

would only condemn us both, and I still have no reason to trust you." Releasing Amir, the guard stood. "Just know that if you live through today, you have at least a temporary ally."

"Fair enough." Amir took a deep breath. Pain shot through his ribs. He was beaten, but not beaten enough. "You will have to leave marks on my face that will make them believe we are having a less civil conversation."

Nadir cracked his knuckles. "Oh, I planned on it." He plowed his fist straight into Amir's cheek. Stars blanketed the room.

Another blow.

Copper flooded Amir's mouth. The room spun. Somehow, he ended up on the floor, but he didn't remember falling.

Nadir opened the door. "Bring this rat to the sultan."

They dragged Amir down the hall. Pain coursed through his knees every time they were raked over a seam in the gold-plated floor. Once inside the throne room, they threw him prostrate before the sultan. Badra and Aladdin stood on either side of the throne as Amir pushed himself up to a kneeling position. Every guard had a weapon drawn and ready.

"Jai'far, you have brought shame to yourself and to your vestments." The sultan's voice was more authoritative than Amir had ever heard. "Relieve him of his robes."

Amir didn't remember getting dressed, but they stripped him back down to his sleeping garment.

Aladdin took the staff from Salem. Amir eyed the snake idol. If he could concentrate hard enough, he might be able to reach out and call to the crystals, using his powers to compel the staff to meet him halfway. But the sight of Badra gave him pause. Her face was streaked with tears, her eyes dull and lifeless. She must have thought everything they'd shared had been a lie.

"*Princess*," Amir pleaded.

"Do not address her, Sorcerer," the sultan ordered.

Amir started to reach for his staff again, but he stopped and looked toward Badra. A pain far deeper than his injuries swirled in his gut. "Let me explain." He tried to stand, but the guards threw him back down.

The sultan's face was nearly feral. "She cannot save you. You have taken advantage of her womanly vulnerability for the last time. You are hereby sentenced to…"

"Wait!" Badra placed her hand on her father's arm. "This creature must not make monsters of us all. As an engagement gift, I ask that his life be spared, that he may live all his days in abject poverty as punishment for his crimes."

The sultan raised his eyebrows. "You have chosen a husband, then?"

"Yes, Father. My heart belongs to Prince Aladdin, now and for all the days of my life."

Amir winced as if her words were a blade being dragged over his flesh. She smiled at Aladdin, but her eyes were still lifeless, her eyes glistening.

The sultan clapped his hands. "Then make quick work of throwing out this trash. We have a royal wedding to plan. In one month hence, my daughter will be wed to Prince Aladdin of Noblis!"

No! This can't be!

Aladdin bowed. "I am most humbled, sire, but I would love a more expedient ceremony."

Amir growled. Of course he did.

The sultan waved his hand as he exited the room. "Nonsense. We need to make plans, invite the neighboring kingdoms. This will be a huge celebration!" He disappeared into the hall.

The guards pulled Amir from the floor as he yanked against his shackles.

He spat at Aladdin's feet as they dragged Amir to the door. "This isn't over, street rat!"

The atrocious boy simply laughed and waved goodbye. Ignorant fool! He had no idea who he was dealing with!

One month. The sultan had unknowingly given Amir one month to save them all.

The guards dragged the former vizier through the kitchen and out the servants' entrance. Once outside, he called up all his strength to ward off the pain as blow after blow rained down on him. Badra must have known he would face such a beating at the mercy of guards.

Did she care? Some part of her must have. After all, it was only by her mercy that he was allowed to keep his head. Somewhere inside, maybe deep inside, *his* Badra still existed, maybe even still loved him. He could still save her if he could survive the next few minutes.

Groggy and unable to support himself, Amir closed his eyes as he was dragged from the palace grounds and through the very gate that he and Badra had snuck out from only a few nights before.

He waited to be thrown to the street to fend off rats driven mad by the scent of his blood, but instead, they fastened his shackles to the saddle of a horse.

He blinked up at the rising sun. Where were they taking him?

"Prince Aladdin thought you may enjoy a tour of the city, oh wise vizier," Salem said, slapping the horse's rump.

"No, wait!" Amir cried as the horse took off at a slow trot. He tried to keep up, but one of the guards kicked his knees out. People made way, laughing as he was dragged along behind the beast, his skin scraping through the hardened sand streets. Searing pain turned into a dull, numb ache as he gripped the rope and pulled himself back to his feet.

"That's no fun," someone said before kicking him down to drag behind the horse again.

One stab of pain blended into another until every part of his body screamed in agony.

As they passed into the market, street vendors threw spoiled fruit at him, calling for points if they hit him in the face. After time he rooted for them to win. The cool fruit soothed some of the burn on his cheeks and arms.

By the time the horse reached the outskirts of the shabby district and the guards released him, Amir's undergarments hung from his shoulders in shreds. Blood dripped from just about everywhere, and his eyes stung, caked with grit.

He collapsed at the edge of the street, struggling to take in a full breath as the sand caked in his wounds and stabbed him with the slightest movement. He needed healing and so much more.

Gritting his teeth, he tried to draw the constellations in the air and speak the sacred words, but he couldn't steady himself, he couldn't focus. There was no way he could will himself back to the temple and even if he did, he had lost Iago back at the palace. There would be no one there to help him.

Pulling up to his knees, Amir crawled toward the alley. Each placement of his skin-less knees against the ground was a new lesson in agony, a new pinnacle of the depths of what torture could be. His mind numbed to the world around him. His ears rang and his heartbeat drummed in his ears.

So many years of precise planning had brought him to this place in utter failure. It would have been more merciful to have died as a child on that ship in the quiet, painless depths of the sea than to know such agony, such defeat. Flopping to the ground, he took in one labored, shallow breath and struggled with the next one. If this was the end for him, he had only one regret, and that was the promise he'd broken to a beautiful princess, now a prisoner, whose only crime was wanting to be free.

Shivering in the dark, Amir cuddled into a ball. Each movement cracked wounds trying to heal, opening them anew. His pain was meaningless, though. Badra was the true victim in this plot. Was she inside herself, aware, screaming to be free, or had Aladdin found a way to break into that amazing, unbreakable mind?

He shivered anew. He'd underestimated the boy, and now they would all pay the price.

Once Aladdin married Badra, the only thing standing between him and the throne was the sultan. Would the boy wait a few weeks after the marriage to avoid suspicion, or would he kill the old man at the first opportunity? And what of Badra? Would he tire of her, discard her like the trash once he had the crown he desired?

Lovely, strong Badra standing up there, beside the throne— her tears still haunted him. Part of his soul had chipped away, lost forever with each glistening droplet that ran down her cheek.

She loved her people so much that she'd raced for money in disguise, only to give her winnings to the poor. She deserved a better future, as did Iman, a child whose only sin was losing a father, and having trouble keeping his family fed. Aladdin would ruin them all, treat them as acceptable casualties to achieve his ridiculous idea of a perfect society.

Amir leaned against a wall. Hadn't Iman suffered enough? What would happen when there were no travelers needing help to water their horses, and no merchants to steal from? He shuddered, gazing up at the golden dome of the palace peeking out proudly over the rooftops.

The poor people of Bisnagar had no idea what was about to befall them. The kingdom still bustled, holding on to the last dregs of prosperity. They had no idea how fragile an economy was, and how quickly it could decline under the worst of circumstances. This kingdom had no idea that Aladdin was about to take control and destroy everything the people had struggled to achieve.

Yes, Bisnagar had shortcomings. Yes, there was poverty. Yes, there was despair. Amir could have bettered these lives, though. The equality that Aladdin proposed was novel, but thrusting that upon people would cause chaos. The merchants would move on, leaving nothing but the unskilled poor to fend for themselves—more likely to kill each other for the scraps.

What Bisnagar needed was more work and training for those without skills. A formal decree to repair buildings and roads would create jobs and make Bisnagar even stronger. Amir would have done this, and so much more. Now, Bisnagar was cursed just as much as the ignorant would-be prince who was about to take the kingdom as his own.

When sunlight warmed his face, Amir limped back to the *khan* where Xerxes was being boarded. Walking in, the other patrons stopped talking and gasped, staring. He was in nothing but his shredded undergarment and his torso and legs were skinned from being dragged through the streets. He could barely see out of his left eye, so he was sure it must have been swollen shut. What a sight he must be. He made his way up the stairs and found his room locked.

"Can I help you?" a gruff voice spoke behind him.

Amir turned to see three men in the hall, folding their arms and trying to appear intimidating. After being beaten by guards twice their size and dragged by a horse, the intimidation wasn't going in their favor.

"I just need to get into my room."

"If it's your room, you should have a key to the lock."

Amir gestured to his garment. "As you can see, I've had a bad night and my clothes have been taken from me, so I don't have the key."

"Well, the rent for that room was due the day before yesterday."

Ah, so these were the collection agents. Amir didn't know how long it had been since he had taken a full night of sleep, nor was he sure of how long he had been unconscious in that alley. He had no idea what day it was. These gentlemen could be perfectly within their rights to beat him to death.

"I assure you, this is my room. I haven't been late on my rent before now."

The smallest of the three gigantic men stepped forward. "Do you think we care?"

Apparently, common decency was beyond these men. "I'm sure we can—"

Amir buckled over as one of the other men punched him in the gut.

A twisted smiled crossed the shorter man's face. His eyes were hollow, lifeless as he sneered. "Prince Aladdin says *hello*."

A flush of adrenaline washed through Amir, but not fast enough to skirt the blow of the wooden chair leg that the short man had hiding behind his back. Amir coughed as the man slammed the chair leg into his ribs again.

The three of them dragged Amir outside. A hard blow to his left temple left him stunned. Blow after blow came down on him until he stopped fighting back.

Dizzy and awakened to a new world of agony, he hung limp in their arms until they threw him back into the street. His body seemed to splinter when he hit the compressed dirt.

How many times had he passed a beggar, or a beaten person lying in the street, and barely noticed? How many living souls passed every day of their lives in such torture?

Using the wall of the tavern to steady himself, he got to his feet. Blood streamed down his chest. At least one punch had hit him squarely in the nose. He was probably unrecognizable at this point.

He heard a familiar neigh and looked up to find Xerxes tied to a cart and being led away by the man who had knocked Badra from her horse at the races.

"Stop!" Amir yelled. "What are you doing with my horse?"

"I just bought this animal from the innkeeper. You should have paid your rent and board, you disgusting leach."

"Xerxes will never race for you," Amir called after the man.

"Then he will make a fine stew." The man kissed his fingertips and laughed.

Amir summoned all his strength and ran after them. He couldn't leave Xerxes to such a fate. He was a good horse, kind and gentle. He deserved better.

When he reached them, the rider turned and pounded a giant fist into Amir's already battered face. The world spun as Amir slammed back to the ground. Xerxes whinnied in protest and pulled violently at the rope tethering him to the cart. The man grabbed hold of the reins and flogged Xerxes with a reed. The horse reared up, shrieking. The sound of the reed whipping through the air was punctuated by a snap every time it struck dear Xerxes's hide.

Amir reached up, only able to see silhouettes. "Xerxes, don't fight. It will only make it worse." He stood and spit blood into the dirt at his feet. "I will come for you, I promise!"

Yet again, he'd made a promise that he was no longer sure he could keep. His vision wavered. His knees exploded in pain, and he realized he'd fallen again. The ground rushed up at him as his sight faded to black.

Amir groaned. His back burned as if knives scraped him. He opened his eyes and realized he was moving. Dragging. Someone was dragging him by his left foot.

"At least get him out of the way. He can die over there where no one has to step over him," someone said.

The sky above him wavered and blurred. He was vaguely aware of an animal—a dog, maybe—licking his cheek. A cool drip splatted on his face, then another. He opened his eyes to dark clouds overhead. Rain pelted him, and a stream thick with mud ran down the gutter beside him. He slumped over, letting the dirty water run into his mouth. It was cool and refreshing, spreading through his body as he swallowed greedily. He ignored the dirt running down his throat. He'd done worse in the name of survival. Rain was rare in the desert, and he would not refuse such a gift.

He shivered in the deluge and forced himself to his feet, stumbling through the flooded streets. Each step was a new lesson in agony. Blood painted the puddles he stepped in, only to be washed down the streets with the rest of the garbage.

Long, too long he stumbled, blinded by the rain until he found shelter under the eaves of a building where some stray dogs had huddled together. They didn't seem to mind him inviting himself into their home. Thanks to their hospitality, he stayed warm and survived the night. By morning, the freak desert storm had passed, and muddy puddles pooled in the streets, steaming in the desert sunshine. His sides ached, not only from bruised or broken ribs, but also because he could not remember how long it had been since he had eaten.

Stumbling to the well he'd watered Xerxes in the day of his

arrival in Bisnagar, he approached an older woman in long, brown robes drawing water to give her goats.

"Please, madam. Would you please allow me the use of your bucket to wash my face?" She drew back, twisting her lips and nose as she urged her goats to hurry away. Looking down into the water below, he could barely recognize the twisted figure that peered back at him, a man with one eye swollen nearly shut and a discolored face. He held out his arms and considered his blood-crusted chest. He was every bit the monster that poor woman thought him to be.

Going to the stable, he found some clean water in the troughs and washed himself as best he could. He was able to examine himself and see that his wounds were at least trying to heal before the stable master yelled profanities at him for dirtying his horse's water.

Amir walked through the marketplace, asking anyone who didn't shy away from him if he could work, if not for money, then for room and board. Not a single person was interested in hiring a half-naked, scab-covered street rat.

On the parapets around the palace, red and black flags still flew. If tradition rang true, that meant that Badra's father was still sultan. Amir had no idea what Aladdin's colors were, but he was sure those flags would change the instant Aladdin had the throne. His arrogance would allow no less.

Knowing Badra was still unwed was some consolation. Not much, but some.

In the evenings, he returned to his friends, the dogs, who taught him to dig through piles of garbage behind a restaurant. Casting his pride aside in favor of filling his belly, he would sort through the discarded muck to find the least disgusting bits. The dogs were less generous when it came to sharing sustenance, but Amir always managed to choke down a few bites of partially eaten vegetables. Sometimes he would get lucky and find a little raw animal fat or a few clumps of rice. He used to dine at establishments like this as a patron, every night eating like a king. Each day that he picked through the trash made that seem more like a fantasy than a memory.

No matter. He shoved a piece of chewed and discarded fat into his mouth and swallowed. A meal was a meal. He wiped his mouth and turned his attention to the sound of a disturbance in the marketplace, a child screaming, pleading for mercy.

"I can pay you for it as soon as my master comes back; he owes me two week's wages!"

"Lying thief!" the bread merchant roared.

"I swear to you, I can get you your money!" That voice—the boy who'd helped tend to Xerxes!

"Iman!" Amir ran toward the sound of the commotion. "Stop! I am his master." Amir shoved the mountainous brute that had a hold of the boy. The man barely budged.

"You're his master?" Red veins riddled the merchant's eyes.

"Yes, he looks after my horse. But I was robbed, and I haven't been able to pay his wages yet. I'll give you what I owe him as soon as I can. Please, let him go."

"You street rats need to learn what happens when you don't pay for what you take. Get him!" the merchant shouted, pointing at Amir.

Two men grabbed Amir while two other men rolled out a thick section of a fallen tree that was scored with chop marks and stained with a dark, coppery tint. The merchant took the boy's arm and held it across the stump. Iman shrieked, his eyes wide and pleading.

No! This could not be allowed!

But then again, it could. The laws gave the merchant the right to punish crimes committed against him.

"Take mine instead!" Amir twisted free of the men's grasp

and rushed over, pushing the merchant back. "I'm the one who really stole from you by not paying my stable boy. It's my hand you should take."

"Is that so?" the man said through clenched teeth. He nodded toward the stump, to which Amir responded by shoving past him and putting his wrist down over the score marks.

"No!" Tears streamed from Iman's eyes. "I did it. I stole from him. Don't do this, sir. Please!"

Amir gritted his teeth. Without a hand, that boy would never be able to feed his family. He'd done nothing but be faithful and hard working. Amir, however, after the life he'd led, deserved everything coming to him.

He sneered up at the merchant. "Have your revenge."

The merchant huffed and raised his scimitar.

Amir returned his gaze to the boy. So young...not far from the age Amir had been left alone to fend for himself.

For you. Amir clenched his teeth tighter. *I do this for you.*

The blade whistled through the air as the merchant slammed the scimitar down with a thump.

The spray of blood hit Amir's face. He stared, gaping as his arm ended at the red-smudged blade lodged into the wood. On the other side of the foul weapon, his hand slipped off the block and fell into the dirt.

Amir's heartbeat drummed in his temples. One beat. Two beats.

Had this actually....happened?

He fell back, blood shooting from the severed limb. Amir grabbed his wrist and screamed as the pain finally registered and exploded in every nerve.

Bright red blood pumped from the stump as Amir held it up, watching the crimson stream flow down his arm. One of the men grabbed him and held the flame of a torch to it, scorching the arteries shut. Amir screamed and pulled his burnt stump to his chest.

"The debt to your stable boy is paid." The merchant picked up Amir's hand by the pinkie finger, dangling the dead flesh from his fingers before dropping it into a bucket beside the block. "Unfortunately for him, he still has a debt to me."

20

THE MERCHANT YANKED THE BLADE OUT OF THE BLOODIED log. The world around Amir spun. His pulse throbbed in his temples as he stared at the bucket his hand had disappeared into. He hazarded a look at his burned stump. Somehow, his fingers still blazed in pain, even though they were no longer there.

A scream registered behind the throbbing in Amir's head. He shook away the fog as one of the men tied a thick cord around Iman's wrist.

"W-Wait." Amir tried to get up but fell into the dirt.

A second man pulled the rope, stretching the boy's arm out across the log as a third man held Iman down.

Iman kicked and wailed, tears turning to mud as they streaked through the dirt on his face. Amir reached out, but his hand fell, as useless as the one left in the pail.

The merchant lifted the blade once more and brought it down across the boy's right wrist. The *thunk* reverberated in Amir's ears.

No. Skies, no!

The shrieking filled Amir's world, an agony he knew all too well. He clawed at the dirt with his remaining hand. Lost, helpless.

Iman's screams ceased as he passed out, but when the

flames seared the bleeding flesh, he revived and his screaming began anew.

Amir held his own stump to his chest, unable to move. This was the worst of bad dreams. He begged to wake up, but he knew this was a nightmare of his own making. There was no rescue from horrors brought on by destiny wrought from a lifetime of arrogant and vengeful choices.

The boy lay in a pool of both their blood, clutching his burnt, hand-less arm as Amir crawled over and flopped beside him.

Iman held up the nub. "H-How will I feed my sisters...my mother?" The boy's eyes rolled back. His mouth hung open as his head lolled to the side.

Amir hugged him tightly to his chest. In the face of such pain, this boy had the strength to worry about his duty to his family above all. Amir, at least, deserved what had befallen him. How cruel a world this was, that would punish an innocent child.

"This is not the end for us, boy." He put his forehead against Iman's. "We aren't cast aside so easily."

He scooped the boy up into his arms and stood on wobbly legs. Nadir stood just inside the crowd. His eyebrows were drawn together in concern, but he stood firm.

The guard captain could have stopped this. He could have saved the boy, if not Amir. But of course, Nadir had to uphold the law, and the law allowed punishment for stealing.

Amir stumbled toward the city gates. When he got there, one of the guards shoved him from behind, causing him to drop the boy's unconscious body.

Amir sprang up and turned, ready to fight despite missing a hand. The soldiers drew swords. A few days ago he would have laughed at such insolence, but now?

Iman groaned at Amir's feet. The boy had only one chance,

and Amir wasn't going to waste it on his own bruised ego. He lowered his arms and backed up a step. Instead of sheathing their swords, though, the guards advanced.

"Stop!" Nadir ordered. "Let him go."

"But, sir, the boy won't survive if he takes him out there," Salem said. "I don't think that child is his son."

Nadir rested his hand on the hilt of the sword at his hip. "We know next to nothing about this man. I saw him try to save this boy. I don't know why, but it's not our business. I am ordering you to let him pass."

So the brutish warrior has a soul, after all. Amir nodded to the captain.

Nadir bowed, this time with genuine respect, maybe the first bit of respect he'd received from any of the palace guards. It was appreciated, but it was also far too late.

Collecting the boy in his arms once more, Amir set out into the scorching desert. Once over the sand dunes and out of sight of the city, he dropped to his knees and filled himself with intention.

Nothing happened.

He held up his hands to make the symbols of the constellations that would take him back to the temple, but only one set of fingers came into view. Constellations needed to be draw with two hands. The patterns needed to coalesce at the same moment!

He cursed at the heavens at the top of his lungs.

But what did the purveyors of the dark arts care if he had hands or not? Such a trifle wouldn't have stopped the great sorcerers of old. How would they have overcome this, though?

He remembered his mentor, sitting on a hill as Amir shivered, unable to light the fire they needed to survive the night. "Sometimes," the sorcerer had said, "we overthink things. We look for a complex answer to our problems. In most cases, the easiest solution is the most powerful path to take."

The easiest solution... *Blast the sands!* The easiest solution would be to have both hands! But if he didn't, and *since* he didn't...

Holding up his burnt stub once more, he closed his eyes. Visualizing both his hands in front of him, he began making the symbols just as he would have if he had both hands, imagining his fingers, where he would place them, what he would write in the air. He spoke the incantation and felt a tremor, like an earthquake. Placing his remaining hand on the boy, he screamed the words out into the universe. When he opened his eyes, he was back in the temple. The boy lay beside him, as well as several feet of the sand that had surrounded them.

No matter. He'd beg Iago for forgiveness another day.

He rushed to the shelf and searched for a regeneration spell he had seen during his research. He found the scroll and spread it across the floor next to the boy. Amir read through the incantation as quickly as he could, then gathered the items he needed to regrow a limb.

Amir fumbled with his remaining hand, filling a basin with various herbs and potions, and then mixing the ingredients with blessed water from an upper shelf. He spoke the magic words until the mixture bubbled and a pink smoke rose from the bowl. Hopefully, that was the correct color.

Not that it mattered. He'd seen the worst that humanity had to offer. Death would be a welcome respite from this world if he'd made a mistake and mixed the potion incorrectly. Of course, he wouldn't resign Iman to more torture, if that was the possible result. Grabbing a few loose cloths from the shelves, Amir soaked up the liquid from the bowl. He wrapped his own nub first, and when he didn't fall to his knees screaming in pain, he then wrapped Iman's scorched stump. That was the most he could do for the boy. That, and hope the ancient dark sorcery worked.

He splashed the remainder of the potion on his own face and torso, then rubbed some into his legs. The last bit he sipped from the bowl, tilting his head back so as to not waste a single drop.

His wrist began to tingle. He held up his bandaged stub, considering the sensation before stabbing razors cut through his flesh.

He grabbed his wrist, holding up the bandage as bones sprang forth, molding into a skeletal hand. He screamed through clenched teeth, shaking, tears streaming from his eyes as muscle spread over the bones, then a layer of fat and skin. The burn intensified. He fell to his knees, screaming at the sky. A hum surrounded him that overshadowed his own voice, and then it disappeared, leaving him in silence.

He jumped, hearing the ever-present drip in the far reaches of the temple. His fingers twitched within the bandage. He willed them to curl, then reopen, and they responded.

He'd done it!

He wiped his brow. Yes, he'd done it, but at no small cost, considering the pain.

Iman groaned, rolling over in his sleep. Amir shivered. No child could live through that kind of agony twice in one day.

He jumped to his feet and hollered at the shelves. "I need a spell that will keep him asleep, and unable to feel pain for thirty minutes!"

Two scrolls jumped into his hands. Iman's brow furrowed. He twitched.

Amir opened the scroll and began reciting the words without checking their meanings first. A black vapor rose from the scroll, spiraling above Amir.

Iman sat up, his eyes bolted open wide as he screamed.

Amir pointed to him. "The boy!" he commanded. "Help him sleep through the pain, but no longer than thirty minutes!" He'd known better than to trust dark magic. If he didn't specify, Iman might never wake up.

The vaporous specter jumped into Iman, and the boy fell back to the floor. Amir checked for a pulse and sat back, breathing a sigh of relief. The boy breathed easily as bones grew from beneath his bandage.

Amir opened and closed his own new hand. How many impoverished were left in a worse state, or just left to die for no better reason than not having the means to survive? How could one living soul remedy injustice with compounded injustice?

He rubbed his chest, cataloging his own sins—the countless people he'd stepped on or otherwise abused in the name of increasing his skill and bringing him closer to a kingdom of his own. He shuddered. Maybe he should have let the merchant take *both* his hands.

He growled at himself, standing. He hadn't come so far to question himself now, or to curl up into a sweltering blanket of his own self-pity. He was a man of action. One who looked ahead, never behind.

The tides had already begun to change in the kingdom, though. The air in Bisnagar hummed with the power of the jinni. Aladdin was probably already blind to what his perfect world was turning into.

Amir rubbed his chin, considering Badra's family flags still flying over the palace. As long as she hadn't married Aladdin, she was still safe, and with the sultan's stiff attention to law and tradition, Aladdin would be hard-pressed to become Badra's husband in less than the required month-long engagement. Unless, of course, the prat coerced them with magic.

If he were going to, though, he'd have done so already. The

marriage would be complete, and the flags would have changed. Hopefully, Amir had at least one more week to ready himself.

Somehow, though, Aladdin had started his plans of the *perfect society* in motion without even taking the crown. The boy was formidable, indeed.

This made the streets even more dangerous, especially for Xerxes. This was the first promise Amir needed to keep. Out of all the time constraints set upon his shoulders, Xerxes's time had the most chance of running out early with the horse out there alone in a world riddled with hunger.

Amir tried not to imagine the animal's terrified screams or the horse-master licking his dry, cracked lips as he prepared his dinner. Amir nodded to himself. Saving Xerxes would be twofold. It would fulfill his promise, save his friend, but of the utmost importance, this would be an excellent test of his power before he faced Aladdin and his jinni.

But first, he needed to attend to his youngest friend. He crouched, checking Iman's pulse. The boy smiled, hopefully lost in a wonderful dream. Amir ran his fingers over the boy's two beautiful, perfect hands. Anyone who thought all dark sorcery was evil was sorely close-minded. Mystical arts could do magnificent things in the hands of those not prone to abusing their power.

Closing his eyes, Amir spoke a simple incantation, sending Iman back to his home. Hopefully, the child would wake up in his bed, thinking today had been nothing more than a bad dream. Now, to become all Amir was meant to be.

Amir reached his arms out to the temple and took a deep breath. Focusing, he allowed magic to course through him. Swirls of sparkling light formed on his palms, wiping away the last of his injuries. The oldest of magics embraced him, welcoming him home. His power deepened and emulsified, his anger feeding the darkest depths of the sorcery, filling him with something new—strong, deep, and menacing.

The walls of the temple quaked as he lowered his hands. He breathed slowly, magic tingling through him, ready to be released.

He turned toward the scrolls. "What will I need to save Xerxes?" A parchment hovered to him, then a tincture flew into his hand from the vast darkness he had yet to explore. He considered the murky liquid inside. "I would like to remind you that I am your new master, and if Iago has any poisonous traps, I hereby curse this place to go down in flames should I die from a tincture given to me in this archive."

The potion in his hand flew across the room and shattered against the stone wall. The contents spilled down, bubbling and eating away at the stone.

"Clever, Iago." He turned back to the darkness. "The correct potion, if there is one?"

Two different bowls on the table shook. Amir checked the scroll and mixed the two ingredients in water. This was a simple tincture, probably because the spell only lasted a few minutes. He filled two bottles and placed them in his pack.

He took a deep breath, then released it slowly. He'd soon discover if the spinning sensation inside him was an indication he'd returned to full strength or not.

"Xerxes," he whispered, closing his eyes. "Take me to him."

A sparkle rose in his chest, and when he opened his eyes, he stood before a stable. He smiled. Maybe getting back into the palace wouldn't be as hard as he'd thought.

Amir walked through the double doors. Manure littered the floor. Buckets of molded meal, some fallen over, lined the walls. The pungency of death and decay hung like a veil. The scraping of metal against metal rang through the space as someone sharpened their tools.

Amir quickened his pace as a high-pitched whinny and a struggle ensued in the back of the stables. He pulled the tincture from his satchel and gulped it down, wishing he'd thought to bring extra water to ward off the taste.

"Easy now," a man said softly.

Amir rushed to the doorway, but it was too late. The sound of a blade slicing flesh was followed by a wet gurgling whine and a series of thuds as the horse fell to the ground.

It was him...the man who had pushed Badra from her horse at the races!

"Stop." Amir's voice echoed with an odd power that compelled the man to freeze in place.

The racer held a blade in his hand, ready to cut open the animal. But he just stood there, paralyzed.

"What's happening?" the man asked, clearly trying to sound more angry than afraid.

"For the next few minutes, your body will feel the need to do anything and everything I say. Your mind is fully aware and capable of protesting, but unfortunately, the mind is not of much use without a body to carry out its commands."

The man sneered. "Who are you?"

"My name is of no consequence. About a week ago, you acquired a black Arabian stallion from an innkeeper. He belongs to me, and I'll be needing him back."

"Is that so?" the man said, shaking as he struggled against the spell in an attempt to put his hand down.

"Is your arm getting tired?" Amir enquired with feigned concern. "Bring it down as hard as you can."

The man obeyed, plunging the blade into his thigh. His eyes widened as he screamed and fell back, holding his leg.

"That was unfortunate." Amir's brow wrinkled as he circled the whimpering man. "Where did you say I could find my horse?"

"You might find some bones left in the scrap heap outside the restaurant." The man chuckled and spit. "I'm not afraid of your black magic, Sorcerer."

"You're lucky I can tell that you're lying." Amir smiled. "Give me that knife—carefully please; and don't even think about touching your leg."

The man pulled the knife from his wound and shrieked as blood poured out.

"Do you wish to stick with your story as I allow you to empty the contents of your veins onto the floor, or are you going to tell me what I need to know and save us both some time?"

His face turning pale, the man finally surrendered. "The stall at the end." He pulled a leather string from his neck that held a key.

"Thank you, sir." Amir patted the man's cheek. "Better see to that wound, my friend."

The man turned his attention to his bleeding leg and Amir made his way back into the stable. He put the key in the lock and pushed the door open. Covering his nose and mouth, he entered. The smell of disease and excrement hung thick in the enclosed space. Xerxes's ears perked up when Amir entered, and the horse struggled to get to his feet.

Choking back the ball building in his throat, Amir opened his arms as the horse rubbed his head against Amir's chest.

"I told you I would come for you." Amir embraced him. "I'm sorry it took so long."

Holding tight to his old friend, Amir whispered the incantation to bring them back to the temple.

Xerxes bucked up, neighing at his new surroundings.

Amir held up his hands. "It's okay, my friend. I'm going to make some medicine. I'm going to heal you."

He neighed again, stomping his feet, but Amir ran his hands over the stallion's back until he calmed.

Amir grimaced, tracing his fingertips alongside red, swollen lash wounds, still weeping pus and stinking of infection. He'd promised Xerxes long ago that he would never be beaten again. "I didn't mean to break that promise." And he'd do his best not to break it again.

While rubbing salves into the horse's wounds, he pondered his next quest: saving Badra. Fighting the jinni was a given. Amir wouldn't allow her to live under Aladdin's thumb. She deserved better.

He'd have to place a new scroll in the royal library, one that would free her and allow her to marry whomever she chose. Maybe even fashion the wording in a way that would allow her to be sultan.

Amir smiled. Bisnagar would become the golden city of progress, rather than just being known for wealth. Yes, Badra would like that very much. If any woman had the ability to rule, it was her.

He would have loved to stand at her side when she took the crown, but he was not royal. She deserved far more than a sorcerer who'd spent the last fifteen years plotting to take over her kingdom. Yes, he could still use magic, but for the rest of his days he'd know that what they had was not real. He wasn't sure he could live with that, and he was done with breaking promises.

He'd do everything he could for her, and then leave Bisnagar forever.

Amir patted Xerxes's neck, offering the horse some water as he surveyed his temple and the bountiful scrolls. The knowledge of the ages was at his fingertips. Now, he just needed to figure out how to find what he needed to fight an omnipotent adversary without the help of Iago.

21

THE FOOD TASTED A FEW DAYS OLD. NOT THAT BADRA would complain. If she didn't like what she'd been served, the cook might be thrown out into the streets—or worse. She rubbed her neck, easing some of the sting from the golden collar.

"Tell me your most secret desire." Aladdin's dark eyes invited her to open her soul.

"What do you mean?" The princess perused her breakfast and continued moving it around the plate in hopes that he wouldn't notice that she wasn't eating much.

"Tell me something that you've always wanted, that you've never been allowed to have." He leaned forward and braced his elbow on the table.

A pang of guilt needled her, but she resisted the urge to visibly squirm over her discomfort. She wanted to say something noble, but the truth slipped from her lips. "I wish I could walk outside the palace." She shrugged. "I've always felt like a bird in a cage."

"I want to make all of your dreams come true." The prince reached across the table and opened his hand.

"You are my dream now." She smiled as she placed her hand in his.

"I will inform your father that I am going to take you out to meet your people." Aladdin stood and marched off, his shoulders back.

"Sweet prince, so little you know," Badra whispered after he was out of earshot.

When he turned the corner, she unclasped her collar and let it fall to the table. *Sands!* It seemed like the bauble got heavier and heavier each day.

"Shall I take that for you, Highness?" her red servant asked.

Badra waved her hand. "Yes, please."

The servant girl wrapped the collar in a napkin and scurried in the direction of Badra's room.

Somehow, the air seemed cleaner once the necklace was gone, as if it were suddenly easier to breath. Badra sat back and took a sip of water.

Aladdin was sweet, but her father would never let her outside the palace walls.

She wasn't about to tell Aladdin how ridiculous his request was. It wasn't her place, after all. Still, her curiosity got the best of her. This was a conversation she wanted to overhear.

She crept down the hall to the entrance to the throne room and stood just outside, straining to listen.

"Absolutely not!" Her father sounded shocked at the mere question, as expected. "Princess Badroulbadour has never been beyond the palace walls and she never will. If anything ever happened to her, my life would lose all meaning."

"In Noblis," Aladdin said, "I have nothing to fear from my people."

"Bisnagar is a different place altogether." Her father's tone softened. "I'm sorry, but it simply isn't safe."

"Sire, your people would love you if you gave them the chance to know you. The hundreds who swarmed in to take advantage of your hospitality are not any more noble in their hearts than the people only a stone's throw away living in poverty."

"The poor will always blame the authority for their misfortune. I'll not have them take their frustrations out on my daughter."

"Sire, the people need to see that we care about them. I don't plan on being the kind of sultan who sits behind these walls and cares nothing for the goings-on outside."

"Is that how you see me?" Her father's tone grew dark. Badra flinched. He so rarely got angry.

"That is how the people see you." Aladdin didn't waver in his conviction. "Now that I have come, I want to change the public view of the royal family. This will endear us all to the people under our rule."

"You are young, and you do not understand loyalty as of yet." Her father's voice was stern, harsh.

"We cannot demand the people's loyalty without showing them that we deserve it."

This, to some extent, made sense, but Aladdin's ideas were such a far cry from the way things had been done in Bisnagar since before her father was born.

Footsteps sounded across the floor. "I will not let anything happen to your daughter, I swear to you. This is not only about fulfilling her fanciful desire. Rather, it is a necessary political maneuver. The people must know us and we must show them that we are not going to spend our lives cowering in our palace while they suffer."

There was a long pause. "If I allow this..." Badra held her breath hanging on her father's words. "Twenty of my most skilled bodyguards will surround you both at all times."

"I assure you, that is unnecessary, sire," Aladdin interjected.

Badra slapped her hand to her forehead. Was he a fool?

Her father had just agreed to the unthinkable! Leave it be and be happy with achieving the impossible!

"However, I understand and respect your reasons for insisting," Aladdin continued. "I thank you for your flexibility, Your Majesty."

Badra held her chest, breathing heavily.

"If you are to be the sultan, I must allow you to begin exercising your authority. But this will be planned. Security will map out your route, keeping my daughter's safety as the top priority."

Badra's heart pounded against her hand, and her eyes began to sting. She quickly suppressed her excitement and leaned casually against the pillar as Aladdin walked past.

"Impressive," she said, only to catch his attention.

"A spy?" He came close and propped himself against the pillar. "What is the punishment in Bisnagar for spying on a sensitive political conversation?"

She mimicked his playful tone. "The future sultana doesn't have a right to listen in while men stand around deciding her fate?" She put her arms around his neck. "How disappointing. What if I promise to never do it again?"

"Then I shall forgive you this once." He leaned in to kiss her, but she turned her head.

She wasn't sure why. Suddenly, kissing him just seemed wrong.

His expression was no longer playful but visibly insulted. He glanced down to her bare neck.

"I'm going to find the perfect outfit to wear." She kissed his cheek and slipped under his arm.

"My love," he called after her with a sternness that made her stop and look back. "Don't *ever* eavesdrop on me again."

Surprised at his tone, she stared blankly for a moment, waiting for him to smile or do anything to reiterate that he was only joking, but he just stared back at her. A chill swept over her and she felt an intense fear of his displeasure. Hands shaking, she nodded and forced a meek smile before turning to walk back to her room.

The golden walls seemed to close in on her. What had just happened? Why had he been so angry?

She pushed through her door and closed it behind her. Taking a deep breath, she leaned against the gold scrawl work. Even the walls in her own room appeared smaller, stifling.

Looking down, she choked out a sob as she tried to control her trembling hands.

She knew it was completely out of character for her to not only allow a man to speak to her that way, but to actually be made to feel as if she were in the wrong for simply expecting to be treated as an equal.

She looked into the reflection in her mirror and remembered painting over the bruises she'd suffered from being battered at the races. How horrible would it be if she someday needed to paint over bruises that came as a result of her disobedience to her husband?

22

Holding his arms out to the side, Amir called out to the library. "Tell me everything I need to know to fight one of the jinn."

Several scrolls whisked off the shelves and drifted into his hands. Most of the documentation was unclear. Some appeared to be written by madmen, maybe those cursed by the jinn themselves. One scroll chronicled a man who had unlimited wishes—until the lamp had been taken by another. However, the second man only got three wishes. The author speculated that if you found the lamp on your own, the jinni was your slave for all time, but if the jinni was taken from the master, the thief would only be granted three wishes.

The unknown was: had Aladdin found the jinni, or did he steal it from another? It was completely possible that Amir would be going up against cosmic power beyond recognition, limited only by the power of a street rat's imagination.

Amir rubbed his temples. This challenge seemed impossible, but all the scrolls agreed that using the power of the jinn for your own gain invited a darkness into your soul. The few who had good intentions and tried to use the lamp for good, eventually lost themselves to the darkest parts of their own nature. So the longer Aladdin had the lamp, the more base he would become, and the more dangerous. Amir needed to work quickly.

Above all, he needed to get back into the palace. He called to the balcony in his former room and felt himself waver in the dark before rematerializing in the temple.

Interesting. Next, he tried the trees in the back of the garden, again to no effect. He tried Badra's room and the spell held, wavered, pulled him in, and then spat him back. Amir flew through the air and slammed against the archway before falling to the hard ground.

"Blast it!" He punched the tiles at his feet. The boy had put some sort of psychic boundary around the palace, the strongest around Badra's room. Clever.

Amir could appreciate someone who thought through every possible contingency, especially since Captain Nadir would have reported back that Amir had walked out into the desert, carrying a boy, and both of them were missing hands. Amir scowled, imagining Aladdin's mirth over hearing of the apparent demise of his adversary.

He was soon in for a disagreeable surprise.

Getting back inside the palace would be more complicated than he'd originally expected, though. With a magic barrier intact, he needed to think less like a sorcerer, and more like a common thief. As his instructor had told him, sometimes the simplest answers were the best. So he summoned himself some lock-picking tools and fashioned a new black cloak. If only he had the materials needed for a new staff... But there was no sense dwelling on the things he had no control over.

His next challenge would be the princess. Whether through the jinni or some other trickery, Aladdin had found a way around Badra's ironclad mind. Amir needed to start fulfilling his promise to save her by breaking this curse.

He turned to the shelves. "How would one free another from magical influence or mind control, even if that influence was the result of a jinni?"

A scroll flew down to him. He nodded, reading the ingredients. They were all basic and readily available. The agent of the spell, though, needed to be an item of great value to the sorcerer, thus representing a sacrifice. To ward off the strongest of curses, the vessel needed to be a gemstone of sapphire, amethyst or...lapis lazuli.

He startled, holding up his hand. A thin white band marred his finger where his family crest had been for most of his adult life—a grouping of ships sailing about a lapis lazuli sea.

He'd given the ring to Iago. *Sands!* What had the demon done with it?

He rummaged through the shelves, finding nothing but herbs, ointments, and unlabeled tinctures. He slumped onto the chair at the table, holding his head. To combat a jinni, the spell needed to be at its strongest, and he couldn't recall owning nor caring about a sapphire or amethyst. He needed to find that ring, but where?

Across from him, small bowls of frequently required ingredients sat perfectly spaced from each other, ready for use. One bowl was slightly askew. Amir pulled the bowl closer and pursed his lips. It contained red feathers. Useless.

Iago said he needed the ring for a spell, but he hadn't said what kind of spell. In Amir's exhaustion he'd simply handed his most precious possession over. He should have asked more questions because the next time he saw the demon he'd conjured himself inside a bird.

Amir balked—a *red* bird. He grabbed the bowl of feathers. Beneath the plumage, in a thick, clear goo, lay the ring. Amir laughed, wiping his eyes. The eccentric demon had used the lapis lazuli to possess the parrot!

Rinsing his only piece of jewelry with blessed water, he held it up to the light. The ships sailed around the blue jewel, stalwart, as usual. This ring was a symbol of his family and all that he had left of his father. The stone was simply a possession, though. A reminder of a past he needed to let go. Only then could he achieve a future that would have made his parents proud.

After mixing the potion and speaking the words, he waited for the brew to sparkle and smoke. Satisfied, he pried the stone from between the sailing ships and dropped the lapis lazuli into the potion. While the concoction simmered, he fashioned a non-descript leather cord that would act as a chain. Once affixed, all he would need to do would be to get the bauble around Badra's neck without her screaming for her guards and asking for his head.

He rubbed his throat. Beheading was one punishment sorcery couldn't return him from.

Placing the bauble into his pouch, he took a deep breath and transported himself to the dark alley where he had been left to die a few days earlier. Ducking around alleyways, he made his way through the marketplace toward the palace.

Of course, he wouldn't be able to waltz up to the front gates, but the time he'd spent watching the guards, learning their timetables so he could ferret himself and Badra away on frivolous escapades, now proved to have had a much more nefarious purpose.

Using his lock picks, he jimmied his way into the underground passages used to maintain the sewers and found his way beneath the sultan's bathing chamber. If they got out of this, he needed to make sure this entrance was fortified. For now, though, these sewers would be invaluable.

The room was filled with steam and through the grate, Amir could see Aladdin sitting with his back to the drain. The prince was talking to that cursed demon monkey.

"She's gorgeous and I have her completely under my control, but she's taxing my resources. Her resolve is tiring me."

The monkey screeched. "Then what are you waiting for?"

Amir cringed, hearing the shrill, inhuman voice.

"I can't let anyone question my ascension to the throne until it is too late for them to do anything about it. Once I am sultan, her father will slip into a peaceful slumber from which he will never wake." He drew water into his hand, and allowed the droplets to trickle from between his fingers. "After she births my heir, Badra will do the same." He sighed. "It's the kindest death anyone could ask for. Kinder than the fate they would wish upon me if they found out my plans."

"Master shows mercy." The monkey bowed his head.

Sands! The monkey is the jinni! For some reason, Amir had expected him to be larger, and more...human-looking.

"It's for the greater good. Soon this palace and all its riches will be divided up amongst all the people of the city and poverty will be done away with forever."

Amir shook his head. As the son of a merchant, he knew how commerce worked. Of course, the current class system was unfair. Amir had experienced firsthand what it was like to be on the bottom of the social ladder. However, if all wealth was to be simply redistributed, the people would have no need to work to feed their families or aspire to something greater than what they began with. Sure, for a certain time it might seem like a utopia, but it would not take long before human nature took over, leading to theft, deception, and murder. Then, the entire kingdom would crumble. What Aladdin had envisioned was pure folly and no magic in the world could make a society thrive under those conditions.

He continued down the tunnel. There was one last thing he had to do before he could make his way back to the temple and come up with a plan.

23

THE WATER IN THE FOUNTAIN SPARKLED A LITTLE LESS these days. Badra closed her eyes and breathed in the scent of the jasmine flowers. Those, like the water, didn't soothe her as they once had.

A guard glanced at her from the edge of the trees, and another from the entrance to the garden. At least they'd stepped back a bit, giving her more room to breathe. Ever since the morning they'd banished Amir, the guards had been hovering, nearly suffocating her. Aladdin had insisted the source of the vizier's sorcery had been in his staff, and that staff was now in her father's possession. What did they really think one man could do, stripped of his power?

The guards were definitely giving her more room, though.

She shivered. Could that mean they *knew* Amir wasn't coming back? Could something have happened to him?

Her father had granted her wish. He would not lead her to believe Amir had been set free if he had been executed. But out there, in the city, anything could have happened to the former vizier.

No—not just the vizier. Her friend. Amir. She had to remember that he was not a nameless member of her father's staff, but a man—a man who had shown her what it was like to truly live.

A shadow of doubt crept into her heart. Amir had appeared worn and beaten when they'd pushed him to his knees before her father. He'd wanted to explain, even pleaded to her, but she'd refused to listen. What if he'd had a valid reason for lying to them? Not that she could think of a good reason for lying, but she'd never even given him a chance.

Shifting her weight, she scanned Amir's former balcony. It was strange, how the former vizier filled her thoughts now, but a few hours ago, when she'd taken a meal with Aladdin, she hadn't even thought of her former friend. Is that what love did to you, made you forget everything in the world that mattered to you, but this one person?

Maybe it was common sense taking over. She'd completely let her guard down with Amir. She'd trusted him like she'd known him for a thousand years. But that wasn't her fault. It was the sorcery. His treachery had probably started the first time they'd met, and he'd made her look into the eyes of that ridiculous snake staff.

She kept playing each memory over and over, though—each conversation, the times they'd snuck out for little adventures. She knew he had only been after the throne, but her heart couldn't be convinced that what they'd felt for one another wasn't real.

Perhaps she just needed to go out and see the races on her own. That might cheer her up and remind her that she didn't need a man to live life to the fullest.

Although that seemed a little disrespectful to the husband she had agreed to give herself to. Maybe together they would travel the world. She tried to imagine that idea being exciting, but she wasn't sure anything would ever compare to sneaking out of the palace, without guards, and without a care in the world.

"Badra."

She could still remember Amir's voice as clearly as if he were here.

"Badroulbadour!"

Cringing at the sound of her full name, she spun, ready to inflict dagger-like words meant to disembowel the speaker. Instead, she fell mute, clutching the edge of the fountain as her gaze fell on dark skin and the most stunning eyes she'd ever seen.

She gave herself a moment to revel in the joy of just seeing Amir again, until the harsh reality of her strange new world flooded back in, smothering her.

"Are you insane, showing your face in here?" she whispered. "I wouldn't be able to save you a second time around. Not that I would want to." She winced, the lie digging into her gut like a knife.

Amir stepped out of the trees, with no regard for the guards lurking about. "I'm willing to bet my life that you wouldn't have saved me in the first place if you didn't want to."

His smile penetrated her defenses. Again!

More sorcery?

She turned away. "You disgust me! You made me think I was special and different and you probably said those same words to dozens of women."

"I haven't always been a man worthy of your ear, but I pray you..." Amir sat beside her. "I wasn't honest with you when I first walked through the palace gates. Yes, it was my intent to take the throne as my own. Falling for you was not part of my plan."

She shoved him away, but he grabbed her shoulders. "But I did, Badra. I fell for you when I watched you tell that noxious prince that he would never win your hand. I fell for you when I discovered that the hooded rider who gave his winnings to starving children was a princess in disguise. I fell for you when you pulled me into the fountain." He pointed his chin toward the water. "It didn't happen all at once. I fell in love with you every day that we spent together and now that it's over I need you to know that."

"Why?" Her eyes welled up. "Why can't you just leave me alone and let me be happy? I'm going to be married in a few days and you're the last thing I need to be thinking about." Even though she couldn't stop thinking about him any time she was alone.

"That's the thing," he said. "I would rather you marry the old Vizier Hazim than Aladdin."

"I bet you would!" She yanked back, and he finally let her go.

"Not because I'm jealous, although I am..." Amir rubbed his eyes. "I hate to see you marry anyone. But Aladdin is no better than me."

Badra scoffed. "You can't be serious."

"I am afraid I am."

A guard came out, looked right at them, and then ducked back into the trees.

Her eyes widened. "Why didn't they come arrest you?"

His smile dazzled. *Blast it all!*

"When they look at me, they see Aladdin. It's a temporary enchantment. I don't have much time."

"Good. You shouldn't be here, impersonating the prince."

He shook his head. "But he's not a prince. He, like myself, is an imposter. He intends to murder you and your father as soon as he has the throne. He, also like myself, is using magic to manipulate the situation."

"More lies!"

"No. I was unable to hypnotize you. I tried, the first day we met. I ordered you to forget our conversation, but you…" He smiled, as if recalling the fondest of memories. "You batted my scepter aside and shot venom at me. You were too strong for my magic." His posture slackened. "Unfortunately, Aladdin's source power is more sophisticated."

"Right." Badra folded her arms and narrowed her eyes. "All that stuff about your family…"

"Was true. I thought I'd spoken too freely; that's why I wanted you to forget." He gulped. "You see, the truth is, I was not born into a noble family. My father was a merchant and my mother was born a slave."

She brought her hand to her lips. "You're joking."

"Unfortunately I'm not, and because of this, I know we can never be together, but I would rather die than see harm befall you." Amir held up a blue gem dangling from a silken ribbon. "Take this. It will help you resist Aladdin's influence."

"And how do I know you won't use that to control me like you tried to do with your staff?"

"First off, I could have already placed this on you without telling you, but I didn't."

Badra fiddled with the edge of her sleeve. "And?"

"And nothing." Amir hung the necklace on the outstretched hand of a statue and backed away. "Some part of you believes me, because you haven't screamed for the guards."

"Oh, so just because I don't want to see your head cut off, you think I believe this nonsense."

"No, you don't want my head cut off because you're in love with me. And you believe me because you're too smart to let his magic control your every thought, no matter how powerful it might be."

Her nose flared. "You think I'm in love with you?"

He closed the distance between them and whispered in her ear. "I've never been more sure of anything in my life."

His lips covered hers, and the sweetness of his touch left her lost, floating in a mist of all that was great and good. For a few seconds, all in the world was right. Until he drew away and exhaled a warm breath on her cheek.

Voices cast across the garden. One spoke her name. It was Aladdin!

Her breath hitched. They couldn't find Amir here with her, not now!

"Go!" She pushed him into the trees.

Amir obeyed, disappearing back into the shadows from whence he came. The necklace still hung from the finger of the statue.

Did she dare trust him, after he'd all but admitted his guilt? Could she afford to trust Aladdin?

At the sound of the prince approaching, she grabbed the necklace and hid the jewel in the folds of her dress.

"My prize!" he cooed with his arms outstretched. "You must come and sit with me in the throne room. I have a company of European actors ready to enact a modern play for us."

"That sounds lovely." She hurried to his side.

His gaze drew to her neck. "You're not wearing your collar."

"It was starting to hurt." She touched her throat. "It rubs every time I turn my head and I was getting a red—"

He stopped walking and snapped his fingers. Nadir stepped forward and bowed.

"Go to the princess's chamber and fetch one of the necklaces I've given her," Aladdin said. "Any one will do."

"Yes, sire." Nadir bowed again. His eyes lingered on Badra for a moment, as if asking permission to leave.

She felt her own eyes widen, begging him to stay, but his lips thinned. Alas, he was only a guard. He'd been given an order. If she did not command him outright to stay, he had to listen.

The guard gave her a curt nod, bowed, and backed away. She'd never felt so horrified to be alone with someone.

Aladdin smiled, but it wasn't soothing, as she'd grown accustomed to. "The necklaces are a symbol of our love, Badroulbadour." His hand tightened around the back of her neck and she could have sworn his fingers felt longer than they had been before. "I like to see them on you." He spoke through clenched teeth, his eyes manic.

"Of course, my love." She forced the words out. "I-I'll put it on as soon as the play is over." *Or never. Sands!* She'd never felt so threatened standing next to him. Where was the love, the security?

"You'll do it now." He snapped his fingers, and Nadir appeared. The guard gaped, wide-eyed and standing there, holding the thick, gold necklace. He handed it to the prince.

"Ah yes, my favorite." He held up the bulky monstrosity. "I know you said this one is uncomfortable, but women are so much stronger than they are given credit for." He snapped the collar around her neck. "The things they endure for the benefit of those they love, it's extraordinary, isn't it?"

"Y-Yes." She gulped.

The metal tingled. Her breathing slowed.

What was she worried about? Everything was fine. She smiled and leaned on his arm as they walked.

He patted her on the head like a puppy. She loved when he did that. "That's my girl," he said.

When they reached the throne room, Aladdin sat down and motioned for Badra to come sit on his knee. There were so many comfortable chairs, but there was nowhere else she'd rather be.

Once she was seated, the actors began the play.

Aladdin pulled her closer to him. "I've heard that the wedding night can be exceptionally painful for the bride." His hand swept forward and gripped her hip. "And of course, there will be the births of our children. So many sweet things bring pain, don't they?"

She cringed. What an odd thing to say.

"Sit at my feet." He shoved her, and she landed on the hard tiled floor.

Badra stared at him, agape, before a warmth spread over her again.

At his feet was where she wanted to be, as long as it pleased him. She could massage his toes, make sure he was comfortable. She adjusted her skirt, and her fingers grazed over the bauble she'd hidden there.

Amir! Amir had been here! She needed to give this cursed jewel to Aladdin right away.

She gripped the small stone to pull it out and hand it over when ice shot through her veins. She trembled, blinking as if she'd been in the dark, and someone had lit a candle. She gripped the stone harder, as if her life depended on not dropping the jewel.

She was sitting.

On the floor.

At the feet of *a man.*

Her hand trembled. Her life may not have depended on not losing Amir's gift, but her mind certainly did.

The ice in her veins turned to fire. The red-dressed servant handed her a glass of wine, and it took all of her strength not to throw the drink in Aladdin's face. How many times had she humiliated herself like this over the past several days?

Skies above! Amir had said her mind was too strong to control, but just yesterday she'd lain beside Aladdin, placing grapes into his mouth one at a time.

The prince reached down and scratched the back of her neck like a favored pet. She gripped the stone even tighter. Everything Amir had said was true. She, her father, and this entire palace were under a horrible spell.

They had fallen for the most grievous of betrayals, and she was the only one in the palace who knew.

ONCE HE WAS A FEW YARDS BEYOND THE PALACE WALLS, Amir picked the lock on the drain cover in an alleyway in the middle of the city. Replacing the cover and erasing his footprints, he set out toward the market to find some food. Conjuring money cost the spell caster a price he was unwilling to pay, but no matter, the restaurants and their trash piles were always available.

The dogs wagged their tails as he approached. He'd have to start giving them all names if they were to be good friends, like this.

"Sir," Iman called out.

Amir's cheeks heated. He backed away from the trash, glad he wasn't already on his knees, rooting through the filth for a meal. "Hello, boy."

Iman held up two perfect hands, flipping them back and forth. One of his sleeves was still stained with a coppery tint. Blast it!

"I wasn't sure I'd ever see you again," Iman said.

"I wasn't sure, either." Amir pressed his lips together. "I still owe you for a week's work, don't I?"

The boy shrugged. "Two weeks."

His gaze carried to the dogs in the trash, then drew to Amir, then back to the dogs. His eyes widened with awareness, blast it!

The child's expression became determined. "Come have dinner with my family, and we'll call it even."

Amir shook his head. "I couldn't impose."

"Please, sir." Iman tugged on Amir's sleeve. "It would mean a lot if you would meet my mother and sisters. A hot meal and a roof over your head for the night is the least I could do after... after everything." He wiggled the fingers on his new hand.

Amir gave an uncomfortable nod, hoping the boy would continue being cryptic about the new hand. He followed Iman to a lowly hovel that had apparently fallen into disrepair without his father present to do proper maintenance. Amir ducked through the doorway and entered a small, dimly-lit room.

"Light another lantern, Lina. We have a guest," Iman said cheerfully.

"A guest?" A little girl no older than five or six years, appeared from the adjoined room. "Who?"

A second little girl who appeared identical to the first followed behind. "I'll add some water to the soup!" she said with a smile as she ran to the black pot suspended over the small fire. "It'll be done soon," she added, stirring a few cups of water into the contents of the pot.

"Twins?" Amir pointed at the girls.

"Lyla and Lina." The boy gestured for Amir to take a seat at the table. "I picked their names."

"Beautiful names for beautiful girls." Amir sat down.

"In a few years they will be old enough to marry. Do you have any wives?" The boy wiped out a bowl with the edge of his shirt.

"I do not. However, by the time they are old enough to marry, I will be too old."

"They could still cook and keep house for you."

"I am not the sort of man to take ladies young enough to be

my own daughters as wives. You should let them choose husbands for themselves. They should each be treated like princesses by someone young, handsome, and brave."

"Someone brave enough to sacrifice their hand to save a boy they barely know?" Iman's eyes were wide in the light of the fire.

"I don't know what you mean." Amir stood up to leave.

"You are the one who saved Iman and gave him back his hand?" One girl came to him and took his arm, pulling back the sleeve to examine the thin white scar that remained on his wrist, barely visible. "Iman has a scar here too. Don't worry. We won't tell anyone. We wouldn't want someone to cut it off again." The little girl went back to the soup. "It was hard enough for Iman to convince everyone that the boy who lost his hand was someone else who looked like him. He says the bread merchant still watches him like a hawk."

"He doesn't watch close enough," Iman said, producing a loaf of bread from the inside of his cloak.

Amir slapped his hand on the table. "You didn't learn your lesson the first time?"

"Losing my hand didn't fill my sisters' bellies." He broke the bread into four equal pieces. "If life says we have to eat, then we have a choice to either risk a hand or starve with all our limbs intact. So I say, if my hand gets cut off again, I'll take it with me and throw it in the soup."

"You're disgusting, Iman!" The other girl slapped his arm. "I'm not eating your hand!"

The boy raised his spoon. "Good, more for the rest of us!"

"I'm with Lina." Amir put his hands up. "You can have the hand soup all to yourself."

The girls laughed and Amir couldn't help but join them. Iman just smiled and shook his head. "No hand soup today."

Lyla served them each a bowl of watered-down vegetable

soup. After they ate, Iman went into the back room with a bowl of broth and a small piece of his own bread.

"Iman likes to spend time with mother in the evenings," Lina said. "He makes her eat and talks to her. She mostly only gets up when she has to."

Amir stood and walked into the bedroom where Iman sat next to his mother on a blanket spread out on the floor. The woman was far too thin for a woman of her age, her skin an odd, indiscernible color. Amir's stomach clenched. How had this mere boy managed to keep her alive in this state?

Iman glanced over his shoulder before continuing his work. "If you can grow back a hand, can you heal someone's mind?"

"I'm not really sure spells work that way."

Amir sat next to him. The woman just stared at the wall as the boy spooned broth into her mouth and cleaned up what dribbled out.

Iman dabbed her cheek with the edge of his sleeve. "If you're ever curious or want someone to practice on, I would try anything if I thought it might make her go back to the way she was."

"If I could do something like that for anyone, I would do it for you." Amir put a hand on the boy's shoulder.

After the bowl was empty, the girls and Iman all laid their blankets near the fireplace. The two girls shared a blanket so that Amir could have one for himself. He felt guilty denying such hospitality. It always seemed that those who had the least offered the most.

He stretched out, listening to the three children tell stories to each other about brave heroes who fought evil wizards.

Amir knew these stories well from his own childhood. These were the kind of stories where good always triumphed over evil, and the line between the two was as plain as night and day. If Amir had learned anything in his life, it was that good and evil were not so black and white, and most people existed in the massive gray expanse between the two.

When the chatter had completely ceased and he knew that all the children were asleep, he transported himself to the temple and retrieved the scroll that held the spell of regeneration. He took a few moments to prepare the potion and re-familiarize himself with the words before transporting back to the hovel. Tiptoeing into the mother's bedroom, he poured the liquid into her mouth and performed the spell, channeling all the power of his astral body into an effort to heal her.

Afterward, she continued to lie there perfectly still with the same steady breaths as before. He plopped back onto the dirt and rubbed his face. That was the most he could do for her. Hopefully, it was enough. He took the blanket they'd loaned him and put it over the twins before closing his eyes and returning to his temple to rest and gather his wits for the battle ahead.

Soon, he would fight for people like Iman who wanted to work and make better lives for themselves. They deserved that chance...every single one of them. He had to stop Aladdin before it was too late, or else there would be no future for anyone in Bisnagar.

RED SWEPT BADRA'S HAIR UP INTO AN INTRICATE TOUSLE
of curls adorned with fresh jasmine flowers.

"You look lovely, Highness."

Yes, she did. She hoped Aladdin approved. Otherwise, her
servant might pay the price.

Badra shuddered, remembering the heated look in his eyes
when he'd caught her eavesdropping. His temper seemed to
intensify by the hour. Servants had begun giving him a wide
berth. She wished she had the same luxury.

Hanging on the golden vines that adorned the edge of her
mirror was the blue gemstone that Amir had given her. If
Aladdin found out that she had accepted something from the
man whom they'd thrown out of the palace, she'd have a great
deal of explaining to do.

So be it. The risk was worth the protection the stone gave
her. Snatching the necklace off the wall, she shoved the stone in
her brassiere over her heart. If anything, the stone gave her clarity, and clarity was what she needed in the days to come.

She had been convinced she loved Aladdin, but when she
returned to her room at night, the feelings had faded, even
before Amir had given her the blasted stone.

The gold collar Aladdin was so fond of glinted in the
sunrays falling on her dressing table. She shivered, imagining

the clasp clicking around her throat again. Everything felt right when she wore it. Too right.

Her stomach roiled and she stood, shaking her head to clear it. Today was a good day. She was about to walk into the city without a hood hiding her face. Aladdin had asked what she wanted and then had made it happen for her. It was a wonderful gift she intended to take full advantage of. Maybe, if she got lucky, Amir would find a way to contact her or sweep her away and save her while they were outside the palace walls.

It was a fantasy, but a good one. Even if Amir was not out there, waiting for her, she wouldn't miss a chance to leave the palace as herself rather than the hooded rider.

Still, she wrapped a traditional shawl around her shoulders, concealing her bare neck as they walked down the hall to the main receiving rooms. If they got far enough from the palace before Aladdin noticed she hadn't worn her collar, he couldn't send one of the guards back to fetch the necklace for her. As long as she fawned over the prince, he'd never even think to check.

At least she hoped not.

Nadir and his finest guards gathered and walked in formation around them as the palace gates opened. Badra beamed as Aladdin took her hand and they made their way through the streets. He watched her react to each new sight as if it were the first time she had seen it.

Seeing the boy who had taken care of Amir's horse, she called one of the guards to come near. Untying a small coin purse from her belt, she handed it to the guard. "Could you please give this to the boy standing near the bread stand?"

"No." Aladdin pushed her aside. "Darling woman, you would be treating the symptoms rather than curing the disease. If we are to truly spark great change, we must fix the problem at its source." He put both hands up. "Citizens of Bisnagar, hear me!" Badra glanced around and folded her hands, looking as meek as she could. "A time is coming when no man will be wealthier than any other and we shall all be equals." Aladdin took a loaf of bread and gave it to the boy, who then backed away, disappearing into the throng.

"Are you planning on paying for that, Your Highness?" The bread merchant bowed but stared daggers into the prince.

Aladdin ignored him and continued playing to the crowd that gathered to listen. "Once I am sultan, none of you will fall asleep with empty bellies." He glared at the bread merchant. "We will all learn to share what we have—or be left behind along with the archaic notions of class and nobility." He held his hands in the air over the people. "The days when greed was the beating heart of this kingdom are coming to an end. Mark my words: a new world lies ahead!"

The spectators broke out in applause. Aladdin took Badra's hand and guided her around in a circle as if to display his prize. She gritted her teeth, not relishing being treated like a show pony, but she wouldn't dare dishonor him by protesting while everyone watched. She looked down, hoping that no one could see her reddening face.

After his speech, the guards had to hold the masses back and Badra began feeling uneasy.

"Why has it taken this long for someone to do something?" one voice shouted.

"A delicate flower like her has no care for those living amongst the thorn bushes," said another.

"Finally, a royal who will be worth something."

The voices made her feel as if the world were closing in around her again.

"May we go, my love?" Badra entreated.

"What are you talking about? The people love this."

"I'm just feeling a bit overwhelmed, that's all."

"Of course. I'm sure this must all be very strange to you." Aladdin put his arm around her before turning to address the people once more. "Stay strong, my brothers and sisters. Change is coming!"

Half the guards lagged behind to keep the admirers from following too closely and the other half surrounded Badra and Aladdin with their weapons at the ready as they entered the palace gates.

"Wasn't that the most exhilarating thing you've ever experienced?" he asked.

"It *was* exciting."

Badra interlaced her fingers with his. That wasn't entirely a lie. Anything outside the palace was exciting. She simply wished she'd been with someone else.

She adjusted her shawl. "How are you going to do it?"

"What do you mean?" Aladdin grabbed her hips and pulled her toward him.

"If the nobles are no longer going to be noble and what is theirs is to be given to the poor, and the merchants and businesses will no longer be getting paid for the things they sell, so they won't be paying the people in their employ..."

"What are you trying to ask?"

"Once the money that's been given away runs out, what will be the motivation of the bread makers and the farmers if not to receive payment?"

"You need to have faith in the love of all mankind. They'll work in harmony because it is the right thing to do." Aladdin placed a hand on her cheek. "I know it's not a concept you have had the chance to experience or witness being cooped up in the palace, but it's a powerful thing." His hand moved down her throat, his fingertips tracing a line down and drawing the scarf away, exposing her bare neck.

He frowned. His eyes lanced hers.

His hand still rested a finger above her breast.

She pushed him away with a girlish giggle. "We are not married *yet*, My Prince." She kissed his cheek. "I am the one thing you are not allowed to explore just yet."

He pouted. "I think you enjoy watching me suffer."

"Maybe a little." She winked at him before disappearing down the hall. As soon as she was in her room, she took the jewel out from its hiding place and rubbed it against her face. Breathing hard, she realized how little sense the prince's words really made. In fact, looking back over most of the things they had discussed since his arrival, it all seemed more like a bunch of nonsense he was making up as he went along.

A knot tightened in her stomach. This man was about to be her husband. He was going to be given ultimate authority over the entire realm and he knew nothing about how a strong economy worked.

Badra rushed to the balcony and vomited over the side. Waves of anxiety crashed over her and the more she thought about Aladdin, her father, the kingdom, the more she worried that there was no way to reverse what had already started. She couldn't tell her father. He never listened to her even when he wasn't under a spell.

But if she was the only one left in the palace with their wits about them, she needed to do something. She couldn't sit here and wait for everything to happen to her, as a good little woman was supposed to do.

She leaned back, wiping her mouth. What could she do, though?

A pair of yellow birds fluttered in their cage below, rushing at the bars as if trying to free themselves. She shivered. Amir may still be her only hope. If he was really a sorcerer, he could battle Aladdin, maybe save them all.

If he'd even agree to come back again after they'd thrown him out without letting him defend himself.

Badra touched her lips. His kiss had been so warm, so pure. He still cared, and yes, he was right. She loved him. Now he needed her trust, more than ever.

She straightened. She needed to find a way to help him. But how?

The fountain trickled below her, and a butterfly fluttered at the edge of the garden path where she and Amir had walked the day they'd first met...the day he'd tried to bewitch her with his staff.

The staff!

They'd told her the staff was his source of power. That was why her father had insisted they take it from him. Maybe if he had his staff back, he'd be able to help her take back the kingdom!

It was a long shot, but it was something.

A cool breeze whisked across her face. She'd have to be stealthy, but the hooded rider was all about stealth, and no one would be expecting an attack on the kingdom from the inside.

26

Amir's gaze carried over the three empty fruit stands in the outer market. At midday, this section of town should he bustling with foot traffic. Instead, a brisk wind whipped up a sand spiral.

People cheered in the distance. Perhaps there was a festival he was unaware of?

"Sir!" Iman rushed to Amir's side. "The prince who is engaged to the princess just took this loaf from the bread merchant and gave it to me in front of everybody. He's going to force people to share what they have for the good of everyone!"

Amir frowned. "Did he pay for that?"

"No. You should have seen the look on the merchant's face." Iman's eyes were wide as he jumped and gestured wildly.

"Iman, we have to go back and pay for that bread. The merchant will have it in for you more than he already does."

"He wouldn't go against the prince." Iman shooed away a fly. "He had no choice but to accept it. I really like this new prince."

"He's an idiot." Amir scowled. "What he proposes might sound ideal at first, but what will happen when you can't collect a wage for the work you do?"

"It won't matter because I won't have to pay for food." Iman held up his hands like it was the simplest solution in the world.

"And where will you get food if no one wants to make it for free?"

"Bakers still have to bake. It's what they do."

Amir ruffled the boy's hair. "You think you know everything, don't you?"

Iman wrinkled his nose and scurried off back toward his home, where he would share his complimentary bread with his mother and sisters.

Ah, to be so young and naïve.

What this boy—and Aladdin—didn't understand was that everything came at a price, no matter what the laws stated. The bread merchant might not be able to get to Aladdin, but he could certainly get to Iman.

Closing his eyes, Amir said a small incantation he'd memorized in case of emergency. He blinked, his eyes stinging. The scroll he'd read this spell from had warned that this particular incantation had a price. It stole time from one's life. Speaking it was unthinkable, but this, decidedly, was an emergency.

He held out his hand and fingered the five shiny coppers he'd conjured. Five coppers for five hours of his life. He trembled. The time was of no consequence if it saved Iman from more harm.

Confident in his decision, Amir walked to the marketplace to search for the slighted bread merchant. The bread cart had closed up early. Odd, with the sun still so high in the sky and people still mulling about, many gossiping about the new prince and an exciting future.

Fools. They had no idea what was about to befall them.

Below the bread cart, a rat chewed on what otherwise appeared to be a perfectly good roll.

Amir's stomach sank. What if the merchant closed to go find Iman?

He bolted back to the boy's home. Through the window, he watched Iman sitting down to eat with his sisters and breathed a sigh of relief. A woman handed each girl a bowl of soup from the pot—their mother. Amir smiled, warmth spreading through him. Of all the spells he'd ever cast, that one seemed the most satisfying. He'd made a family whole again, and Amir couldn't remember seeing anything so wonderful as a family sitting down to a meal together, and the smiles on those children's faces.

There was an unease filling the air, though, signaling that another storm was on the way. Only this one felt different, something dark and foreboding carried in on the unnatural wind—the power of jinni, it had to be.

Amir whisked himself back to the temple. He needed to be ready for whatever was coming. Too much was at stake for him to falter now. With the fate of the entire kingdom and Badra's life hanging in the balance, there would be no room for error. It was time for him to do what he was best at.

His chest tightened, and he scratched at the thin white line on his wrist, a permanent reminder of how quickly the balance of power could be tipped. He needed to keep that balance in his favor, no matter the cost.

Closing his eyes, he whispered the words and summoned a hundred coppers, the equivalent to four days of his life. He opened his eyes and grimaced at the coins. He understood the warnings. The coin came far too easily, and life was already too short.

Grabbing the coins, he sent himself back to the market. A dog barked, running through the streets. Both of the herb dealers' doors were locked. The crystal dealer nodded to Amir as he left his own shop.

"Closing early today?" Amir asked.

"As are many." The crystal merchant motioned to the many

closed doors and empty carts. "Several have already decided to move on." He shook his head. "This new prince..."

Amir nodded. "I heard." He couldn't really blame them. Those who got out early could make shop elsewhere, rather than leaving en masse later, struggling to stake claims in neighboring lands.

Slipping into an alley, Amir whispered a spell that whisked him to the city of his birth, where he easily obtained the herbs, crystals, and various ingredients needed to prepare himself for the imminent battle with Aladdin and his jinni. He spent a full day brewing potions and filling small vials, then securing them in his satchel.

The continuum potion, a tincture that would allow him to reverse time for three minutes, took a full day to boil, and then another twelve hours to cool before the mixture could be bottled.

If Iago were here, he may have known an ancient method to speed up the process. The last time he'd seen the demon, he'd been thrown against the wall by one of the guards for having tried to help Amir. For all he knew, the bird was dead, and Iago with him. He supposed that was of little consequence at this point. There was no use in dwelling on the loss of someone who'd been officially dead for well over a thousand years, especially when so much was at stake.

Reaching into his pocket, he discovered the original five coppers he'd conjured—enough to pay for Iman's bread, and then some.

Checking the coals beneath the simmering potions, Amir conceded that he'd done all he could do, at least for the moment. He needed to make good with the bread merchant to clear Iman's name.

Closing his eyes, he ferried himself back to the marketplace.

He gaped at the people walking the streets. Many stumbled, holding their heads. Some had red eyes or were coughing, and many of these afflicted wore fine clothes, not the rags of peasants. The poor were already starving and many times were afflicted with diseases they could not afford to treat, but now the wealthy?

More shop doors stood closed as he moved through a street devoid of horses or the sounds of merchants calling out their wares. Had it really been such a short time since he'd first arrived in the golden city?

He glanced up at the palace. The sultan's flags still flew high. Maybe these merchants felt the same tingle in the air that Amir had...the abhorrent breath of the jinni floating over the city.

He paused in front of the bread merchant's stand, the shelves empty like most of the others. Amir shook his head. Iman was so certain the merchant would always make bread *because that was what bread merchants do.* What the boy didn't understand, and Amir knew all too well, was human nature.

Amir stared at the coins in his palm. If the merchant had moved on, it might be better for all of them. Human nature also told him that some people held a grudge, and the bread merchant, he was certain, was the kind to never forget.

He moved toward an alley and prepared to recite the words that would whisk him back to his temple. With things progressing as they were, he needed to take what potions and spells he could and stop procrastinating. Aladdin's power grew, despite still being just a prince. Amir shivered to think what the boy might do once he actually could wield absolute power.

"Get out of the way!" someone shouted in the street.

The bread merchant strode toward his cart, wiping splatters of red from his forehead. His scimitar hung at his hip, poorly cleaned and still stained with blood.

Amir's stomach sank. His heart raced as he flung himself through the streets, shoving past anyone who slowed him down as he sprinted to Iman's hovel. As soon as he burst through the door, his heart shattered at the red stains on the dirt floor and the desperate sound of the two little girls, weeping.

The twins screamed as he entered, most likely expecting a hulking man with a sword.

"Amir!" Lyla threw her arms around his waist.

The last time he'd seen this child, she'd been alight and happy, offering her home and her soup, despite their own destitution. These tears, they were too much to bear.

Their mother sat in the corner, holding her knees. "You're the one, aren't you?" She sobbed, peering through matted, dirty hair. "You're the sorcerer who saved my boy the first time?"

Lyla cried into his tunic. Amir tried to swallow the dryness in his throat.

The girl wiped her nose on her sleeve. "Amir can fix this! He's more powerful than the sultan!"

The woman brought herself up on shaky knees. "You saved us once. Won't you help us again, please?"

Pushing the girl away, Amir eased over to where Lina clung to Iman, facing the wall. Gently turning the boy over revealed his ghostly white face. Both Iman's hands had been severed at the wrist, this time without the decency of cauterizing the wounds. Someone had tied a gray-stained cloth tourniquet on each wrist—cloth the same color as Lina's tattered dress—but blood still wept from the wounds.

"By all that is holy!" Amir hung his head. His chest clenched and thickened. "I told him he would get caught if he stole again."

"No, he didn't steal. The prince gave him the bread." Lina sobbed, pointing at the door. "But the bad man came and..." The girl's face twisted as she wept uncontrollably.

The bread merchant—doling out punishment on the wrong person, on the only one who he could reach.

"I am going to try to help him." Amir scooped the boy into his arms. "There's no time to waste. You must all promise not to speak a word of what you are about to see to anyone."

He didn't wait for them to answer before transporting himself and Iman to the temple. "Hold on, boy." Laying him on the floor, Amir rushed to the alchemy table and began mixing the ingredients for a potion to bring the boy back from the brink of death. Regrowing Iman's hands would do him no good without any fluids in his veins.

The potion to replace blood was slow working, and once he'd gotten it down the boy's throat, Amir set to work to regenerate the hands. After the fingers were fully formed, Amir reached out and took the boy's hand. It was cold to the touch and Amir prayed out loud to anyone who might listen.

"Spirits, demons of the wind, earth, and sea, I ask that you deliver this child from death. My invitation is open to anyone with the power to heal him. I would be in your debt. One day, I will be the most powerful sorcerer in the world and my gratitude will be worth infinitely more than it is right now, I swear to you."

The boy remained pale.

The man Amir had been a few short months ago would have brought down a storm of unholy wrath on every one of these vile parasites that had reduced the beautiful city to squalor. But the man he was in that moment, kneeling at the side of a boy who had nothing with which to repay him, only wanted to make right all the wrongs that had been caused by Aladdin and his cursed lamp.

Iman moaned in his sleep. Hopefully that was a good sign. There was nothing more he could do for the boy. Picking him up and holding him close, he returned him to his home. The girls crowded, sobbing their thanks.

"He'll come back," Iman's mother said. "If we don't come up with the money, he promised to take all our hands."

Amir's nose flared. "Not while I am living."

Speaking an incantation, he summoned a spirit into his hand before running his forefinger and middle finger around the edge of the doorway.

"Let no one who intends harm enter these walls."

"Yes, Master," the tiny voice hissed from the creature in his palm.

"You will be safe as long as you stay inside," Amir told Iman's family. "I'll be back when I can."

"Will Iman live?" Lina's big eyes shone up at him in the dim light of the oil lamp.

"I hope so." Amir lowered his head. Never had any words been so true. This was no longer about a power struggle between him and Aladdin. This was no longer about his love for a woman he had no right to care for.

This was about Iman, his family, and the hundreds of families like them who had nowhere to run. When the rest of the merchants left, the poor would be butchered and pawned by those left behind to fend for themselves. They'd already seen the worst humanity had to offer, and Aladdin's laws had not even taken effect yet.

Amir's fists clenched and the darkness in his heart deepened, hardening him. Any other day these people would cower at the feet of a sorcerer. Sands, any other day he may have welcomed their prostration, but today was not any day.

He'd wanted a kingdom, and he'd failed. Somewhere along the journey, though, it had become less about ruling a kingdom and more about making Bisnagar a better place.

He could no longer be sultan but he might still be able to

save the innocent left behind. He closed his eyes and let the sorcery flow through him. The comfort of the darkness took hold...the same darkness that had sent him on this journey. Failure was not an end, but only a new beginning.

These people needed a champion, one who was not afraid to meet their tormentors on their own terms—and the time for waiting was over.

27

Sitting at her dressing table, Badra rubbed her thumb over the blue jewel Amir had given her. The collar around her neck pulsed, coaxing her to throw the stone away and be done with it. She quaked, gripping the jewel in her palm. It was getting harder and harder to resist, even with Amir's help.

"I hope you never lose that stone, Princess." Red pulled Badra's hair into a messy ponytail.

Badra almost asked why, but she knew why, and asking her servant to speak the words aloud would lead to nothing good. Badra was more like herself when she had the stone. She felt even more like herself when she returned to her room and took off the putrid collar.

She shivered again. There was a darkness closing in on the palace, squeezing her, and she had no way to escape. When she was with Aladdin, though, the world became bright again. All of her cares drifted away.

She hated that—because it wasn't real. *None of this is real!*

She fumbled with the clasp on her collar. She needed to get it off. She needed to be rid of this thing, but the clip tightened, refusing to budge.

"Wait, Highness." Red popped the fastener, and the collar bounced off Badra's lap and dropped to the ground. Red reached for it.

"No." Badra rubbed her collarbone. "Just leave it."

She took a deep breath and straightened, as if she'd been held under a weight.

She stared at the golden necklace on the floor. Fairy tales always romanticized love. Maybe love was a magic all its own, and that was what she'd been feeling. The prince was kind overall, gentle and loving...as long as she did as she was told. Too many times she'd seen the dark spirit harbored deep within him, maybe the dregs of a sordid past or a bad relationship he'd had with his parents. Still, the rage in his eyes had frightened her at times, and it was becoming harder and harder not to agitate him by saying or doing the wrong thing.

More than anything, she worried for her father. He had been coming to the throne room to handle matters of state less and less often. When he did manage to drag himself out of bed, he could barely stay awake long enough to address the most pressing issues at hand. Dark circles crept under his eyes and his once-round face had thinned.

She rubbed the sore skin beneath where the necklace had been. Strange, how she hadn't even worried about her father earlier when she'd seen him. She glanced at the collar again. "Could you maybe put that on the other side of the room?" she asked.

Red grabbed the collar with a cloth, barely touching the flashing gold. Maybe the servants were wiser than any of them gave them credit for.

Badra's head started to clear. She needed to spend more time with that dreaded jewelry tucked away. It was impossible to deny the influence of the gifts Aladdin had given her. Her father had one, too. A large stone on a ring that Aladdin had given him a few days before her father had started granting him more power.

She shuddered. How easily the prince had come in and taken control of everything.

She needed an ally, but who could she talk to and address her concerns? The guard captain—Nadir—he'd looked at her strangely whenever she hopped to Aladdin's bidding. He also seemed very agitated whenever Badra lay at the prince's feet. Maybe she could talk to him, ask him to keep watch over her father?

Could she even trust the guard, though, in this strange new world?

Raising her gaze to the mirror, she focused not on herself, but on the servant behind her. The girl appeared wilted, like a flower that had been plucked and abandoned to the elements.

"What's wrong? You look horrid." The princess turned and put a hand on the girl's boney shoulder.

"Forgive me, Highness. I do not mean to offend. I will come back to clean your room when you are gone." The girl made for the exit.

"No, I wasn't trying to send you away." Badra placed herself between the girl and the door. "Tell me what's wrong."

"I'm just feeling a little weak. I'll be all right."

"Are you ill?"

"No, Highness."

"Well, for goodness' sake, tell me what's going on."

The girl trembled, her eyes as big as saucers. "Please, Highness, if you make me talk about these things, my whole family could be executed."

Badra stared, realizing her mouth was open. "On whose authority?" Badra tried not to shout, but her patience had grown thin. "Your only duty is to myself and my father and neither of us execute people for telling the truth."

The girl looked at the floor. "The prince has made it clear to all the palace staff that no one is to discuss the state of the kingdom in the presence of you or the sultan. He said he doesn't want you to worry."

"The prince does not sit on the throne."

Red held out her hands. "Yes, but with your father's declining health, and no Grand Vizier, the prince had no other choice but to take charge."

Her eyes narrowed. "*No other choice*. Is that how Aladdin put it?"

Red nodded.

Badra took in a deep breath and released it slowly. "This is a direct order from your princess. You will tell me everything that is going on in the kingdom."

The girl's shoulders slumped. Her eyes teared up. "It's horrible, Highness. A plague has ravaged most of the noble families. When the last heir of each household expires, Aladdin has instructed that possessions of the dead are to be distributed amongst the poorest citizens. It's unclear how many deaths have been due to disease and how many are the result of greed. There is talk of a curse."

Skies! Badra considered the frail girl. "Has this plague taken a hold of you?"

"No, Highness, I just..." The girl paused. "I haven't eaten in a few days. The market has closed down completely. Many are giving away all they have in hopes of being spared the curse. The farmers and butchers are no longer doing business."

"This isn't possible." She walked to the balcony. Everything appeared just as it always did for as far as she could see. Which, she supposed, wasn't all that far. She wished she was in her father's room, with its view of the city and the outer fringes of the market.

"The palace will run out of food in a matter of days, Highness. The staff has been beaten or worse for removing as much as a discarded roll from the coffers, but food is becoming harder and harder to come by, even if you have the money to buy it."

Famine and plague in Bisnagar, one of the richest kingdoms in the world. How was this even possible?

Badra's hands curled into fists. She knew exactly how it was possible. "This is the end of everything...isn't it?"

She'd worked so hard to do what she could to better the lives of the poor, but now it seemed even those in the palace would starve.

She couldn't sit in her gold-plated room and just let this happen, though. She might be powerless, but just like at the races, she could help the few while she was still able.

"I am extremely hungry," she said. "Bring a full meal to me, please."

"Yes, Highness." The girl bowed and disappeared into the hall.

Aladdin could not have known his attempt to bring balance to the class system would have resulted in everything spiraling out of control. At least Badra hoped not. Hopefully, he was working hard to fix this.

When the girl returned she stumbled and balanced herself against the wall. "Sorry, Highness, I..." The tray wavered.

Badra grabbed the platter of assorted fruits, vegetables, cakes, and a plate of curry roasted hen. She placed it on her meal table. "Are you okay?"

The girl nodded, her eyes filled with tears.

Badra positioned her vanity seat at the table beside her own before taking a different seat. "Now, I want you to sit and share this meal with me."

"Highness?" The girl backed away, shaking her head.

"You will do as your princess commands," Badra asserted. "I wish to share a meal with you, my oldest friend."

Tears rolled down the girl's cheeks. "I don't think I should. I'm just a servant."

And there was no reason for her to feel that way. She was a person, as much as Badra was a person. She had the right to eat as much as anyone. She had the right to live her life and be who she wanted to be. She was certainly more than...Red.

Badra's cheeks burned and her gut clenched. Maybe she was part of the class problem without even realizing it. But she could remedy that mistake. "I have never asked your name." The girl's eyes were a deep, rich mahogany brown. Badra had never taken the time to notice that, either. "I am so terribly sorry. I have always felt at odds with everyone around me, and I see now that I was partly to blame for my own unhappiness. What is your name?"

"Myra." The girl put her hands over her mouth as she quietly sobbed.

Badra put her arm around Myra's shoulder. "We may very well starve together in a few days, but I'll not eat another meal without you."

"My family..." The girl's face fell into her hands. "I can't eat while they starve."

"How many are there?"

"Three, Highness: my mother, father, and little brother."

"Bring them into my service. I will write a letter for you to take with you that will allow them to come through the gates. They will eat with us."

"The prince will notice if you take your meals locked in your room with your servants."

"I'll deal with Aladdin. I am still an unowned woman." Badra smiled with feigned confidence, the statement tasting like a lie as it passed her lips.

A knock sounded from the hall and Myra answered. Nadir stepped inside. He beckoned her to close the door.

Badra stood. "What is the meaning of this?"

He sighed, bowing. "The prince has requested your presence in the garden." He considered the elaborate display of food. "Shall I tell him you are occupied?"

She laughed. "Not if you want to keep your head." She tried to walk past him to the door, but Nadir grabbed her wrist. She bristled at his insolence until she met his eyes.

His gaze did not waver. "I would much rather lie for you, Princess—tell him you are ill—than watch you come as called like a dog."

How dare he!

Myra huffed behind her, as if she were holding back a sob. Badra stepped back. The servants...the eyes and ears of the palace, were trying to help her. Goodness knows they knew more about the world—and what was going on in her own home—than she did.

"Thank you, Nadir, but it is best to keep him happy, for now."

But now she knew she had at least two allies in the palace. She met his gaze. "The sorcerer Jai'far had a snake scepter."

He nodded. "Yes, Highness."

"Do you know where it is?"

His lip twitched. "It is with your father's collection of foreign trinkets."

That would place the scepter in her father's bedchamber. "You are well versed in the hidden walls in the palace, yes?"

"The means to save you and your father in case of evacuation." It was a statement of fact, rather than a question. "Of course, I am the captain on His Majesty's guard."

Badra played with the edge of her dress. "My father has quite a collection. He'd hardly miss one little scepter should it go missing."

His grin widened. "No, Highness, I do not think he would."

Excellent. She'd said nothing to incriminate either of them should they be questioned with magic. Hopefully, he understood her request.

She glanced at the table, then back to the captain. "When was the last time you ate?"

He grimaced. "Yesterday."

"Fine. I order you to help Myra clean all of this up." She lifted her chin. "You may take as long as you need, in case any of these insolent cakes should fall into your mouth by accident."

He bowed. "Her Highness is most gracious."

She headed for the door.

"Highness?" Nadir's brow furrowed. "The prince asked me to make sure that you wore your golden collar."

Of course he did.

She snatched the gaudy necklace from the drawer Red...no, *Myra* had shoved the horrid bauble inside and pointed the trinket at them both like a weapon. "Keep the door locked until you are both done *cleaning up*. And don't take anything home with you. I might not be here to keep you from losing your hands if you get caught."

They both bowed.

Steeling herself, she clicked the collar around her neck and stormed down the hall.

The prince must have been terribly afraid to tell her what was going on if he had gone to such lengths to hide the state of the country from her. She wanted to speak frankly with him so they could work together to find a way to heal the kingdom. However, she wouldn't incriminate Myra. Her best chance of fixing all this was to get Aladdin to come clean and tell her himself.

She found him in the garden, lying on a blanket spread out

in the sunshine. A pitcher of sweet wine and a plate of grapes were waiting for her.

He held out an arm. "Come to me."

Aladdin was so handsome, his golden skin and dark eyes smiling at her mischievously from beneath his wavy, black locks. He was dressed differently today; a long purple shirt with gold trim and tan riding pants. He was even more attractive without the pretentious turban.

As much as she knew it was warranted, she couldn't bring herself to hate him for all the misery that had befallen her kingdom. She couldn't even be sure that it was his fault. Perhaps this was all simply unfortunate circumstances that happened to coincide with his arrival.

Deep down, she knew better. Her skin tingled beneath the collar. She cringed before her entire body relaxed.

As she stretched out beside him, she found herself completely enamored by his every movement. Nothing made sense—nothing had to. She loved him. And if the world was in its final days, she was thankful that at least they would face the end together.

28

THE RAGE BURNING THROUGH AMIR'S HEART PLACATED HIS soul like an old friend. During his time with the princess, he had allowed his heart to become weak and heavy with the extraneous yet wonderful emotions he'd forgotten a human being was capable of.

The wounds left by the loss of his family had faded into a dull ache, but the attack on Iman had reopened them, allowing all the hatred and vengeance to spill out and once more reignite the fire in Amir's belly.

Those who had been profiting by victimizing the innocent would be held accountable, and the night of their reckoning had come.

He transported himself to the alley and walked through the square. When Amir reached the wide street where the marketplace had once been, the rain had already started to fall in torrents. When he had been lying half-dead in the street, the first mouthful of rainwater from the gutter had tasted like a gift from the heavens. That storm had probably saved his life. That trench in the road was not far from here.

Now he was back again, dressed like an aristocrat and walking through the streets where he had begged and scavenged for scraps with the dogs.

The rain didn't bother him in the slightest. He found it

thrilling now that his powers were fully recharged and he had a whole arsenal of spells and potions at his disposal.

Thunder rolled through the heavens and Amir smiled, knowing the storm would cover the sound of the bread merchant's screams. The stand where the man sold his wares was still empty but for the bloody chopping log.

Amir wrinkled his nose. No more. This sort of outright contempt for one's fellow man was intolerable and inexcusable.

He broke a flask on the ground, and a yellow vapor rose up between the raindrops.

"Take me to the bread merchant."

The smoky entity twitched before flying through the street. Amir ran to keep up until the vapor hovered near the corner of a house, where three dogs crowded around a bucket. One animal drew out a dismembered hand and ran into the night while the others snarled and snapped over whatever remained.

Amir steeled himself. He required a clear head for what needed to be done.

The vapor shifted across the front of the dwelling and stopped outside the door. A soft, yellow glow emanated from the window.

He smiled at a spell well cast and waved his hand. "You've done well. That will be all."

The smoke twitched again, then dissipated into the rain as Amir took another bottle from his satchel and held it up to the light. After actually tasting the potion once before, he took a deep breath, knowing that it would taste even worse than it smelled.

Dumping it into his mouth, he forced himself to swallow, then waved his hand in front of the door. The wooden panes swung open, welcoming him inside.

The merchant sat at his table, eating a large plate of food. He jumped to his feet when Amir entered. With another wave of Amir's hand, the door slammed and locked behind the sorcerer.

Amir scanned the plates of food. "Good to see the famine hasn't had an effect on your table, sir." Amir smiled. "Please pardon my intrusion and sit back down to your fine meal."

The man cocked his head before he slumped into the chair. "What is this?" He took a bite of his meat. "Some kind of sorcery?"

"The darkest kind." Amir circled his hand in the air, a trail of black smoke following in his wake. "Dark sorcery is really the most fun, isn't it? Although you probably don't know much about sorcery." Amir took another step toward the table. "You are a respectable working-class man. Selling bread isn't your profession anymore, though, is it? Tell me." He sent the swirl of smoke to wrap around the merchant. "What is it that is putting food on your table these days?"

"I find people who have what I need. They can either choose to give me what they have or I take it."

Amir gritted his teeth. So the merchant stole from others... the very crime that the man punished on a daily basis without mercy.

The merchant took another bite and swallowed. "I also called in on my old debts. Any who couldn't pay paid in other ways."

"So simple, and what an honest way to do business." Amir sat across the table from him. "How many hands did you take today, do you think?"

"Seven, maybe." He scowled, probably realizing that he was answering questions rather than spitting fire.

Yes, the smoke had the man well under Amir's control.

The merchant's eyes widened. He pointed a chicken bone at Amir. "You...You were that beggar who was with the boy who grew back a hand."

"Your memory is better than you let on." Amir leaned back and watched the man shovel the last bit of food into his mouth. "What is your name?"

"Rashid," he growled, his eyes ablaze.

Ah, the look of anger. It was so satisfying, knowing the man was in there, feeling as powerless as Iman must have when he'd left him for dead.

Amir took a calming breath. The last thing he needed was to let his own emotions take over. "Rashid, I am going to make sure you don't take another hand again as long as you live."

"Get on with it and kill me, you piece of refuse." Rashid glared at Amir. "Before this spell wears off and I take your head to mount on my wall."

Amir laughed mirthlessly. "We both know that is not going to happen."

Rashid sneered. "I'm going to chop you up and feed you to the dogs."

"How will you do that?" Amir leaned forward and stared into the man's eyes. "You won't be able to hold a blade after I'm done with you. You are right about one thing, though; this spell won't last forever, so I had better just get on with what I came here to do."

"And what is that?" Rashid spat.

Amir handed the merchant the thick cleaver poised on the edge of the cutting board. "I want you to cut off the thumb on your right hand."

The merchant's eyes grew wide as he lifted the blade. He whimpered as the tip of the cleaver slammed down against his will. He screamed as the bone crunched and blood splattered his shirt.

"I'll kill you!" he cursed.

"I know it seems cruel, but a point needs to be made here." Amir placed his elbows on the table and clasped his hands in front of him. "Now, I need you to do the same to your pointer finger."

The man's eyebrows rose. His eyes widened. "No, no!" He raised the clever again and wailed as the blade came crashing down.

Agape and breathing heavily, Rashid stared at what he'd done.

"What is your favorite part about cutting off a person's hand?" Amir braced his chin on his fingers and listened intently like a child asking for a story. "Is it the blood?" Amir's throat burned, remembering the impossibly large red stain on the floor of Iman's home. "Is it their faces as they gape at the bloody stump left behind?"

"It's the screams." Rashid's eyes widened again. "I like the sound of my blade cleaving flesh and bone. And I love the sound of their screams as they watch."

"Interesting." Amir nodded as he processed Rashid's answer. So this man liked to hear screams..."Next finger please."

"No, please, stop!" The man shrieked, repeating the process with the next finger.

Blood started to flow across the table, so Amir fashioned a tourniquet from a curtain cord and tied it around the man's wrist to keep him from bleeding out.

"Why don't you just let me die?" The man's bloodshot eyes were heavy and imploring. Weak, like those he'd taken advantage of.

Amir walked around the back of the table and patted the sick excuse for a man on the back. "Don't worry. That option hasn't been taken off the table yet. Keep lively, though."

The man sat unnaturally straight.

"Good. I can't have you passing out on me while you still

have a few digits left. Now, let's get rid of that ring finger. You won't be needing that."

Amir paced the room and kept Rashid engaged in conversation while the merchant cut off the remaining digits on his right hand. The merchant sobbed, the word "please" occasionally breaking through.

Amir knew that the potion would be wearing off soon, although the man's will was so broken at this point, he didn't have anything to fear. It was time to finish what he'd started and end Rashid's miserable life.

"Take the blade in your fist," Amir ordered.

The man's cold, already-dead stare met his own. There was nothing but anger, desperation, and evil there before his eyes welled with tears. Then a sense of calm overcame the merchant, as if he realized his torment was about to end.

Amir considered the severed fingers on the table and the man's screams. Oddly enough, the sound of the man's pain hadn't soothed the ache in his heart for all the atrocities poor Iman had seen in his life. It didn't seem enough. This man's death would repay that debt to Iman, and everyone else whose hands lay in that bucket outside, feeding the dogs. Yes. This was the only way.

Badra's smile crept into his thoughts, the way she'd laughed when she'd won that doll the night they'd gone to the races, and how'd she'd given the toy away to a sad child. She would be mortified if she knew what he had done, despite this man's wrongdoings.

If she were sultan, the severing of limbs as payment for a crime would be one of the first things she'd abolish, yet here he stood, doling out the same punishment.

Amir shook the thought away. This merchant was not a man. He was no better than an animal.

No, animals were far better than him. The world would be

a better place without him. He wished the blade to the man's neck, and the merchant's hand trembled as it rose to his flesh.

What right did Amir have, though, to be this monster's executioner? Badra's dream was of a kingdom better than what Bisnagar had been. She wanted laws the people on all levels could believe in and abide by. She'd hate this.

She'd hate him, but not more than he hated himself at the moment.

Amir blinked, and the merchant dropped the knife to the tabletop.

"I'm going to leave now." Amir yanked the tourniquet on Rashid's wrist tighter before he turned toward the door. "If you bring harm of any kind to another human being, if you command someone in your employ to harm another person, I will come back and we can have a conversation about your other hand. Tell me you understand."

"I understand." Rashid's eyes raked over the bloody carnage he'd committed on himself.

"Do you have a doctor in your debt?" Amir asked. "Someone who can tend to this for you?"

Rashid swallowed hard. "Yes."

"Good. Hopefully, he is not one of those whose hands are outside in that bucket."

Amir left the merchant's house and ventured back out into the dregs of the storm. The rain had stopped, but an odd, swirling wind still whipped through the city.

He expected to feel better after leaving this place, to be avenged and hopeful that he'd made the world a better place. He felt neither.

A deep disgust welled up inside him. Yes, he'd removed a predator from the realm of the helpless, but Amir had lost a little of himself in the process. This wasn't the way to make things right. He wanted to fix everything in one fell swoop, to make a fair, honest world where anyone could better themselves, no matter what caste they'd been born to.

He looked down at his hands and the magic tingling on the edge of his fingertips. That kind of miracle was outside even his formidable power.

He hoped beyond hope that somehow his prayers had been heard and Iman would be all right, that at least that small part of this intricate, fading puzzle could be completed.

Skies, the boy had lost a lot of blood.

But Iman wasn't even the largest issue at hand. To his left, the door to the oil merchant's shop hung ajar. To the right, a cart that had sold goat's milk lay on its side, the wheels missing. The city had fallen into ruin far too quickly to be natural. Those with enough food remained inside their homes, hiding from the lawlessness. The only safe place seemed to be within the palace and how safe that was remained to be seen.

The most logical choice was to join the more forward-thinking merchants and flee the city.

He nodded to himself. He should take Xerxes from this blasted place and never look back. This was no longer the golden city of his dreams. He'd wanted to rule a spectacular kingdom, one he could be proud of. This new Bisnagar boasted bloodshed taking place in the open streets in broad daylight. The people were starving and becoming more and more desperate every day.

The domes of the palace peeked over the tops of the buildings. The sultan's flags still blew in the wind. One ripped off and flew out into the desert. Another hung on threads, ready to tear away at any moment.

Badra and her father would not be long for this world if Amir didn't get ahold of Aladdin's lamp and put a stop to all this. The solution might appear plain, but Aladdin had been a mere street rat with ideals of ending poverty for his fellow citizens, and the lamp had made him into a sadistic egocentric madman. The jinni's power had defiled someone who at one time had had the most admirable intentions.

Amir shivered, the sound of the cleaver slamming down on Rashid's fingers still fresh in his mind. He had to get the lamp, but Amir had already strayed into the dark on his own. Since he was already so far gone, what sort of savagery would the lamp evoke in him if he were to touch the ancient relic?

He studied the flags still flying over the palace on massive, stout poles. His future didn't matter. Not anymore. He just needed the lamp long enough to take back the kingdom. Once he'd saved Badra, the darkness could have him. Goodness knows, he deserved it.

29

BADRA STEELED HERSELF AS ALADDIN LEANED BACK ON the throne, lazily running the edges of her dark curls through his fingers as she sat on the floor at his feet.

Myra approached, her head low. "My Prince, the high cleric has fallen terribly ill and will not be able to perform the marriage ceremony tomorrow."

Badra's breath hitched as a flutter of delight ran through her. Could it be possible—a few more unexpected days to try to get the scepter into Amir's hands before she married away the kingdom she loved?

Aladdin sat up, shoving Badra's head out of the way. She moved quickly to his side. It was her fault for being too close, and she needed to make up for the error. Maybe she could massage his feet for him?

She cringed, reached into her pocket, and rubbed the stone. The ridiculous thoughts slipped away, and she gripped the stone tighter. What would have become of her if Amir hadn't given her this heartfelt gift? She needed to find a way to hold it at all times to keep from losing herself to the power of this horrid collar.

Aladdin's eyes darkened as he faced the servant. "That won't do. Send over the palace physician to see to him."

"The doctor was killed in a riot at the university two days

ago, My Prince." Myra flinched, as if afraid his next words might be to order her beaten.

"How unfortunate." Aladdin glared at the girl. "No matter. I will summon my own cleric who accompanied me from Noblis. Better than a cleric, a proper *imam*."

"A foreign priest cannot perform a royal wedding." Badra pushed up to her knees. "It won't be valid." And she didn't want anyone negating her marriage. Once she gave herself to Aladdin, it was forever.

No! She gripped the stone more tightly. It was beginning to get harder and harder to differentiate between her own thoughts and the thoughts Aladdin wanted her to have.

The prince tapped his fingers on the edge of the throne. "These are extenuating circumstances and the *imam* is from the future sultan's homeland. I'm sure your father will grant us permission." Aladdin touched Badra's golden collar, as if to remind her of her place. He started going on about how he wouldn't be able to take care of all the problems in the kingdom until he was sultan.

She worked at keeping a smile on her face and a glaze over her eyes. It would be so easy to believe him. Too easy. All she needed to do was throw the stone Amir had given her way.

But where would that leave Bisnagar?

A dark figure darted behind a pillar. She ignored it at first and tried to pay respectful attention to Aladdin's tangent, but her gaze was drawn back to the shadow just in time to see Amir's face disappear behind the column.

What is he doing here? He's going to get himself killed.

"Red girl, you are dismissed for the day," Aladdin announced. "I want to spend some time alone with my betrothed."

"Yes, Highness." Myra glanced at Badra. Her brow wrinkled before she backed out of the room in a bow.

"Is something wrong, my love?" Aladdin asked.

Badra forced a childish smile on her face. "I can't believe our wedding is tomorrow."

"Not having second thoughts, are you?"

Of you dying a slow and painful death? No, none at all.

She slapped his shoulder playfully. "No. Are you? You'd better not back out a day before our wedding."

"I wouldn't dream of it."

A planter toppled near the pillar where Amir had been. A cold sweat coated Badra's brow as Aladdin turned toward the noise.

"Good." Badra jumped into his lap. "We've been waiting long enough already, don't you think?" She licked her lips and narrowed her eyes like the fire dancer had at the festival. She must have done it right because Aladdin forgot about the noise and smiled at her.

He ran a single finger down between her breasts. "You have been very insistent on preserving the purity of our wedding night."

"And you have continued to respect my wishes to do so."

Aladdin placed his hand on the small of her back and pulled her against him. "We still have one day left and you're not making it easy to keep my thoughts pure."

The shadow loomed again.

Was Amir out of his mind? He needed to get away. Preferably to her father's room, where he'd hopefully find his scepter. She needed to give him more time. Maybe he'd happen upon Nadir or Myra, and they would let him know where the scepter was.

She licked her lips again, looking into Aladdin's eyes. "Do you think my thoughts are always pure, My Prince?"

He grinned and leaned away. "You are the worst of tormenters." He gave her a kiss on the nose. "But I've grown accustomed to this game. I made you a promise to wait, and I intend to keep it." He eased her off of him. "However, I'd be more than happy to speed up the marriage timeline. I will speak to my *imam* about it." He turned to walk toward the dark hall where Amir hid.

She had to stop him, but she couldn't keep holding the stone in her hand. Pulling the gem out of her pocket, she shoved it inside her top, pressing the stone against her heart. The gem tingled, soothing her, but she didn't have time to wait. Aladdin was almost at the pillar.

"Stop! Don't!" She ran to him, grabbing his arms.

He raised a brow at her.

She opened and closed her mouth three times, searching for a reason. "Don't...leave me in this state. I-I miss you so much."

Her heart began to race. Amir peeked out, his lips twisted in a sneer. Their gazes met and his eyes widened. He nodded, thank goodness. The last thing she wanted him to believe was that she actually meant any of this.

Her eyes teared up as she thought about all the things weighing on her: the kingdom, her people, her father... Her eyes teared, and she used this to her advantage.

Badra walked away from the pillar, hoping he would follow. "I think about you all the time, My Prince." Her tears were real enough, the words just needed to keep his attention for a few more seconds. "I'm sorry. I'm not normally like this." She wiped at her eyes.

Aladdin made his way back to her. "You're a woman. You can't help but get emotional the day before your wedding."

"It's not the wedding." She sobbed. "It's everything else."

"What do you mean?" Aladdin huffed, his brow darkening.

She needed to do something...anything to give Amir time to get out of there.

Grabbing Aladdin's face, she smashed his lips against hers with as much enthusiasm as she could muster. She squeezed her eyes shut and tried to disconnect from what she was doing. His hands slid down her sides and cupped her backside forcefully. His tongue squirmed into her mouth and she opened to the invasion, trying her best to reciprocate.

Opening her eyes, she could see Amir hurrying down the hall toward Aladdin's room. *No! He's going the wrong way.*

Before she could protest, Aladdin's hand slipped up under her brassiere where she'd hidden the blue jewel. She gasped and put her hand over his, but he frowned, pulling out the leather cord she'd stuffed into the folds of material.

Badra shivered as he tugged the cord, and the stone popped from its hiding place.

He held the necklace up. "What's this?"

Skies! Sweat broke on her brow. "Do you...like it?" What could she say? What would he do?

"Why were you hiding this?" His face grew dark and she started to feel her will blowing away like footprints in the desert sand.

"The jewel is pretty, but I can't wear a leather cord with my gold collar. Don't you think it would look odd?"

His lips thinned. His eyes grew darker than she'd ever seen. "I'll ask you again: why were you hiding it?"

"I didn't mean to make you angry." The truth billowed out. *Oh no!* Maybe if he asked the right questions, she could still answer without lying.

"Where did you get it?"

"It was a gift."

"From whom?" His eyes whirled, like an unearthly darkness had filled him.

Skies! The collar pressed into her neck, forcing the truth.

Without the gem, she started slipping away, like she'd fallen down a hole and reality was shrinking from sight.

"Please!" Badra started to cry again.

He grabbed her face in his hand, digging his fingers into her cheeks. "Who would give you a gift that you would have to hide from your husband?"

"I gave it to her." Myra rushed over and knelt beside them. "It was my grandmother's. She wore it for luck and protection. She lived a long life and after she gave this to me, she died the next day. The princess has been so kind to me all these years; I gave it to her to protect her from the plague. Please forgive me if I have offended you, My Prince."

"Is that true?" Aladdin let go of Badra's face.

She grabbed the jewel from him and rubbed her face with the stone. It cooled her skin, and her breathing slowed. "I knew you'd think it was ridiculous superstition, but I thought it was a sweet gesture and I like keeping it close to my heart."

"Badra." His tone became apologetic, but he still acted like it was her fault he'd reacted the way he did. "You should have just answered my question."

"Yes, My Prince." She bowed. "Forgive me. I will leave you to find your *imam*." Hopefully, his cleric would be a good, pious man and refuse to marry them. She doubted she'd be so lucky, though.

Partway to her room, Myra stopped her. "Let me help you, Highness."

A click scratched her skin, and the weight of a thousand worlds fell from her neck. Myra folded the collar into a cloth napkin.

Badra rubbed her throat. "You have been a true friend to me."

Myra bowed. "As you have always been mine." She pressed

her hand on the door. "Now let's get his horrible thing out of sight."

As the door opened, Badra jumped to find a man standing there until Amir's warm smile brought her back to a simpler time when they'd dunked each other in the fountain and snuck out past the guards.

The trials of the past days hit her all at once. The guilt, the fear, the uncertainty, the helplessness. Bursting into tears, Badra threw herself into his arms. He was tall, warm, loving, and everything that Aladdin wasn't—and she'd thrown him out, allowed him to be beaten and goodness knew what else. She didn't deserve this last chance to hold him or anything else she was about to ask him to do for her.

"I will watch the hall." Myra pulled the door shut behind her, leaving them alone.

"I'm so sorry." Badra peppered his face with kisses. "For everything."

He brushed the hair from her eyes. "You've been under a spell since he came here. You aren't to blame."

A commotion erupted outside. Myra shouted, "No, please!"

"So help me, I will see my daughter!" The sultan's voice boomed.

Badra gasped. "My father? But he's been sick. He barely gets out of bed."

Amir touched her shoulder. "It's nothing to fear. I had a servant slip him a potion that would counteract Aladdin's hold on him. He should be vexed by the boy no longer." He handed a small bottle to her. "If you take this, you will no longer need the stone."

She hesitated before grabbing the bottle. "I have no intention of putting that horrible collar around my neck ever again, but just in case..." She gulped the clear liquid back and gagged, holding her breath to keep it down. "You could have warned me."

He snorted and gave her the sweetest of kisses. "Then you might not have taken it."

The door blasted open and the sultan marched in. He stopped short, finding Badra in the arms of his former vizier. "What is going on here?"

"Father, I can explain." She held up her hands, hoping her hushed tone would tell him to keep his voice down.

"What is Jai'far doing back in the palace?" He turned to Amir. "And why are you touching my daughter?"

Badra tugged at her hair. They didn't have time for this. "Father, forgive me, but I need to do something."

She took his hand and yanked off the gaudy ring Aladdin had given him.

"Aladdin is the real imposter. He's been controlling us with enchanted jewelry." She threw the ring across the room. "While you've been ill, the kingdom has fallen into chaos. The people are starving, and a horrible plague has wiped out most of the noble families. There are only a few guards left and the wedding is tomorrow."

Amir stepped forward. "Aladdin has a magic lamp that conceals one of the fabled jinn."

"A jinni?" Her father folded his arms. "That's ridiculous."

"Ridiculous, but true, sire. From what I can tell, he found the lamp on his own, which means the jinni is his slave until Aladdin's demise or until someone takes the lamp from him."

Badra shifted her weight. The jinn were fabled to have unlimited power, basically gods on Earth. They'd made the trees grow and the rain fall, and had kept balance in the universe—until a brotherhood of sorcerers had captured and imprisoned them in lamps.

The dark years followed, with sorcerers using their

captured jinn to rage war on each other, nearly destroying the world in the process. Eventually, they annihilated themselves as efficiently as they'd overtaken the jinn. The poor jinn remained chained to their lamps forever, though, cursed to grant wishes to whoever possessed their vessels.

Badra shivered. These events had been handed down through children's stories through the centuries and eventually chronicled by scholars, but she'd never dreamed they could be real.

A cloud of smoke rose into the sky, skewing the view from her balcony. She trembled. Her country was in ruin, all because the power of an ancient race was once again in the hands of someone incapable of wielding it wisely.

Amir saw the same billow of smoke and grimaced.

She'd never seen such determination on a man's face. "You're going to steal the lamp."

Amir nodded. "However, as a thief, I will only get three wishes. Then the lamp will return to the Cave of Eternal Sadness, if legend holds true." He turned to her father. "The goal of the jinn from the beginning of time has been to destroy." He held out his hands, as if encompassing the kingdom. "Bisnagar will continue to fall apart as long as Aladdin is in a position of power."

Badra rubbed her arms. There was already so much death, so much loss. "The jinn weren't inherently evil, though," she said. "They were corrupted."

Amir looked at the floor. "I, too, was told those stories as a child. The scrolls of the sorcerers told a different tale." He returned his gaze to her. "I promise you, what is in that lamp is a malevolent spirit bent on destruction."

The smoke outside billowed higher. The country had fallen so quickly, but the solution might be simpler than they thought. "But we can save Bisnagar with our wishes." She touched her lips. "Or maybe make two wishes, and then give me the lamp and I will get another three."

"It's not that simple," Amir said. "We have to get rid of the lamp as soon as possible."

"Why?"

"The longer a person possesses the lamp, the more the power of the jinn corrupts them. I don't think Aladdin intended any of this, but he's had the lamp too long." He held her chin. "Even the most pure hearts have been claimed by the darkness of the jinn. I won't allow you to touch that lamp."

"That explains why Aladdin has become so volatile." Badra rubbed the bruises on her face from where he'd grabbed her.

"Did he hurt you?" Amir touched her cheek—the lightest of touches, but filled with meaning after so long under Aladdin's harsh grasp.

"Nothing I can't handle." She held her head high. "What will we wish for? We should be ready."

"Wish for Aladdin to disappear," the sultan said.

"No, that could have unforeseen consequences." Amir began to pace. "It could make him merely invisible, or it could alter the past so that he was never born and put someone far worse in his place."

"What about the plague and the famine? Wish for the kingdom to be prosperous and for everyone who died to come back to life."

"Think about that. The dead are buried. They'd come back to life underground, only to suffocate to death. The wording needs to be extremely precise."

"How is it you know so much about the power of the jinn?" the sultan asked.

Going into the details would take too long. "He's well educated, Father," Badra began. "He was Hazim's apprentice, remember?"

"No more lies." Amir stopped pacing. "Your Majesty, I was also an imposter. I was born the son of a trader and a slave girl, but my father was an intelligent man. He saw my potential and made sure I had the tools I needed to educate myself." He stood even taller, and Badra's heart swelled for him. "I have studied many subjects in my life, and I would call myself a scholar. However, I have also been a practitioner of magic since I was a boy." He took a deep breath and then released it. "I came here with the intention to one day sit on your throne. But I've realized the error in that thinking. I only want things to go back to the way they were. Once that is done, I will leave Bisnagar and never come back."

Badra grabbed her chest as a deep gash cut into her soul. She'd known Amir was common, but his heinous admission would be more than her father would be willing to overlook. Now they could never be together, even if she could convince him to stay.

The sultan stared at him, his eyes cold. "I think you leaving would be for the best, Jai'far. You seem like a fine man, but after everything that's happened..."

Amir's head lowered. Had he hoped her father would react differently? Maybe.

She understood her father's distrust, though. Their kingdom was falling down around them from one sorcerer, only to find they stood in a room with another. What he needed was proof that Amir could be trusted, sorcerer or not.

The panel beside her fireplace shifted, and a hole opened in the wall. Nadir stepped out. "Princess, your father..."

"Is right here!" The sultan crossed his arms. "What is the meaning of this? How dare you sneak into the princess's room?"

Badra stepped between them. "He's here at my bidding, Father, and with not a second to spare."

She pointed to Amir, and Nadir's normally stoic face broke into a grin. "You lived."

Amir raised his hands, wiggling his fingers.

"Impressive," Nadir said.

Men were odd. She'd have to ask them about that strange exchange later.

"Did you get it?" she asked.

"I did." The captain bowed to each of them. "Forgive me, Highness, for entering your room unbidden."

He reached into the opening and withdrew the sparkling snake scepter.

The sultan's eyes widened. "Stealing from me? How dare you?"

"Not now, Father." Badra grabbed the staff from Nadir. "We need help. We need our sorcerer." She held the staff out to Amir in both palms. "We've been awful to you, and we don't have the right to ask you for anything, but in the name of my people, I implore you. Help us."

30

THE EYES OF THE EGYPTIAN IDOL WINKED AT AMIR LIKE an old friend coming home. He'd written the scepter off, figuring they'd melted the idol and thrown the staff in the fire to ward off its evil, but there it was in all its dark, wonderful glory.

"I will not have this insolence. He is a sorcerer, a man with nefarious intent!" The sultan approached Amir, sticking out his chest.

Badra darted him a glance so cold and forceful that her father stopped mid-step.

Sands, she's beautiful!

The sultan blanched, stepping back. "Then again, I've learned that my daughter is an excellent judge of character."

Amir flashed Badra a coy grin as his fingers wrapped around the soothing warm fernwood. He bowed to her, and to the sultan. "I am, and always will be, your servant, Your Majesty."

The sultan lifted his chin. "We'll see. I believe in the here and now, and I'm willing to forget the past—as long as you can secure our future." He pointed to the scepter. "What can you do with that monstrosity?"

A dark smile crossed Amir's features as he stared into the snake's flashing eyes. "Oh, so many glorious things."

He'd spent so much time creating potions and learning spells to channel a fraction of the power he'd amassed in this staff over the years. The idol, as formidable as it was at trans-fixing someone gazing into its eyes, wasn't the true danger. He ran his hands over the wooden base, originally a walking stick, a simple companion, but the sorcerer who'd taken him in had shown him how to use the staff as a repository, keeping him strong while others may grow weak. Strength may seem mean-ingless in the world of sorcerers, but a tired mind couldn't focus and a lack of focus could lead to one's death, especially if the sorcerer was foolish enough to challenge a jinni.

"How can I help?" Badra stood strong, tall, and completely unafraid.

Maybe she would be afraid if she knew what he'd learned about the jinn in the ancient tomes, and not the glorified stories depicted in children's bedtime reading.

Amir glanced at the still open wall that Nadir had emerged from. "That passage took you from the sultan's room to the princess's room." He turned to Nadir. "Can I trust that it will also lead to Aladdin's room?"

The guard captain smiled in wicked solidarity. "Right into his dressing chamber." His smile morphed into a frown. "But he takes his secondary meal in private every day. I hear him in there talking to that confounded monkey."

Amir sighed. Not a monkey, but an ancient, incredible formidable power beyond any of their imaginations. Gazing into the eyes of his staff, he stroked his beard. Another conver-sation with the monkey was the last thing they should allow. "We can wait no longer." He grasped Badra's hand. "As much as it pains me to ask…"

"I am not a child." Her eyes turned to fire. "This is my king-dom, and I will risk anything to save my people from this pestilence."

Amir nodded…save the people, not simply her kingdom. Never had he met anyone more deserving of a crown. "Then I will need to ask you to be a distraction." She nodded, and he turned to Nadir. "While the princess is keeping Aladdin busy, the captain and I will purloin a small, insignificant-looking lamp."

"What can I do?" the sultan asked.

Keep out of sight? Don't die? Either of the most important options would offend him, when Amir needed the man's trust the most. "Do anything in your power to stop the wedding."

"And I?" Myra twisted her hands.

"Gather any servants you are sure are not under the prince's influence. We might need all the friends we can find before this is over."

NADIR LED AMIR THROUGH THE NARROW SECRET PASSAGE, the glowing snake eyes of the staff lighting their way. The light cast odd shadows as bugs or other small vermin scurried along the walls.

"I didn't know that monstrosity could be used as a torch," Nadir whispered. "What else can it do?"

"Not much, for a common man." But in the hands of the right sorcerer, its powers could be unimaginable.

Nadir's breathing filled the narrow space. "How did you get your hand back?"

"I should actually thank you for that, my friend." He turned to gaze at the guard.

"Thank me?"

"Great sorcery is birthed from the greatest of trials. I'd thought I'd lived those trials. I'd thought I was the most powerful sorcerer in the world. I was sorely mistaken."

"And now?"

"I lived in the dirt with dogs. I begged. I pissed in the

streets. I was beaten, spat upon, and left for dead, yet I still gave my hand in hopes of saving someone who could not defend himself."

"The boy?"

"Yes."

"Did he live?"

"Yes." But only to have both hands cut off later. Amir started walking again. He should have stayed with Iman and his family. He should have made sure the boy recovered.

Bile rose in his throat. His life was filled with a thousand and one things he should have done. Some he regretted, some made him a better person, some made him a better sorcerer. *The trials of one's life make you who you are.* Amir only wished he had a better grasp of who his trials had made him become.

A light shone from beneath another hidden door. Nadir moved ahead and Amir held the scepter high as the guard captain manipulated a series of locks. The captain had dexterous hands for a man so large.

Nadir made to open the door but turned, his face alight with a demonic glow from the snake's eyes.

"Did it work?" he asked.

Amir frowned. "Did what work?"

"You had the power to grow back a hand. We both know that is impossible—unless you achieved your goal. Are you now the greatest sorcerer in the world?"

A valid question, but one he didn't have the answer to. Power coursed through him. He was one with the sorcery, as if he had been born to the dark arts. And now, with the staff holding a life of knowledge and strength, he was all the more powerful.

The answer was, though, that he didn't know, and the lack of that small tidbit of knowledge made his stomach lurch. "If we don't get our hands on that lamp, I will have to fight the jinni."

"And if you do?"

Amir glowered. "People will die, no matter how strong I am."

Nadir's face twisted, then he punched his own chest with his fist. "For Bisnagar."

Amir nodded, but it wasn't Bisnagar he did this for, but for Badra, for Iman and his family, for all those people whose hands lay in the merchant's bucket.

Still, he nodded. "For Bisnagar."

Nadir cracked open the door and eased through.

Amir took a deep breath and passed his hand over the snake's eyes, whisking the light away. The darkness pressed from all sides, but he stood firm, listening.

He once looked at this palace for the value of the gold-plated walls, for the beauty spoken of by accomplished travelers. Bisnagar was so much more, though. The people who lived here thrived in a culture all their own, creating festivals, games, and art. He'd never felt as alive as he had when he'd first strode into their midst. Yes, they had problems, but problems could be overcome. They deserved the chance to try. They deserved the right to survive.

Nadir's silhouette appeared in the cracked doorway. "The prince is seated on his bed. I didn't see a lamp."

"It's not large, and it's not what you would expect it to be." Amir moved toward the door. "You've done all you can. Go protect the sultan." He bowed to the guard captain. "You've been a good friend."

He snorted. "I left you to die."

"No. You left me to become what destiny chose. Thank you." He tapped Nadir on the shoulder and slipped into the room, cloaking himself in silence.

He peeked around the corner of the dressing chamber. As the captain had said, Aladdin sat on the edge of his bed, rubbing his eyes. The smell of smoke wafted in with a cool breeze coming from the balcony.

Were there vines on that balcony he could climb down for a quick escape if necessary? He wasn't even sure that this room opened out to an area in the gardens.

A knock sounded and Aladdin's door opened.

The boy straightened. "How dare…" His posture slackened as Badra walked into view. "Good afternoon, my love."

Amir sneered. He doubted the boy was even capable of love anymore.

"My Prince." She moved to him smoothly, confident, wearing one of those obscene outfits with transparent pants and a tight top barely restraining her womanly curves. She wore the confounded collar, but of course his potion had rendered that useless. Her choice to wear the hideous trinket was a good one. Aladdin would believe she was still completely under his control.

"I owe you an apology for earlier." He scratched the back of his neck. "I only reacted that way because my love for you is so strong. I couldn't stand the thought that you were keeping a secret from me."

Ugh. The power of the jinni must be formidable for Badra to have believed such dribble.

"It was all a misunderstanding." Her eyes flicked to Amir, then back to Aladdin. "I am not going to judge you based on a single mistake."

Pushing Aladdin's head back, Badra kissed him. Power tingled under Amir's fingertips, and the snake's rubies began to glow. Amir closed his eyes, gritting his teeth. She was acting, distracting the street rat as he'd requested. Amir needed to keep a hold of his emotions or he'd make a fatal error.

"I'll forgive you if you promise to never lay a hand on me in anger again," she said.

Careful, Badra. Don't be too bold.

"I swear to you," he whispered.

Like his word was worth anything. Imbecile.

"Good." She smiled. "Because I'm really looking forward to our wedding night. I don't want anything to ruin that." She touched the tip of her tongue to his bottom lip.

Amir cringed as Aladdin groaned. "One day seems like such an eternity.

Amir bet it did, especially when the lying snake saw all his plans of world domination coming together without challenge.

"Yes, tomorrow does seem far away." She smirked, whispering in his ear. "But maybe we can spend some of that time bending the rules."

Amir's stomach sank. Aladdin snickered in a way that had Amir recalling the spells to strip skins off a carcass. They should work perfectly fine on a living person.

The would-be prince pulled her down to him, devouring her mouth with kisses.

Amir's chest burned as flashes of light passed before his eyes. His hands shook, his power sizzling beneath his skin. He would kill this boy slowly, and in the most painful way possible.

Badra opened her eyes, and her gaze met Amir's. Disgust glazed her expression before she closed them again, deepening the kiss.

Amir bit back the need to vomit. She did nothing that he did not ask her to do, but the pain welling in his chest was almost too much to bear. This woman had power over him more potent than the oldest of spells. He would protect her until the end of time if she'd let him, but first he needed to save her from this boy with his sights on her kingdom.

Amir turned his attention to scanning the room for the

lamp. He needed to focus on the task at hand, avoid watching... Badra brought a thigh up on either side of Aladdin.

Sands of time, her tenacity had no bounds! He'd asked her to distract Aladdin, not make him deaf and dumb!

Maybe she was enjoying his touch. He was younger, closer to her age. Could she have changed her mind?

Aladdin moaned, and Amir's chest cinched. His magic yearned to reach out and wrap around the camel dung's scrawny little neck.

Amir drew in a deep breath, and then released it through clenched teeth. There would be a much better time to cut the little rat into a million unfathomable pieces. First, he needed to remove the protection of the omnipotent being that had caused all this trouble to begin with.

He moved into the room, keeping out of Aladdin's line of sight. The boy would want the lamp close, but not easy to find.

Sweat broke out over Amir's brow. This room was larger than Badra's, a dwelling space constructed to impress visiting dignitaries. The lamp could be anywhere.

The monkey thudded onto the balcony. Its eyes widened when its gaze fell on Amir. It hissed a high-pitched shriek.

"Wha...?" Aladdin started to turn, but Badra pushed him back onto the bed and crawled over him with all the agility of her hooded rider persona.

"I don't want to wait." She moaned into his ear.

Aladdin groaned, grabbing her posterior and grinding her onto him.

I. Am. Going. To. Kill. That. Boy!

The monkey's eyes left Amir and darted to the bookcase.

Ah, so that was where the impudent street rat had hidden his greatest treasure.

Amir bolted toward the shelves, and the monkey screeched again, bounding after him.

Hitting the shelves first, Amir whispered an additional spell of quiet and tossed the books aside. There, on the second shelf, sat an old, dented, worthless-looking oil lamp. He snatched the handle with two fingers and pulled it out, but the monkey grabbed it on both sides.

Curses! The jinni had been ordered to protect the lamp from theft!

Amir's brow furrowed. The jinni could have lashed out with its power, but it didn't.

However Aladdin had worded the wish that made the monkey protect the lamp, it must not have been specific enough to make the jinni use all the power at its disposal.

Ice flooded Amir's veins. *Why* wouldn't the creature use all its power? The jinn were selfish, destructive. It was so close to its goal of condemning Bisnagar to irreparable doom.

The monkey's eyes swirled. Not in anger, not in hate—but in something akin to desire.

Amir's heart skipped a beat. The jinni knew what Amir was.

Aladdin had been no more than a street corner magician and look what the jinni had done with him. What would the creature do once it had its claws in a full-blooded sorcerer?

The vile creature shrieked again, apparently not so interested in Amir that it was incapable of fulfilling its current duties, within reason.

"What is it?" Aladdin said from across the room, but Badra's body now lay between him and the bookshelves, her back toward Amir and the monkey.

Badra—powerful, confident, impetuous, rash, and utterly reckless Badra—brought her fingers to the back of her brassiere, released the clasps, and threw her top to the side. The room went silent. Even the monkey gaped at her bare, flawless back as she leaned down to kiss Aladdin again.

Amir's heartbeat slowed in his temples. He could rip her off him, slit the brat's throat before anyone was the wiser. His breaths became coarse, his jaw ached and...

The monkey shrieked again, yanking the lamp back and away from Amir and jumping on the edge of the bed.

Sands! If Aladdin made a wish, it could be the end of them all. Clenching his staff, Amir reached out his hand and called to the lamp.

The monkey showed its tiny, pointed teeth as it wrapped its entire body around the lamp. Amir repeated the spell in his head, and the monkey's entire body elevated, still holding the cursed vessel. The blasted creature shrieked again, and Amir winced at the high pitch as the monstrosity grabbed the bedpost with its tail.

Again, it squawked, this time the reverberation sounding all too far like, "Master!"

Aladdin sat up, holding Badra in his lap. His gaze met Amir's.

"You!" Aladdin growled as he threw the princess to the floor.

Amir cast a spell to cushion her fall, but a wave of cool sweat coated him when he realized his folly.

"Throw me the lamp," Aladdin ordered.

"No!" Amir deepened the spell, calling to the ancient relic.

The monkey snarled, shredding the energy surrounding Amir's spell and throwing the lamp with enough force to blur the object before it landed in Aladdin's grip.

The prince's eyes darkened when he grasped the soiled, pocked metal. His gaze never left Amir. "I wish..." A cruel smile crossed his lips. "I wish for the princess to be completely submissive to me."

No! The potion he'd given her only broke the current spell she'd been under. This new wish was so much more cruel, and a testimony to how far Aladdin had fallen from the man he may have once been. Badra's physical body would be a slave to his every whim.

Aladdin pulled a knife from his belt and placed the blade in Badra's hand. "Put this to your throat."

She accepted the blade and held the sharp point to her neck.

"Wait!" Amir held out his right hand as if in surrender, while gripping his staff tighter with his left. He called to the power within.

"Don't hurt her." Amir stepped forward.

"I would prefer not to hurt her." Aladdin reached out and touched her still-exposed breast. "She wouldn't be as fun if she wasn't warm and breathing." He stepped behind her, using her as a shield.

"What is it that you want, really?" Amir kept his eyes on Aladdin. "The spirit in that lamp will never bring anyone true happiness. It thrives on watching people destroy themselves. Like now. It wants you to kill her. You can't marry a dead woman, which means you'll never be sultan. All of this will have been for naught."

"It's not for nothing. I'm in control now. Bisnagar is as good as mine."

Insolent fool! "Have you looked past the palace gates? Have you seen what the darkness of the jinni has done to the city? Is this what you really wanted?"

Aladdin's nose flared. "Right now, what I want is for you to leave and never come back."

That certainly wasn't going to happen. "I will never leave her at your mercy."

Amir glanced at the jinni. If Aladdin used him, the creature could wipe Amir from existence. Yet he didn't. Was this arrogant little boy trying to win by his own means? Touching, but foolish.

Aladdin's eyes darkened over a malevolent grin.

Amir gripped his staff, drawing in extra strength and fostering a shield between himself and the jinni. If he could ward off the creature's first blow, surprise may grant him the only chance to strike back.

But instead of making a wish, Aladdin swept Badra's hair away from her neck and leaned close to her ear. "If he's not gone in less than a minute, I want you to slit your own throat. If you see him again, you will take your own life immediately. Do you understand?"

"I understand, My Prince," she said coldly. Her expression was blank, but tears streamed down her face. *Of all that is holy!* She was a prisoner in her own skin. She was inside, screaming, probably clawing to get free, but her body no longer did her bidding.

Amir wanted to run to her, hold her, tell her everything would be all right. Instead, he stepped back, staring into her eyes. How could he fight this? How could he possibly save her without her seeing him?

Aladdin snickered. "What was that about never leaving her?"

Amir's eyes darted to the street rat in prince's clothing. *This is far from over.*

Amir drew in more power from the staff. The deepest wounds of his childhood bolstered him, working through his cells and tainting every part of him in darkness. He welcomed it, every last stitch.

"Thirty seconds." Aladdin smiled.

Badra adjusted her grip on the knife.

"Fine." Amir held up his free hand.

Aladdin pointed his finger at the staff. "Oh, and leave that here."

Curse this brat! But he had no other choice. The scepter floated to the floor.

The princess closed her eyes, her breathing heavy.

"Badra?"

Her eyes sprang open, and he concentrated on the strength in his gaze. There was so much he needed to tell her. *I love you. I need you. I can't live without you.*

But maybe most importantly, *Don't give up. I'll figure this out.*

In truth, though, he had no idea what he was going to do. Aladdin had cast the perfect spell. He had no other alternative but to comply.

His knees weakened, and he stumbled back. His head spun. He had to solve this. He *needed* to solve this.

"Fifteen seconds."

Amir's stomach hardened. His lungs refused to fill. *I will find a way to come back for you.*

The drapes and tapestries around him faded into starry blackness before being replaced with the towering bookshelves of his study. No spoken incantation, no hand gestures necessary. Maybe he was the most powerful sorcerer who'd ever lived, but it still wasn't enough to save her.

31

Badra inwardly trembled as she held the knife to her neck. The point dug into her skin, making her want to cough. She tried to call out to Amir, to beg him not to give up the staff, but the snake scepter floated to the floor as if placed down by an invisible hand.

She could do nothing but stand like a statue while she screamed on the inside. *Please don't give up. You can still save us!*

Amir's eyes filled with pain, anger, and loss. Then he faded out, as if he had never been there. Part of her faded away with him. She'd placed too much hope in what might have been a hopeless plan. Maybe Aladdin was too strong for any of them.

Aladdin circled around, his gaze raking over her still-bared chest.

Inwardly, she shivered. She'd thought her plot to distract him had worked. It may have, if it weren't for that horrible monkey.

"You can put the knife away now," Aladdin said. "Keep it somewhere handy in case you need it."

The only place she wanted to put the blade was deep into Aladdin's heart. But instead, she ripped some of the sheer mesh from her pant leg, made a loop, and placed the knife at her hip.

Aladdin frowned. "No, you'll end up cutting yourself." He took the knife belt from around his waist and buckled the soft leather around hers, then placed the knife inside. "There. That's better. There's no use hurting yourself unless your wayward sorcerer comes back, right?"

He leaned in and gave her a kiss. She wanted to spit at him, but she couldn't move.

"Remember, love." He petted her head. "If he comes back, your death will be all his fault. If he truly loves you, he will stay away."

Monster—trying to play this all off like this is someone else's fault!

He picked her top up off the floor and handed it to her. "Cover yourself, my love. I'll not have you being humiliated any more than you already have been."

She grabbed the fabric and quickly fastened it around her bosoms. For the first time, her desires matched her actions. For a brief moment, she felt free. Her womanly curves still nearly popped out of the top, but at least her dignity was still hidden.

He glanced down once more as she snapped the front of her top back into place. "Too bad you won't enjoy our wedding night as much as I'm going to. Just remember that Jai'far took that from you, not me."

Like she would ever enjoy a night with him! Nothing in the world would ever make her choose Aladdin over Amir. Of course, that didn't matter now. Her body no longer obeyed her commands. She would do or say anything this false prince asked, and on their wedding night, she would give him everything.

She wanted to vomit. She wished she could. Even that would be welcome, so long as it was something not done by his will.

"Of course, I could be nice and snap your collar around your neck first. Then we would both enjoy ourselves." He kissed her cheek. "Would you like that?"

No! She shook inside, begging her hand to rise and slap his face, but nothing happened.

As he walked away, Badra blinked warm tears from her eyes. How would she ever live the rest of her life like this?

"Go back to your room and stay there," he said over his shoulder.

At once, her body turned and headed down the corridor to her room. She tried to stop. Maybe she could find Nadir. Maybe he could...what—form a team to overthrow Aladdin and his jinni? Not even an army could stop this.

Halfway down the hall, she tried to reach out and knock over a lamp just to see if she could do one thing without him telling her to, but she walked right by. She was a puppet, and he was the one pulling the strings, leaving her no better than a spectator of her own life. Her heart raced, but the only sign of her fragile state was the tears streaming from her eyes.

She would go mad within days if left like this. She needed to fight, to build up her mental strength, just as she had built up her physical body for the races.

Yes, she would fight this. He may have her body—for now. But he would never have her mind. Inside, she would fight him till the end of time.

She pushed through the doors, and the comfort of her room enveloped her: the smells of the gardens flowing in from her balcony, the sheer curtains on her bed, the trinkets her father had given her through the years sprinkled across the tables.

This was her sanctuary. He couldn't touch her here. She made for the back of the room to get out of this ridiculous outfit, but her legs didn't move.

What?

She tried again, but she stood frozen in place in the center of the carpet. She tried to take a deep breath, but even flexing her lungs seemed beyond her control. Myra came in and quietly closed the door behind her.

"Highness?" she asked.

The only answer Badra could provide was a solitary tear running down her cheek.

Myra shed tears of her own. "Oh, Highness, what has he done to you? Can you not move?"

Another tear. *Oh, Myra! How has it come to this? I wanted to do so much. I wanted to save you and your family, but now I am no better than a statue decorating the halls.*

"Fear not, Highness. I am here for you."

She unclipped Badra's top and shimmied off the transparent pants. Taking a sponge, she carefully bathed the still-standing princess, and then dressed her in the most soft, comfortable lounging dress from her closet.

Myra stepped back. "Maybe I could call Nadir, and he could place you onto your bed?"

But what if this was what Aladdin wanted? Maybe he wanted her to stand here all night as punishment. If Nadir and Myra helped her, they could be executed. No, she couldn't allow anyone else to suffer for her.

Gritting her teeth, more tears fell, but she managed a slight shake of her head. She breathed out, exhausted.

"You do not want me to call Nadir?"

She tried again but couldn't manage the movement. She'd done it once, though. She'd eventually be able to do it again. For now, she moved her eyes from side to side.

Myra nodded. "I understand, Highness."

She lit an oil lamp, casting a soft glow across the room as the sun went down.

Myra held up the blue jewel that Amir had given her. "You left this in your room."

Yes. Her outfit had been too tight to hide the stone, and she was supposed to be protected by Amir's potion. She'd hated the control of the collar, but now she wished for that torture to return. At least it gave her the ability to move freely.

Myra knelt at Badra's feet. "You are always gripping the stone, not wearing it as a necklace, so I removed the cord. That should make it more comfortable, and easier to hide." She slipped the jewel into the side of Badra's shoe.

The cool stone brought her some comfort. Badra concentrated on the feeling of it on her skin. She sucked in a single intentional breath and held it for a moment. It was only one breath, but it was a small victory. Some small part of her still had a choice. She'd concentrate all night if she had to. If there was a way to overcome this, she'd find it.

32

THE SHELVES AND SCROLLS OF AMIR'S STUDY SHIMMERED into view, and he fell to his knees, screaming his fury at the ceiling. Xerxes poked his head out from behind a bookshelf and pranced over, nuzzling Amir's neck.

Amir clutched his oldest friend for a moment, steeling himself. Aladdin had won this battle, but the fight was far from over. He used Xerxes's ballast to help pull himself up.

He needed to keep calm. He needed to think. Right now, Aladdin was probably proclaiming victory, but he underestimated his opponent if he thought Amir would give up so easily.

His skin tingled as he opened and closed his hand. He'd amassed a great deal of power preparing for the jinni to strike. More power coursed through his veins at this moment than at any other time in Amir's life. It was wise for the boy to take Amir's staff, but the scepter had already fulfilled its purpose.

To what end, though? The darkness crept through him, a power meant to be expended, not held inside. Dark sorcery could corrupt just as easily as the power of the jinni. This could very well be the end of him.

No matter. If Amir died freeing the princess, his soul was a small price to pay. Saving her was still in his power. He just needed to think things through.

"The jinn are extremely literal. That is why so many

unlucky lamp holders have fallen ill so quickly." Amir paced the room. Xerxes turned his ears toward him, listening, if not understanding. "There is always a loophole. One just needs to find it."

If you see him again, you will take your own life immediately.

"If she *sees* me." He rubbed his beard, rifling through the scrolls. "Potions of invisibility are complicated and take weeks to prepare even if you have all the ingredients, which are near impossible to find. Some of the plants needed have been extinct since before I was born."

Xerxes whinnied.

Amir shook his head, as if the horse had asked a question. "It doesn't matter where I go if the component I need doesn't exist." He paced the length of the room. "Could I summon the ingredients or create them somehow from a relic left over from a time when they existed? A grinding stone or a bottle that once contained the components might work."

He shook his head. How would he even know what he was searching for?

His hands fisted, and he shouted at the ceiling. "Blast it, Iago! Where are you when I need you?"

He slammed his fist onto the alchemy table.

Iago had amassed a world of knowledge, and he'd forced Amir to memorize and repeat spells Amir had thought ridiculous, but the demon priest must have had his reasons.

He put his hands on the table and tried to recall all the scrolls Iago had forced him to read, but all that came to mind was Badra's lost expression as he'd left her there with Aladdin and the jinni.

She was alone, enduring the worst kind of torture, and there was nothing either of them could do to stop it. He ground his fingernails into his palms. He needed to focus. That was the only way to save her from this vile fate.

Returning to his pacing, he knocked a large hourglass off the edge of the table. He grabbed the device a fraction of a second before the glass chamber hit the floor. The sight of the sand slowly flowing fluidly around inside the transparent globes gave the illusion of time slowing down.

One of the spells Iago had taught him, the priest had simply called 'Stop.' It was an easy spell, but it only stopped time for ten seconds.

"What good is ten seconds?" Amir had asked.

"Ten seconds could mean the world, at any particular time," Iago had told him.

Amir nodded. Yes, if he were in the palace, and Badra were about to see him, he could stop time. Ten seconds might be enough to hide, thus saving her life. It was a simple spell to speak, but the forced, pinpoint concentration had been hard for Amir to master.

"Prohibere omnes," he whispered.

Xerxes waved his tail. Time, apparently, continued. Blast it!

"Prohibere omnes," Amir repeated.

Xerxes stared at him. His ears twitched.

"Gah!" Amir held his hands to the sky.

Xerxes lowered his head, probably thinking Amir's obvious frustration was for something he had done.

Amir stroked the horse's head. "You are fine, my friend."

Closing his eyes, Amir centered himself. This might be the most important spell of his life. The spell that would save the woman he loved. He needed to master not only the words, but his focus, his intent. *"Prohibere omnes,"* he said again.

He opened his eyes. Xerxes stared at him, fixed. His tail held in the air, mid-flip. The torch beside them glowed, but the flame did not flicker.

Sands! I've done it!

Xerxes's tail fell, then whisked across his back again. Amir threw his arms around the horse's neck. "Thank you for the assistance, my friend."

Focus. Amir needed to remember to focus above all things. Too much depended on it.

Invisibility, though, was still a goal. The chance of Badra seeing him was far too great.

He walked in front of the shelves. "The ingredients for invisibility no longer exist. Is it possible to be invisible?" Not that he expected the air, or his horse, to answer. "Show me the scroll that can teach me how to become invisible."

The torch flickered brightly in the silence.

Maybe a different query. "Has any great scholar written about invisibility?"

A scroll whisked off the top shelf and flew into his hand. Amir unfurled the document on the table and scanned the words. Thaddeus the Second of Avernacia in the third age had worked with spells that had made objects enchanted with invisibility reappear.

Amir shook his head. "This isn't helping me. I need the opposite." But if this scholar could make things reappear, had he done any work on the opposing incantation? "Are there more scrolls written by Thaddeus the Second within the same time period?"

The library didn't respond.

Amir leaned over the table and rubbed his head. There had to be something somewhere. A few words at the edge of the scroll caught his attention. Simple phrases that Thaddeus the Second had used. The words translated to 'appear to me' and repeated three times in three different languages. Above this was a dissertation about intent.

He'd learned well about intent. Some spells were more complicated, requiring not only a skilled sorcerer, but a sorcerer fully focused on his task. The scepter had helped with that, but now he had only himself and his will to bring the focus he needed.

Amir skimmed down to the simple phrase again. Thaddeus had found that the words *appear to me* repeated in three languages brought an invisible object to light.

Could it be so simple?

The languages appeared to be Latin, Aramaic, and Egyptian. That seemed easy enough. Perhaps he could construct his own spell, using his knowledge of languages. "*Hide me. Hide me. Hide me,*" he whispered in the three languages. Xerxes met his gaze. "*Invisible,*" he repeated again in Latin, Aramaic, and Egyptian. Still nothing. "*Unseen.*" The horse reached over and nibbled his ear.

Amir rested his forehead on the parchment. There were millions of words in the languages of humanity. The right combination could be anything.

Trickles of energy danced under his skin. With this kind of power within him, if it were possible to create an incantation, he'd be the one who could do it. This wasn't for him. It was for Badra and all her people. Too many counted on him to fail because he could not come up with a spell to make himself hidden.

Xerxes reared up on his back legs, screeching.

"What is it?" Amir stood.

The horse spun, his eyes wide.

"Xerxes? What?"

The horse looked left and right but never at his master. Amir held up a hand to pet his friend but saw nothing. He looked down at his chest but saw only the floor.

He'd done it!

Xerxes reared back again, and Amir's hands appeared in front of him.

"It's okay, my friend. I'm here." The horse settled.

But why had Amir reappeared? And what had he said to bring the required results? He thought of everything, repeated his phrases, but nothing happened.

He slumped back to the table exhausted. Some *greatest sorcerer* he'd turned out to be. Able to do wonderful feats once, but he could not repeat them. Maybe he needed another way to remain hidden.

Xerxes squealed again, backing away but with less terror than before. Amir looked at his hands and saw only the table. Once again, he was invisible. *Hidden*—he'd thought the word both times he'd disappeared.

After several hours of experimenting, he discovered that with severe intent, he could make himself disappear, but for very short periods of time, similar to how a potion worked. So there was no spell necessary to reappear, and he could never be certain when his reappearance would happen.

The caveat his experimentation showed him was that he needed to wait approximately thirty minutes between spells before he could try again, meaning he had only one chance to use his invisibility at any given time.

More of a concern, though, was the lessening of the tingling beneath his fingers.

It seemed his magic may have an expiration as well, at least until he could recharge himself with the scepter. That meant the time for experimentation was over. He couldn't chance depleting himself when he would soon face the jinni.

He shuddered, considering the ramifications of popping into existence right in front of Badra. He still needed to try to avoid her at all costs.

As a failsafe, he mixed the regeneration potion that had

regrown his hand and brought Iman back from the brink of death. The amount needed was far too much to carry, though, so he set the potion aside. Hopefully, he wouldn't need to use it.

But what if Badra *did* see him? The time it took to bring her back to the temple might be the few seconds he needed to save her. He couldn't risk it.

As a backup plan, he whipped up another potion that would render a person deaf and blind. The thought of committing such horror against the woman he loved made his stomach turn, but if Badra couldn't see him, she wouldn't be compelled to kill herself. And if she couldn't hear Aladdin's commands, she couldn't submit to them. Her hearing would return before her sight, giving Amir added time to hide, if needed.

It was a risk to hope that these loopholes in Aladdin's wish were exploitable, but Amir knew it was his only hope. He couldn't simply leave Badra and the sultan at the mercy of the street rat and his jinni any longer than they needed to be.

He took an opportunity to meditate, knowing that he had to keep a clear, focused mind before returning to the palace. He fully accepted the possibility that he may not walk away from the oncoming encounter. He may never see another sunrise. Though the only sunrise worth reliving was the sunrise he'd seen beside the guard tower with Badra.

Amir drew in a deep breath through his nose, then released it slowly from his lips. He'd walk into this battle to secure her chance of seeing the sun rise on another day, even if that meant seeing it without him. This was the right thing to do, coming from a man whose past was riddled with a mountain of things done wrong.

He gathered the potions he'd created days earlier, wrapped each, and placed them in his pack. Taking another deep breath, he prayed to whoever might listen for courage, strength, and ingenuity in the struggles to come.

All his hours of careful planning were over. This would be his last chance to set things right.

Or die trying.

33

Every muscle in Badra's body ached as Myra entered her chamber. A few moments ago, the lamp had extinguished and the soft, natural glow of sunlight filled her room.

"Prince Aladdin said it is time to get ready for your wedding, Highness," Myra said.

The princess immediately went to the mirror and started brushing her hair. Apparently, others could bring messages from him and she would still obey. She considered a full change of appearance for the occasion. She eyed the scissors in her drawer and tried to reach for them. Of course, she couldn't. Aladdin had not given her permission to cut off all her hair.

Badra wondered if someone were to lie to her about one of his orders if she would still be compelled to act, or if she had to truly believe it was something he desired. She wanted to have Myra help her test the theory, but she still couldn't utter a single word.

"Did you stand here all night, Highness?"

"Yes," Badra's body said.

Myra placed gold slippers at Badra's feet. The princess slipped them on, and Myra moved Amir's jewel from her old shoe to the new.

Badra's body readied to tell the girl to throw the stone away, but Badra fought, concentrating on the stone. A force pressed against her. She swallowed, holding her breath.

This was one tiny thing, a trifle to make her happy. She would not lose it. She refused!

The words slipped away, and she released the breath. Finally, a small victory.

Myra put a gentle hand on the princess's chin and turned her face toward her. "Are you still in there somewhere?"

All she could do was breathe slightly harder and faster, hoping that Myra would understand.

Myra's brow furrowed as she helped Badra out of her sleeping clothes. "From the look in your eyes, I'm willing to bet that you're aware of what's going on. I honestly wish you weren't. We'll figure something out, Highness. You have my word. We are trying."

"I don't want you to do anything that would displease Aladdin." That much was true. She didn't want anything bad to happen to Myra. However, her face rotated to the servant unbidden. "You must never speak like this to me or anyone else ever again. Do you understand?"

Curses on Aladdin! That isn't what I wanted to say!

There really was no way for her to break free of this. Even with the help of Amir's jewel, she could only hope that her body wouldn't tell Aladdin that Myra had been helping her, or that the girl had lied about being the one who'd given her the stone.

She watched the mirror in hollow agony as Myra dressed her in a red gown with gold foil stitching and pulled her hair back with jasmine flowers. If this really were her wedding day, she'd be excited. She may even think she looked beautiful, but she never wanted to look beautiful for Aladdin. She wished she could run out into the garden, roll in the dirt, and soil her hair. If she could do one simple rebellious thing, maybe she could feel somewhat alive again.

Instead, she grabbed the sheath Aladdin had given her, and pulled it around her waist. The click of the buckle reverberated in her ears. Of course, she needed her weapon. She needed to be good and ready to kill herself if Amir came to save her. She grimaced inside. Her world had ended, and she was trapped forever. The fiery pits of Jahannam could never be this horrible.

Each step taking her through the hallways to the throne room sounded like a gong within her head. Her body smiled at everyone she passed, but inside she screamed, *Help me! Stop this!*

Too many didn't even meet her gaze, though. Those who did held sympathy or a complete lack of hope in their eyes.

Myra led her to the main receiving chamber. The few remaining palace guards lined up on either side of the gold-inlayed carpet leading to the empty throne. Aladdin's *imam* stood in flowing black robes on one side of her father's chair and Aladdin stood on the other. She shivered inwardly. They looked more like executioners than a wedding party. Especially the *imam*, who bore an unsettling resemblance to that cursed monkey.

She nearly stopped short. Or she wanted to, but her body kept walking. Her soul quaked as the *imam* spun the staff he held and two bright jeweled eyes gazed at her from within a golden idol of a snake. Amir's scepter!

Badra made her way between the two rows of guards and stood near the base of the six steps that would lead to her father once he arrived.

"Ah, my love." Aladdin came down the steps and kissed both her cheeks before the mirth left his eyes. "Give me the stone that you've been hiding from me."

Oh, no! No! She crouched and pulled the stone from the side of her shoe. Her hand shook as she handed it to him.

This couldn't be happening. It wasn't fair.

Bile rose in her throat. That stone was the one thing she had to remember Amir by, and now she had nothing.

Aladdin held the jewel up between two fingers. "Last night it occurred to me that I'd seen this stone before." His gaze lanced hers. "In Jai'far's ring." His eyes became feral. "Where is he? Have you seen him? Is he coming to stop the wedding?"

Yes. And he's going to kill you. At least, she hoped so.

She lifted her chin. "I do not know where he is. I have not seen him. He cannot stop the wedding because if I see him, I will kill myself." Of course, that was the truth. She'd never be able to lie to Aladdin again.

He closed his fist around the jewel. "Good. Let this be a reminder to you that there is nothing the sorcerer can possess that I cannot take away from him."

He marched up the steps to the *imam* and wedged the stone between the teeth of the snake atop Amir's scepter.

Aladdin lifted his chin as he returned to her. "Don't fret. Maybe I'll mount the scepter on our bedroom wall so you can remember every day that your precious inept vizier was unable to save you."

She managed to grind her teeth. Amir had stared into her eyes as he'd faded from existence, staying with her as long as he could. That was not the act of a man who had given up. He'd find a way out of this. Until then, she needed to keep fighting, strengthening her mind. One day, Aladdin would make a mistake, and when he did, she would be ready.

"All hail, our great and mighty sultan!" a guard called.

All bowed as her father walked up the steps and took his place beside the *imam*. She desperately tried to convey to him that she would rather die than give the throne to Aladdin. Instead, she turned to her betrothed, and her body smiled.

Aladdin bowed low to the sultan, then turned and addressed the mostly empty room. "My *imam* will be performing the ceremony since your high priest is not well." He smiled with that grin that she'd found fetching before he'd dug his claws into her kingdom. "I want to let you all know that in Noblis, the *imam* take a vow of silence, so he will not be speaking during the ceremony. He will bless the sacred relic you know as the Sultan's Eye."

Bless it? More like taint it. The Sultan's Eye had been quarried by her great-great-grandfather's people and handed down to each son thereafter. It symbolized purity of spirit and goodness of heart. There was no goodness left in Aladdin's heart, if any had ever been there at all.

Aladdin looked away from the stone. "After witnessing our vows, my *imam* will consecrate the marriage and pass the Sultan's Eye to me, proclaiming me your new Sultan Apparent."

Apparent only. That was some respite. As long as the sultan still lived, there was still a chance. Her father just needed to keep his wits about him and not allow Aladdin to take so much control again. They could still get out of this. They *would* get out of this.

Aladdin took Badra's hand and guided her to the base of the steps. The betrothed faced one another and Badra managed to break eye contact and look up toward her father. The *imam* held out an open hand, waiting for him to offer up the Sultan's Eye. Badra's father produced the plumb-sized ruby from the folds of his robe and considered it with a frown.

"Aladdin," her father began, "I cannot offer you this. You seemed like a bright young man when you first came here. But seeing the state of our kingdom since your arrival, I cannot entrust the wellbeing of my people to you." He swallowed deeply. "Nor can I condone giving you my daughter, whom I love more than anything on this Earth."

Badra gasped. *He'd taken away consent! The ceremony was over!* She tried to pull away from Aladdin, but she remained frozen.

Aladdin smirked at his *imam*, who nodded and approached the throne. Her father looked into the eyes of the serpent on Amir's staff.

The scepter Amir had tried to hypnotize me with. No! She started to tremble, her body nearly collapsing on the steps. Was Aladdin losing his hold on her? She focused her mind, tried to take a step, but her body still didn't obey.

"I appreciate your feelings on this matter, sire." Aladdin kept a hold of Badra's hands, pulling her back to her feet. "Surely, you will reconsider, knowing that I also love your daughter more than life itself. No one could ever make a better husband for her than I."

Her father blinked, then turned to Aladdin. "Of course, you're right."

No! No, he is not right. Father, please, fight him!

Instead, the sultan reached out to offer the stone to the *imam*, who snatched the jewel and turned his back on them. Her father sat back and watched as the *imam* said a silent prayer over the jewel.

A lurid smile coated the *imam*'s face as he nodded to Aladdin.

"Princess Badroulbadour, full moon of full moons," Aladdin said. "I vow to be the best husband you could ever hope for. I will never lie to you or treat you unfairly."

Ha! What lies! She would never trust him. How could she ever? And did he actually believe that he was treating any of them fairly now?

Her body straightened. "I vow." Badra swallowed and tried

to clench her teeth, but she couldn't. "To be an obedient and submissive wife to you. I will bear you many sons and I will serve you as my sultan faithfully until my final breath."

No, I will not! I will hate you until my dying day! I will spend every second of every day strengthening my mind until I find a way to break this spell. You cannot have me, and you cannot have my kingdom!

Tears rolled down her face as the *imam* took a small ceremonial blade from his robes and cut both her and Aladdin's palms. She winced. Her knees wobbled, but Aladdin held her firm as the *imam* took the ruby and placed it in Badra's upturned hand. He then placed Aladdin's bleeding hand over the top of the jewel. He held up a gong and struck it, signifying the end of the ritual.

A smile burst across Aladdin's face. "We are now married by law. Bow before your next sultan!" Aladdin shouted as if expecting a great crowd to cheer.

The guards exchanged glances, shrugged, and bowed like idiots. What was wrong with them? They didn't need to bow to the Sultan Apparent!

Aladdin clapped his hands. "A banquet has been prepared in the great hall. My bride and I will meet you there shortly."

With the few visitors in attendance, it didn't take long before she stood alone with Aladdin, her dazed father, the *imam*, and a few guards. An air of dread hung in the hall.

They were married. Amir hadn't come for her.

Then again, if he had, she'd have taken this knife at her hip, and sliced the blade across her throat. What could Amir do, but stay away?

Aladdin took her hand, and drew her close. He leaned in and whispered to his bride, "Now, as your first submissive act, my love"—he kissed her cheek—"you will kill your father."

No!

No, no, no!

Badra's eyes widened and she struggled against her body, trying to stiffen her limbs, but she still pulled the knife from the sheath at her side. She turned toward her father, who looked at the ground, his eyes half coated with worry, and half still entranced.

Get up, Father. Run!

She gripped the knife more tightly. The guards stood still, like nothing was amiss. *Don't you see me? I have a dagger! Protect your sultan!*

But they didn't see. She held the knife close to her leg, within the folds of her gown, and she was his loving daughter. What was there to fear?

She marched up the steps. The *imam's* eyes swirled with excitement.

Please, no! No! I won't kill my father. I won't. She willed her body to stop, fighting and gnashing from inside, but she kept walking. *No!*

Her father turned to her, and the glassiness left his eyes. His gaze filled with love, and she loved him, too, more than life itself. This couldn't be happening. She had to stop this. Amir had said she was too strong to hypnotize. *Stop!* She raised the blade.

Her father's forehead creased. "Babedra?"

She wept, hearing her mother's pet name for her, as she took the last two steps toward him and plunged the knife into her father's chest.

Nooooo!

His eyes widened with shock as blood coated her hand.

Curse her strength training! Curse her climbing the trellises. Curse her riding horses! Curse everything she'd done in her entire life that left her being strong enough to do such a horrible thing!

She gasped, her chest heaving.

The guards cried out. One grabbed her and pulled her back. Aladdin laughed as she landed at the bottom of the stairs and clawed her way back up to her father.

She choked out a sob, reaching for him. *Father, I'm so sorry!*

His gaze met hers, his face pale. "Oh, my sweet Babedra. Your mother loved you even before you were born. Don't blame yourself for this." He blinked tears from his eyes. "I should have protected you."

And I should have protected you. *I should have known this was coming. I should have prepared us. I'm sorry. I'm so sorry!*

Her chest clenched as his eyes rolled back and closed. She wanted to scream and wail. She wanted to cry and grieve for her father, the man who tried so hard to give her the best life he could, the man who only wanted his daughter to be happy. But she couldn't cry. She couldn't scream. She could do nothing that was not Aladdin's bidding.

She pulled the knife from her father's chest, wiped the blood on her dress, and returned the blade to its sheath.

"That was cruel, I admit." Aladdin leered. "But now, at least, I know you are actually under my control and not pretending anymore."

Skies! Was this her fault? Would he have done this if she hadn't accepted the jewel from Amir, if she'd worn her collar and been his faithful lapdog?

The guards stood around their sultan, agape, arms slack.

"Come." Aladdin held out his hand to her. "The royal bedchamber awaits."

A cold dread swept through her body, a chill deeper than the loss of her father as she took his hand. Her father had been her life, but Aladdin now looked to take her soul.

He couldn't have it. He couldn't have *her,* yet her body smiled as he drew her from the room.

She turned back, but she could no longer see her father, only the red streaks of blood dripping down the once-pristine white steps.

34

Within the secret passage that ran alongside the throne room, Nadir struggled against Amir's hold.

"I'm going to kill you, I swear!" the guard captain promised.

"Then you'd be killing the wrong man!"

Nadir peered through the crack in the panel, to where the sultan lay in a pool of blood. "The sultan! She killed her father!"

"It wasn't her and you know it."

The large guard relaxed, but only a little. "Why won't you let me try to save him?"

"Because Aladdin will have you killed. He wants the sultan dead so he can have the throne. You should have expected this."

Nadir finally pulled away. "Yes, but I expected...I hoped..." He swallowed. "I'd hoped that you would come back to stop this—not come back to allow that abomination to kill our sultan!"

Amir tried to control his own gaze, to relay a hope that wasn't truly in his heart. "You said we could be allies if only to save the kingdom."

"That was before your plan was to let the sultan die."

"He's not going to die." Amir rubbed the back of his neck. "At least I hope not. I'm going to do my best to save him."

Nadir frowned. "I want to trust you, Jai'far, but all I see is another sorcerer, and my beloved sultan bleeding on the throne steps."

"Aladdin is arrogant beyond measure."

"Tell me something I am not aware of."

"In his arrogance, I am counting on him leaving the sultan where he lies."

Rage reared in Nadir's eyes. "Why is this supposed to comfort me?"

"Because that is when we will save him."

Amir pointed through the crack in the wall as Aladdin led Badra from the steps and out into the hall. The throne room emptied more quickly than he'd anticipated, but that was all the better.

Amir and Nadir pushed through the door and bolted to the sultan's side.

"Majesty?" Nadir's voice was pleading, desperate.

Scarlet stained the sultan's robes and the white marble beneath him. Amir pressed the side of the sultan's neck. A weak beat pumped far too slowly against his fingers.

Myra ran up the steps, slipping once on the blood as she reached for the sultan. "No!"

Amir held out a hand to her. "Come, girl. We could use your help."

She knelt beside them, and Amir called to the temple. The world faded out, then brightened again in the center of the high-ceilinged room surrounded by scrolls.

Nadir jumped to his feet. "What sorcery is this?"

"The most devious kind, I assure you, but this magic is mine. You have nothing to fear."

Xerxes whinnied and backed away.

"Sorry, friend," Amir said. "It will be close quarters for a while."

"Majesty! Majesty!" Myra held the sultan's hand, seeming unfazed by the incantation, if she'd even noticed at all.

"Strip his robes!" Amir grabbed the prepared regeneration potion, stirred the contents, and poured half over the sultan's bare chest. "Tilt his head back," he told Nadir.

Amir slipped a tube down the sultan's throat and used a funnel to pour the rest of the potion directly into his stomach.

Myra pushed back her hair, streaking blood across her forehead. "Will this save him?"

Amir lowered his eyes. "I'm not sure, but I have seen this work miracles before."

Looking at Nadir, Amir held up his once-severed hand and wiggled his fingers. The guard's eyes widened, and he nodded. The guard looked back to his sultan, hope crossing his features for the first time.

This potion had regrown hands and saved a woman from disease-caused madness. Could it save someone so close to death?

Amir steeled himself. He'd already asked too much of any gods who might answer. *But please, if anyone is out there who still believes in what is just and good, please help this man to live.*

Myra shrieked. "He moved!"

Nadir placed his hand on the sultan's chest. A smile burst across his face. "He's breathing!"

Amir closed his eyes and faced the ceiling. *Whoever you are, thank you.*

He drew in a deep breath and released it. "I should stay and watch over him, but the princess..."

Nadir stood, pushing out his chest. "Go. We will care for our sultan." He placed his hand on Amir's shoulder. "You are powerful, my friend. More powerful than I think you know. You can save us. You can save Bisnagar."

Amir wished he shared the guard's conviction. "I will try."

Nadir pointed at him. "No you *will*."

Amir nodded, but his uncertainty was warranted. His chances were probably fifty-fifty. If he didn't return, he couldn't leave the four of them here, trapped.

He raised his hands, saying a spell that would ferry them all safely to Bagdad in one day should he not return. This was the most he could do for them, now.

The color returned to the sultan's cheeks, and Amir straightened. So far his luck had held. He needed to move before things changed.

The library faded out of view, and the dank passages of the sewers below the palace shimmered into existence around him. He'd taken far too long, and Badra was in more and more danger as each grain of sand ran through the hourglass. By now, Aladdin may already have her with child. No matter. He would save her from this horror. No woman should be forced to give herself to another. Amir would rather die than allow that abomination to touch her even one more time.

Conjuring a hole above him, he climbed up into the hidden passages. *"Illuminae nas,"* he whispered into his hand, and a slight red light appeared, leading him to the crook beside the royal bedchamber. Amir took a deep breath and peered inside.

"I want you to have an honest conversation with me." Aladdin reclined on the bed with Badra beside him. Both were blessedly still clothed. The gods of luck were still with him.

Badra propped herself up on an elbow and faced him. Daggers shot from her eyes. At least Amir knew she was still inside there, hidden in that submissive shell.

"I will be honest with you and I want you to speak to me as you would if I had not wished for a submissive wife. Can you do that?"

"Yes," Badra said.

Now might be his only chance. He could freeze time, grab her, and carry her through the tunnels to safety. If he could get her back to the temple, he could take his time trying to break the spell on her. He needed to be swift, though. He only had ten seconds.

Amir cracked the door open, prepared to step out, and recited the spell.

"If I wished my jinni to free you, do you think you could you ever love me?"

Blast it! Amir tried the incantation again.

Badra's nose flared. "You used me to murder my own father, my only living family. I could never love you."

Aladdin folded his hands. "I suppose I deserve that."

Yes, you do. Amir sneered. *You deserve that and the world more.*

"While I have the opportunity to tell you," Badra continued, "I would rather die a slow and agonizing death than bear sons for you. I only wish I could be here to see what becomes of you when Amir comes back and picks his teeth with your bones."

Amir cringed. Did she *want* him to kill her?

Amir spoke the spell again. Aladdin was too close to her. He could grab her dagger at any moment. He didn't need Badra anymore. Didn't she realize that?

"You really are in there somewhere," Aladdin said.

Confound it! Why wasn't the spell working?

Focus. He needed to focus!

"It's actually nice to have you back. I thought I would enjoy you submissive, but you're like a doll. It disgusts me."

"Trust me." Badra's voice seethed in menace. "The feeling is mutual."

This wasn't working, and Amir had precious little time. The lamp sat on the nightstand, within Aladdin's reach. The fool probably thought he was safe, that Amir would never appear where the princess might see him. He was about to be unhappily surprised.

I will save her. I will eradicate the kingdom of this pompous brat.

Calling all the power coursing through him, he thought the word, *Hidden.*

He held up his hands and saw only the room. The spell did not hide sound, as far as he knew. Neither did he know if the *silence* spell would have any counteractive effect on invisibility, so he eased forward, thinking through each step.

"I wish..." Aladdin started to say something but stopped. Amir sighed with relief.

"It doesn't matter what you wish anymore," Badra said. "You have an afterlife paved for you in Jahannam."

Aladdin sat up. His expression went blank as he pondered her words. "Unless I find a way to cheat death altogether." He slipped off the bed and started pacing, bringing him farther from the lamp but walking directly at Amir.

Amir jumped back and stilled, sure he had made a sound. His heartbeat drummed in his ears.

"I could wish myself immortal, but it would have to be a quality kind of immortality, not an eternity as a hunchbacked, decrepit old man. I need to be someone who is smart enough and powerful enough to enjoy myself until the end of all things."

Keep dreaming, brat. Amir headed back for the lamp. All he needed was to grasp it. He would not make the same mistake as he had before with the monkey. He needed to hold the base of the lamp in his hands, not just the handle. He needed to possess the relic totally.

"Maybe I'm thinking about this the wrong way." Aladdin

started toward Amir and the lamp. "I wish to be the most powerful sorcerer the world has ever known."

The brat's eyes widened, his gaze latched onto Amir's. "You!" The boy's face twisted into a sneer.

Blast it! The spell wore off!

Aladdin turned to Badra and smiled. *No! He'll call her name...make her look this way!*

"*Prohibere omnes!*" The words reverberated off the walls of the room.

Aladdin stood before him, still facing Badra, his lips open to speak.

Amir had ten seconds. Not long enough to grab her now that he'd lost the advantage of surprise. Badra, as always, was his utmost concern.

Pushing past Aladdin, he took the blinding potion from his satchel and put a few drops of black liquid in each eye and also in each ear. "I'm sorry," he whispered, kissing her frozen lips.

"That was a waste of time." Aladdin scoffed. "You could have used that ability to grab the lamp rather than kiss your lady love goodbye."

"Maybe." Amir straightened. "Or maybe I'm up for a bit of sport. Now that you're the most powerful sorcerer on the planet, what happens next?"

Aladdin looked around the room before bursting into maniacal laughter.

"What's wrong, street rat?" Amir smiled. "All that power and no idea how to use it?"

Realization crossed Aladdin's face. He'd wished to be a sorcerer, but he hadn't wished for the knowledge of how to use sorcery. Amir needed to act quickly before the idiot realized he only needed to make another wish for knowledge.

"I can still kill her before you can chant a spell, Sorcerer!"

He lunged for Badra, still sitting helpless, deaf and blind, on the bed.

"*Ignis verberaque!*" Amir shouted, and a torrent of fire shot from his fingers toward the boy, who dodged, rolling across the floor. *Blast his good reflexes!*

"That's a neat trick." Aladdin patted his sleeve to put out a small flame. "Let me try. *Ignis verberaque!*"

He'd repeated the incantation poorly, but his intention and the power he'd channeled was enough to summon a roiling wall of fire. Amir cast a protective spell to cover Badra as the waves of flame poured out of the street rat's hands, engulfing the rest of the room.

Heat blistered Amir's palms as he pressed the flames back until they winked out.

"That was fun!" Aladdin cackled like an insane child. "I may not have the knowledge of how to use my new gifts, but I have a feeling I could stand to learn a lot from you."

Amir gritted his teeth. He wouldn't make the mistake of speaking an incantation aloud again if he could help it. He had no knowledge, though, of which spells needed to be spoken, and which only needed thought. In a war of sorcerers, a moment's hesitation could mean death.

Aladdin glanced at the princess. "Badra, get up."

She didn't respond.

Aladdin's eyes narrowed. "What have you done to her?" He reached toward her, but as his hand tried to enter the protective invisible barrier, he jolted back, screaming. He turned to Amir, his eyes ablaze.

Amir grinned. *Go ahead, street rat. Try to touch her again.*

Aladdin pursed his lips. "That's an interesting one." He pushed to his feet. "I don't want to kill you, Jai'far."

The boy blurred and was on top of Amir before he could move, throwing a series of hard punches into Amir's face and stomach. Amir repeated a protection spell in his mind but still fell to his knees.

"We are the same in a lot of ways." Aladdin threw a last punch. "I just had the advantage of my jinni to help me get to where I wanted to go."

"We *are* alike in many ways." Amir coughed, holding his stomach and pressing healing energy inward. "I came here, like you, with the intention of taking the throne and remaking the kingdom to accommodate my own vision. If we had met under different circumstances, we might have been on the same side."

Amir staggered to his feet but kept hunched over. He had the best chance if the boy didn't find him a threat.

"But the jinni's darkness has infected you. You're not the same man you were before you had that lamp." Amir clutched at his stomach. "I highly doubt the man you were would have forced another human being into slavery the way you did with the princess, nor would he have forced her to kill her father with her own hands."

"You have no idea what kind of man I am." Aladdin's eyes began to glow a furious yellow. Thunder rolled in the distance.

"Yes, I do, Aladdin. It is in my power to read your heart." That was a lie, of course, but Aladdin didn't know that. "And I know that before the lamp corrupted you, you were a good man and you loved this city."

Aladdin clenched his jaw. "You. Know. Nothing." Growling, he hit Amir again and again.

Amir buckled over, even though most of the blows didn't get through his shield.

"This city is a cesspool of despicable human waste," Aladdin said. "The worst parts of humanity thrive here. I was weak and pathetic thinking I could make a difference. I wasn't ready to make the hard decisions that one must when it falls to you to rule."

Amir held out an arm as if to protect his face. "You gain nothing by threatening the princess. With her father dead, you are already sultan by default. Let her go and get rid of the jinni and I will teach you how to use your powers to make the city whole again."

The yellow in the Aladdin's eyes began to whirl, not unlike the monkey's. "I will bring this whole palace down on top of you both before I let her go!" Aladdin roared.

The jinni had too much control. The boy had to see this. "Why?" Amir asked. "You don't need her!"

His head arched at an unnatural angle. "She embodies everything I've always hated about nobility. She sits up here in her golden palace, oblivious to the suffering of her people."

Wind swooped in from the balcony, swirling through the room. The drapes ripped from the bed. Badra's hair stood out behind her as if she sat in the midst of a gale storm.

"She does care!" Amir shouted. "She's been sneaking out into the city for years, giving money to the poor in secret."

"You'll say anything to stop me from tearing this all down." Aladdin raised his hands.

The ceiling shook. Something unimaginable roared outside.

Amir's feet slid across the tiles, pulling him toward the balcony. "Do you want to know the real reason I know you love this city?" he screamed over the wind. "The jinni wants to see you destroy yourself and everything you love."

The gold dome from the throne room crashed into the balcony, sheering the mortar right off the side of the royal chamber. Aladdin gaped.

Amir held out his hands as best he could, countering the wind with every spell he could think of. "Look around you. The city, much like the palace, is falling apart. The princess hates you and is trapped inside her own mind like a caged animal. You made your first wishes with the intention of filling your life with the things you always dreamed of. You wanted to be a part of all this beauty and instead, you've destroyed it."

The roof above them cracked. Part flew up, exposing churning black spiraling clouds.

"It's too late." Aladdin's face contorted. "I've already come this far. I might as well finish this."

Amir reached for him. "No!" But despite his incantations, the wind pulled him back. He slid farther toward the gaping hole where the balcony had once stood.

Amir's heart ached as Aladdin's frame expanded, bloating out in unnatural angles. The rest of the ceiling broke free, revealing not clouds, but an enormous black cyclone. A cage of birds swooped up from the gardens and vanished within the spinning mass. Several screaming guards twirled higher and higher before they disappeared.

The dressers sailed into the air, taking the lamp with them. The bed shifted, and Amir bolstered the protections around Badra, cementing her and the mattress to the floor. Setting his jaw, Amir repeated the word "hold" both aloud and in his mind as the other pieces of the room around him took flight.

One of the massive flagpoles that held the sultan's family banner flew up into the cyclone, the flag still flying as if clinging to a past that no longer promised a future.

Aladdin's skin turned a horrid pale blue. His body extended, becoming bulbous as his massive form grew out the top of the ruined ceiling and into the sky.

Above, the cyclone wavered, showing two yellow glowing orbs—eyes. *The jinni!*

The lamp rose toward the shining eyes.

Could it be that the jinni had what it desired? Did the foul creature see the destruction of the golden palace as fulfillment of its true purpose, and was it ready to cast itself back to the Cave of Eternal Sadness?

As Aladdin stretched toward the heavens, he opened his ever-widening jaw to reveal row after row of jagged, sharp teeth as he became as monstrous on the outside as he was within.

The flagpole whisked around the cyclone once more. This time the sultan's banner ripped free and whisked up into the heavens as the tall pole disappeared around the back of the cyclone again.

"You are weak, Jai'far," the new, horrible Aladdin screamed, his voice booming like the thunder. "And now you will watch all you love die."

The eyes in the cyclone pulsed as Aladdin pointed at Badra.

"No!" Amir threw another protection spell over her as a bolt of lightning charged from the sky, exploding across his shield.

The energy ricocheted and sizzled across his hands. Another blast came and Amir fell back, slamming onto the tiles. The edges of his cloak smoked, the tang of charred cloth burning the inside of his nose. Another blow like that might be the end of him.

He held out a hand to ward off another attack and prayed Badra was still deaf and blind—and unknowing of how close death loomed over her. She must feel the wind, though, and sense the furniture moving. Maybe Amir's curse had made things even worse for her. She didn't deserve this. She was good and kind and everything a princess should be.

Another blast. His shield buckled. Dust from the crumbling walls kicked up, choking him. The powder seared his lungs, making each breath harder than the last.

The energy field wavered over the princess. She was going to die, and Amir would have to watch. He wasn't powerful. He was nothing, and now Badra would pay for it.

A spray of red howled past, along with curtains and a serving tray, all swept up in the circling winds.

The tray shone brightly, still gleaming from the last polish. Bisnagar's treasures were strong, like its people. The tray banked around again, still unscathed—resilient, like this land, like the princess.

Amir's hands clenched into fists. He bolstered the spell as bolt after bolt of lightning came raining down from Aladdin's massive finger, but each blast that hit Badra's shield reverberated back on Amir with more force than being beaten in the streets.

The smell of burning hair filled the room. Smoke eddied from holes in his cloak. Amir's breath caught, the sting deepening as his magic inched away with each strike. He was losing time. He needed another avenue, a new spell.

Above, the serving tray and the spray of red whisked around the outskirts of the cyclone, driving higher. Next, the lamp crossed directly over the cyclone's menacing yellow eyes. The walls ripped away, and Amir gasped. Desert sand surrounded them on all sides. The palace, the city, all Bisnagar...wiped from existence.

Another bolt hit the shield, and Amir fell back. His chest tightened. He tried to focus, but the unending desert haunted him. All those people...Iman.

Little parts of his soul chipped off, and he imagined each piece drifting up to be swallowed by the beast.

He took one last look at Badra as another bolt shattered across her shield. His sight glazed. Once he lost consciousness, his shield would falter. She'd die, like the rest of her kingdom. Amir had failed. He'd failed *her*, and that was more than he could bear.

The flagpole took another turn around the cyclone but hovered as the tray and the red flurry behind it whisked past.

The pole rose as if held by a huge hand as Aladdin pointed downward with death in his eyes.

"I tire of this," Aladdin said. "I wish the sorcerer dead."

No! Amir's shoulders tightened. He pressed his hands out, bolstering his protection spell.

The jinni's yellow orbs blazed and the pole flew free—not down on Amir, but up.

Aladdin's eyes widened before the projectile lanced the would-be prince through the chest. His head whipped back. His mouth opened in a deafening roar.

*I wish the sorcerer dead...*but he hadn't specified *which* sorcerer.

On all that was holy, the jinni had what it wanted, so it had used Aladdin's wish against him, just as the texts had promised.

Still roaring, Aladdin pointed at Badra. Another bolt of lightning exploded over the shield, shattering the last of Amir's defenses. The princess fell to the ground and didn't move.

"I wish," Aladdin choked. Black liquid foamed from his mouth. "I-I wish..." He pulled at the pole in his chest while the cyclone whirled into the shape of a massive face and laughed, the sound booming from above over and over.

The lamp rose, glowing. The serving tray circled past the laughing jinni, followed again by a spray of red. As they passed the lamp, the platter tilted, casting a mirror image of Iago's twisted face.

What mockery is this?

The tray sucked into the cyclone, and the fluttering mass of red became a large bird. The creature twitched, flapped, and worked against the wind current. The parrot inched forward, fell back, then gained once more until its gray claws reached out and grasped the handle of the lamp.

Amir's breath hitched as the laughing stopped. The jinni snarled as Aladdin stumbled back, still holding the pole in his chest, and slammed to the ground. The earth shook from his fall, and the last of the palace beneath Amir and Badra crumbled.

Above, the lamp stopped glowing, revealing a gorgeous red parrot fluttering against the wind, dragging the lamp like the heaviest of burdens.

The face of the jinni morphed as its cheeks filled with air, blowing at the brilliant red and blue parrot. The stench of a thousand lifetimes rolled across the land. Amir retched, then righted himself. He wouldn't succumb so easily. He reached out his hand to the lamp, but the words wouldn't come to him. His head spun.

The bird fluttered, being pushed back faster than he moved forward. But Iago had seized the lamp. He should have control of the jinni—but, no. The creature only had the handle, not the base of the lamp.

"Iago!" Amir shielded his face from the whipping wind. "You need to hold the sides of the lamp!"

The parrot screeched, its eyes rolling madly, its tiny claws cinched about the rounded handle. The bird squawked a series of words that sounded somewhat like Latin before Iago spun as if someone were whipping him in circles. With a final squawk, Iago flung the lamp through the air toward Amir.

The jinni roared, a massive hand shot out of the cyclone, reaching for the lamp.

A dull ache ripped through Amir's heart as the enormous hand advanced. The lamp couldn't return to the Cave of Eternal Sadness. Not yet! Amir stumbled forward, his legs leaden.

"*Fugere ad me!*" Amir called out, reaching with all the intent of a lifetime. No, a thousand lifetimes, one for every man, woman, and child swept away by this monstrous evil.

The jinni's fingers grazed the lamp.

"Fugere ad me!" Amir called out again.

The lamp sparked and shot toward Amir. The jinni roared again, smashing its outstretched hand into Iago while it reached with the other. The parrot slammed to the hard sand with a deafening thud, its neck twisted at an unnatural angle.

Bile singed the back of Amir's throat as he held out his other hand, pressing with all his might. The lamp fought against the wind, advancing, but then blowing back.

"You will not kill again." He ground his teeth. His jaw ached. "You will not kill again!"

The jinni's eyes blazed, and Amir's hand shook under the weight of a creature larger than a dozen palaces of gold.

"You will not win this!" Amir shouted.

The jinni growled. Wind and rain whipped around them.

"I will save them." Amir wiped the water from his eyes. "I may rot in the pits of Jahannam, but I will see this undone. My life will be a small price to pay." He took a deep breath. *"Fugere ad me!"*

The jinni balked, its eyes wide, as the relic shot into the sorcerer's hands.

Amir gasped, his body trembling as the winds died. The ancient metal cooled his palms, as if already sucking the life from him, but he grasped the metal harder. He couldn't drop it. The risk was far too great.

The world hung suspended, as if time had stopped. Amir stood, panting. He clung to the small tarnished vessel. The silver tray had made another pass around the cyclone but now hung, frozen in time. Lances of rain held like darts thrown at the ground. After so much violence, after the open cacophony of sound, the silence seeped in, more chilling than the rain.

Amir wiped back his dripping hair and stumbled toward Badra. She lay on her side, her eyes closed, but her chest rose and fell in slow, steady breaths. Amir choked back the tears. He'd saved her, but for what?

The desert went on forever, an expanse of dead sands that once held such life and wonder.

"Your wish is my command." A low sinister voice drew Amir's gaze to the other side of the crumbled platform that had once been the floor of the royal bedchamber. In the corner, where the changing room once resided, stood a shadowy figure darker than the black sky that loomed overhead.

Shaking, Amir held up the lamp. "I was doomed the moment I touched this, wasn't I?" An itching sensation swept across his skin as he imagined the creature smiling, dreaming of ways to use someone with Amir's power. It wouldn't be long before he became no better than Aladdin. He needed to do what he'd promised, before he no longer had the strength of will.

"I wish for everything and everyone else in Bisnagar to return to the physical state they were in before Aladdin found this lamp."

The ground rumbled and the world around him churned. The walls about him rose as if invisible masons worked at a million times their normal pace.

Badra sat up. Her eyes widened and she grabbed her chest, taking in the scene. Amir ran to her, but she screamed, reaching for him as she faded from existence.

No! What had he done? He'd thought his words carefully. She should be fine!

Heat flooded Amir's veins as he turned toward the jinni. "Where is she?"

The creature's eyes darkened. Sands, it would use the wish against him—send her to wherever she was before Aladdin had taken possession of the lamp. What if that place was now under tons of rubble and sand?

The broken floor beneath his feet rumbled. The roof grew from the outer edges, all sides reaching for each other until they joined in the center. Through the windows, other buildings rose. Carts that had been ripped apart by the cyclone streamed back together. A tree flew past, then another. It was like watching the past several hours rewind.

Keeping a strong grip on the lamp, Amir walked out onto the balcony. The sun peeked through the clouds, and from the sultan's veranda, he could see people stroll into the streets of the marketplace, most stumbling as if confused.

Tears welled in his eyes. He'd done it. He'd saved them.

"You still have two more wishes, Master." The jinni put a cold hand on Amir's shoulder.

"Where is Badra?"

"Do you wish for me to tell you?"

"Ye—No!" Tricky creature.

Amir shivered and twisted away, walking back into the room. The cold of the jinni still hung with him like the grip of death. He'd almost lost a wish. He needed to be more careful. No questions. No conversation.

The lamp seemed to ice beneath his palms, pulsing, waiting for him to make a grave error.

He shuddered. Two more wishes. Two more chances to lose his soul. He closed his eyes and summoned his courage to do what needed to be done.

35

Badra drew in a long, deep breath of jasmine flowers. Her eyelids fluttered open and the sun warmed her skin. She sat on the edge of the fountain.

She jumped to her feet. She spun around, taking in the garden. Why was she here?

"Amir!"

Her heart throttled in her chest.

Aladdin. The jinni.

Her father!

She bolted toward the royal bedchambers. Aladdin had arrived and taken everything from her, and she'd allowed the guards to throw out the one person who could protect her. Amir hadn't given up, though. She'd sensed his presence, felt his warm lips on hers.

She must have fallen asleep, though, until she woke with the castle growing around her, being built by invisible hands. Amir had stood in the center of her father's bedchamber, holding the lamp.

Of all that was right and good in the world, Amir had fulfilled his promise to save them all, but at what cost? Just touching the lamp would be enough to draw him into the same downward spiral that destroyed Aladdin.

"Princess!" Nadir called from down the hall, racing toward her with Amir's scepter in his hand.

She didn't stop. "Amir has the lamp! We have to stop him!"

When she reached the door, she yanked on the handle, but it didn't open. She banged on the frame. "Amir! Amir, stop! Drop the lamp. Don't touch it!"

Nadir came from behind and handed her the scepter. "Get out of the way, woman!" He slammed against the door once, twice. On the third try, the hinges gave, and he kicked the door down. They pushed into the royal chamber.

Swirling darkness surrounded Amir, coating him like a veil. The creature stood before him, tall and shaped like a monkey shrouded in a billowing cloud of death.

Badra's heart sank, and she dropped to her knees. She'd lost him. He'd been her champion, and he'd given his life for the good of all, just like in the storybooks.

Amir held up the lamp. "Jinni of the lamp, you are no longer a slave. I wish for your freedom."

The jinni's jaw fell as Amir handed him the lamp. The creature took the relic and held it to its chest. The air about the being pulsed with a slow, steady rhythm. The smoke churned as if a thing alive, easing over the creature's skin like a wanton parasite.

Badra grabbed her chest. Amir had freed the jinni. They'd won!

The creature's gaze lifted from the lamp. It sneered, baring sharp teeth. "Sorcerer!"

It threw the lamp, shattering the mirror on the far side of the room, before it lunged at Amir, snapping and hissing.

"Jai'far!" Nadir dove for the creature. He grabbed the monkey from behind, but the jinni already had Amir by the throat, lifting him from the ground.

"No!" Badra raised the scepter over her head, charging at the beast, but before she could club him a large, clawed foot shot out and kicked, flinging her into the wall.

Her head cracked against the stonework. Stars flashed in her eyes.

She blinked, struggling to focus as the creature raised Amir higher.

The sorcerer's feet kicked. He tried to speak, but only a rasp escaped his lips.

Nadir punched blow after blow into the monkey's six-foot frame.

But why? The creature was free. It should have been happy.

The monkey seemed furious, though. It had called Amir *sorcerer*.

Badra shivered. It had been ancient sorcerers who'd condemned all the jinn to slavery.

This jinni was no longer a slave, though. It should have returned to its original state, just as Badra had been ferried back to the garden after Amir made his wish. Here the creature was, though, snarling, still taking revenge.

The scepter lay at her side, the red stone eyes winking at her. Amir's blue jewel still lay wedged between its teeth. The stone had been her friend, a personal, hidden ally against her tormentor.

Had the stone protected Badra from Aladdin, though, or from the power of the jinni? Had it really been the power of the ancient being fueling the evil, or had the curse bent the jinni into a sick, twisted opposite of its true nature?

The creature grabbed Nadir's neck with its other hand. The guard captain grunted and kicked, but the jinni just hissed through those awful pointed teeth.

Amir's face darkened to a sickly blue.

Blue, like the stone...the stone that had saved her from a spell that had controlled her mind and made her no better than a slave.

Could it be so simple?

Badra dug her fingers into the snake's mouth, but Aladdin had wedged the jewel between the idol's teeth.

Amir's head bobbed. His eyes fluttered as if weighted.

No! She would not be beaten by Aladdin. Not now.

A drop of blood fell from her hand, the wound in her palm reopening. Her blood had bound her to Aladdin. Could it also set her free?

She squeezed her hand over the stone, red covering the blue. She pressed again and the jewel shifted but didn't free. Badra cried out, slamming the staff on the floor. There had to be a way to...

One of the red eyes popped out and bounced across the tiles. She lifted the scepter and found the blue jewel lying on the floor, lustrous in the rays of the sun.

She huffed out a breath before snatching the stone and bolting toward the jinni. The creature turned, baring its pointed teeth, and she slapped the stone against its forehead.

The creature stepped back, still holding Amir and Nadir.

"You were not always like this." Badra continued to press the stone against its skin. "You used to be a creature of faith, hope, and light. Amir freed you. He is not one of the horrors that doomed you to the lamp." She pressed harder. "Feel the strength of the stone and remember!"

The men fell to the floor. Nadir held his throat, gasping for air. Amir lay still, his face turned toward the wall.

Her gut twisted, pain rising into her throat. *This has to work. There is no other option!*

Snarling, the creature raised its claws to her face.

"Remember!" she screamed.

The monkey's nails pressed into her cheeks.

"Princess!" Nadir stood but stumbled.

The jinni blinked. Its eyes widened. It drew its hands back

as if burned, then dropped its arms. The yellow in its eyes swirled twice before it faded to blue.

Shaking, Badra lowered the stone.

"No!" Nadir grabbed her wrist, forcing the stone back onto the creature's brow. "Whenever you lost the stone, Aladdin took hold again."

Amir sat up, holding his head. "Nadir is right. The curse is eternal. I made the wrong wish. I only freed it from the lamp. It's still evil."

What had they done? Badra's hand shook as she pressed the stone against the creature's head.

The jinni's gaze rose to hers, not the eyes of a monster, but the eyes of a frightened child.

"How do we kill it?" Nadir asked.

"No!" Badra kicked the staff to Amir. "Use your magic. Do something to help him."

"Do what?"

She turned to him. "I don't know. You're the sorcerer."

Sighing, Amir used the staff to pull himself to his feet. He held one hand out and the other on his scepter. Fire shot from his fingertips, lashing the jinni between the eyes. The heat singed Badra's skin and she stepped back, cradling her burnt hand. The creature's eyes rolled before it slammed back onto the floor.

Badra gasped. "Stop! What are you doing?"

The fire abated, and Amir slumped onto the staff. Nadir grabbed him, holding him up.

Her stomach turned. "I said not to kill it. It didn't know what it was doing. It had no more control than I did when Aladdin made me kill my father."

Amir closed his eyes, huffing. His head lolled.

Nadir slapped his face. "Stay with me, Sorcerer. There'll be no dying today."

Except for the jinni.

Bile rose in Badra's throat as she dropped to her knees beside the creature. For days she'd been lost, hidden inside herself, frantic and unable to stop what Aladdin had made her body do. Was that how it had been for the jinni, millennia after millennia?

She reached out to touch the creature and the jinni sat up. She scrambled back as the monkey's gaze latched on to each of them. In the center of its forehead, the stone glinted, shining like it had absorbed the fire from Amir's staff. The flesh around the gem was red tainted with blue, like the jewel had melted to its face.

A black fog formed around the beast. Badra covered her nose as the stench of rotten eggs filled the room. The jinni's eyes settled on her. The air thickened, pulling her toward the pulsing mist.

"Stand back!" Amir pushed Nadir away and pointed the scepter at the jinni. The light of a thousand suns flashed in the room.

The dark smoke circling the monkey pulsed like an animal breathing before the vapor fell to the ground with a whoosh and spread across the tiles like black sand.

The jinni held out its hands, looked at its palms, and laughed. It jumped to its feet, wide-eyed. Continuing to laugh, the creature raised its face to the ceiling and shrieked. Badra covered her ears as the jinni ran out onto the balcony, grabbed the roof, and climbed out of view.

Amir rubbed his bruised neck. "You're welcome," he rasped.

"Did you save it?" Nadir asked. "Is it still evil?"

Amir shook his head. "I felt the spell dissipate. As long as that stone is lodged in its skull, it is no longer cursed." He raised his hand and the ruby lifted off the floor and returned to the empty eye socket of the snake idol.

He turned to Badra. Deep circles bruised the skin beneath his eyes, and several cuts on his forehead had crusted over. His hair hung thick with grime, and his beard was singed off.

He'd never been so handsome.

Badra grabbed his face, peppering him with kisses. "I thought you were dead."

He pulled him to her. "Frankly, Your Highness, so did I."

Badra folded into his arms. "I never want to be without you as long as I live."

Nadir smiled at them, then grimaced, staring at the balcony. "That thing looked insane. What have we loosed on the world?"

Amir laughed, still gasping for breath. "A problem for another day."

Her father appeared in the doorway, blinking his eyes and stumbling until he saw them.

"Babedra!" His face lit up.

Tears filled Badra's eyes and her chest clenched. She ran to her father and hugged him. "You're all right!"

He shook his head. "I woke up in a strange place with my guard captain and your red servant." He blinked twice. "Then suddenly I was in the throne room. Everyone looked as if they'd seen a specter."

"I'm so sorry, Father, for everything." She wiped away her tears. "I've never meant to be a bad daughter. I know I've never been the easiest..."

He held up a finger. "No, you haven't. But I'm proud of you and I wouldn't change a single thing about you."

They turned to where Amir was about to slink into the hidden wall within the changing room. Was he...leaving?

Her father's voice boomed. "You, Sorcerer, have some explaining to do."

Amir backed away from the wall. "What's to explain, Your Majesty?" He held his hands to his sides, one holding the scepter. "I am whom Aladdin said I was. I wanted to rule this city for all the wrong reasons. You were right to cast me out."

"Yes." Her father nodded. "And since then, you have saved my kingdom, my daughter, and my life—through no small risk to yourself, I might add."

"Thank you, sire." Amir held his hand over his heart and bowed.

Badra's chest ached. Was he really about to disappear through that door, vanish from her life forever?

"Jai'far, I gave you forty days to prove yourself, and I declare that you have done myself and Bisnagar proud. As we discussed, I will make you my Grand Vizier."

Amir's lips parted. "But, Your Majesty..."

"There are no *buts*! I am Sultan. My word is law!"

Badra held her hands over her smile, but she knew it would show in her eyes. This meant he could stay...he could stay with *her*.

"And, after careful evaluation of the scroll you gave me... that was real, wasn't it? No sorcery?"

Amir bowed again. "I would never be false in the written word, Majesty. I am a scholar."

The sultan nodded. "Good. Then, as I said, after careful evaluation of the scroll, I agree with my ancestors. You will marry my daughter and sit on my throne until your heir is ready to take your place."

Amir's eyes flicked to Badra. "With all due respect, Your Majesty, I'm more interested to know what your daughter wants."

Badra drew in a deep breath. Her chest ached. Amir was

just offered everything he'd wanted, yet he was giving her a way out...just like he'd promised.

He took her hand in his. "I would love to marry you, but marriage and children have never been something you wanted for yourself. Not only that, I am far from well-bred. I'm not worthy of this honor."

Badra frowned. "I will decide who is and isn't worthy of my company." She smiled. "Besides, I haven't been asked what I want by someone other than a servant in a long time. You considering my wishes means more to me that you can ever know."

The sultan stroked his beard. "If I have learned anything from this horrendous mess, it's that the world is a much bigger, more complicated place than I ever imagined. I don't want to die without having seen some of it." He nodded, his thoughts far off. "I think I would like to step down and do some traveling. Of course, I can't do this unless my succession is planned." He turned to Badra. "So, dearest, I ask you, with all respect to your wishes: What would you like to do?"

All eyes fixed on her. She had their attention. All of them. Even her father.

A ball formed in her throat. She'd spent the last day a prisoner, completely devoid of free will. She'd thought her life was over, but here she was, left with the ability to choose her own fate.

Amir was right. She resented being thought of as nothing but a vessel to birth more royalty. For this, she spurned marriage and every suitor who'd tried to win her. Maybe marriage didn't have to be that, though. Maybe it could be stolen nights by the watchtower, or sneaking out to play games at the festival, or dunking each other in the fountain.

Amir smiled at her, humble and waiting for an answer. Whatever that answer was, he'd accept her choice, because he loved her. He was a good man, regardless of what he thought or what his original intentions had been, and she couldn't imagine spending the rest of her life with anyone else.

Badra ran her fingers through Amir's singed whiskers. "Your beard is not long enough to be sultan."

"Good." Amir kissed her. "Because you are going to look amazing with a crown on your head."

36

Amir adjusted his weight in the saddle and Xerxes whinnied as they stood on the edge of the palace gates. The hooded rider sat at Amir's side on a striking white mare, her cloak tossed back so all could see her.

She petted the horse's mane. "Are you ready, Cleopatra?"

Her horse snorted, and they headed out, Nadir and Salem riding behind them.

Amir called over his shoulder to the guard captain. "I told you, you can stay home with your family."

"And miss The Great Sorcerer and Her Majesty riding into the market for the first time ever? I don't think so, Your Grace."

Amir snorted. "You don't need to call me that."

Nadir bowed low on his horse. "Of course, sire."

Amir shook his head, knowing his friend spoke mostly in jest. When Amir was crowned his first order of business was to proclaim Badra the true power in Bisnagar. She now ruled this land until her death as sultan, a title that his lovely wife was very particular about. Being called *sultana* almost incited her wrath as much as someone using her full name.

When Amir renounced the crown, Badra immediately named him Grand Vizier, a title and position he was more than happy to accept, although many still referred to him as *Highness* or *Majesty* out of respect.

The red and blue crimson rosella flew down from the guard

posts and alighted on Badra's arm. All the birds in the gardens had been set free, but none had left the grounds. Artisans had built perches, baths, and ornate bird houses to keep the new inhabitants of the gardens happy, and Myra's family had been brought into the palace as their keepers, cleaning up after the birds' droppings and making sure they had more than enough to eat—both the birds, and her family.

As they passed into the market, people cried out to them and waved. The royal couple wasn't mobbed. The people kept back a respectful distance.

While Amir's first order of business was to make her sultan, Badra's first public decree was to proclaim the victory of her sorcerer. Most had seen Aladdin's huge form rise into sky, and the howling cyclone that had whisked their world away. Badra had seen fit to make all aware of who had fought that menace and won.

News of the Great Sorcerer of Bisnagar had spread quickly, so when laws were passed outlawing the taking of hands and granting the common people more rights, none of the aristocracy balked. Bisnagar was not yet perfect, but the golden city was well on her way...all because of its incomparable and lovely new sultan.

Enhancing his hearing, Amir caught voices on the wind. He dismounted. "I'll be right back."

Turning the corner, he saw the bread merchant, Rashid, handing Iman four loaves. "It's no problem. Enjoy your meal and pay once the Great Sorcerer gives you your wages."

The man straightened and his gaze met Amir's. The color streamed from the merchant's face.

Alas, like the others in the city, he had a full memory of what had happened under Aladdin's rule. He held up his hands pleadingly, and Amir smiled, counting ten fingers.

He threw the merchant a coin purse. The money clinked when Rashid grabbed the leather bag.

He hefted it in his palm. "This is enough for two hundred loaves, maybe more."

Amir nodded. "Then make sure the next hundred people who come to you unable to pay are fed. Then send them to the palace for honest work."

The merchant nodded, his lower lip trembling. "I will, Your Grace. I promise."

Iman held up the loaves. "Look, sir. A feast!"

Amir rustled the boy's head. "Indeed."

"Come have dinner with us, sir."

Badra came around the corner.

Iman's smile broadened.

"Will the hooded rider be racing this month, Majesty?"

She smiled. "You can count on it, but this time, without the hood."

Amir smiled, knowing he'd have to hex the other riders to do their best. Otherwise, they may be afraid to truly race against their sultan. Either way, a woman, her long mane of curls flying behind her, would be quite the spectacle. He was sure Bisnagar, and the world, would never be the same.

"You can come to dinner, too. Please?" Iman asked Badra.

She smiled. "I'd love to."

"It's settled, then!" Iman started toward his hovel, and the royal couple followed.

Again, people bowed to them in the streets.

Badra stopped several times, saying hello to children and passing out alms. "This is only to get you through the day, though." She turned to the people. "I hereby proclaim poverty a thing of the past."

A hush fell over the gathering. The people looked at each other.

Badra leaned closer to Amir. "Can they all hear me, even in the back?"

He waved his scepter over the masses. "They can now."

Badra raised her chin. "We are going to rebuild the outer rings of the kingdom. If you need employment, come to the palace. There is more than enough work for anyone who is able. We will train you, make you master artisans, and together we will build a Bisnagar we can all be proud of."

The crowd erupted into cheers. Badra's eyes glistened, but she blinked the tears away.

Amir's heart squeezed in his chest. Every time he thought he'd reached the pinnacle of his love and admiration, she found a way to make him love her more.

He choked down the painful ball building in his throat. All his life, he'd strived to be something better than what he was—always learning, always researching. He'd been a perennial scholar, but now the only thing he wanted was to help his wife fulfill this dream.

Oddly enough, that idea bloomed inside him like a seed of hope. He would bring all of Badra's ideas to fruition. This was home, and his life was now devoted to making Bisnagar the best the golden city could possibly be.

Iman pulled Amir's wrist. "Come. Our bread is getting stale."

The people made way, chanting, "Bisnagar!" over and over.

Smiling, Amir threw a small fireball spell into the air, exciting the children in the outskirts of the crowd. Their laughter whisked away Amir's memories of nearly bleeding to death in the alley. Those days were over. Important, and a necessary part of his past, but not an unpleasantness to dwell on.

The ground beneath their feet hardened. The shabby district still lay in disarray, but not for long. The people would soon have the funds to rebuild, and the training and skills to keep their properties in good repair. Iman's home, though, appeared just as bad as it had been before.

"Iman," Amir said. "I thought I found you work. Do you still not have enough to fix the holes in your walls?"

"Not yet, sir, but I will. Artisan Kellis is coming tomorrow. I asked that my training be started here so he can show my sisters, too."

Amir smiled. "Good thinking."

They ducked into the house, and the girls screamed with glee to see their new sultan. They immediately sat and chatted about dresses and balls and palaces and boys. Badra laughed, answering their questions and asking her own.

"Where is your mother?" Amir asked.

Iman looked at the floor. "She fell ill again when the world returned to normal." He swallowed before his smile returned. "It's okay, though. This is a small price to pay to have my sisters and my home back. I am still forever thankful, sir. I would never ask that..."

Amir placed his hand on the boy's shoulder. "Iman, there is nothing that you cannot ask of me." Amir held out a palm, and a small vial shimmered into existence.

The boy's eyes widened. "You are getting better at that."

"I suppose I am. Go give this to your mother."

"I will! I will!"

Amir brought Badra to the small table, and they scrunched around the battered wood, sitting on the dirt floor. Badra enjoyed her first meal of watered-down soup and shared loaves of bread with a smile on her face, all the while congratulating the girls on their superior cooking skills and inviting them both to the palace to show the cooks their secrets.

The girls nodded, wide-eyed, and Amir looked forward to

the day when the palace staff served peasant soup. Oh, what an interesting night that would be.

The parrot cawed on Badra's shoulder, and one of the girls shared her own bread with him.

Sharing for all, from the wealthy to the most meek. This had been his dream all along.

After a few stories and games, Badra gave each child a kiss and told them to be good.

Amir checked the back room, where their mother sat up, blinking her eyes. Good. Let the family reunite, once more.

When they took their leave, the sun began its descent to the sands. Back on their horses, Nadir and Salem followed the royal couple toward the main gates.

"Are you sure?" Nadir asked as they left the city.

Amir scanned the sky. "Oh, most definitely."

Xerxes's hooves crunched in the desert sand. The bird took flight, circling ahead of them until darkness fell. Then he returned, this time alighting on Nadir's shoulder.

"Feathered menace," Nadir complained.

Badra cocked a brow at him.

"That would be a lovely, wonderful, cheery feathered menace, of course."

Amir snorted and tossed a handful of nothing into the air. A fireball appeared, floating ahead and lighting their way. Badra steered Cleopatra closer. "This would be romantic if we could lose the guards."

Amir glanced at the men behind them. "Would you like me to enchant them back to the palace?"

She blinked. "Could you?"

"Yes, but then we'd have to deal with the lectures when we returned."

"That doesn't sound like fun."

"I agree."

A group of horses charged at them at great speed. The glint of raised scimitars caught the light from Amir's fire ball.

Swords unsheathed behind them.

Amir held up a hand. "There is no need for that."

"But, sir!" the guards said in tandem.

"Sheathe your weapons," Badra ordered.

Amir glanced at her. She was so much more beautiful when she took charge.

Amir called the light closer to completely illuminate his and Badra's faces.

"At least take this," Nadir said behind him, holding out Amir's scepter.

Suppressing a grin, Amir placed the staff across his lap, making sure the golden snake head caught the light.

The bandits skidded to a stop, piling sand at their horses' hooves.

The leader's eyes trailed to the scepter, an unfathomable prize for any bandit. His jaw dropped.

"You...you're him," the lead rider said. "The Great Sorcerer."

Amir called up a smile, raising the fire ball with a flick of his finger. "I am. May I help you, gentlemen?"

The men looked at each other, pale as they lowered their weapons.

"N-No," the leader said, backing away until his horse hit an invisible wall behind him.

"Be nice," Badra whispered to Amir.

Ah, yes, his days of wickedness had ended when he'd put on a wedding band. He forced another smile. "I'm not sure if you gentlemen are aware, but thievery is illegal."

They looked at each other again, wide-eyed.

"If you are in need of work, we can teach you a skill." He pointed to each of them. "You all seem to have nice, strong backs. There is plenty of good, paid labor available in Bisnagar."

The leader gulped. "But we are not from Bisnagar."

"The golden city is open to anyone searching for a better life," Badra said. "As long as they are honestly in search of improving themselves."

The man gawked. "Truly?"

"The time of the thieves is over," Amir said. "Throw down your swords and find honest work. The sweat of your labor will reward you beyond measure."

All of their swords hit the ground at the same time. Amir balked. He couldn't have timed that so precisely if he'd used a spell on them. Luckily, what he offered seemed like magic to most.

They bid their farewells and the would-be bandits headed toward Bisnagar.

Once they were out of sight, Amir got off his horse and turned to Badra. "Are you sure you want me to do this? It's a lot easier the other way."

She shook her head. "No. I want to see it."

"Fine." He raised his scepter into the air over the desert and shouted, "*Videtur!*"

The ground rumbled. The sand shifted in waves. Leaves sprouted from the Earth as the pointed obelisk rose into the sky. Badra clapped her hands. "Do it again!"

Instead, Amir flicked his wrist, and his wife floated off her horse and into his arms.

"Do you think you can charm me with your magic?" she asked.

He kissed her. "I believe I already have."

Amir led her through the garden, down the slick steps and into his sanctuary. Badra glanced back at the slime-covered steps, grimacing.

"I told you there was an easier way to see my study."

"It takes more than a little unpleasantness to dissuade me. You should know that by now." She kissed his cheek and turned to the shelves. "So this is it?"

Amir nodded. "In all its glory." *Well, Almost.* "Iago! Stop pretending you don't know we're here."

The demon priest materialized right beside Badra. She cried out, stumbling beside Amir.

"That wasn't nice," Amir said.

Iago rubbed his hands together. "Maybe not, but it was so much fun!" His gaze alighted on Badra. "Ah, so this is the only thing in the world worth dying for?"

She blushed, turning away.

The demon elbowed Amir. "Very nice."

Amir raised a brow. "Yes, *she is* very nice."

"Enough about me." Badra whistled, holding out her arm. "We brought a present for you, ancient one." The red and blue parrot flew in and landed on her wrist.

"Pestle!" Iago said.

Amir frowned. "Pestle?"

"That's what I called him. You know, mortar and pestle?" Iago's translucent form darkened until he was whole again. The parrot flew to him, landing on his shoulder and nuzzling his cheek.

"The bird comes to you of his own free will," Badra said. "But he is free now, as is all of Bisnagar."

Iago's eyes narrowed.

"That means he is not your slave," Amir said. "If he chooses to fly you out of here from time to time, that is his choice, not yours."

Iago smiled, and the bird leaned in and nibbled his ear. The demon wiped a dark gray tear from his cheek. "When I woke up here, I couldn't see out." He turned toward Amir. "I had no idea if you caught the lamp, or if the jinni had destroyed you." He looked away. "It seized Aladdin's soul. The boy is gone— lost to eternity. I thought you..." He shook his head. "I didn't think I..."

Amir put his hand on the ancient keeper's shoulder. "You were wrong."

The demon smiled. "Obviously. You have become the most powerful sorcerer in the world. You fought a jinni and won." His eyes widened. "This must be chronicled!" A pen and parchment popped into the air, and Iago grabbed them. "Quickly, tell me everything!"

Amir smiled. "Another time. My charming wife and I have a date with a sunrise."

Iago wrinkled his nose. "Sunrise? There are always sunrises. There is no scholarly significance in a sunrise."

Amir brushed Badra's cheek with his fingers but spoke to Iago. "There are certain things, my friend, that I fear you are no longer capable of understanding."

"What does that mean? I am the keeper of the scrolls. There is nothing I do not understand!"

The parrot squawked as Amir led Badra from the temple.

"Amir!" Iago called.

Amir led Badra up the stairs. "Just keep walking."

She snorted, looking over her shoulder as Iago grumbled in the darkness.

THE SUNRISE BLASTED ACROSS THE DESERT, MORE spectacular than if Amir had conjured the colors himself.

"It is certainly a new day in Bisnagar," Nadir said behind them.

Yes, that it was.

Badra's face was alight in the glow of morning's arrival, more vibrant than he had ever seen her. Although he thought the same thing every morning.

Amir had come to Bisnagar with thoughts of conquest. Little did he know he'd be the one conquered so completely. He smiled, allowing the sunlight to warm his face. Never had conquest been so sweet.

EPILOGUE

Cloaks drawn over their faces, they re-entered the city. With two guards riding behind them, none were fooled. However, the people only waved as they passed, rather than approaching, seeming to understand that the royal couple wanted their privacy.

Amir pulled back on Xerxes's reins as they approached a *hana.* "Would you care for a drink after a long journey, Majesty?" he asked.

Badra's gaze carried over the rusty sign and pitted door. "Here?"

The smell of stale spirits clung to the entrance, as if the establishment hadn't been cleaned in some time. Absolutely disgusting. No sultan in her right mind would be seen in a place such as this.

Her eyes lit up. "What fun!"

Amir helped her from her horse as two children ran behind the building.

"We're going to miss it!" one child said. A third boy scampered past and disappeared behind the *hana* as well.

"What do you think is going on?" Badra asked.

Amir shrugged. "It's your city. Let's find out."

They moved around the back of the building and froze. The sun backlit a man holding a scimitar high overhead and a child's arm in his other hand. "I will take your hand for stealing!"

The child tried to pull away, pleading while two other children rolled out a chopping block, huge grins on their faces.

Heat coursed through Badra's veins. This was not happening in Bisnagar. *Never again!*

She grabbed Amir's arm. A ball of fire appeared in her sorcerer's hand as another child pushed through the others.

"No!" the boy said. "He's my servant. I didn't pay him on time. This is my fault. Take my hand instead!" The child's gaze met Amir's, and his eyes widened. Amir's ball of fire winked out when the boy pointed at him. "It's him!"

Everyone froze but the man with the blade. He spun, dropped to his knees, and touched his forehead to the ground. The sword dropped into the sand...a scimitar woven from reeds and clay. A toy?

One of the children kicked the man. "Aladdin, get up!"

Badra gasped and moved closer to Amir as the man raised his head. A million terrors came rushing back as the former prince looked up at them, his eyes wide and searching. He wore a peasant vest, leaving his chest bare, and soiled breeches that may have once been white.

Her shock withered as a coursing heat flushed through her body. "You!" Badra screamed. "How dare you show your face in Bisnagar after all you have done?"

Aladdin raised his head only partially. "After all I have done? What do you mean, Majesty? I'm just teaching children—"

"You know exactly what I mean." Badra made a move to kick him, but Amir held her back.

"I'm not sure he does know what you mean," Amir said. "Stand, boy."

"Your Majesties." The former prince placed a hand over his

heart. "I beg forgiveness. This display was not meant to offend. We aren't ready for an audience yet. We've barely started rehearsals."

"Rehearsals?" Badra asked.

Aladdin stood and scratched the back of his neck, like he had so many times in the palace. "This is my players group. I've been working with the children, acting out stories and trying to keep them out of trouble." He looked back at the youngsters. "Right now, they only want to act out the Fall and Rise of Bisnagar." He bowed again. "Please forgive if we got anything wrong, Majesties. I hit my head and can't seem to remember any of it, so we've created our play from the accounts of others."

Could it be possible? She turned to Amir, who smiled back at her. Yes, apparently it *could* be possible.

She considered the children, some in clean clothes, but most in rags. "You're teaching them the arts?"

Aladdin nodded. "I grew up on these streets. I almost lost a hand on more than one occasion, so I wanted to create a safe place for the children." He shrugged. "I guess they don't need it now as much as they used to."

"Nonsense." She took a step forward. "They need it more than ever. Bisnagar needs this." A few of the children wore belts with false scimitars at their sides like the guards. One girl had long, black hair and royal robes. The princess, perhaps? She smiled. "Our land needs to thrive with art and culture. This should be encouraged."

Aladdin sighed. "Unfortunately, most of them are leaving."

Badra's hair whipped over her shoulder as she turned to him, eyes ablaze. "Why?"

"They are all going to learn a trade to help their families and to rebuild Bisnagar."

Badra glowered. "What? I forbid it."

Amir leaned closer to her. "It is your law, Majesty."

She glared at him. "Well, that's not what I meant. Children should be in school. They should be playing. Certainly we have enough adults to rebuild."

"The parents don't see it that way," Aladdin said. "If a child can earn, they want them working."

Badra folded her arms, gritting her teeth. She would not have her laws bent and twisted for unwarranted gain. But after so much poverty, she could understand the parents' concerns. "Then you will pay them."

Aladdin gaped. "I'm but an orphan myself, Majesty. I have no way to..."

Amir tossed him a purse. Aladdin stared at the satchel, wide-eyed. "As of today, you are the head of the Royal Players' Guild. Any child who wishes to learn the art of a player, will be taught by you and be paid for learning their trade, and then for performing, like any other job in this land."

Aladdin's eyes widened further. "You must be joking."

"We're not." Badra lifted her chin. "You will take the next forty days to form your troupe. On the forty-first day, you will debut your play in the palace." The children began to cheer.

Aladdin's face reddened before tears welled in his eyes. "Is this real? Am I dreaming?"

"I assure you, you are not," Amir said.

"You should also find an assistant to help you teach," Badra said. "Because I plan on building you the grandest theater in the world, and I want you to help with the planning." She turned to Amir. "You will see this done. Add it to the renovation plans."

Both Amir and Aladdin stared at her.

"What?" she asked. "Are either of you not up to the challenge?"

"We are, Majesty, we are!" Aladdin laughed, holding up the purse for the children to see. They celebrated, dancing and singing as Badra and Amir eased back to the front of the building.

"You told me Aladdin had been a street magician." Badra stopped in the alley and grabbed her husband's arm. "Your second wish, before you freed the jinni..." She held out her hand to the celebrating players. "You gave him this?"

Amir looked back on the merriment. "It could have easily been me, lying there in the sand, defeated and soulless." He turned to Badra. "All he wanted was a better Bisnagar. He wasn't evil at heart. He'd been corrupted. I couldn't leave him wallowing in Jahannam for all eternity." He smiled as the children cheered, again. "Aladdin needed a purpose. A good purpose. I gave him one."

She lowered her eyes. "When I saw him, it all came rushing back to me. I wanted..." A bitter tang coated her tongue. She shook her head. "I wanted to hurt him."

He ran his fingers down both her cheeks. "I know."

She drank in his love, soaking in the warmth from his touch. How was it that such a simple gesture could give her such peace in a city still reeling from their barely-survived brush with a jinni?

"Why is Aladdin the only one who doesn't remember?" she asked. "The rest of the city has perfect clarity."

Amir pursed his lips. "Would you want to remember if you'd let yourself fall to such evil?"

Of course, her husband was always thinking of others. This was one of the many reasons she loved him.

She kissed his cheek. "You are a good man, Amir Haddad."

The sun rose high in the sky as they made their way back to the palace. The dirt graduated to clay, and the clay graduated to gold beneath their horses' hooves. Even the road would need to be renovated, ensuring all sectors enjoyed the same comforts. That was fine, though. More renovation meant more employment. More employment meant more trade. More trade meant more of everything for everyone.

She nodded to each of the guards at the palace gates as they entered the receiving room.

Amir helped her from her horse. "Where would you like to break your fast, Majesty?"

She rubbed her chin. "What would be the perfect end to this lovely adventure?" She played coy, but her plans were already set.

Badra glanced at Myra. She wore blue today, rather than red. It suited her.

The girl nodded. Her face reddened as she pressed her lips together.

Holding back her own smile, Badra said, "I'd like to sit by the fountain."

Badra kept her face serene as her sorcerer led her out to the garden. The fountain rose into the sky, the spray glinting in the sun. As Nadir had said, a new day had dawned for Bisnagar. For the first time in her life, she was the ruler of her own destiny.

She kicked off her shoes as they neared the pool. She had plans for that destiny...grand plans. The first, however, was decidedly selfish.

Amir sat on the edge of the fountain and gestured to the space beside him. She leaned down to kiss him.

He was so handsome, so trusting. Maybe far too trusting. She pushed him, and he flipped head over heel into the water.

Badra pressed her lips together as he sputtered, "It's cold!"

She laughed, leaning over. "Of course it is. I had them ice the water this morning." Amir wasn't the only one who could scheme nefarious plots.

His eyes darkened and her feet left the ground.

"No!" She screamed as her body hovered over the fountain. "Don't do it, Amir! Don't you dare!"

An evil smile crossed his lips. "Oh, I dare."

She floated into the stream, the pulsing fountain streaming iced water over her. She shrieked, the frigid torrent soaking through her *lehenga,* until the spell broke and she fell into his arms.

She swatted at him. "That was mean."

He laughed, then kissed her. It was sweet, warm, and everything a kiss should be. She melted, his touch taking away the sting of the cold.

"I love you, Badroulbadour," he said.

Badroulbadour?

She raised a brow and leaned in to kiss him again. Before their lips brushed, she shoved him back under the cold water. He was still spluttering when she climbed out of the fountain and ran.

The servants snickered as she passed.

Myra clapped her hands. "Run, Your Majesty, run!"

Nadir shouted jests at her husband as Amir stomped on the tiles behind her.

Badra laughed. Yes, she was the master of her own destiny, and she intended to enjoy every moment.

ACKNOWLEDGMENTS

This book was a labor of love, and a lot of people helped make this happen in record time.

First and foremost, I need to thank my husband, the domestic god who cooks all the meals, gets my kids to school on time, and makes sure the house does not fall apart. Also thank you to Grandma, for chipping in with the laundry. (Don't laugh. I have three teenaged boys in sports. It's an entire day of washing and folding!)

Writing is usually a solitary affair. *How to Kill a Street Rat* was a group effort of many wonderful friends and professionals that were equally as excited about bringing this story to life.

I had a clear, concise vision of what I wanted for this story, but my original visualization had some empty spaces. Thank you, Heather Cardona, for plugging the holes in my outline to make sure everything flowed nicely.

Crystal Wood, I think you were just as excited about this concept as I was. Iago was your brainchild, and it was a brilliant one. I have to admit, I was very apprehensive at first, but the demon caretaker of the scrolls took on a life of his own (as evil demons will). And yes, you were right; Amir needed a friend and mentor in all of this.

Sometimes, it is hard for a writer to know if they are relaying the emotions of a scene onto the page to create the right mood. Sharon Hughson, you are always there, pom-poms waving, ready to help read the completed story and point out where things are lacking. You always challenge me to deepen the intensity of the pivotal scenes. Please never stop being critical. You make me strive to be better in all the right ways.

Jenny Michaud, you and Sharon agreed, and I took action. The new beginning of this book is all thanks to you two. You are both good at reining me in and making me ease into a story, rather than starting with an explosion.

Scarlet West, I took a chance on you because I'm a sucker for someone working toward a goal to better themselves. I was super pleased with your manuscript analysis, and I appreciated you pointing out the places where I could tighten the story.

Amy McNulty, thank you for jumping in as a new member of my team and getting the copy edits done within my deadline. Someday, I might actually learn to place the comma in the right place the first time.

Tandy Boese, you have been my last line of defense for a few years, now. Your proofread sparked a fun (and even more confusing) discussion on Facebook as to the right and wrong places to capitalize the words prince, princess, and sultan. You'll be happy to know that after consulting as many experts as I could find, and finally turning to the Chicago Manual of Style, you were right.

Christian Bentulan, you captured Amir and Badra beautifully in the cover art. Thanks for putting up with me, right down to the angle that the bird was flying. It's the little details that count!

Nicole Conway, I wanted something special for the interior

design, and you made it happen. Thanks so much for my little magic lamps!

And, finally, a special thanks to my readers for sticking with me while I tried some other things. I'm back where I belong, and I'm happy to be here. I look forward to creating more stories that everyone can love.

Hugs all around!

—Jennifer

ABOUT THE AUTHOR

Jennifer M. Eaton hails from the eastern shore of the North American Continent on planet Earth. Yes, regrettably, she is human, but please don't hold that against her.

While not traipsing through the galaxy looking for specimens for her space moth collection, she lives with her wonderfully supportive husband, three energetic offspring, and a duo of poodles who run the spaceport when she's not around.

During infrequent excursions to her home planet of Earth, Jennifer enjoys long hikes in the woods, bicycling, swimming, snorkeling, and snuggling up by the fire with a great book; but great adventures are always a short shuttle ride away.

Read more from Jennifer M. Eaton

www.jennifereaton.com

Chapter 1

The dry, black-spotted leaves crumpled in Damon's fingers. A slight breeze wafted the particles from his palm and scattered them across acres of similarly blackened foliage. Just last summer, this land had provided half the *cara* fruits in the kingdom. Now...this.

A boy strode across the field toward him. One of his guards advanced, but Damon held up a hand and crouched to the child's height.

"Did the sorcerer send you?" the boy asked.

Damon nodded. "He did."

"Can he fix our farm?"

Pursing his lips, Damon scanned the ravaged fields. Sending fertilizer and farm hands was one thing, but how could they combat utter desecration?

A man approached more slowly, gripping a worn brown hat between weathered hands. "Sorry. He don't mean no disrespect. We're hungry, that's all." He shooed the child away.

Damon stood. "It's not a problem. Is this your field?"

"Aye. Thank you for coming. We're at a loss."

Unfortunately, so was Damon. He'd heard stories, but this was so much worse than he'd expected. All he could do was report back to Binal, and hope his father would send someone who actually knew something about plants.

Damon took in the farmer's sunken cheeks. "When was the last time you ate something?"

The man looked away. "I had a bit this morning. My wife and I agree, it's more important that the children eat."

Stars, had it really come to this, in the mightiest kingdom in the land? He grimaced. *Not while I still have strength to do something about it.*

Damon turned, walked back to his horse, opened his saddlebag, and pulled out the ration packs.

"What are you doing?" the guard holding the horses asked.

He held up the food. "What do you think I'm doing?"

"What are we supposed to eat on the trip back?"

Was he serious? "We'll manage."

"That's not enough to help. You can't feed all the people yourself."

Damon pushed past him. "Maybe not, but I can feed a few." He handed the pack to the farmer. "Bring this back to your family. I'll report what I've found, and see if I can send a botanist to help you."

The man clutched the pack to his chest. His eyes filled with tears. "Thank you, my lord."

Damon grasped the man's shoulder. "Save your thanks until we get you a bountiful crop."

The man smiled, lifting his chin. "Long live Esparon."

Damon's chest clenched as his gaze trailed across the dying fields, again.

He whispered, "Yes, long live Esparon."

The timid voice of the child and the tears in the farmer's eyes traveled with Damon along the road back to the castle, blocking out the complaints of the two guards forced to ride without rations.

Blast them both. He doubted either of them had been hungry a day in their lives. Not that Damon had, either. Binal would never let him starve, but at least Damon knew enough not to complain in the face of others' suffering.

That child was young—too young to know such hardship. Damon needed to make sure Binal understood how serious the blight had become.

When they reached the stables, Damon handed off the reins and turned to the page. "I need to speak to see Lord Binal immediately."

The page lowered his head. "I will pass on that you have returned."

In other words, find something to do and wait until you are called. Typical.

Damon sighed and waved him away. It certainly wasn't the page's fault that his father was occupied. There was no reason to make the man's thankless job worse by arguing.

His two guards gave a slight bow, then walked away, shaking their heads. Let them be annoyed. They will have full bellies within an hour—more food than that farmer's family would probably see in a week.

"Hey there, Doxion." Guardsman Rayhan patted Damon's horse's nose. "I see you managed to bring his highness back in one piece." He turned to Damon, and his smile melted into a frown. His eyes widened. "Was it really that bad?"

Damon nodded, pulling off his gloves. "If this keeps up, we're all going to starve."

Rayhan moved closer. "Word has it that the battle mages are scoping potentials." He looked over his shoulder. "Maybe we're finally going to do something about those blasted witches cursing our country."

Damon blinked. "I don't know that there is any truth to that." He certainly hadn't heard about any attack on their eastern neighbors.

His friend shrugged. "You wouldn't be able to tell me even if you did know, but I'm okay with that." He smiled. "I threw my name out there, just in case."

"You what?"

"If we're going after the witches, I want to be right there in front. Someone needs to make them pay for what they've done to our land."

Damon squeezed his gloves until his hands ached. Nefarum's witches had been a bane to Esparon since before his grandfather's rule. They needed to be stopped, that was for certain, however... "War isn't always the best answer for a kingdom or her people."

"Sir?" A young boy in servants' livery hovered by the side of the stable.

Damon turned toward him. "Yes?"

"Lord Binal has requested your presence in the war room, sir." The boy wrung his hands. Damon's stance softened. His father intimidated the mightiest of soldiers. This child was lucky not to have soiled his pants in the presence of the high sorcerer.

"I'll be there shortly."

The boy bowed and disappeared around the front of the building.

Rayhan held out his hands. "The war room. You see? Rumors are not to be taken lightly."

"It's the day after quarter moon," Damon pointed out. "My father always holds council on the quarter."

"Yes." Rayhan pointed a finger. "But for the first time in seventeen years, he's invited you."

Damon's stomach fluttered and he grabbed the side of the stall. His friend was right. He'd always been sent on errands at the quarter moon, traveling Esparon and engaging the people, like today. Normally, his father would discuss his decisions and tactics with Damon in private, but actually being called into the room with the war chiefs?

"Congratulations." Rayhan punched his shoulder. "It's about bloody time."

Bloody. An interesting choice of words. He nodded and headed toward the castle.

Rayhan's voice came from behind him. "Put in a good word for me. I'd make you a great general!"

Damon gulped, and shivered despite the heat of the late day sun. His friend was too eager to see combat, but Damon was afraid that day may come sooner than anyone had hoped.

Anya sidled to the edge of the cliff. A thick ball roiled in her throat, and she forced it down. This was the same precipice her mother had fallen from. Resisting the urge to look down and see the place her body had been found, Anya closed her eyes and steadied herself as a gust of wind tossed her long, dark hair in her eyes. The airstreams could change at any time, and she needed to be prepared. The village could not lose another priestess.

Anya drank in the cool air and took in the clouds billowing across the crisp blue sky. Green, growing glory greeted her right up to the edge of her warding spell. On the outside, the grass darkened, turning browner in the distance. *That* was why she stood atop this mountain—to keep the death and gloom of Esparon on the outside where it belonged.

She closed her eyes and stretched her hands outward. Her fingers traced sigils in the air. An *antecedum* for power, the *triglenterum* for fortitude, the *carcelemnum* for joy, and the *veridas* for goodness. Her mother had taught these spells to her from the time she could walk. Anya just never thought she'd have to take her mother's place so young.

Closing off the ward with a swirling *kavas* string, her family's own signature spell, she stepped back and watched her ward bolster, grow, and connect to the neighboring wards in the distance. The shield was a tapestry of sorts, each village priestess weaving her own blocks in the quilt. In the east, the red swirling bands of Naomi, in the west, the mottled, blocky patterns of Armana's sigils filled the sky. Here, Anya's weave was neither colorful nor uniform. 'Sturdy is better than pretty,' her mother had always taught.

Anya wasn't sure that her ward was sturdy, and it definitely wasn't pretty, but none of the sorcerer's spells had broken through from the outside, so she must be doing something right.

With a flick of her wrist she conjured up a spider sigil in the air—a sinister little bug of her mother's design that crept along the ward, checking the weave for holes. Her mother probably wasn't the first person to say that *luck favors the steadfast*, but this, too, was an adage ingrained in Anya's very being: always recheck your work.

Mistress Lixiss would inspect Anya's ward again in about an hour. It wasn't that she or the high priestesses didn't trust Anya, but everyone knew the consequences of failure.

Anya looked out on the dry, dusty plains beyond the trees on the outside of the ward and shivered. She understood their caution. With so much at stake, it would have been better to pull in a priestess from a neighboring village than elevate Anya before she'd had time to prove herself. There just wasn't anyone else, though. So here Anya stood, sole protector of her stretch of the ward, like her mother before her.

Anya let her hands drop to her sides, her fingers curling into her white linen dress. Dirt clung to the hem, as usual. It wouldn't be a Warding Day without Lixiss reminding her about the importance of appearances. She released the dress, allowing the fabric to scrape the ground, again. What did it matter, when she'd get even dirtier on her way down the mountain?

She whispered the words to a locater spell, searching for the one soul who'd be happy to see her, no matter what she looked like. The incantation cascaded through the air, swirling and peaking until it burst over the grassy fields outside her village.

She padded down the path that led back to the valley, avoiding sharp rocks that would slice her bare feet. The countless journeys up and down this hill since her childhood made the otherwise perilous trip easy, which may have been one of the reasons they'd elevated Anya so soon—no one else was willing to climb these peaks.

Anya smiled, kicking a stone and watching it bounce down the decline. They had no idea what they were missing.

Circumventing the mountain path, Anya stopped as the sky opened over her province. No matter how many times she walked this path, the sight never failed to steal her breath.

Below, a team of winged horses in brown, black, and mottled gray tones grazed in the vivid green pasture. She grinned and bounded down the rest of the steep path at breakneck speed, the special bundle in her pocket bouncing against her thigh until her feet hit the soft grass. The cold, damp blades made her sigh, close her eyes, and raise her face to the sun. This is where she truly belonged. *This* was home.

Several horses moved toward her, their wings a riot of colors and textures. They were all beautiful, but only one held her heart. She scampered towards the tall, white stallion that all the other horses gave a wide birth to. The magnificent creature stared her down as she skidded to a halt in front of him. Anya bent in a theatrical, formal bow and then straightened.

Entor nuzzled her black hair, which seemed even darker up against his milky wings and pale coat. Anya giggled when the huge winged horse snuffled in her ear.

"Stop, that tickles." She tucked back her hair. "I have something for you." She pulled an apple from her dress pocket. "Just don't tell Finn." She checked the guard tower but saw no sign of the old man, who was probably snoozing again.

She couldn't really blame him. Guarding the horses had to be a boring job. Nothing had attacked these beautiful creatures in her lifetime, and thanks to the priestesses and the wards, that would never change.

Entor sank his teeth into the apple with a crunch. Another pony snorted behind her. She turned to find several horses inching closer, and one foal ventured near enough to reach his nose into Anya's pocket.

She jumped back. "Oh! I'm so sorry. I couldn't bring enough for everyone." She turned out her pocket to show them. "Perhaps if I enchanted my cloak to hold more?" A palomino mare tossed her head in annoyance while a feisty brown neighed and sniffed at her pocket, as if not completely believing it was empty.

Anya held back her grin. "I'll bring more next time, I swear!" The horses would hold her to that promise. She'd need to find a way to smuggle more fruit from the kitchens.

Anya leaned against Entor and laughed as a playful colt nipped her sleeve before she and the remainder of the horses dispersed, finally convinced Anya had no more treats to enjoy.

Entor remained at her side, his all-knowing eyes surveying her, as always. Most felt belittled beneath that gaze, but Anya met his stare. Entor didn't judge her age or lack of ability. To an extent, he was the only one that didn't look down on her and expect her to fail. At least that's what she told herself.

She kissed him on the nose and turned toward the simple dirt trail that led past the guard tower and through the trees. Reality lay within, and she needed to face it sooner or later. She tapped his flank. "I guess I'll see you on the other side."

Anya trudged along the path, across the field, and pushed through the gates leading into the village. The dark red roofs absorbed the sun's light, making them look like tarnished coins. The smooth stones of the worn-down road cooled her feet, soothing away some of the anxiety over making a public appearance.

Her mother had liked the socializing part of her station and had been a great conversationalist. Anya never inherited that gift. She felt all wrong and couldn't find the right thing to say when the townspeople approached.

"Good morning, Priestess," Mrs. Todd, the butcher's wife, had a basket beneath one arm. She smiled at Anya with a strange glint in her eyes. The people she protected looked up to her, maybe even marveled at what she could do, but none realized what a heavy burden magic could be.

"Good morning," Anya said with a small nod.

Her mother would ask Mrs. Todd how she was and about her three children, calling each by name. Instead, Anya quickened her pace, avoiding the issue.

Kiera and Cillian, the village newlyweds, and former schoolmates of Anya's, approached with their hands linked and their faces alight with smiles.

"Priestess," Keira said, giving a curtsy.

Anya cringed. In a time not long ago, they would have said

"Hey Anya!" and asked her to roll down the hill with them to see who could get to the bottom the fastest without vomiting.

Those days, it seemed, were long gone.

"Can I trouble you for a blessing?" Keira smiled at Cillian. "We're trying for our first child."

Anya's eyes widened. Their first child? Grace of the moon, they were barely out of school! Then again, so was Anya.

She forced a smile. "Of course." She raised her hand over Keira and whispered a few words she remembered her mother speaking when the Parson's pigs hadn't been breeding. The magic unfurled within her, small threads inching their way through her arm and out her fingertips. The sensation prickled like hitting her elbow on something.

Keira jumped and stepped back, Cillian steadying her.

"Well met," Anya said. "I wish you a house filled with happy, laughing children."

The couple hugged. "Thank you, Priestess."

Anya nodded. Hopefully, their child wouldn't come out squealing with a pink, curly tail.

An older man and a middle-aged woman had stopped to watch the blessing, but now scampered away, wide-eyed.

Her stomach hardened. As a priestess of the order Anya would never truly belong among the villagers, again. She looked back to the happy couple walking hand in hand. She could have had that, in another life, one where her mother hadn't been taken from her so soon.

She wiped the burn from her eyes and headed out along the path towards the temple, rubbing her sore shoulders. She didn't remember her mother seeming so tired after reinforcing the ward. Maybe it was the extra effort of blessing Keira. Her mother had made spell casting look so easy. She'd made everything look easy. Maybe in time, Anya would get the hang of her new station.

She glanced up a familiar hill, and warmed, remembering the small cottage and white fence she knew sat on the other side. Too bad she couldn't return to her old family home after tracing her spells each Warding Day. A nice nap would have been helpful before returning to the temple.

Another family lived there now, though, and her brother's family had moved to Hecit Valley on the other side of Nefarum. There truly wasn't anything left in this village for her but her duty.

Entor swooped down to land in front of Anya, his wings creating a gust of air that stung her eyes. A cloud of dust puffed around them and she coughed into her hand.

The tinkling of delighted laughter behind the trees made her grin. The children of the village were not supposed to approach the winged horses. They were especially not supposed to be outside the town border, but they loved Entor. She remembered her own glee, the first time her mother's horse, Zaman, had flown into the valley to claim her mother as his spirit match.

Of course, Entor hadn't claimed anyone, and probably never would. He was 'the bold white,' 'the wild winged stallion.' He was the horse that made the others scatter, and people point and watch, wondering what he might do.

His free spirit must have called to the children, just as it called to Anya, though. She, like this amazing horse, and those children hiding where they should not be, had no intention of conforming to what others considered civilized boundaries, much to Mistress Lixiss's and probably to those children's parents' chagrin.

As Anya strode alongside Entor's clopping hooves, the ornate shimmering blue roof of the temple peeked out over the treetops. The arching gables towered over every other building in Nefarum, and with good reason. The temple was the heart of their small oasis, the seat of the high priestess. Everyone in Nefarum understood the order's purpose. The protection of magic meant the protection of the world, and nothing was more important.

She wove her fingers into Entor's mane, soaking in the power that radiated from his presence. It seemed unfathomable that there were those in the world who would hunt him down and destroy him, just because of what he symbolized and the power he bore. But this was one of the many reasons she climbed the mountain each Warding Day: to keep the sorcerer and his cursed taint, out.

Chapter 2

Damon paused on the war room's threshold. Voices rumbled from within.

As a boy, he'd pressed his ear against the thick oak door trying to glean what the kingdom's most powerful voices were plotting.

Who was he kidding? He'd done this only a few weeks ago, but now his day had finally come. The famed high sorcerer had finally decided to allow him to stand at his side.

Damon inhaled and pushed the door open.

His father leaned over the edge of a long, warped wooden table. Binal had rough, strong features and dark eyes centered on what may have been a map. His long hair was the same dark shade of brown as Damon's, held back by a circlet inset with a stone imbued with power. Binal straightened to his full six and a half spans of height—an intimidating warrior in addition to a master sorcerer... Damon's polar opposite in so many ways.

The seven war chiefs from Esparon's territories looked up when he entered, and silence flooded the room. Damon shuddered, and resisted the urge to step back out. He'd waited too long for this. He was the prince. His voice deserved to be heard.

"Ah, Damon." His father offered a rare smile.

Damon gave a slight bow. "I've just returned from the north farms as you requested, sire." He took a few steps inside. "I fear it's worse than we suspected."

Binal gestured to the empty chair at his immediate right—a place of honor reserved for whichever chief held Binal's favor that month. Around the room, men shifted their weight. A few twisted their lips, some lancing him with a glare before looking away.

"Sit," Binal ordered.

Damon wiped the sweat from his brow as he took the offered chair. The eyes of the most influential men in Esparon were on him. Many of these men had sat in on his training. A daring few *educated* him one on one, taking far too much pleasure in beating down the son of their sovereign in the name of *toughening him up*. His knuckles whitened on the arms of his chair. He wouldn't give them the satisfaction of balking at their presence. He was no longer a child. Still, his mouth turned to chalk.

"As I was saying," Binal said. "We must expand our borders if we're to survive the winter."

Damon blinked. "Expand our borders? Respectfully, father, we need to see to our people before we drag them into another war. The crops..."

"Are failing," his father continued. "Krut is too far from Nefarum to feel the witches' wrath. Scouts tell me their crops are bountiful. I've decided they should share their good fortune."

Padraig of the Southern Hills cleared his throat. "With respect, my Lord, the boy has a point. Do we have the resources to mount an attack?"

Jeers and derisive laughs filled the war room, and Padraig's face reddened.

"With our army and my magic, we cannot lose," Binal said. "Unless you doubt Esparon's might, Padraig?"

The color ran from Padraig's face. The Southern Hills were a recent addition to his father's empire. For him, the sting of the sorcerer's might was all too fresh.

Padraig shook his head. "No, my lord. You're correct, of course."

Damon would have pitied the man if he hadn't personally toured the Southern Hills last month. Padraig's farmers were heavily tithed and suffered beneath his rule. After Damon had reported his findings to the court, he'd hoped his father would put an end to his people's unwarranted distress, but more pressing matters always seemed to get in the way.

"Liam, you will commit your land's warhorses for our soldiers." Binal addressed the oily man with crooked teeth that ruled the coastal region.

Liam bowed his head, his long nose almost touching the table. "Of course, Lord Binal. We would be honored."

Damon held back a snort. Liam had been kissing Binal's posterior for years, dangling his daughters in front of his father, hoping for a union. Most recently, those same daughters had been dangled in front of Damon. His father certainly had to see through such power plays and groveling.

Binal turned to Damon, his eyes narrowed.

Had his father sensed his misgivings? He sat beside the greatest sorcerer their land had ever known. He should have spent more time learning to create a wall around his thoughts.

"What say you about my plans, son?"

Damon licked his lips, glancing down at the map of Esparon and the few surrounding kingdoms his father had yet to conquer. What Esparon truly needed, was a swift end to any campaign, and a return to focusing on their people.

He met his father's gaze. "Have you considered sending an emissary, telling them of our struggle and asking for their help?"

The chiefs watched Binal, waiting for his reaction.

"That would be an excellent plan," Binal said, and the chiefs began nodding in approval. "If I wanted to risk people on a fool's errand."

Damon's face warmed.

Perhaps his father purposely brought him here to make a fool out of him? He'd tasked him time and time again to go out and interact with the people, always making promises that his father never followed through on. How could he think Damon wouldn't put the people first?

His ideas were sound, though. He just needed to approach them from a new angle. Maybe one his father could understand.

"They could kidnap the king." Damon stood and pointed to Krut's castle on the map. "And ransom him for land rights."

Binal leaned his head back and laughed. The war chiefs joined in, the sound raising in a cacophonous symphony.

"You still have much to learn, my son." Binal's smile faded. "Always trying to avoid bloodshed. You must realize that carnage is inevitable in war. You must cut some throats to make the rivers of victory run red."

Damon held his grimace back and gave a stiff nod as he eased back into his chair. "Yes, Father."

He sat in silence as the chiefs and his father plotted the demise of the western country. He didn't understand why avoiding needless waste and violence was so repellant to these men. The old ways of war and death had not served them well

—their people were suffering. A different approach might mean their survival, if they would only consider other options.

The meeting ended and the war chiefs filed out. Damon began to stand, but Binal clapped a heavy hand on his shoulder.

"Stay, Damon. We must discuss something of importance." Binal took a deep draught of his ale.

Damon sat back down. "Yes, Father?"

"In truth, our attack on the western kingdom is nothing more than a stopgap. As you have confirmed, magic is swiftly draining from our land. We must take more drastic action to ensure Esparon's survival." Binal leaned towards Damon, his dark eyes pinning his son in place.

Damon had seen men die under that stare—grown men reduced to sniveling children, hardened warriors stripped to lifeless husks, twitching on the ground gasping for their last breath.

Refusing to flinch, Damon met his gaze. "W-What sort of action?"

"First, I must gain your vow that you will do whatever it takes to bring our country back to its former glory."

A muscle in Damon's jaw twitched. "Of course, you have my vow." How could he think any less of him? Esparon was his legacy, the people his own. He'd die for them, and his father knew this. At least, he'd thought he'd known. Damon shifted in his seat as his father's eyes continued to bore into his very soul.

Let them—let his father search his mind. The only thing he'd find was undying loyalty to his people. No, Damon had no taste for bloodshed if it could be avoided, but that didn't make him a coward. He would fight and die for Esparon if he needed to.

"Excellent. I should have generals as devoted as you, but I do not. I can trust only you with this task." Binal leaned back.

"You're always spouting about a peaceful end to conflict. Well, I give you one. Do this one task, and I will spare Krut."

Really? Damon straightened, lifting his chin. "Anything." Krut wasn't his responsibility, but war meant casualties on both sides. Sparing Krut meant sparing not only the soldiers, but the innocents living along the borders.

"I'm sending you into the heart of Nefarum."

Damon's eyebrows shot up. He grasped the arms of his chair, fairly certain his heart had stopped beating for a moment. "Nefarum? With how many men?"

"Alone."

Now his heart *did* stop. His hands tightened on the chair.

"You will smuggle a winged horse through the witches shield and bring it back to me."

"A-a horse?" Bringing back one creature wouldn't be difficult. He'd been riding since before he could walk, and winged or not, a horse was a horse.

Binal nodded. "Do this, and our lands will be fertile once more. Our crops will be abundant and life will flow back into our country."

Damon looked down, digesting his father's words. "How could one horse..."

"Leave that part of it to me."

Damon nodded. His throat parched as he swallowed. All Esparon needed was for magic to flow through the land once again. He could save the people, and stop another war. It seemed like such a huge gain, for such a small...

"You only need one horse?" Damon asked.

Binal's booming laugh filled the room. "I appreciate your confidence, but don't be foolish. These horses are not normal animals. They wield a great power. The witches will protect their source of magic to their deaths." He ran his fingers over the edge of his goblet. "One is all I need."

So be it. "What if I run into a witch?"

Binal slammed a hooked dagger onto the table between them. "Kill her."

Damon shuddered. Perhaps he could ask for a horse? Surely if they had so many, they would be willing to give up just one.

"Da-mon." His father drew out his name. His eyes turned to lances again.

"I-I won't let you down, Father." He grabbed the dagger, shoving the blade into his belt.

"I know, Damon. I have complete faith in you."

Damon gulped, taking in the slight indent in the table where his father had slammed down the knife.

Certainly his mage tutors had reported back Damon's countless failures. Unless they were toying with him and never tried to teach him at all. What Damon had mastered were mainly parlor tricks and simple spells—nothing of the caliber of his father's war mages, and definitely nothing like the power the sorcerer himself wielded as easily as walking.

"You're underestimating yourself again."

Damon cringed. Of course his father knew his every thought. "I'm sorry, Father. I'm just not sure why..."

"Faelar tells me you unwove his battle shield last week." Binal smiled. "He's quite impressed. He's not sure how you did it."

Damon pursed his lips. "It's a deconstruction spell. It's useless in battle. It takes far too long. I..."

"What is around Nefarum?"

Was this another trick question, meant to take him off guard? "The witches' shield."

His father's smile changed, it seemed almost...proud?

Damon's breath hitched. "It's a shield. A giant battle shield!"

Binal nodded. "They are ready for an army, not a small, temporary hole. You will cut through their shield, and let it reclose behind you. The hags won't even know you're there."

Damon gaped. He was right! Damon could do this!

Binal got to his feet. "Make your preparations. You leave at first light." The sorcerer swept from the room, leaving Damon alone at the table.

A slow drip echoed through the chamber, and a breeze whistled across the cracks in the foundation.

Damon swallowed at the lump in his throat. He would do anything to keep his father's favor and save his people from their fate. His hands curled into fists on the table. He could do this. All he needed was one horse, and he would be lauded for all time as the prince who saved Esparon.

Did you enjoy this preview?
Find buy links for this and more great books
From Jennifer M. Eaton on Goodreads
Or visit www.jennifereaton.com